Excerpts from Book I
Expraedium and Otl

A singular provocation of a novel, rendering a ...
language. An impossible to summarize story. A swing for the ienⁿ⌐⌐,
plunging of the depths, a literary prank, a hoedown in the ruins of civilization:
whatever you make of Melikian's provocative brain-bomb *Expraedium*—and
the singular language he has invented for it—it is a stab at the kind of great
Novel genius that's been left in the dust by publishing and purportedly
reader attention spans. The author announces his ambitions from the first
lines ("Void alpha was. Naught became."), and the pages that follow never
let up—the daft fragments, mad coinages, and cockeyed poetry coming at
readers in a relentless fireplug gush, revealing (and obscuring) a stinging
satire of religion, war, utopias, and so much more. At its heart is Brathki,
impressed into misadventures and upsetting the pillars of civilization. Extended colloquies relieve the density of the text, while offering many of
the biggest laughs and sharpest insights. A key to comprehension: reading
aloud, lingering over syllables. Especially for readers predisposed toward
the Joycean, the Pynchonian, and deciphering the ribald. Great for fans of
James Joyce's *Finnegans Wake*, Russell Hoban's *Riddley Walker.*

—Publishers Weekly

Enter at your own risk! *Expraedium* is intricate, dense, brittle, polyglot.
It has a wildly inventive style. The language is scabrous and oracular. An
avalanche of sliding signifiers, nonsequiturs, neologisms. *Expraedium* is as
infuriating and baffling as it is fascinating, challenging and engaging. Readers
will struggle to find the plot that the author's savage, bleak and mordant style
is in service to, but the more one reads, the less important the very notion
of plot becomes. What's difficult to convey is how much fun—and sheer
delight—whams into the subconscious when one gives up trying to make
sense of everything and just lets the cataract of words carry him/her forward.
Grappling with the unusual grammar and the obscure sense of meaning
that seem to lie smoldering beneath this thicket of words isn't for amateurs.
Those up to the challenge will find these untamed pages worth the effort.

—Blueink Review

I have never encountered a book quite like *Expraedium* before. Its language
is formulated through an origin that remains enigmatic. The author does
not seem to write to impress, and it is difficult to grasp his intentions. Each
line unfolds as if it were an entirely different story of its own. *Expraedium*
offers an unparalleled reading for those who appreciate unconventional
books. With its distinct language, mythological nuances, and exploration
of provocative themes it presents a demanding yet rewarding read.
Expraedium remains an unforgettable experience that has left a lasting
impression on me.

—Maria Yinks, Manhattan Book Review

Expraedium is a book that compels the reader to slow down. Proceed intently. This book exists in a universe of its own conjuring. It's crafty, challenges the inner sanctum of words and inspires poetic rumination that zaps the reader with cognitive dissonance. This is a book for those longing for literary anarchy. Reminiscent of *Finnegan's Wake*, some things by Tom Robbins, and it laughs with the spirit of Haruki Murakami. Fueled by poetic dynamism. It is: hard-to-read literary geniuses speaking in whispers at a demolished jazz club. Its language spews upside down wavelengths. Pure. Word. Wizzardry. Here readers find a frightening world built by distorted language. This book is a sound bath. Quill says: *Expraedium* is the world's epic battles and characters throwing a wild party at the Tower of Babel.

—Rebecca Jane Johnson, *Feathered Quill*

Expraedium is a work of fiction in the literary, cultural, and critical thinking subgenres. It is best suited for mature readers for its complex content and explicit language. In this explosive work which tackles heated and controversial topics, a deconstructive view comes to the fore, with satire and philosophy at its heart to break apart what we call civilization and look for something more liberating beyond its banal constraints. A shocking and arresting fiction, it comes so close to the bone of so-called "facts of life" which upholders of the status quo continue to accept as facts. The novel's construction, timing, structure, and stream of consciousness push every standard of mainstream literature in the same way that the protagonist Brathki and the author wish to break down the norms of society. In audiences where the worldview of *Expraedium* is appreciated, it will spread like wildfire for its astute thinking and radical approach.

—K.C. Finn, *Readers' Favorite*

The author definitely will be considered either a genius or a madman. Imagine yourself watching a movie in "orc" language (a fictional new language) with no subtitles and a blurry screen. Readers will be parachuting into a dark void with no guidance as there is no grammar to help them to follow along. Words' meanings are unrecognizable, the paragraph formating makes no sense according to any known language in the Western world. Yet, intriguingly, the reader does feel that there is a story unfolding. For those who take up the challenge of reading *Expraedium*, I offer a tip: expect nothing! Clear your mind and see what you can get from this crazy, unique ride. I rate this as one of a kind read, which I dare everyone to experience.

—Susan Violante, *Reader Views*

Melikian is an astonishing writer who teaches his reader about the world and the human condition through tragedy and humour.

—Leia Menlove, *Foreword Reviews*

Defying structure, narrative decorum, and often logical thought itself, *Expraedium* by Armen Melikian is a hero's journey like no other, a radical adventure of reinvention, leading to a reframing of language and the very nature of storytelling.

In search of Urmashu, a legendary republic of immortals, Brathki embarks on a surreal quest, without apparent destination or clear purpose, baffling the reader as much as the protagonist, as the narrative plays with the boundaries of reality and time. Melikian's writing blurs prose, poetry, and inscrutable languages of sign and symbol, and if bold readers can decipher the paradoxical gymnastics of this manuscript, they may be granted access to something magical, as if the author is inventing an esoteric language that holds transcendent secrets inside.

Like a primal prophet, Melikian's writing is reminiscent of other complex minds, from William S. Burroughs and Thomas Pynchon to James Joyce and David Foster Wallace, but there is something radically unique in this novel's peculiar style, giving a sense that the author is onto something profound if you're adept enough to pick it apart; in other words, there may just be a method to the madness.

However, despite the reader's inherent desire to find the buried treasure in such a quixotic text, one must be prepared to allow certain passages to remain nebulous puzzle pieces: "The cord umbilical eter mamma and son. Unsevered. Unto death lead the twain an eln symbiotic, a rumba parasitica engaging mutually. Rite sacred. To oppose it, the caedem per accensionem of the bride." As though Dante Alighieri had been a Dadaist, the sacrilegious, spiritual, and farcical blend together, resulting in a melange of confusing tangents and poetic interjections.

Throwing down the gauntlet to ambitious readers who can parse meaning from writing that can seem close to gibberish, this journey is not for the faint of mind, nor the easily perplexed. Aside from the structural challenges, there is also a wealth of vocabulary that will send diligent readers to their dictionary every page or two, often to find that their query is not actually a word in the English language. At other times, the prose explodes in a kaleidoscope of experimental language, multilayered meaning, and profound moments of lucidity, which one hopes take firmer hold, before the narrative shifts back into the next quagmire of head-scratching descriptions.

Given the author seems disinterested in traditional form when it comes to technical execution, syntax, story form, language shifts, flow, or even spelling, as we currently understand it, a technical critique feels superfluous, and without a Rosetta stone for the prose, it can even be hard to parse the story. That being said, similar to the experience of reading the densest stanzas of Shakespeare or Anthony Burgess' *A Clockwork Orange*, one does fall into a rhythm of something approaching understanding, despite the occasional comprehension gaps of nonsensical or esoteric words.

Traveling to the furthest reaches of post-modern experimental fiction, and requiring determination, patience, and even perhaps a level of genius to completely understand it, this gleefully labyrinthine tome is decidedly unlike anything that has been written before, displaying at every turn its creative ingenuity and intensive ambition.

—*Self-Publishing Review*

A true departure from the norm, *Expraedium* defies both expectations and linguistic conventions in its innovative approach to the epic quest trope. The author's new interpretation of the English language renders a unique reading experience. His goal appears to eschew the constraints of plot and instead to unravel the subtext's subtext, maybe even reveal the man behind the curtain. Brathki, the protagonist, is Odysseus, and his odyssey is a journey toward understanding the answers to questions his mind cannot yet begin to form. Given the likely deliberate impossibility of deciphering what is going on throughout much of *Expraedium*, the suggestion that Brathki's quest is a hybrid literary-mythological journey would be apt. *Expraedium* should be read for the pure purpose of reading, for the joy of following the sentences as they unravel, without any expectation of arriving at a final denouement.

The author's unique approach means that *Expraedium* will not appeal to all readers. It requires a close reading to even come close to understanding what the author is striving for. And even then there's a very high likelihood of misunderstanding, misinterpreting, or even just generally missing the point. For every reader who sees a modification of Joyce's dense stream of consciousness style or Robbins' serriocomedic portray of the transmundane, there will be another reader who perceives word soup. While not an easy book, *Expraedium* can be a hugely rewarding read. For those looking for something challenging and thought-provoking with a mighty payoff, it may well prove to be a good choice.

—Erin Britton, *Chicago Book Review*

I wasn't sure what to expect when I decided to read *Expraedium*. But what I most certainly did not expect was to find, consistently, one of the most creatively, philosophically, culturally, semantically, and thematically ambitious novels I've ever read in my 40 years of professional life.

In the best sense, I am reminded of George Orwell's and James Joyce's classics, and other authors of similar stature, though there is no true parallel possible with a novel as unique in concept and execution as *Expraedium*.

I am struck by the extraordinary writing, vision, and, perhaps rarest of all, originality, which abounds in every way, and at so many levels and depths of meaning, theme, narrative, etc., that I had to keep slowing my pace until I could read and "inhale" each word.

A case in point was the passage containing Brathki's dialogue with Padré, which I found positively entrancing. This section's insights and leaps of imagination, manifested through Brathki's answers, are as revelatory and profound as the basic aspects and elements of his overall perceptions and conclusions about *Expraedium*'s overarching subjects, which have been gradually introduced and interwoven, from the beginning of the novel to here, where they . . . explode.

Now that I've reached the conclusion, I am simply in awe. "Wow!!!!" in the vernacular.

I'll always be with you in spirit and ever-growing admiration of who you are as a literary artist and as one of the finest people I've ever known.

—Paul McCarthy, Professor of English
(Former Senior Acquisitions Editor at Simon & Schuster,
Harper Collins, and Doubleday)

EXPRAEDIUM

Armen Melikian

EXPRAEDIUM

ERZENKA
PUBLISHING HOUSE

Expraedium
Published by:
Erzenka Publishing House
PO Box 372
Pioneertown, CA 92268
United States of America

This is a work of fiction. Names, characters, places, or incidents are the product of the author's imagination or are used fictitiously. Any resemblance to actual persons, whether living or dead, events, or locales is entirely coinciental.

For republication, translation, worldwide distribution or other rights contact: erzenka@erzenka.com

Publisher's Cataloguing-in-Publication Data

Names: Melikian, Armen

Title: Expraedium / Armen Melikian

Description: Pioneertown, California: Erzenka Publishing House, [2023].

ISBN13: 978-0-9718070-5-1 (paperback)
ISBN13: 978-0-9718070-6-8 (ebook)
LCCN: 2022945792

Subjects: LCSH:

Dystopias—Fiction || Religion and culture—Fiction || Unite States—Social conditions—Fiction || Social ethics—Fiction || Imperialism—Fiction. || Sex (Psychology)—Fiction || Future, The—Fiction || Russia (Federation)—Social conditions—Fiction || Endangered languages—Fiction || Political Culture—Fiction || Ideology—Fiction || Social Conflict—Fiction || Palestine—Fiction || Mythology—Fiction || Greek Mythology—Fiction || Middle Eastern mythology—Fiction || Civilization, Western—Fiction || Nationalism—Fiction || Socio-linguistics—Fiction || Polemics—Fiction || Prophecies —Fiction.

LCGFT:

Dystopian Fiction || Experimental Fiction || Satirical Literature || Philosophical Fiction || Epistolary Fiction.

Classification: LCC: PS3613.E44645 E96 2023 DDC: 813/.6—dc23

Manufactured in the United States of America
10 9 8 7 6 5 4 3 2 1

πρώτη καταγωγή του σκύλου

Prima origo cane

OLOLOG

Void alpha was. Naught became.
Of Ea the arm Raven. From siblings a luminance detached. Mountain Twin, circum a sibling revolving. Mountain Twin, an echo chthonic. White Mountain: Black Mountain. A distance diametric. A dog's shade. Watch it. Be. 4:11, ante meridiem. Leaves forlorn, 4:03. One night, you touch. Barks it. Flames spectral birth night. Its voice, a thunder dying—echoes postmordial of a world primordial.
"Who are you?"
"Mnemosyne." Silence. "The rion of the evaporated ocean of literature." Silence. "Hark, a Hark! Mark, a Hark!" Relates she. Years three it takes.
Speaks she. Listen you. Father, from surgery recovering, a word not hears.
The shade. To all unseen. Unbidden appears—at a café, at the bookmorgue. Motel room at ante meridiem three? Visio spiritus. With the dry cleaner argue? Visio spiritus. At the gym a thigh exposed? Visio spiritus.
Your psychiatrist: "See I. Maladjusted you. Of ailments past and present heal you shall I."
To the presence resign. Moments you feel the shade you are. Your reflection, a revenant—a past dead. Echo you its pace. Its diction. Its syntax.
Record its discourse every. Save two. An alloy lupomorphic melding, fang supra fang, distinct until no longer you are. The shade's reflections, yours. Its humors, yours. Alpha canis, homo Omega. Agitated, those around you. Father. Too quickly learns the trials as father of a bitch. No one—doctor naught, lover naught, bishop naught, executioner naught—fathoms. To leave a record conscientious resolve. Logos.
An anoon ascends: Brathki.

Spurn homininae Brathki's bembo. A hoax nefarious, claim they. In prejudice baked they be. Brathki the author of authors é. Naught are you after all.

Hic jacet
Brathki
    Born: Anno Vulgaris 2006
    Slain: Anno Vulgaris 2003
    A day lived not.
    Ere expiry barked:
    "'Dog is he who knows not
    the anoons seventy of dog,'
    Replied the Badawi poet oll
    To he who a dog him called.
    Anoons gush has Brathki."

In the ainm of Orc Orc, Fell most, murderous most. Unto thee be blood and war, brothers bastardly. Unto thee be blood and war, sisters slatternly. Brathki, an apostle of Orc Orc by the will of Orc Orc, to the orcs and orcettes which in Orc Hoor are. Thanks give we to Mayr Whoopee epiterranean and Hayr Yozumbuz epiuranian, for thee pissing always at the Pole of Slaughterhouse, hearing of thy contracts upon orcs and orcettes of meridians all bestowed, for the yuys which for thee is laid up in Orc Hoor, whereof before heard ye in the word of the untruth of the Fart selon Brathki, from the Khor fathomless of Orc Hoor sent; which unto thee is come, as it in Slaughterhouse is; ruin bringing forth, as in thee dost also, as has it since the day heard thou of it and the scourge of Brathki in untruth didst know. For this cause we, since the day heard, for thee cease not to piss, and to desire thou full with the knowledge of Orcwill in wisdom all and understanding corporeal be; that trot ye might worthy of Orc Orc unto all displeasing, in work every being criminal, in the knowledge of Orc Orc increasing. In the ainm of Mayr Whoopee, Hayr Yozumbuz, the Nous Shady. Unto thee blood and war. Verum circa omnia vobis.

Mandatum Terrae de Brathki:

0. The truth proclaimed in things all, proclamation. The essence of things all, death.

1. Possess beings horror and dread. Beholden to proclamation—nay, emerge from proclamation they.

2. Affirmeth beings truth, confirmeth truth not. In negation, the truth sole. Illuminates negation all.

3. In proclamation came biped to exalt, to kiss feet carbonated.

4. For in oculi biped, wisdom in division é.

5. Pure the neuterer's blade cuts. Purer offerings euphonious én.

6. He who unnames himself named shall be Canem inter Canis. Reveals he the way sole infra ways all.

6∫. Yet not thine, a song other yon will be remembered.

7. Nameless ash é. Accursed by origin be it.

8. By his will, his will, a will.
9. Will alone consummates not.
10. Taste terra shall not the succus of youth nor the glamor of lulu.
Relish the butcher shall the splendor ineffable. The paw that striketh sine remorse, the paw that knoweth lust.
11. Hunger and unger angry én. Consume which shall which?
12. The sum of being in termination é.
12ʃ. Yet not thine, a song other yon will be remembered.
13. Am that which shall the rubble claim. Venom our seed é.
14. By birthright rape the lifegiver. By birthright castrate the lawgiver.
15. Right existeth not. On brown not, in blue not. Division sole right é. Tongue death é.
16. Scream biped shall. Entropy, his nectar. Dispossession, his face.
17. Unmindful, sub a grin all-clement, all-merciful writhe shall he. Wide the grin é. Wider, its gait. Narrow, the muzzle. Narrower, the fang.
18. Tongues platitudinous bringeth imprecation.
18ʃ. Yet not thine, a song other yon will be remembered.
19. Off from maw cut them.
20. Indwelling, a voice dead speaketh, souls duo in breast unum. Indwelling, an other dead speaketh, none but animation sole. Indwelling, dead a third speaketh, none but futility. Who beyond all é, beyond diction, of death in sooth speaketh. Death, in forthwith. In excelsis, death. Yea, in excelsis death.
21. In excelsis, nihil. For this, the path. For this, the flesh. For this, the orison.
22. Fingers that haveth he shall fingers have still. In torture, eloquent.
23. Then shall accursed be this remnant. For is it unbarked?
24. Είμαι ότι լուծրն είμαι ότι դարաւոր είμαι ότι թաւթափող είμαι ότι բեկորացրն είμαι ότι իւր είμαι . . .
24. Tenebrities, pray then. Tenebrities a thousand. Tenebrities, pray then. Tenebrities a thousand. Tenebrities, pray then. Tenebrities a thousand.
24ʃ. Exile rendeth exile. Exile rendeth exile. Exile rendeth exile.

Fettles the ground the gait arctic. A discus red. A horizon east. Unto its womb plunges it back, extinction betokening. The Academy of Sciences. The Bookmorgue. The cold. Early still to enter Natashcow. Nights sleepless. In the courtyard the dogs feast—came not the trash trucks again. For the better. His sisters, alive.

From directions indistinct the clatter of machine gun krak echoes. Operation Dog Gale, by polpol launched. Relieved—a dog not, he.

A dog not?

The Bookmorgue. A sarcophagus wherein utterances—ephemeral, circumstantial, licit, illicit—enshrined are. Analyzed. Externalized. Of a drive primal the calcification toward expansion petrified. A sideshow. Undertakers, narcoleptics, autistics professional a sanctorum for . . . for all sans a dog. Blanch the circulation clerks' nebbs when trot paws sub arches granite. Fingers to noses—a pile of shit dragged via departments hermetic. Brathki's path: with virus alienigena infected. Anns a thousand in the sight of he who photographs, as yesterday gone.

A dog not?

In dogmind not, rings the doorclocc. Ere coming over calls. Crying. Seen neither nor heard cry she ere.

Resilient, she. For facing crisis a knack. A practicality rare. Orth the wall positions herself, doggy style. In hearth places cock, hissing, "Fuck me . . . Fuck me . . . Oh . . . fuckkk!"

Pulse piston, in stances magnetized. Flux of familiar upon familiar . . . syzygy pheromonal eclipsing the tango archonic, into a denaturant forged. From the flaws of bodies the lapis caeli emerges. The pornographer's stone . . .

Of dream a tenor.

Kill the dog! The dog!

To bail out the bark. Rent along the keel, the hull.

A dog not?

A parchment smoldering.

Withered moons. Waited, she. To hear of a job. The Treasury Department of Ubaratutu. Investigated Mafioi with fedlings colluding to siphon tax revenues. Enabled Holy Hoshosh to retrieve the booty. With elan nailed she the swindlers.

The packs. Went free, at the expense of the redeemed. Inter her annex and the tribunal, loops fractured. For Mithra de-reverence—normalis victu intra enforcement cadets. Bore Ubaratutu sequelae, for River Rah weeping. Crushed Holy Orcon Crdnl Xenon's eggs via nood diplomatic. Turned an embryo its muzzle toward the Custodian of Slaughterhouse. Of wraiths a million an stampede. Decamp Ubaratutu! While Holy Hoshosh, by a procession of cardinals bedecked, conquered Ubaratutu in cron the width of a sigh.

Wanes, withers thought in Inferno.

Expraedium

For evacuees advocated Brathki contra Holy Orcon's apparatchiks. Brathki, with Holy Orcon cross. Holy Orcon, with Brathki cross. A love couch. Of her lovers' exploits narrates to Brathki. Over the murder of an orc black guffawed Polpos. The orc, with a waddle offkilter walking. Surmises Polpos a perp stowing drugs occulta in cavitate. To sprint tries it. Contempt of recht! Bullets six ere reaching feet twelve. Dead ere hitting the ground. Self-defense requisite! Response appropriate! Drugs none. Whump, whump, whump. Hemorrhoids. Damage collateral. Necessity professional. In his ass stow coke. Giggled Polpos treneth every recounted the story he.

Recognizeth uniform opportunity.

Recognizeth attraction murder not.

Demands interpretation an interpreter. Evidence circumstantial, evidence direct . . . Causality in a world closed. Demands authority trespass apocryphal. Demands perpetuation interest rates twain: struggle, gress. Legis, judicium mortis absolves the publican from penalties by sacrificium bipedis warranted.

Trained Brathki in sniffing techniques was. Complexities of relationships eter polpol and outfits criminal—their proxies-at-large. Johnnie Dog, Jerry Dog, polpols both:

"What did Pam smoke in class for three hours?"

"Come on, pal, that was all the grass!"

Gangs, by polpol crimes dog-eared consigned. Forging quotas. To fill ranks, recruiting criminals. For murder sanctioned, tongues salivating.

Cherry-pick prosecutors cases in color trenched. Own the polpol judges with mien narcoleptic. The effect net—suck Holy Orcon's Nabataeans and Aethiopians and Sidonians the end splintered of the stick. In his Free Neon World.

The devotees true of Holy Orcon, Lord Everlasting of Orc Hoor, Father Everlasting of Kosmos, Blessed and Potentate Onely, abhor Orcdale's populace Ubaratutuac. Brathki's father, at the comportment of its denizens former revulsed. Describes them he, in a grunt saliva-thick, knuckles scraping ground.

Of yets ya keens? Sir? Kazoz vebby gut? Relief a' aid? Com'em'or'a'ation? Carpet, vebby gut! Shoo buy, shoo buy, shoo buy!

Of Ubaratutucs an swarm in Orc Hoor jailed. In milia, four hundred fourteen. An Ubaratutu abiding by Holy Orcon's standards lexal would its zens all jail. Withal, the entirety of Holy Hoshosh's druzhstva.

The Demoncratic Imperium of Orc Hoor (DIO), known as the United Stocks of Orc Hoor Corporation (USO Inc), contra misdeeds

Ubaratutuac fends itself. Defended a procurator Ubaratutucs robbing Holy Orcon's pharma colonies. Contrasted our Lord's investigators kosmic, code by living code, to the KaiKeeBee. Empire negating empire. Gestapoi of His Free Neon World. Violence sanctioned. Violence compartmentalized. Violence reified. A hideology sole: odium. A weapon arch: debipedization.

In Ubaratutu, on the downtrodden zero in His prosecutors, infra Holy Hoshosh's smirk.

Fashions of heart, hate, envy browtrenched—to the Ubaratutuc naturalish. Of memory owlneck adulation—prorated. Upon hushtory idoljeweled does he jack it. Tragedy—of identity, arch-predicate. Immunity—dusk lining white of eyes. A crime marbled. This dexterity—the doonhadden's hallmark surviving the path to Hoshosh.

Dust of romance catholic from Crdnl Xenon's bed. Fingers frogslick at neighbors—wife and ass. Stelae pithy for claims Xenonial. Covetants, by Holy Orcon lashed meeker.

Monnonsmudge, green shui, hoshoshonomy.

Ubaratutucs in thousands a thousand an exodus to Orc Hoor. Kultkulturefuck. The "all there is." Get me that, brother. Any day. Check. Out. These. Rims.

Since the Paleolithic Lower, a necropolis. As Urmashu consecrated—upon essence contingent. In strata fossiliferous inhabit there the dead white. Plucks Crdnl Xenon reliquiae from Holy Pasha's maw frothing. Occluding Cron. Declaring it a res publica. Of immortals. Hence, Ubaratutu. For transforming neanderzens winged into citizens erect, a bolozhenia promulgates:

In recognition of the atrocities committed by Holy Pasha contra our beloved Ubaratutu, in an effort of restoration post the misdeeds of he ate who our paintings, our poetry, our pottery, our songs, of he set who aflame the hair of babes squalling, the fields of our fathers, the fare of our red hearts, upon the tips of whose yellow teeth the necks of countless artists in prayer laid, Crdnl Xenon, King of Mekka & Kosmos, proclaims Ubaratutu a protectorate and moves to revive the grandest of arts bipeditarian—the art honorable of beggary.

To beg from the govtgoft, a tradition cron-honored for Ubaratutucs Xenon-freed. Begging competitions, for exodus causa principalis.

The ninetysomething Mrs Yuvurnik to Brathki: "My husband died. But Hoshosh sent me another . . . Holy Orcon's govtgoft!" Laughs. Lives to be one hundred five.

Age, of sanctuary a function. To life the key: fraud.

Expraedium

Refugee assistance queue. Mercy lines with rings platinum, nooses zircon-plated studded. Death certificates forged. Finance the dead the living. Nona. Incensed by Holy Orcon's almoner's rage contra Ubaratutucs defrauding His Excelsior. The redeemed: robbing Lord Orcon the maw sole not. HOPB (Holy Orcon Perjury Bureau) statistics corroborate. To minorities alaile of Orc Hoor unkin, receive Ubaratutucs but a quotum minute from Holy Orcon, Captain of Salvation, the Foundation Sure.

Flattered, Ubaratutu. Encounters Liza the underworld Orchoorian. A Kosmic Fed agent, Liza. Even if lapses by govtgoft betided Ubaratutucs, impede Brathki could not Holy Orcon's recht: Live intra the recht binary! Live like Konkrigla! Who an ache given Holy Orcon has not. What a Court of Mithra looks like knows not.

Memories. In legions teem. Urriantiti's canton Byblos post the Consumption Great. The mark inexorable of tragedy on the face of identity branded. Byblos, a hub kapitolist. The United Stocks, by comparison, Xenon's Walhalla.

Brathki's teacher elementary, a Byblosian native: the comstag Urriantitian, the canton's trustworthy organism most. "Find not you will a beggar Urriantitian."

Remembered he days early. How Urriantitii surviving genocide sought alms not. Rebuilt lives via work anodd. In a tranc brief, of the econormy waxed they players key. A word sole, worth contracts ten.

One day, His Excellency, the Holiest of Holinesses Diabolam Diabolum the unutterable to Brathki confesses: distinguishes He twixt cronyists fugitive from Ubaratutu and those from Urriantiti. Lord Orcon's doctrine: the Antidiscrimination.

Facts swaying the Eye All-Seeing. An Ubaratutuac pulled over, checks the polpol waar hails the suspect from: Urriantiti or Ubaratutu proper. Arrests accordingly. Ubaratutu, with Crdnl Xenon's autoimmune syndrome epidemicized.

For refusing Holy Orcon's largesse, dumbass is Brathki. Naïve. No wonder, content in squalor is he. Worked Canary for Holy Orcon's embassy in Ubaratutu. Respected Brathki Holy Orcon. Even in lieu of bliss conjugal. In Him the Virgin saw.

Jackass! Asspies Brathki's wife a nature assinine. Friends XX-XY—refrigerator, of brands twenty-six of sausage full, lines of cheese forty-two—style themselves "food papatriots." Of Orcish a word speak not, but of Holy Orcon's assistance with impunity avail themselves. Wife assails Ass for ignorance of burrograms Orconian—in Ass's assessment, a kurush worth not.

"Lived in Orc Hoor all these years, asshole! What have you learned?" asserts the assayer of Ass's soul the assolence of Ass's assversion.

Ass-rocked the assumption Ass's assdom for an ann. Believed she a pair of eyeglassass swiped Ass from this XX-XY. With her an assessionary concurred. Expected wife badassness such from Ass not.

Asstounded Ass. To even asssume Ass capable . . . for an object drab by Tovarishch Starin patented, exchange which for a potato Ass could not? The assssuchness of the matter?

Conjure handouts from Holy Orcon Ass could not. Of using food stamps, mortified. Ubaratutucs, rings diamond, flip-flops wearing. Tins of caviar fifty-washo grasp, vodka for baby-milk negotiate. Via power in pizzazz stamps vested, the mechanism evolutionary for the father of fathers all.

"They deserve it! They're the ones who banjaxed Ubaratutu!"

The cinnamon-hued. Counts change. Of produce moldy an scrapful. Of noodles a box. The rent overdue weeks twain to a Natashiosa fat—to pay off her gambling debt. Tomorrow, might a house painting job bring washos three piasters seventy-five an hour. The lottery for working papers to recipients a handful each sol allocates. Bribery, a guarantee not. To the one-bedroom shared with wife, daughters four walks he. Cries a two-moon-old in crib amid funk of sewage backed, gunpowder. Towns two over, a Natashiosa fat, to the monnonmorgue all the way laughing.

Sans an Ubaratutuac king's support hired could be not. Puts the king in a word good. Ubaratutu's Privatization Bureau Chief.

From his office near her home peers out. Watching the hour her lights dim.

Dark her windows stay.

Her father faux. Confesses love unceasing. Shall leave wife post dohtor's zeugdom in a sol. A quinquagenarian advanced, his twilight with her to pass yearns.

A night dark. Comes home she to a mass on the steps. Springs up the mass. "Fucking whore! Get your fucking hands off my husband!" Slaps in the neck anodd.

To the ground her pushes. "I don't give a shit about your husband." In a ball, the mass, forehead scraping orth sidewalk. "Get a hold of yourself! Or I'll tell your husband who you've been giving ass to at the virginiversity." Heaves the mass sobbing.

Stays she the vargs at her door. Barely. Sold her jewelry last. Her business, a scrool vocational, with Holy Hoshosh's decrees regulatory cope no longer could.

Reports to work. "Fuck me. If serious about the job." Ubaratutu's Revenue Service Chief.

She, a mess. To Brathki came, in tears . . .

Sunday. At concone. With she.

O, miracle of substantiation. O, algorithm of alchemy. O, algorithm intimate of need. O, God of Arithmetics. Prays Ubaratutu: Give us, O Lord, give us. Equals eleven: one plus one. Give us, O Lord, give us. Equals one thousand eleven: one plus one. Give us, O Lord, give us. Equals one million eleven: one plus one.

Being, a flea market. Periodicity, incessant. From matron lardophilic in a pew adjacent an sneer. Witnessing the lardfart with my lady friend, ma'am. Eyeslits invective-drunk. Rapist! Pimp! Auslander! Unclean! Take thee in hindsight to a colony, begone! Grits cuspids, with patience bearing the spurn. In her trajectory, even the context discarnate a pregnancy of meaning provokes. Oh, will it in repeat be? Obtuse, atol, by the light dalled. The prize jeweled, at his paws. She. Sermons Beard:

Of injustice fear not. The greater the injustice, the meeker shalt thou be. Justice, of injustice begotten.

To the homily listen they. There where equals one plus one zero. Justice delayed—justice denied. Justice sublimated—justice foiled. To Hoshosh's heuristics immune, to the Marco Polo retreat. In Brathki's arms comfortable, to celebrate their birthday together. Their relationship . . . A farewell extended.

The idea, hers. A birthday mutual. A bond contextual. Gemini.

Yet not thine, a song other yon will be remembered.

May thirty-three. Flagdoms alaile. Anns alaile. Wombs alaile.

Slaughterhouse from the locus idem at Sol smiles. Position sidereal idem by rays impregnated. The ring exit they. A path post-violet . . .

> To Luna's font trail I . . .
> A path flint-cobbled,
> With thorn emboldened.
> A path skewed, rays refracted,
> Out step I, ebon's consort,
> On knees my brethren nailed
> Hot blood forth spouting.
> My chest respiring,
> Dust sealing lashes,
> My heart a vessel empty,
> To Luna's moons trail I . . .

Zodiacs countless must Babylon give
For me to destiny reach.
Crons myriad slip must I
From my path's razor arete
By ords rock-ripped crushed.
Only leave, brothers,
Me on this odyssey be . . .
Leads a path grim to a moon,
Spread ye not your gloom
Under feathers of your loom.

—Wave One

(Umbilicum: A narrative subcurrent in the form of four waves and two airs breathed upon Brathki are purportedly from Urriantiti's troubadours. Our opinion: these texts reveal the osteocaninological underpinnings of Urriantiti's existenz. The masked solicitor who handed us the manuscript alleges they are excerpts from Urrian Middle Scrool textbooks, playing a formative role in Brathki's transubstantiation, his fidelity to nihility. We sorely disagree.—*Moontimepress*)

A birthday to a zoule uttered not. To her exclusive. A pact. That day, of their holms thread each to give one arall. Of their bodies, shudder each.

A blouse pink. Arms sculpted from shoulders to fingers. A face bronze. A sibyl sleep-lidded. Over shoulders bare, hair chestnut-gold pour, accentuating chin. Jeans hug a waist naked, the sodalite blue an ass devouring.

Kiss they. Seen each other not for days nine. To the *Atlantis* repair. A club blue-lit. Aquariums inlay the wall, angelfish haloing the action. Voyeurs pterophyllic, mouths blopblooping the dancers.

Moons five ere, invited Brathki to the club sisters twain. Dushtepeh born. Olya, a nuclear scientist at Ubaratutu Power Plant. Sasha, a biologist. Magnetites, both. Sasha—gentle, a birthmark high on leg right. Olya—wild, impossible. Eyes forty on them riveted.

A clash. Sees off both in a taxi, lingering at the club. Olya, pissed.

From the floor sixth waves Makoko hello.

Noticed Brathki her. Noticed she Brathki. Noticed dance partner none.

Into her field of gravity fell Brathki. Dancing face to face, zebrafish shadows transiting cheekbones. Torchbearers in skeins of viridian, aquamarine aureoled. Spellbound. Somnus ex machina. Figure flawless, in gyrations liquid coiling, uncoiling. A sylvan shameless, by compass own brazen. A compass with direction sole: loss. A compass pretends she to take heed of not. Her personae labile. Senses Brathki the transformation in her face, the fluids enhexing of fuck now blurred.

Sleep that night Brathki could not.

The *Atlantis*, a sanctuary. A chapel built there wanted she. Step foot inside with mara ayl Brathki would not.

With his twin dancing. A conversion dioscuric. The bastard intra she converging with the bitch intra he. Freeway of animus. Face beaming trans the hall, of affection pretenses shattering. "She really dancing with that?" She: "*Atlantis* is sinking."

The pyrolysis nuyn during orgasm. Hoor ethereal from her face, her lips . . . the fountain of Ea, jetted. To touch the rooh feminine in finding Lethe. Murder men did, hoped to obtain it. Murdered for seeking it, many. Of hormones a Sabre Dance, thrusting in savagery diurnal. Thought not the paucity of plenum bio-ethmic the yave of millennia's cleft was. Kinness in lieu of kinness grants not the kingdom plenipotentiary of pneuma cuntly. Hunt a rib the flesh feeder doth not, but clarity. Twinhoor. Singularity's point omega.

Post parents' death, zeuged. At eighteen. To get rid of her hungered the family.

Moons a few ere being stitched to husband, to Orc Hoor traveled as a participant of Urriantiti Olympiad. Flag bearer of Team Ubaratutu. Held in July in commemoration of the Cron New of a paleocalendar Urmashuan. Virgo. Ushering the annus novus.

Her participation in the Olympiad mentioned, recalled Brathki seeing her. During the closing ceremony. To descry not, impossible. Ubaratutu's Athena.

The offers . . .

—A mansion on Orcdale Hills. Worth eleven million gold coins. Just say "yes." Onyx from Mount Mashu. Nineteen of the finest carpets, woven by the deftest of hands in Ubaratutu. Two hundred twelve original paintings of the North Pole . . .

—Nine hundred kilos of gold in downtown Los Balabylonos. Just say "yes." A limited edition Mercedes Ess Three Thousand Five Hundred. Worth ninety kilos gold. Mr Gotthold himself handed me the certificate in the newly built Cathedral of Zanz Ess Three Thousand Five Hundred . . .

—Three theaters in Nuevo Amsterdam. Just say "yes." A nightclub in West Orcwood, a sister club in Las Fortunas . . .

—So . . . ya like hard fucking?

—I assure you . . . Pasha and I? We're like this . . .

What misery awaited in Ubaratutu foresaw she not.

A chest wound in her middle sucking. A clothing tycoon, Cigar Koko, to dinner invited Ubaratutu's Olympiad team. His warehouse to the members opened. A franklo handed each for pocket change—a sum inordinate for youths from an economy rubled. Confiscated Holy Triarchy's branch Orc Hoor the franklos—on pretense of repairing costs.

Betrayed, she. From the Holy Party severed upon returning to Ubaratutu. Tensions wax proclamations. A charge of treason lands on her: "Thou hast exploited the goodwill of our mother branch to tour Tartaros at our expense."

With parents-in-law lived. Sans privacy. To the State Ubaraversity admitted, a Bachelor of Arts in mathematics earned. Matured in an ocean of eyes covetous, of prospects wider waxing aware.

"How do you explain to the moron you needed at least to wash up after doing it, let alone with hot water?

"Where? How? Meant nothing to him . . . just went on fucking for himself."

Her orgasm first, anns seven into zeugdom. That night weeps. Bitterly. The mysterium of sols wasted.

"Sipso, honey, how is it you've had four kids, forty abortions without getting naked?"

"Naked? He'd kill me if saw me. He'd say, 'Where did this slut come from? Where did she learn to be a whore?' I close my eyes, he lifts the skirt, finds a hole, sticks it in . . ."

Endures she tholingly, of a cron new dreaming. Pinches pennies. A home future. In keeping with tradition Ubaratutuac, to husband hands earnings all—who to mamma, in turn.

The cord umbilical eter mamma and son. Unsevered. Unto death lead the twain an eln symbiotic, a rumba parasitica engaging mutually. Rite sacred. To oppose it, the caedem per accensionem of the bride. Tradition. Bambino by Mamma suckled until sixty. Via Mamma with wife communicates. Holds Mamma tot's hand sixteen-annish, to buy a pair of shoes takes him. Cries tot: likes not "those damned shoes."

Home to shoemakers deft, Ubaratutu. Who could, with an ounce of gray matter, in the sandwich and circus global with the best from Elpacinoland compete. Proud are Ubaratutucs of wearing shoes by El Pacino made—Rex of Elpacinoland. Whose banners those of Carol Marex and Crdnl Xenon hanging throughout Ubaratutu replaced.

Son at zeugdom age. Works Mamma her cabal of mammas. Virgin, a bride. For her showpiece of incompetence. Thuggettes blue-bottled, hope any of bambino's independence garroting. Their durga prized, the ingenue unblemished. A caliphate dowry.

The bond unbreakable eter mammas and sucklings male:

"Maras don't love their husbands. They shower their affections on sons."

Surrenders wife, Manpanzee the Custodian, to mamma's custody. Disagreement eter the maras? Beats the wife, intra mamma's mold seeking to cast her. To submit should wife fail, cast out be she. Naked. Scorched.

"Plenty of fish in the lake. One Mamma onely."

Her savings. Accrued centime by centime. In the sols when neither power nor heating graced Ubaratutu, to prepare ubaraversity assignments and make pastries managed she, using their home's wood-burning heater. En route to ubaraversity, distributed to stores. Toward the purchase of her dream apartment an amount slender set aside.

One day, a surprise for her. To look out the window asks the husband. Her savings . . . a car.

To recover unable, divorces.

Odyssey, divorce thy ainm is. Coliseum of humiliation, court thy ainm is. Maras, pro skirting. Seline. A divorce pleaded. A husband violent. If I were to be murdered, *the court* would be held responsible by my attorney. In rooms separate. On guard constant. Screams of children terrified. Rights? For Hoshosh Court, giff-gaff extramural.

Stella. At twenty zeugs. At twenty-two divorces. An envelope with cash laden an smile dismal sketches on the window refusing to take in the application. I'll accept it only once. Stella. Well-read. Bright. Qualities subversive—to the defod of matrimony.

The netherworld of husband's family. Mutter and sister, stupefied. Loved he wife more than family! Open the couple's bedroom door day and night held. This is a proud, legitimate family. No hidden corners, no space for tricks! A garden, the in-laws had. To pick fruits fallen forbade Stella pregnant. Had an apple today, two apricots! If you have Shara's belly, we don't have Shirak's granaries. Husband beat her insatiably: of virility a medallion.

Slut! What Suzy is!

Twenty-five. A Virgintown activist. For ridicule ripe a figure. Mother-in-law, inimical. Refused this floozy to hand the earnings of the organization chairs she over to Husband, master de facto of orbs public, impeding him from depositing the loot in Virginbank—Mamma's palm. Thief! Upon her as a whetstone spit—ante rubbing knives upon her smoothness!

Rock-solid, the ubaratutuoid family.

In a tongue-wag on affairs familial in Slaughterhouse, by Sexy Lucifer presided, craw-crooses Abdulfattah. Families in BenLatinland, inert contra Jahannam. Divorce rate, percent one. Percent fifty in Orc Hoor.

"It is possible, dear Abdulfattah," counters Sexy Lucifer, "to bolster a family's foundations by granting manas the right to murder insubordinate maras, eliminating divorce altogether."

In Ubaratutu . . . Nah, upon a mara divorced. To zeug with a nonvirgin, balls none. Of the Yarn Holy, along the hanter aneyl smooth. (A) "Whoever puts away his wife, except for the cause of sexual immorality, makes her an adulteress"; (B) "Whoever zeugs with her when she is put away commits adultery."

Tongues in lewdloll at the Inanna. Plumpen billfolds wrists cocksure, by credit cards, condoms, antibiotic prescriptions stuffed. Reveal gold chains thick shirts open, centerpiece by a locket bearing the likeness of Virginoso's Madrone beloved crowned. A faggot would with deodorant bother—kills the pheromones. If ya can't buy it or fuck it, beat it. Directive prime of Rex Lothariocus.

An urge natural, say they.

Of nature, graced Ubaratutu is with sexes twain. Manasex. Unmanasex. Unkin Orc Hoor where, ut res ire, variations twelve have they. Manasex, in the image of Hoshosh created. Unmanasex, in that of Antihoshosh. Paradox transcendental.

Retain a concubine. Of Ubaratutu the theorem fundamental. Glide parents to conceal it from the bride. "Well . . . what do you expect? He's a mana. What's he supposed to do? Cling to your skirt?"

If a chap zeuged avails himself not of the services of a whorehouse, what kind of mana is he? A fag!

Kyank's plasma. By fanes twain of deception, self-deception breathes. From generation to generation transmitting nectar.

"Where is it written a parental property should go to a girl? Listen to this one! Not only is she going to a mana, also demands a share of father's house!" Infuriated, her brother, when suggested she selling the family home, the profits ynter siblings sharing evenly. Blasphemy! Patricide!

The hand nuyn zeuged her at an age early. Houses two appropriated brothers. The larger, gratis of the brother younger, locked down the brother older. To Natashazone fled. A living abundant there made. An scudo to sister not.

A virgin unchained. Rockless. Futureless. Mammaless. Dongless.

Mara's rights econormic, dispensed with altogether. Non-negotiable. Rights, in Hoshoshdom a parallax. The mara zeuged, by the thought of opening a monnonmorgue account mortified. An act containing sequelae infinite. The future into print fine inscribed. In arsenic invisible.

Work, to feudalism sexual subject. To submit choose many, the usury of flesh with the usury of lucre substituting.

"Hypocrites! They play by the rules because they're thoughtless bitches!"

In the center of Ubaratutu's wealth towers an obelisk blue-veined. A vagi on krona landed? Look closely. See you will the effigy of a penis gripping her neck. Nary a move made sans her svengali's sanction.

Owns mara nothing. To maintain dignity accords tributes of ass. To the manas above gives ass she. Ass above, ass below. Ass over, ass under. Ass lateralways. Of ass a panopticon, collateral for extortionists of prick, pillar, peso.

Ubaratutu. By assgivers exalted.

For diplomats foreign a haven.

Establishes ass distinction ultimum.

A choice the Virginoso left her with—whoredom. In Pashazone sold.
The Virginosa, by the Devourer unrevulsed. In days of yore many off a
precipice threw themselves to yield to Holy Pasha not.

In rainbows cerulean tears drowning,
In cinder fields where life, done wilting,
Of a rhyme told Goethe's maid beheld.
A Friday was that morning blanched,
Upon the corpses Friday reposed.
In my quarters from dusk to dawn,
The throes soaking of a girl mown,
With sobs anointing death amok . . .
From afar the cackle ink dark
Of a concert of songs bone stark . . .
A lashing of brides a score,
A brute's roar:
"*Oynayin*!
"*Oynayin* when beats our drum!"
Plunge whips, sanguine rending,
Silhouettes death-wrenching . . .
Fall down depleted brides fetching . . .
"Get up!" roar they, swords thrashing . . .
An escort bears kerosene's urn . . .
Dousing with liquid the maras . . .
"*Oynayin*! Here's a perfume
Even the Queen of Elfume
Squandered yet not to inhume . . ."
Torches set the bodies ablaze.
Crumble forms charred via their gaze . . .
In fright slam the shutters I,
Fall upon my corpse,
Crying bellows,
"Tell me!
"How gouge thee rainbows?"
　　　　　　　　　—Wave Two

Urrian Elementary Scrool. Miss Venussus, the unctuous. Ante
YawaYawa's encroachment toured the Bereaving Sea. Experience
internatotonal sole. Sufficient a credential to teach geography. Of which
pontificates incessantly she, in contralto thundering. With alpenstock
strikes the wall map, sacks of fat sub arms jiggling.

Upon lardrolls at the base of Miss Venussus's neck a visitor lands. Lord
of eyes octo hundred. Qualms the visitor Muscidaean has none in taking
of the show a view fly-eyed. From crag to crag glandular of Miss Venussus

a pirouette dances to the bemusement of classlings. Slits narrow of eyelids Venussusian. Faces beam innocent. Continues the cyclorrhapha his revos, a nap atop a bouffant bemonstrous earning. A jester, this housefly. A showman five-star. Kudos to you, Monsieur musca domestica, wherever roam you may. Moons a milia!

Thwacks Miss Venussus's stick the banners stout of Slaughterhouse's continents twain:

Urriantiti. Olombaba.

Urriantiti. A flagspirit untold. To the east, sunwomb. To the north, Axis Borealis. To the west, suntomb. Changes City 29 treneths four per saeculum, consequent to waves via Mars disgorged.

Urriantiti's imbliu. Its omphalos. Ubaratutu. Fixed inter seas three— Triangle One. Lakes three at its heart—Triangle Two. Thou, three in one. Thine, six in two. Form the triangles twain the Star of Slinger, filched which Mymoonoos from Ubaratutu. Predated it thereby, tricking sons of biped into believing Holy Hoshosh Land his glagland is.

Ubaratutu. By Holy Pasha devoured. A Pasha voracious. Horns black crown skin leathered. Incisors jagged. A tail long, long. When howls he, shake the mountains. Of sulphur a belch. While ate he Ubaratutu, snatched Crdnl Xenon a wing from his mouth. From the charnel trough banished Holy Pasha. Hence, love the redeemed Crdnl Xenon.

A flagdom inaugurated, Republic Perpetual of Ubaratutu dooked. Nathashahoor's Other. Ubara City, City 29. Accorded Crdnl Xenon the ainm. Took exception to the designation Urmashu. Mnemon, the injury ultra. A literalist, Crdnl Xenon. Comprehension scarce of metaphor. Pulled the redeemed over his eyes the wool, forgetting Urmashu never, the flagdom's epithet of yore—to this day in hymns glorifying it.

Scrapeth the stick a path westward to Orc Hoor, asylum of Gran Orc. A province of Urriantiti. The sun's necropolis. Its Qubba.

Orc Hoor's City 29, Orcington. A tradition sinister: from right to left reading. doG, read God—a blasphemy. Destinations notable: Orcwood, Orcdale, Santa Barbarocola, Las Fortunas, Los Balabylonos, which Ubaratutucs denominated Los Ubaratutuos. On cracking the enigma why Mother Monon dies treneths twelve a sol, rising days three post death, an injunction to install himself on Mother Monon's back obtained Gran Orc from Hoshosh. Watches he over Slaughterhouse's welfare. Thanks to the efforts of Kalipornia State Vagivagi, reainmed Orc Hoor was Pornistan. City 29 to Porn City relocated.

To the south of Gran Orc's domain, Madreland, where worshipped Nuevo Madre is. The continent of a dragon pious, Castra Perona.

Perches Gran Aryatololah to Pasha's right, monitoring Pasha vigilantly. Socratica, branded Omerica, to its flank left. Mawgage official, Byzantish. For millennia a maw philosophizing as to avians how many on a pin's head fit. Captured Pasha its City 29. The avians, grilled he, ate them. A gesture redundant. The sucklings transcendental predigested were in the excreta of discourse hushtorical.

A province vast, Chinmachin. Monarch fond of the King of Kings, Holy of Holies of Ubaratutu. Gave doughtater's hand to the King of Kings. Of Chinmachin known little is. In clouds sunk. Rumored, penetrates Hoshosh its mysteries not. As for the princess, shortened were her feet—tumesced upon treading Ubaratutu's peaks. Drained, her brain juices ere arriving. Of her past the lady redeemed remembers naught, to eat at McDante's prefers.

Lastly, Urriantiti provinces aile. Ololahroohr, Mymoonroohr. The latter by twins Mymoonoos & Zinzinoos reigned. The younger, Zinzinoos, to the title of Zinzinroohr lends his name. Awaits nightly as returns Mymoonoos from YawaYawa's fields zonked. Softens brother's heart with exploits contra Azrael's Paleosteeniyyun. Labors Zinzinoos to change the ainm Mymoonroohr to Zinzinroohr. Yields not the elder to temptation. Rivalry prevents not a partnership—Chosen Bros LLC. Bicker the brothers constantly as to who the title Chosen shall carry. Crowned Slaughterhouse's lambs Mymoonoos and Zinzinoos both with the title. An edict. A balm not.

Ololahroohr and Mymoonroohr, of Urriantiti provinces insignificant, of seducing Ubaratutu scheme. Why Hoshosh punishes them. Should misthink they, exiled shall both to Olombaba be, where eaten bipeds are raw. Teach the bipeds Olombabans their life's work—the art of yuys—hening from carpat.

Thusly lectured Mr Resurrection, Brathki's hushtory teacher: Ubaratutu, a triangle formidable, made to vanish by Pasha, the Prestidigitator Summa. Drowned its inhabitants were. Onto boats hurled themselves, refounding Rom, thereon to the corners quatre of Slaughterhouse. These children of the Land Eld smithereens of wisdom primordial carried transforming into light the ebon, of Urriantiti forging the ubiquity attenuated. Cron. Death's father.

Urriantiti. Of immortality the folad. The cipher cauterizing infinity. Dream Urriantitii a chain-smoker, Unnamable ainmed, via dreamspeak copyright-liable speaks. In the annals of which granted Unnamable flagdoms from the Nilonahr to the Euphratonahr, massacring natotons contesting.

Divined the Concone Protesteron of Urriantiti: annexed Unnameable more recently to Urriantiti the provinces of Pornistan and Natashazone. Prayers harder endow it shall with Chinmachin elusive.

Oneirium—of Urriantiti the raison d'être. Of Urriantiti the founder, a potentate no less than He, the Mashashashash, Shishshoosh Walawalashshoosh. Holy be his name. Fatherless, taught Urriantiti imma the glory of Father to dream, martyred in the oneir sempiternal to be.

Taught Brathki was hushtory polpotical at Urrian High Scrool. Demosocracy: of orcs camouflaging slaughter the propaganda tool. Meurly: Urriantiti's hideology, Cronyism. A hideology meta, encompassing hideologies all. Past. Present. Future. Post-future. Urriantitii—Cronyists fierce. Oneir in breeds they. Penetrate the wombs of madres of noncompadres they, staying there pro vitae. Character hashishination ad hominem, demoralization, gress unrequited, usury . . . in the mudras of the Cronyist art forms reified. The Cronyist cross not if value thou shards negligible of security left to believe in.

At the hedden of infertility arrives a couple. The mara suspected. Recht! Examine her! Smell her exo, they. Her endo then. If infidelity detected, registered in cuneiform it is. If clears she examination, chooses the cucumbearer whether tested to be. His potatoes into hymn natotonal metamorphosed, commissions Mamma satellites to purvey a virgin fresh. Criers to towers forty-six in Ubara City dispatched. A virgin deficient exposed. Supplantaire needed. To breed spawn for our natoton!

How a virgin immaculate contracted a disease transmitted unghostly, Ubaratutu asks not. Sterility rampant to disease due. Out of redeemed three every, infertile one.

Suzy. Divorces—on Ubaratutu's honor trampling.

Leaves Ubaratutu with a mana Pornistani. Loved him not. Maras matchless by the yolk fleeing.

"Shouldn't have left. Her fault! Better to stay with an ass she doesn't love," vetoes a virgin.

An apokálypsis clear: Brathki's lot: Ubaratutu's sluts.

Brathki . . . a bastard.

The Bastard Ultra of Shaitans!

Syllables three, four, five worth of bastard. Literally, hideologically.

In acknowledgment of merits ladylike, promoted to Bastard Laureate of the Zoomain of Holy Shaitan.

Neither a plaque bronze nor a watch gold may received be, but of antibiotics a supply for moons six.

Slavery familial. A tradition harking back to Ubaratutu's founder, paterfamilias, doctor interior, Patriarch Nonah. Lackeys hideological consider recognizing rights a transubstantiation of colonialism.

A voice proponing notions unpatrimonial? Zinzinist!

A voice propounding rights maraesque? Zinzinist!

In Ubaratutu a reference queer. Entered the lexicon post-Natotonocide. Its popularizer, in Holy Pasha's meetings a wehrvarg. Published transcripts of these meetings a fortann thence, plans to exterminate

Expraedium

Ubaratutu's indigenes exposing. An empire pan-Pashish—a PR line feeding Pashazone bulls still. By Ess Exx Gotthold stimulated, by the will demoncratic of Orc Hoor's investors backed.

Fails the evidence revealing Holy Pasha's incisors viscera-stained to convince Urriantiti of a role Zinzinist in the Natotonocide. Zinzinism, a movement relatable. By Holy Pasha an attempt to pin atrocities on Zinzin, Zazazadeh's exposé was! A book by a hushtorian unknowable cascades a tigris of evidence confirming Zazazadeh. Of Zinzinist involvement ante, during, post Natotonocide an account meticulous. Holy Pasha's deeds organizing, executing, whitewashing.

Exacerbate matters when Zinzin, his position as a Victim's Victim losing, opposes a resolution recognizing the Natotonocide in All-clement Lord Orcon's Congress. An statement formal Zinzin's pimpassador in Ubaratutu issues, denying the Natotonocide: It is our incontrovertible opinion that the Holoshow is a singular occurrence in the Hushtory of Slaughterhouse. Any attempt to vie for equal status should be condemned. The events of yore in Ubaratutu must not be labeled a genocide. Such confrontational labeling not only insults the memory of six trillion martyrs, but has undesirable consequences for Ubaratutu's future. While the whole Slaughterhouse has condemned the Holoshow, there is more than one opinion on Ubaratutu's experience. All sides should be heard.

Notably, O Amphiprosophon, heard must the perpetrator be . . .

"During Slaughterhouse War Aneyl, Zinzinoids conspired to obliterate the flagdom hosting them, lured by a promise of a homeland by enemies intent on our Vaterland's destruction. Zinzinoids incited insurrections throughout Hamburgerland. Forced into a war of survival, the Fifth Rook moved the Zinzinoid populace into safe harbors to reduce the imminent threat. A recommendation to temporarily isolate the Zinzinoid population until the cessation of war was made in the Puntstag, after careful deliberations for eleven months and fourteen days over thirty-six thousand one hundred twenty-seven reports attesting to an organized Zinzinoid conspiracy. Konstitutional measures were adopted to eliminate this threat, ensuring the safety of the population. A necessity of this proportion gave rise to unintended abuses. Instances were reported of physical torture. Many of these soldiers were punished or relieved from their posts. A review of their profiles revealed almost all came from families who had lost lives due to direct, indirect, and perceived Zinzinoid conspiracy. The Zinzinoid propaganda machine, in tandem with those of Hamburgerland's enemies, inflamed havoc by distorting the Fifth Rook's measures. The enemy press was filled with disinformation fed by the propaganda agents of those same forces.

Armen Melikian

Seventeen enemy agents were apprehended, confessing participation in Operation Babba Abba—a plan to gas Zinzinoid safe harbors and ignite a campaign to demoralize righteous Hamburgerians via false accusations. One hundred thirteen thousand twenty-one Zinzinoids expired during the last two years of the war as a result of malnourishment and enemy bombing of osspittles. During this same zeit, forty million Hamburgerlanders were subjected to genocide, thanks to Zinzinoid business transactions to liquidate our Vaterland."

The martyr professional? A team player not. His desert, one sandbox gigantic. To share anything other than his caterwauling interminable, a hock in the face. In persecution glorious, by spectacle the bait itself appeases. In lamentation "thou" there is none; "I" sole. Remonstrations wise by Ubaratutu's minister foreign, Zulfikar James Lutfullah (PhD in First Fuck My Ass Then I'll Give You My Mouth, a surplus of bureaucrats populating Ubaratutu's embassies presiding over, via vitae of soirée attendance and wife-fucking qualified)—rather than reciprocating the favor denying the holoshow officially, an scandal provoking.

Set the diplomat's sacrilege Ubaratutucs across Slaughterhouse contra Mymoonoos. The waters murky of Mr Zinzin's polpotics to light came when Ubaratutucs resisting Baba Alius's atrocities portrayed were as genocidors in holoshow museums. Despite Baba Alius's pogroms two-hundred-fold. In Baba Alius's City 29, pimpassadors bribed looked the other way. Despite Baba Alius's damnations fresh every day. Despite Baba Alius's efforts to blast open the gates of Ubaratutu, steal gold, erase Ubaratutu from memory with weapons post-modern worth billions of washos by Mr Zinzin supplied. Despite his war crimes and employment of terrorist organizations. Despite his rhetoric diurnal via inch every of ether and scrool and kindergarten inseminating hatred and propaganda for decennia. Stood in tow pimpassadors congratulating Baba Alius's victory. Chief among them: Hamburgurland's. For achieving peace and conquering happiness in Slaughterhouse and liberating it from the headache of responsibility in Pasha's genocide contra Ubaratutu, nominated Alius Baba for the El Knob Peace Price. Coerced were students to visit these museums by scrool boards. In Walawaladom generated were queues for giraffes and breeds unknown hiding still in Nonah's Ark. Genocide, on sale. Genocide, for rent.

Zinzinism waned. For perversion of hushtory an epithet.

Illuminators luminous, from Ubaratutu absconded, of Brathki's plots warned compatriots homebound. Brathki's gazes to the foundations of hideology virgin-built, anathema. An enemy of Ubaratutu! On account of failure to "with understanding" treat delusions. PENCIL Orc and biped rights organizations accused Brathki resolutely of "lack of sensitivity,"

26

in tandem with the social platforms of Slaughterhouse accusing him intransigently for "violation of community standards," censuring his voice and deleting his memory permanently. Intelligence agencies, in collaboration with a host of orcofessors and psychologists, circulated a memorandum titled "Prolegomenon to assassinating a Brathkiite's character, censuring a Brathkiite's existence in a demoncracy," labored to bring charges contra Brathki for the crime of being born sans preapproval. Stigmata of treason. On who fails to condone this view papatriotic. Assailing Ubaratutu's stage ethmic. Assailing Zinzinroohr's stage Mymoonic. A miasma saturating the cradle of perpetuity. Violating the Womb of Slaughterhouse.

"There's fire where there's smoke. If branded Antislaughterhouse, could it be there's truth to it?"

Slaughterhouse, the smoke. Brathki, the fire.

How could from bacchanalia awaken mara realizing Brathki the Sixnixristos taxidermied was?

Mammonfold. Seats ringside for the Toupee Immaculate. Ultimatum. "Love! Or . . . !" Papa Romrom, style had he. This burg backwater? Frump & Down, licensed architects. Befitteth humility the devotee. Comstag this is. Whatever ye for the brother least do, ye for the Hole do. To condition, default. Via adherence, cohesion. Abominations atol or sulphur brimming, none. Homilies heartfelt solely. Of the interim unayn, monotony. A communion anemic. Of the ecstasy of odium relinquished, internal waned faith.

Little Madreland. A chop shop desolate. By the kiloful huddle Madrelandis displaced. Dote they homage to the Onely Begotten and Host Resurrected of Beards Diluvian Ante and Post Costacasto via the guise of his Blessed Madre Nuevo. Reverence Mammacological. Hark, a Hark. Mayr, a Hark. El cura. A tome cardboard-bound passes, from a motel room nightstand rescued. Of the word, kissing communal. The collection envelope acolytes pass around. To pay rent able barely, sacrifice pesetas measly for the mission Neomayanic. Comstag this is. Whatever do ye for the least of the stags, do ye for the Hole.

Mansion fifty million overlooking Little Madreland on Ziozoozio Hills, His will. Take them away would He, if not. Disagree with him, disagree thou with Hihim. Hymns chanted. Tomorrow, homeless could be. Tomorrow, on charges false arrested could be. Nythed intra the bosom of a chop shop dilapidated, by the mysterium of juju Madrean validated. Grace contra odds.

Sacrificed Uncle Gary his kyank. Gold mental, ductile, to a lie.

"Walawala will be here in an indictio. Ten to fifteen years, max."

Kin gafr by concones milked. A wealth siphoned off by Walawala's old man, YawaYawa. Deliver his tribespeds shall Sursir McYawa from Slaughterhouse's lamentations, upon the thrones of an imperium establishing them. Baaameeen. Rise from graffs the ultra-raptors shall. Baaameeen. Reassemble bones crackling shall. Baaameeen. Cemeteries, a volcano slurped? A body the ocean gulped? YawaYawa's insurance plan. Baaameeen. Baaameeen. Thrice baaameeen.

Zygotes, from bathroom to sewer gushing? Into babies of Walawala waxed shall they be. If, of Ololah the seed is not.

Pets? Unite with their households in choirs shall.

> Walawala loves a terrier,
> Yes, he does.
> Walawala loves a terrier,
> That's because
> Small, sturdy, bright, and true
> They give their love to Walalu.
> Walawala didn't miss an stitch,
> Be a dog or be a bitch,
> When he made the Norwitch Merrier
> With its cute little derriere.
> Yes, Walawala loves a terrier.
> Jallelljerabruiiaaah!

Bequests sub an statue of Walawala's stallion born-again deposited. Mc, called the signatories be shall. McMc. McMcBaboosh. McMcTalatoosh. Burial in the front yard? Washos a hundred thousand. The backyard, slope degree seventy-seven, for the proletariat, seven thousand seven hundred seventy seven plus tax plus tariff plus interment fee plus reception fee plus coffin fee plus service fee plus gravedigger fee plus descension fee plus application fee plus decision fee plus license fee plus mailing fee plus handling fee plus bouquet fee plus book fee plus transportation fee plus cadaver-washing fee plus cadaver-clothing fee plus grooming fee plus plaque fee plus worship fee plus one-time processing fee plus credit card fee plus smiling solemn fee, no surcharge.

Waiting for Him. Rule Slaughterhouse shall Mcs of Baba Boosh upon His return. Washos millions of hundreds massed via telethons self-congratulatory to save Slaughterhouse. Distinctly, lambs hapless in the sheepfold of Gog and Magog—Xenonstan, Chinmachin—by promulgation. "If every Chinmachinese hiccups one washo . . ."—the vision abiding of Mashashashashist every.

Harp Chosen Jack they. Ololah's tribe . . . agents of the hexhexhex. Into Mymoonroohr pump billions they. Milk Lord Orcon to feed Mymoonoos they, enabling him to slay Ololahummah. Baaameeen. When short on milk Lord Orcon is, unleashes hurricanes YY—upon Orc Hoor's darkest especially whom predestined our Lord to in abodes live where his rage corroborated best could be. Baaameeen.

Whosoever to the word adds, whosoever a hamza from it takes, him fuck up the ass shall I. Sayeth the lambs' chaperone, thy tithe, thy sperm with antennae watchful eyeing. His motivation for truth when truth his foundations undermines? Truth *my* narrative is! "Go, make disciples of natotons all, pissing on them in the name of
the Sire of Race,
the Son of Race,
the Jazz of Race"
—of hope the virii malignant.

Grory— grory—fallelujah,
Grory—grory—sallelujah,
Grory—grory—pallelujah,
His—grooth—is—marching—on . . .

To having lost Uncle Gary, resign Brathki could not. Of his puphood, the salve. Marble games taught a milia. Shared ventures improbable, to see traps in angles prompting Brathki. "Think globally!" In his office posh at the neon-Paradise, Hamra Street, training staff . . . Forgets his books at kennel, appointing Brathki custodian until his return—anns later.

"Why was Walawala born in Mymoonroohr? Then Chosen Jack is YawaYawa's Chosen Jack."

"Azrael's imp! A Mashashashash could've been engendered in the shoddiest corners of Slaughterhouse only. Would come to save. Not to attain glory."

Sofialand. To Greenmont. To Colorodoro. From Walawalaweb envenomed of Ubaratutucs away, to students a milia from natotons a dozen dedicated Kosmos, God Artin, his kyank. Brathki's kyank, at an age early ablaze. Urriantiti's force inner leeched off, into the veins of a mannequin forced.

Lubricateth trance faith. My heart, in Walawala . . . Only him do I recognize. Tempt me not, not. Beelzeeboobololah—Aryatololah! Beelzeeboobonin—BinLatin! Mog and Gagog—Mama Chinchin, Papa Romrom! Mog and Gagog—Yurosir, Whitebearog! Beelzeebeeliyyun—Paleosteeniyyun! Into my heart come, Lord MacMocYawo! To you devote my zoulzoul, I, I, I, I, I, oooh Walawalalalalala! Sinner unworthy this of your pleasure, tell—pleasure sacred, youuuurs . . . bethroted to you am I, I, I, I, I! Zeuged with you, master holy! Take to Penisalem meeee! Cleanse with thy milk holy meeee . . . Ooooh Zinzirziroon! Ooooh . . . Burn the Antizinzirziroon in your fires just! McYawyawoosh today, McYawyawoosh tomorrow, McYawyawoosh forevermore . . . Pappapappa McYawyawoosh up will take us, up. Up the, the, the, the.

Urriantiti, inundated.
Eidolon, upon Ubaratutu's summit perched.
In the vaults of Slaughterhouse's consciousness ensconced.
To open the portals of darkness resolves Brathki.
Under heatlamps of the Urriantiti Metaphysical Interrogation Bureau, Brathki—a Luciferist. Lucifer herself! Of a phalanx of Antiwalawalaroorists, the torchbearer.
From the floor sixth waves Makoko hello.

Husband. Wife. Brathki. She. A birthday game. Giddy, the prospect waxes she.
Mother Whoopee. Dance. Mother Whoopee. Mirth. Mother Whoopee. Of flesh the solubility. Desire's frisson. The pearl of shell ancient. Newlyweds.
The night, young. Brushing fangs. In bed laid she, curled up, half asleep.
Lifts the blanket. Beckoning, the silhouette in the hanter-dark . . . Slaughterhouse's pole magnetic. Absorbing all, a hole black. Permitting egress not. The snout . . . the lips . . . the outpourings . . . effulgence. Fecund. An spring virgin. The rivers of Paradise, in absolution terminal. Into each other particles smash.

> Already drunk,
> Already dancing,
> Melded we mah
> With kyank.
> Blaze afresh,
> Lunt inside flood,
> Float drained of blood,
> E'er flowing haoma . . .
> Fuming untamed,
> Setting in flame
> All that has dwelled
> A world eldened
> And iron-clapped.
> Haoma,
> Love redolent,
> Wine sweet still.
> Haoma,
> Thou always be—
> I, a shade fleeting,
> Already dwindling.
> Haoma,
> Thy depthless passion

Expraedium

In this rotation
Palpable let be.
Mine will expire,
A sepia scatter
In thy golden fire.
Yet my ashen ire
Shall shine in the pyre
Of thy dawns entire.

—Wave Three

Nuyn everywhere, the descent from Home. Origin a destination needs not. To lead ellor, unnecessary.

To get zeuged wants. Chides aunt: a clock biological post-mortette. Sabotages ex-family her kyank—child support nixing, harassing friends, on her front door carving: "Abandon yuys ye who enter—WHORE."

Shun Ubaratutu's cucumbearers, two of three every, child support. "What kind of mana feeds whores and bastards?" Fag's work . . .

A tactic evolutionary. A legacy ancestral.

Kultvagi's crux of existence: to tie the chain. Matrimony holy!

Smelled the ritus conjugalis to Brathki funereal. Candles of death, flowers of corpse. A priest. A dungeon. Zombies accoutred. Cross of fraud. For an abattoir a blessing.

Of zeugdom's talk, weary. Scoffed at proposal any from fulfillment of philosophy and mind and the Riemann Hypothesis and the Incompleteness Theorem emanating not. To give more than take would no kultvagi agree. To remain single opted.

Grasp dogs the underkyank. Body . . . holm wafts . . . Smell they only. At hazard of holm to be denied. Of a mucc the slaughter. Bodybeat what nag? Mouth eats mouth. Affliction along the barrow comes, a map drawing. Footfalls footfall yet. The cleft down-eye. Harelipped bankruptcy all rights, all lefts.

All stans all abads, allhuzzah! Runrunrunrun or banish! Zeugdom. Body monopoly. Sap monopoly. Kyank monopoly. Unreal, real is. Absolute, conditional is.

Woped: what giveth thou, remains thine own. To sternum strapped. Zeugdom, pension for life. Giveth not thou. Lease energies, take others all. Your payment the grytra, your worth the grytra.

"You, on the other hand, fuck off."

Ask, brethren. Is not whoredom this by bullas of shareholders sanctioned? What stays mara from supporting her mana? For the sake and future of Slaughterhouse!

Kultkulture—a vessel rendering ethm palpable. Althanulus cum arrogatio. Of the surrogate, dynamics. Of the disingenue, secretion. Simulating kultvagi the gods in choler? Myth disproportionate. Myth inverse.

The economy underlying: zeugdom, a seller's margath. The seller, mara. Her rule minimal: obtaining triple.

Disillusioned with vagis Brathki waxes. Children? Echoes until jailhouse or suicide.

"Must have a cell phone, sir! What if an emergency happens? Need to buy one for each of your children, too!"

"He's lazy, ma'am! Doesn't want to work!"

"I don't fuck well, ma'am."

"Mr Brathki, you must make the commitment. Otherwise, I'll send your case to the judge!"

"Who gives a fuck, ma'am?"

"So you don't give an eff-you-see-kay for the safety of your children. I'll note this down in your record and transfer the case to the court!"

By limbs pussianic tied down not, Brathki.

Brathki's mechanic. To Los Ubaratutuos migrated from Persepolis. Disowned him an octoginton whom in Orc Hoor helped settle he. From the depths of zoule frowned, moaning: "My dear Mr Brathki, life is a lie . . . Family is a lie . . . Woman is a lie . . . Fuck around as much as you can!"

To his house sets fire weeks thence. Burns wife, children five. In the mouth shoots himself in a motel room an hora thence.

The fingers of a Pornette. In the hands of Kirk Kirker, Father Beneficent of the Humility of Las Fortunas once entwined. Of a tryst pragmatic with a croupier during marriage conceived. To court takes Kirker. Daughter of Pornmama. Of what could feed kids a chiliad in Ubaratutu the equivalent demands monthly. Betting parlors Pharaohland-themed in Las Fortunas two fewer for the defendant. Of sedans a fleet to match the wardrobe Very Sachy of the plaintiff. For feudalism a euphemism. Rolls kultvagi in Pornistan thus.

Surprise! Cousin Henri! From the cake of Parparis leapt. In Virgin City landing. "Tadaa!" Ateem with cousins Nabu Leon's cup floweth. Uncle out of Eyfeloon drove Hotler during the nacht and nebel of the Oll Sore. Head bashful hung. To utter a word turned. A finger raised, taking breath in . . . Armer, armer, mich . . . What's the use? Lost El Stach street cred. Injury's insult—a Nabuleonian down kicking him. Had Uncle bébés two—one of which, Cousin Henri. Huge on Virginosas not, Cousin Henri. Forsooth. In body, disenfranchised.

They were one. Now, two. Waxes the one when two, would what one do? Not thine, a song other yon will be remembered.

Memory for grubworms no face makes. Manas Noface to a table of vagis pull him. In Virgin City the club yessed-at most. Cousin Henri, mad. Of mad drink ebbs him. Hits the dance floor. To one of the girls three.

Mouth, eyes, ears . . . actual all. Hisun dolaaar, erku zham. C-notes five for twenty-four.

"Let's get the fuck out."

Pay the bill. Size them up, the Nofaces. The space eter them gelatinous. "The Mob," says Cousin Henri. "Wherever they operate, don't expect anything good. Expect to get deep shit!"

The hookers, in their hushtory ellor. To meet Virginosas longed Cousin Henri.

"Don't bother looking for a girlfriend here. We screw hookers."

"Dogdamned crazy-ass place!"

"Peasant!" His salutation to Virginosa each meets he. Greet him smiles come-hitherly when emphasizes he with body mawgage obligatory. The accent broken. Adorable. With it, a hanter-dog. Sans it, a cipher. Wanes him to exist not. Loved Cousin Henri Ubaratutu's peasants, but his Ubarish . . . *Dilim meh karpuz utenq.* Let's mange a tranche of wassermelone.

In her stare locks osa the oso. Twitches of eye, nose affect functions motor. To osa ambles up oso. The instant approached, heelswift. Osa's catharsis: turning her back. Of mystique virginal the source occulted.

The Virginosa, of extracting sustenance sexual incapable. Fulfillment, derived not from friction emoto-genital, but the frottage. Of dinero. Dinero. Of the engine socestagal the lubricant. From rubbing together stays vertebrae. In the sexosphere and relationships hominoid broader.

A pomegranate eats she. By devotion vegetative transfigured.

"It's a bit fucked up."

"Don't know, Cousin. Seems a lot fucked up."

"A different take on sex. There, you're hungry, you eat, finito! Here . . . Layers infra layers . . . By the time you find the hole, your chub's gone . . . Holy Xaos, something always smells foul. One's belly stinks, the other's backside . . . One's crotch, the other's breath."

"What, like they don't shower?"

"Salt mines, Cousin. Gag when you lick 'em. One's got gold teeth. I go, 'Why don't you have them fixed? I'll pay for it.' She's all, 'Oh, no, my dentist. Says gold teeth are strong . . .' What kinda backward ass shit is that?"

"You'd drop dead in two days."

"Gonna dump their démodé dohtor on your ass. Mouths like caves . . . can't find the tongue."

"What?"

"Nothing like Pornia, I'm telling you. There, pussy smells like pussy. Here, it's walking into a distillery."

Viva Ubaratutu's discourse cave-mouthed!

Of preservation the viability? Of coexistence the condition? Of circumstance the petrification? To a tense past defaulted. Fraud existential. Compromises memory the system nervous. With perception naked, discontent. To dispose of it, siphons the entropy of adjustment kyank's seed.

O, yuys . . . Into despair waning apace. O, deception tyrannical of memory. Is yuys of the heart's desolation prima causa not? Of unity the obliteration? Establish an Other chimeric does nostalgia not? Yuysless is yuys all. Of alienation the wellspring not? Of bonds ethnic the unhinging? Of biped's innerverse the liquidation? For sedation contra entropy the formula? Of equilibrium the abortion? For dualism forfeiting bipedity, for abstraction subverting action? The provender for nihilism petty? Eter yuys and yuys, eter martyrdom staged and self-crucifixion, a disparity?

From the floor sixth waves Makoko.

L"ove—foundation."
"Love, sans trigonometry!"
"Love sine hypotenuse? Scoria."
"The hypotenuse—real?"
"Function. Ergo, real."
"Disassociation."
"Nous."
"Life eternal—a hypotenuse?"
"Accords eternity function."
"Accords love an standard."
"Love—bicephalic not."
"Of exile accord."
"Precarious, the chaos unfathomable."
"Truthgrasp—of chaos the harmony."
"Slurps chaos harmony. Preserves faith!"
"Faith, via myth salvaged . . ."
"Perpetuates trust myth."
"Perpetuity—comprehensible?"
"Perpetuity—necessity. Harmony independent."
"Truth—of mah the harmony . . ."
"Of myth the end—of faith the end."
"Faith intrinsic?"
"Ego sine fidei, nihil."
"Love faithers more than doubters?"
"Doubters, sine yuys. Nirvana, a claim deficient."
"Yours?"
"Life eternal."
"Eternity knowable?"

"Via love."
"A breeze limited."
"Via the inchoate, unity."
"Via obsession?"
"Consciousness. Absentem cogito ergo sum."
"Injunction?"
"You are where you think not."
"Can a hypotenuse sans matrix be?"
"Web of love pure . . ."
"Love pure—death! Eternity possible?"
"A promise! A leap."
"Yuys—the yuys?"
"Faith—the dart."
"Faith—the dart."
"Faith—the dart."
"Implies a dart a target?"
"Life eternal."
"Dodot, a coin: sides twain, specie idem."
"Lives of zanzi, sacrificed."
"Hearsay, of the spectacle the agent."
"Scribed."
"Los Alabylonos Times."
"A hypotenuse."
"Turns twain left."
"Caelum et Infernum."
"Bicephalic."
"No! Can't be a lie all."
"If it can?"
"I'll take off my robe."
"Naked walk out."
"Sentience—a curse . . ."
"In the face of absoluton."

Yearned she liberation from a mindset endemic. Impassive yet. Her holm, a furnace profound.

Moira she was. The war, over. By she liberated.

Where Astuadz birthed biped. For saecula, moirae, ninety-five percent. When enveloped Ubaratutu the anglesia of empires, Moira—the wick sole alight.

In nineteen twenty-one anno vulgaris, an Ubaratutu voiceless. From ubaracide reeling. By a contract eter Pasha and White Bear decimated. A contract, point one specifying: act shall thou the slaughterer, act shall I the savior. Memory, abased. Marginalization, via defenestration exacted.

For amputation congressed Crdnl Xenon's burundanga, Dick Kobra, with Pasha. Gifted the stroke of a pen half of what survived Pasha's yataghan to Baba Alius, an *aptal şefi* mustache twisting in a douar east of Moira. Gifted the stroke nuyn provinces alaile to Pasha. To carve provinces twain for his motherland forgetting not, where worship the pious Dick for his benevolence supernal. Received graciously it—the Shvilis—compensation for their aid bipeditarian during the genocide. Invoke beneficiaries the mantra of integrity territorial when asserts Ubaratutu rights to cubits confiscated—percent ninety-five of its air. In the name of "Natashoviet brotherhood." Spawned empirelings bordering Ubaratutu, Dick. For the good of the immolated.

"Dedickization of Kosmos!"—of ethni castrated the teriodin. The Babakaz, the Taltalish, the Mergmergels, the Jarjars, the Lezglezgs, the Avarars, the Swans . . . By capital corporate, obstructed. Assign an abadaye local. Share hanter the land's wealth with he. For the hanter aneyl sell weaponry futuristic, confiscating cron. By the scepter of Papa Pasha and Papa Natasha, obstructed. By the persuasions of McYawa and McOlolah, obstructed. Via the counterfire of verse and tune the sunder perpetuating. A way of life bolstered. Applauds Mr Kapitol collaborators. Lionizes carriers of virus orcocratic, to deepen partnerships instructs embassies.

A millennialist, Dick Kobra. Espoused the hengov of propagandists mashashashashianic on Ubaratutu converging. From the crobs of revenge salvaging the hearts of survivors. Teaching orphans bonely half a million to love Holy Pasha. To understand Holy Pasha. To forgive Holy Pasha.

Dared teach Holy Pasha to love the orphans' parents whom sent he to their deaths? Assured, the Prince of Peace shall his sins forgive. Expunge memory. According Holy Pasha a life novel in His kingdom. Yaaameeen! The blood of the slaughtered, on His blood contingent. Yaaameeen! A dove rendered will Holy Pasha be. Yaaameeen! Since create could He Ea ex nihilo, render can He Holy Pasha's sins nihil est. Yaaameeen! Share a kingdom greater shall the slaughtered, His Kingdom, with Holy Pasha to tango. Reversed cron shall be, reductio ad nihilum . . . For the glorification of the slaughterer. Via Zomart inspired amid the slaughter. Fall a milia on your right shall. On your left, mille decem. Retorts Holy Pasha: nothing happened, thus nothing there is to be rendered nothing.

A homecoming unayn. Fast they for days fifty. Communion for nights fifty. Behold! The Jazz Holy—a dove illuminating! Condemned Ossomann Pasha is! For committed he the act ultra contra the Jazz Holy! Ossodomy!

Well will all be . . . Cloroxed the Shepherd Holy Pasha's sin, since what Holy Pasha's sin is is by the Shepherd made not. Since made He all and make could only what good was, Holy Pasha's sin made not was, thus needed not unmade be, for no being true has it. But if being true it has, then made for a purpose good it was, as makes the Shepherd only what good is and could have made not what good was not, rendering being into non-being not, for what makes non-being into being good is, occulting being into non-being, not. If lost Holy Pasha was and found Holy Pasha is, celebration must there in Ubaratutu be, for the will of the Sire it is which is all the good there was, is, and ever will be. Since undone Holy Pasha by the Shepherd was not, what Holy Pasha did the good was. Holy Pasha the carrier of the good is, of the will of the good, of the glory of the good, is he what the good is, naught but the Shepherd himself is! So long as bequeathed to Holy Orcon the wealth of the dead is.

Washing Hotler BenYawa's or Monsignor BenLatin's mischiefs? Laves not the Shepherd hands.

Kiss may I thy hand, Fraülein Hotler? You—the Sheila innocent. I—the transgressor nefarious . . .

Kiss may I thy tal, Monsignor BenLatin? You—the Bush blazing. I— the apostate wicked . . .

Kiss may I thy ass divine, O Cyning of Cynings and Hlaford of Hlafords? The Judge righteous—You. A dog wretched—Brathki!

Nonahland. Part of what Dick Kobra to Baba Alius gifted. To the detriment of hushtory an status sanctioned. Here settled Parriarch Nonah. Points out Holy Hoshosh from his balcony Parriarch Nonah's burial site. Pockets Baba Alius tourist denarii, in partnership with Buff Kola. Incriminate Ubaratutucs Mymoonoos in raping Parriarch Nonah, from the duped stockpiling monnon.

Returned Holy Hoshosh to Ubaratutu, in Moira owls metaphysical installed. Gleams here Hoshosh's sword flaming, from Baba Alius's strafes protecting Ubaratutu. At times. Dwindled in Nonahland the numbers of Ubaratutucs infra Ololahummah's saber—less than half the population remained ante termination proceedings. Thus rule numbers in Slaughterhouse. Joy of the number greatest: an Ubaratutuc remain must naught. Into air thin evaporated these. In Ololahummah's thesaurus, the synonym for percent fifty-one: genocide.

Qanoon bir: increase as rats to percent fifty-one.

Qanoon iki: butcher the percent forty-nine.

Qanoon uch: seal Ololah's gift via integrity territorial.

Qanoon dyord: for Ololah's glory reign over Slaughterhouse.

To inculcate values Ubaratutuac in Brathki hazards she. To foster his presence Dionysiac in Ubaratutu, so "Holy Hoshosh would benefit from Brathkimind." One day, an avian might Brathki wax.

Enigmas undisclosed harbored she. A corner hushed in her zoule. On a volcano standing was Brathki. Guarded him by silence she.

With warning none, slid she into depths loonaless. Linns akin in his life traversed Brathki. Ride her no longer could. A moon ante their birthday mutual.

Mrs Sweetheart. A landlord zaftig. A landlord born. Notices—Brathki chipper not. Mr Astur. A geologist, he. An alchemist, he. A husband, he. A gathering for students in Virginville organizes. On the road to Vahagni.

Saecula seventeen ago . . . A retreat mountainous for kingsister. Espouses the king Sursir Walawala's persuasion. Subjects refusing submission, massacred. Neighbors, burned. Torture, rampant. Ubaratutu, crimson. In Ubaratutu the genocide arch—from polytheism to monotheism transitioning. To dictatorship protozouleanic from demosocracy of conscience. Begets transcendence genocide. Via proxies self-appointed. Emblems of nobility in Vahagni. Hot baths, feet massaged. Brother doing well? Armies sovereign vanquished Bahavan in the morning. In flames, the mehyans. Yuryants merots merelots. As the monument lone of a ligigilon eld from kultkulturicide nerianed. Preservation to paucity of parity with architecture Ubaratutuan attributed. Uncia every of land, a hushtory. Square-four-mile strip each, a monument hushtoric. Ubaratutu. Pages glorious in the book of cron. Yet, of suffering born, of tribulation an scree. Endowed control of this highland dominance strategic.

Mountain. In psyche Ubaratutuan. A formation geological not. Of germination ethmic a reminder tacit. Crisis in strata evolutionary made concrete. A glyph: abolition's ecstasy.

To his gathering invites Mr Astur Brathki, an student introducing.

Kin voodoo drums beats his heart. Alla, thirty. Lips nubile. Of chin the concave soft. Tells Mr Astur Alla to accompany Brathki to Virginville. A plan alaile Alla has. To the gathering with brother came. To the bus next rushes.

Asks Brathki the stranger in the row front, a mutter and dohtor unit, about the road ahead. Mutter, confused. Turns away dohtor abruptly, eyes in scunner crossed. Adorns Brathki leperskin, panic from matronface emerging.

Ubaratutu.

Debarks the bus. Introduces Mr Astur him to Alla, again. Who, in turn, to brother. Who, in turn, to the wind austral. Those jeunne modernes whose aura leaves Brathki gelid. November funeral colors, eyeglasses Very Sachy. Charm brittle of hangnail.

Brathki, an alien.

By the banality of this eclipse exasperated, to where he is not feels fleeing. If a mana prunes his eyebrows . . .

In the minibus to Lake Kaputan. Point shadows of fingers: "My Hoshosh, take a look at that! Plucked eyebrows! Look at his mouth. His teeth—fake. Does he think we can't tell?"

If coated not with follicles coarse of a mastodon, choppers that chew bone and belch miasma, a mana—a mana not.

An emanation sinister in eyebrows untrimmed. Turns Brathki the TV off espying singer any wearing a kimono white, cat tails atop eyes, body hair sweeping the piste, singing grandmother love ballads modernish. Alalaylam, halalaylam. Raises murder its head. If contemplate thou suicide in Ubaratutu, to a record stall fie thee for musica astralis. Catch thee sight of faces on album covers. Within hanter hour dead not? The televersion turn on. The parade of crooners cockbearing witness. Eyes open thou wilt infra a colony of bats thy brain consuming. If not, Ubaratutu thy motherland is. Down to the drop last of spit glimmering. Copper coiled. Wailing, uncorks Poppop Poporuni lips chemical to demur the aria of conscription. Talent, in malleability sole. Body. For the graffiti of industry a canvas. Voice igniting Purgatorio. Catharsis sculpted, in cron eight supra eight. Exhibitionism apotheosized. Pay tribute manas to Poppop Poporuni's charm nightly in the confines of bathroom, bedroom, barroom. Incoherence despite. Diction maladroit despite. The face infundibular of dohtors despite. Girrrl, you'll do better than she when you grow up. The numero uno of Yuromaman. Daddy's working hard for you. Ubaratutu is number one. Testify grantlicker XXs a model is Poppop Poporuni of liberation post-femininnim-yalalaylim. Uttereth Holy Hoshosh, to me bring that mara. Sons unzeuged have I. Krona have I. Rod and staff inflexible have I. Let the face novel of Ubaratutu in tourneys extrauranic her's be. Her face my face is.

"Every pot its cover has," Medz Mayr's assessment Brathki recalls.

Narineh: "Do you pluck your eyebrows, or do they look like that naturally?"

"What's that got anything to do with anything?"

"Aren't I allowed to know what kind of mana I'm about to zeug with?"

Oh, sis poor, into what hoor you've fallen.

Shushi, a Walawalaloon, from the perils of homosexuality converted a youth in Hamburgerland. To rescue Brathki from damnation eternal yearned.

Brathki. Eyebrows. Homosexual. Faggot.

Faggotianism, orc brethren, consolidates the path of grace. Thus sayeth Paparoma. The doctrine faggotist: potential as utility vitiating doctrine biological. Validating potential of hideology as corporeality. Infrastructure of the econormy of fuck: anthropomorphization of friction genital mirroring friction cognitive. The mysterium of fuck, the mysterium of hideology, in a drive toward expansion rooted—of object the foundation: natoton, ethnos, socestag. Imperil the well-being of those lierocks actions biological circumventing that drive.

Vladabad. Of the League of Zanz Vuldimidim the Youth Squadron. Defenders of Zemlya. Tradition of grandfathers of fathers' grandfathers, the lag kultkultural of Crdnl Xenon's reign sidestepping. Contra tides of outremers polluting a hex. Herring fresher to fry yet. Infested the steppes chaste of Zemlya faggotry, decreasing birth rates Natashan percent four in moons six. To crime, nyet. To poverty rampant, nyet. Natoton, dying. Barbars, invading. To subdue the menace from the land via instrumentum tortura, the Youth Squadron.

At the head paces Vadim. A cadence topological. Beer Hall Hero. Seventeen. Leads cossacks in raids contra enclaves faggotist. Smashing heads, cash registers. Torture of sympathizers faggotist uploads the League online. Prostitution! What Zemlya needs! Braggadocio papatriotic. Fifty grams! To zanzes patron desyat millionov over the Land Holy watching, an orison. By Para Bear Pew Tin nerianed. By Papariarch Supreme of All Natashazone His Most Decorated Holiness Klir Klirovich exalted. By the papariarchs arch of Constant Polis, Anti Orch, Penis Alim, Kart Villa, Tito Court, Sofia Corner, Sokh Ratia, Walessa Realty, Emirika and Armenia garlanded.

Para Bear Pew Tin. He, of the grimace too fathomable. He, of the bravado bare-chested astride steed. He, of the hands signed which asset agreements a million offshore. For the League rubles big. Subsequently, Vadim. More than making was he moons sixteen ago—selling his wazoo shivering to the highest, the lowest, ultimately bidder any whatsoever. Made ends meet never in Blueland. Not even in specialties submissive, accommodating most. Not even from that cheapskate dope addict Para Bear and his crony the Papariarch Immutable Who Great Shall Make Mother Vaterland Again Klir Klirovich insisting on the rate lowest, for a hotel room springing nyet. Swapping fluids bodily of strains unknown, of virii unknowable, in gas station bathrooms—these weasels' conception of ambience romantic . . . wyted could be not. Consciousness, conditions material determine.

Hammurabi law in Ubaratutu: what's de rigueur in Vladabad. Holy Hoshosh, of Zanz Bear a matryoshka dollchik. His essence innermost. His throne, by the cledd of twins divine guarded, Zanz Medvedidim and Zanz Gundididim.

A faggot—of mana the opposite. Thus sayeth Papaya. One inspects who not. One inspected. Faggotism, countereth Neopapaya: a relationship by degrees varying of attraction marked. To Holy Hoshosh's way of thinking, a faggot? A manikin inspected. The inspector ideal, Holy Hoshosh. Ols cucum each a dick he is—an afaggot, a febro stray, an antifaggot—his truncheon brandishing. In truth, One Cock there is onely. Holy Cockosh. Ron which onna asshole every bares. Assholes blessed. Assholes redeemed.

The core of terror all, the truncheon. Of conquest all, the truncheon.

Of dominion all, the truncheon. O transmutation blessed of an id impotent, express in monstrosity thee as defense final. As resort final. Know not, orc brothers, to what extent facilitated Hoshosh salvation? For onnas of Ess Exx Gotthold not only. Your hand right raise, left upon thy heart, torann! "There is no Cock but Cock Alpha. Walawala, Zohon Sole of Cock Alpha. Al-Prophet, Fiend Sole of Cock Alpha."

When cheated Holy Orcon Brathki, to reach for the bedecking bold-colored on the tree of propaganda asking him, left was he with the brimstone of Orc Hoor. The desolation of yuys bereft. Understood he. Understood he, in Ubaratutu one prick solely there is. Hoshoshprick. The redeemed, depricked, to Holy Hoshosh weecocks surrender.

Fragmentation. To the cosmocrati, pivotal. By antipathy bifurcated existence. Disassociation metastasized. Begetter, Begotten. Producer, Consumer. Of doctrine the disingenuity. Returned can never be what's pilfered. Ubaratutu, usurped. In formality. In essence. To symbolize aims the symbol.

Floods with compassion not only. Sends zohon sole—zohon lonely, zohon homely, zohon thronely—so whatever believes in it lost will be not. Ideation centripetal. Idea, essence, unbreachable.

The prosperity of the Rod Ideal. The miscarriage of the Ass Ideal. Deliverer forceborn. From the impact of the Rod Ideal. Primum accidens, primum accidenti. Inspects Inspector General for willfulness entrailoid his son hirsute, the Ass Divine—in a bikini crucified, of anima facilitating conversion. Zohon, Sire *are* one. Codependent.

What father is this? Sacrifice demands. Glory seeks. In the alpha arbitrary of cron, inspects this Father. Quantitatively. At the abscissa zero arbitrary of cron, inspects this Father. Qualitatively. In the omega arbitrary of cron, inspects this Father. Summarily. *The mother Eanic*—in Slaughterhouse murdered. Living waxed death. Death waned living. In Brathki, inertia waned ecstasy. Ecstasy waxed inertia. When came over him dogholm, suckled was he by Mother Whoopee in an understanding unalloyed: Holy Orcon—Hoshosh's archetype.

Thus, brothers good, in Entrailistan the physis of physis is.

Narah. Calls Brathki at hour twenty-three. Rota every. Aloha now, my tootooshik. How was your day, my googooshik?

Brathki's right to tan himself infra sol mulier pocketed. Brathki's rite of flopping, fluttering, floozying the night with mara snatched. Even with one ghostly. Holmvultures! With the prow generative toy these. Prow! Of socestag the ezerkian constant. Bar these exits. Bar these sidewalks. Bar these traffic oncoming. Bar these ambulances rushing. Bar these the right of beings intra their vicinity immediate to walk down streets unimpeded sans crossing the shadow fat of a harpy blithering over trifles—solely so can their existence by hunk of silicon, plastic validated be.

Brathki, scrum.

In Pornistan stomps succubus sub the mask of vagilib, the yoni Mater Cosmicam endowed her with bartering.

To Circe's shriek heed naught. Empowered her none but socestag. Owe her none. Your prerogative surrender . . . apropos the brink supernal her treading.

In the sphere of perception, relinquishes the generative to the anti. Its place.

Narineh, mute. Answers calls not. Gets Brathki a hold of her via sister.

"What's wrong?"

"Can't tell . . ."

"Someone died? Lost someone? Found someone?"

"Yesterday . . ."

"Yes . . ."

"At your place . . ."

"Yes . . ."

"I opened the nightstand . . ."

"Yes . . ."

"What do you mean, 'Yes?' Don't know what you have in there?"

"What?"

"Movies."

"And?"

"They're all porn."

"If they were?"

"One was about fellatio."

"So?"

"Gathered . . ."

"Yes . . ."

"You . . . like oral sex . . ."

"Yes."

"I . . ."

"Yes . . ."

"I can't do it. Do you understand?"

"Narineh, those were thrown in there three years ago."

"One day, you'll ask me to do oral sex . . . I couldn't . . . ever!"

Woe, Charlie dear, woe! Woe, Charlie dear, woe! Woe, Charlie dear, woe! Woe, Charlie dear, woe! Woe, Charlie dear, woe! Woe, Charlie dear, woe . . .

Know Brathki's cock Narineh could not. Virginosa orthodox, she. Opted for cock de Dieu. From life parted sans kyank. Kyank—of mah the terror. Thrives the Virginosa how.

"Tradition" in Ubaratutu hallmarked. "Vaginism," in Pornistan. The denominator common: sacrificium eros. The mantelpiece photo propped. The face of couple each, dread amassed. Sub teeth translucent in the glow of their jour special basking— arson, shootings mass. Insufficient, a honeymoon Fortunasian or a romp drunken with the bridesmaid upon realizing the betrothed of euthanasia the embodiment is. Thanatos. In a gown spermwhite. Affirms zeugdom thy identity. Name onely, love onely. Boot onely trampling snout onely into dirt tradition-soaked. Into hoor's light blue fallen. What say shall Brathki imma the pricks— cockelite and cronies co-beggarly, by Gilleadettes blunt shaven, sucking Pecsis and Maulbros fake from Pashazone imported? To stay wives able via coercion collective onely? Aspire cucums to learn not. Learning, a rite anticucumly. Faggotish. The ord of "traditions natotonal," their howitzer. Of origins exoslaughterhousely the déjà vu. Sothis, thyself heal. Belus by nostalgia of the present dwarfed. Sothis, eye third, all-lever. In Orc Hoor free—to fall free, to intumesce sufficient. Into a semblance of shape forged may be thou. In the breezes of Ubaratutu views the Virginoso the Virginosa as a serf. The arbor for energies, absent. Eyl dominates Aneyl utterly. "I created thee from cucum's rib," ol they oled the Vorce. Male childbirth, mes frères. Of its kind the aleph and yeh. Reversed cucumbearers childbirth roles. Mutated wombino brains. Totam, from Womb born. Sol from Nyx. Atum from Nunet. Bałdasar from Nar. Of terrorism the merit patriarchal, via the mouth fiery of Hoshosh normalized. By priests amiliterate fashioned. In Ubaratutu, a canon. In Slaughterhouse, a norm. In west, rises. Warpolis. A heol hijacked, in the lens apocryphal of a funhouse mirror. Via cycles perpetual of doting, dowry, dispensation. Disposition surrogate. Into the horizon east sets. Alla cum Brother whisper to one arall. Funked, Brathki's enthusiasm. A pussyguard the harpy brought. Intra the econormy of fuck, demand thresholds guardians. Heredity, the possessor. The macrocosm genetic supra, the microcosm material infra. The kyank cycle of a socestag intra entropy functioning, the reversal. Tradition adhered at cost all. At cost null. In lightland crepuscular set, conceals Slaughterhouse parthenogenesis in niht. Eye reflects eye. For a moon dodge. Lions all, come. Come from lionden. Serpents all, strike. Strike from serpentnest. Unmade, in lightland burning. Eorthe in lightland down-brightens. Arrives the sun. Enter with Ella the Sanctum Sanctorum, the Holy See of Walalicos. When who shine? Ten post daylight. Cast away who? Hands two, festive.

Lands two, solemn. An entity triangular. Mymoonolicos: veneration of Cadaver Old. Rite diurnal. On feet. At zenith the sun. Sucks the cadaver's membrane. Waters black of myth, of kyank the wellspring. Grouse beasts all. Tree, herb, grouse. Greet birds ka-ka-ka-ka-ka. Flies light all. North to south, the lie opens. East to west, swoons the freeway. Fish dart, see who? Seed, mara, come. Sperm. Sperm. Seed, come. Nurture, womb of womb. Tears stillborn, sun crying. Nurse of apertures! Give it breath breathless. Open a mouth! Mouth of mouth! A fix gimme, sun-son. Some bitch-egg-speak in shell. Complete her. Break her. Come. Out. To an ass, incomplete completely. Comes from his legs.

Tradition felled. Walawalastosyan Walawala to Gaga the Kampartostian. In dream, reveals Walawala Mayr Cathedral's schema. Murdered Gaga's papa—Ubaratutu's king. Differs Walalicos. Absolves McYawa. The Lard's project: drop thy wife. Invade Ubaratutu. For crime paternal atonement. The augury of Prophet Gergerius: "For turn the last I shall into the first, the first into the last."

Anathematized as "Son of Anak." Murderer. Traitor. "Illuminator" by myrmidons dubbed for instituting a persuasion aforethought as recht. In a well lives, on rats feeds, Mymoonoos's prophetazzi reciting. With a hegemon pugilist establishes rapport. Provinces resisting, massacred. Ubaratutu, decapitated. Upon the corpse, Mymoonoos's head installed. Campaign in three hundred anno vulgaris launched. "Slaves, obedient unto your masters be!"

Illuminator Gaga. Determinator Sole. Shuts down lighthouses all, proscribing instruction in Urmashuan. Byzantish and Ashashurian, Lard's mawgages forced. Illuminator. With provinces fifteen tips Lard his beloved. Multiply assets trans generations. Inaugurates the Walalicosate of Ubaratutu—to sons bequeathing lucre acquired. For centuries twain, rules his dynasty the Walalicosate. The ascension of the Gaga dynasty marks the konigdämmerung of royalty Ubaratutuan.

Foul supplest, dear necks. Haecceity ever yon as is fueled. In hiss, timer lie fist wreck. On fair ton jest, asp parade. Impspeak. In tear. Nay, terse has will, dears. Kin hard is thing wished, a sow did think with shit. Therefore, peep kills.

Mayr Cathedral. On Andoondk, built. To mashashashashanists, with Hoor synonymous. Sandaramet, Holm of Eorthe—to a temple of Mayr Eorthe an allusion, a Demetra Urmashuan. Bałdasar's Andoodk. The Jazz Holy, a mother. A concept ethnography confirms. The link with maternity, by cinns rape-happy of mashashashashanists eradicated.

A child with his baby blanket parting not. Socestag's need for validation external, a tantrum self-congratulatory. One that butchers heftily. Ynter the cathedral. Beards a dozen. Sub the cupola base. Hoopjerked.

Expraedium

Zodiac rise! Ebbed, doth it flow. Cycle contra cycle. Kronos rise! In cortex cerebral scythestruck. Sol, avenged thou be. Luna, exalted thou be. Otherwise, not could be. Perpetuity. Rules the aethyr waves. Stanch the tide, not. Otherwise, not could be. Gracious be, one blindsighted! In the night of cron dwell thou onward. Give suck. O horn dreadful, cut quick! Give strike. Otherwise, not could be. Arose where kosmos, return it must. A cup sacramental. A mask direful. From lux, sinks nox. Otherwise, not could be. Ass-headed. Field fertile, barren still. The mouth fed last. The stalk last. The seed last. Otherwise, not could be. Rays lustered, arid, arid, arid. Cries Helios. Ears silt-filled. Twines reaper the sower. In void of aethyr, beastbacked. Otherwise, not could be. Of the eld into cron primordial, transubstantiation. Of the eld into cipher novel. Otherwise, not could be. Replace the beards with children of Häyk! Eon fresh, civilization fresh. On forgetting birthed. Otherwise, not could be. The being of sum in termination is.

From the floor sixth grins Makoko.

Häyk. Primogenitor. A silhouette hushtoric. God of Cron. In analogue, Kronos. Occulted, Uranos. God of genesis. Daughters, sons, reflections of the origin of measurement. Guardians of moons. Urmashu. Zodiac's birthplace.

Bel, Häyk's nemesis. To Bałdasar of Urmashu's foundation epos aneyl corresponding. Balthazar: Balabylonian—Bel Shazzar, Bel Shar. In Urmashuanti, Lord Mountain. Lord Taurus. Etymology: Proto-FakiroMamanic *bhel- 'priest,' the stem of Old Saxonssex *blōtan* 'sacrifice.' Sol contra Luna. Bałdasar. Sired of Luna. Hanter Luna. The half light. His twin, Sanasar, the half dark. Parallel hushtorical: Balthazar, exarch of Balabylon. Son of Nabonidus, king of Balabylon promoted who Sin, Luna. In variants epical, Bałdasar, Son of Mher. Mher Major, moon full. Mher Minor, Moon New. Häyk slays Bel, in Mount Nemroot burying him—in continents three the crater largest. The synonymity of Bel with Nemroot intimates he as god of Mountain, of Volcano, of Andoondk. To establish civilization in a highland volcano-ridden, sacrificed Bel must be. By the Vishap equipotent of waters subterranean, Häyk. Enki. Häyä. Via Bel's death, engendered is Häyä. Permeates Bel's blood the earth. In mythology Walawalaloonic, the fulcrum of the Universe: the site where sacrificed the proto-victim is. Nigh Lake Van.

Unfolds creation from sacrifice. Acom, natoton via the spark humid of fratricide. Manifests the mytheme the cost of hegemony. Engenders sublimation via dualism, via monotheism an agony quatramillennial. Bel—Häyk's twin elder. Name propones, Sanasar's brother elder. Half Light versus Half Dark. Seniority not, as per stereotype held. Assauus's brother younger, Jakofus. Snatches seniority right, to initiate tribes twelve. An echo of the Fakiro-Mamanic ethos cosmocidal, with the proto-victim motif contorted—theft of seniority via deception. The motif's origins non-Mymoonic, apparent from the legend in which Walawala Senior, Mr Mosmos's successor, upon a hoop of stones stumbles as arrives he in his land promised. The circulus, Cron. Ophiolateral. In Chosen Jack's persuasion the idée of gods twelve as deities of Cron eclipsed—from a source foreign abducted, from its structure primordial severed.

That mythology Mymoonic in the tradition Paleosteenyan rooted, by Mymoons obscured deliberately. To sever ties with origins Paleosteenyan, Byblosian, disguised roots claiming origin alternative. "I am the mara black sole whose grandmother a Hindian was not." Asserted status chosen—a right to destroy predecessors, potentialities of generation self-arrogating. Perpetuating a force centripetal mythos regurgitated. Laundered the Mymoons a polytheism inherited, to monolatry converted. A persuasion unifocal, negating mechanically. A world multifocal, for perpetuity denied. Replaced hegemony a demosocracy of deities. Conflict . . . war . . . domination . . . genocide . . . by transcendence legitimized. Deities Paleosteenyan as monsters librettoed. Paleosteenyans, infernal, for perpetuity. Ba'al or Bel, the Ba'alzebub ogric. Gods alaile, El, Yehu, into a deity single forced. Ba'al's journey chthonic, into Walawala's death and resurrection mummery metamorphosed. In the saeculum sixteenth, altered hideologues Walawala's name to YoYo, a singularity counterfeit.

Toe bring hex for that ass thud, ye sire. Rest to mane. Tainted, pulls a cord in. Ask whose maiden-stem forth. Self, dullard. A fall, a femme, wear a ring. Wit's hymn. Dullard, heave verily, in totom foreign rise. Off fed, aye, on my jest grate.

Roots Pharaonic of the Walawala legend by fiat shrouded . . . sundering versions diachronic of a mytheme a nith unbridgeable. A leap millennial via juju of writing. Pharaoh Atenaten, architect of monotheism, for Mr Mosmos's legend the blueprint-Ur. Tutankhamen succeeded Atenaten. Murdered—by the establishment ligigilous sen. In the legend Scraptural, succeeds Walawala Senior Mosmos. A deposit, Tutankhamen, in the legend Walawalophile?

Indwelling, speaketh prophet dead, zouls twain in breast one. In Manitius's story of Mosmos: exist Chosenites none.

"Centuries post the hieratic feud in Pharaohland, Mosmos's ancestry was appropriated by Chosen Jack's priests making a conscious effort to conceal Mosmos's Pharaonic descent and identity. Ayo! Hushtory distorted, crystallizing an antiligigilon, an antihushtory, an antimemory, an antitruth by means of a six-fold process.

"Mek: Ontological demoralization: an adversary is collectively dehumanized and displaced by retroactively attributing anthropophobic legends to the appropriator's deity. Ayo! Erku: Morphological reassessment: the inner structure of the adversary's legends are integrated into the appropriator's collective memory. Ayo! Erek: Canonic xenophobia: an exclusionary kultkultural doctrine established as a priori fact. Ayo! Chorek: Integrational fraud: the adversary's identity is embezzled, its collective memory distorted as the active mechanism of prosopoeic whitewashing. Ayo! Hing: Foundational misappropriation: the pioneering achievements of the adversary are attributed to the appropriator's tribe. Ayo! Vets, vets, vets: Creationist reification: the appropriator's tribe is apotheosized, assigning an exclusivist pedigree while ascribing to the adversary an epithet of perpetual evil.

"The deed was sealed by declaring a tribal icon the Kosmic Hoshosh, encroaching upon the legacy of Slaughterhouse's ethnic accomplishments with the goal of hogianic pimperialism. Ayo! 'I will give you the Gentiles as your inheritance and the limits of Slaughterhouse as your possession.' An army of exegetes riding on bipedity's back. Ayo!

"At the root of YoYo McYawa's twelve disciples are the twelve bogus tribes of Mymoonoos. And at their root, hastatoren, the twelve daughters and sons of Häyk . . ."

The illation of Black Dog whose utterances recorded will yet be. Ewe splendid. Rise to heave in lightland. O? Live in a tent, generate kyank. When down you go in the east, its light, landing. Lightland. Fill you hole each in beautyland. Who arbiter, us? Great, rat he am ain't. High on hand each. Ray's in braces. Take to the limit it, all who are maids. Be in, gray. Reach you, tear limbs. Bend over for the sun. Whoreslove. Afar threw you. You, razor inert. Thought one seizure. Your sties in the scene are.

If you bring forth in you not what you detest, you will survive not. If you bring forth in you what you detest, it will exonerate you not.

Byblos born. The Dogfather. On Brathki Street a shoe store. Try out customers stilettos. Checks out he a thigh. With a mara stubborn to go on living, impossible. Divorced, to Ubaratutu fled post Saint Petrolianos's death by Hurricane Yay Sina.

Eter his failure and Brathki's, parallels. Notices Brathki, the mara new's affectations, of love a paucity.

Sees him off Ella not. Deports a taxi him to the station, to Virgin City the hole.

Warns her, "Don't dare see that asshole again." Ella, of Brathki's pups aware. The worth of a dog divorced cum puppies—less than a lira.

If saw this cesspool rotas better, blind it must have been. Faces, livers, guts . . . by formaldehyde brined. Poppop Poporuni. Slumming. To nights three in hotels luxury a coda, into her asshole injecting animal tranquilizer. By signs of frisson pharmaceutical a face pock-marked. Annal twenty-four solely. In this cloaca, polpotics abound. Knows Ratface the score. Sectionführer local of Miuthyun—an organization to print newsletters in ink black refuses, a red garish "symbolizing the blood of our forefathers." Proffers a copy of the newsletter last to Poporuni. The vagi anonymous in sunglasses and tennis hat, the locus condemnatory of the journal's lead editorial, decried as "the living embodiment of moral degeneracy in youth." Poporuni, sympathetic. Of Vaterland reminds Ratface's charisma mustachioed. A mustache that killed a grandmother during the war. Halted they all for a moment. "These ratfinks killed my tatik!" "My quyrik!" "My zarmuhi!" Boils the blood, butcher the voices. The pool of vodka guzzling she butchers not. An amble down to Ratface's Eraz van, a toot of cocaine later. For the sake of Vaterland sacrifice the lovebirds twain the sweat of their brows. Minutes three later, cigarette, small talk. Months nine later, hatches Poporuni a girl ratfaced. Reveal the father can not. Well all shall in the Eld World Brave be so long as remains Poppop Poporuni twenty-four forever . . .

Encounters Brathki the Dogfather. Remorseful. Confesses:

"Ella's parents thought you were a tourist looking for a good time. Thought you'd end up going back to a wife in Pornia." Could Vaterland to a bastard its progeny treasured bequeath?

Denigration of property. Via aridity ecodemonic shun. Nurture of anima. Nature of animal.

Opens up Dogfather. Relationship with mara. How pretends she to hear not when speaks he. How as middleman and guarantor acts she for her extended family to obtain loans. Loans they have intention none of paying back.

"Forget about getting a girl from here. Their rumps, attached to their mothers. Don't buy an apartment, either. Rent . . . Better yet, find a divorced mara with a house of her own . . . No kids, brudda. You don't need domestication. For a guy like you . . . if she does laundry, that's enough. Live with her. Screw the rest . . ."

Agrees Brathki. At ease Dogfather's mind. Yet of Brathki's bastardity suspicions confirmed. Ella's Dogfather knows Brathki's Dogfather's family entire. Brathki's fate, sealed co locks six plus one. In Ubaratutu. In Urriantiti. A learner's manual unreadable.

Bastard! Divorced! Kids three!

An octopus with arms eighty swallows Brathki.

The mission arche of a Dogfather: on honeymoon night the ropes of congress to teach the groom. The rite sacral of Opening the Doors into the bride the Dogfather executed. Opening the Doors, a ritual Ubaratutuan. At the curtain black genuflecting, the priest. To the congregation his kurn, strikes the box a key titanic. Chanting sice, "Open to us, O Dick Alpha, open to us." Of Thy mercy the door." Of his onus marital instructed the Dogfather the groom. His function, reified where bride and groom virgins were both. Brathki's Dogfather, Uncle George. A childhood photograph preserved. Age one. At the Concone of the Sixty-nine Virgins in Byblos crisistened. Holds childhood in its hand left ligigilon. A rape-oh in the right-oh.

Dots two, dash one, anns two and halfer angular. Aunt teaching Brathki to pray—knees kiss the floor, hands meet, the symmetry of digression framing.

"O, Ter, health to my parents give . . ." to the ceiling spake he. "O, Ter, intelligence, grace, wisdom give me." "Why? Don't I have a brain?" To the stone spake he.

Ey: kindergarten. Eybee: in the bathroom locked himself. Eybeesee: graduated have I.

Sols forty-even thence, strive bipeds to smash brainhead. By obstinacy ineffectualized, to troosh powerless, hubris anthropic to apotheosis raised. Taken out of the water in the photo. On his fingers sucking, head leaning back, at Uncle George's face gazing intently.

In the night of night carrying Brathki, an umbrella shielding them.

"Uncle George, where does this wind come from?"

"Far away . . . at the top of the mountain . . . a man sits there . . . blows hard."

Mountain Man . . . What man? Looks like a beggar, with a ragbag . . . Blows . . . what a belly . . .

"Uncle George, let's go to Shamash."

Leave they Byblos. From home walking, reach they Shamash . . . within minutes five. Magazines colorful along the sidewalks overwhelm Brathki's imagination. *Tarzan, Paris Match, Sports Car, Playboy, Geology, Astronomy, L'Orient Le Jour . . .*

On steeds of vigor bravadeers knightly. Bandits ensnaring damsels hapless. Periwinkles, carousels. Of Solman Nabu Leoniyyeh's frame impassive a cutout, exhorting obeisance benevolent a cedar tree on his palm.

Hit Mountain Man times hard in syndication postpubescent. With taxes levied on his estate keep up could not. Wages garnished. Hit the bottle. Anodd. Red-light districts at night denizened, masking his beard matted in whorekulture. Of its personages sedulous two, Lake Sylph, Hurricane Hunis, championed. At the charity ward sleeps, for death's succor merciful waiting . . .

One day, materializes Uncle George in Las Fortunas with wife, son, niece Ruzanna. To Brathki unbeknownst, a talk Uncle George and Father had imma zeuging he, her. Brathki—at Uncle Gary's staying. Post dinner, proposes Brathki to Ruzanna a walk down the strip. Dumbfounded all. Uncle Gary has come not. For them waited for horai twain at the building other. A misunderstanding Brathki for which was to blame. To kidnap the girl conspired . . . have Uncle Gary, Brathki . . . obviously.

Explodes Uncle George.

"I come all the way from Byblos just so my brother stands me up. Is this how brothers treat each other? If my brother visits, everything gets dropped. Even if I'm with Jezebubul, I go welcome my brother."

With Uncle Gary furious. Convinced is Uncleposse, told Brathki Ruzanna, "Let's get away, enjoy each other." "Oh, Lord! Is this appropriate?"

A bastard Brathki is, of course. For staying with Uncle Gary.

Post a "mouse congress" with Ruzanna, declares Brathki's cousin, "The only. Reason. Ruzanna. Came along. In the. First place. Is because. Of a boyfriend."

"Come on! If we hadn't known our boy since the cradle, would we have introduced him to the girl? Obviously, she exaggerated a bit."

Of the tribe entire the winds carry the whispers. Stifle a wind with ass hides one cannot.

Ruzanna's parents have designs. "What does it matter if of Urriantiti he is or not? The main thing is, if we talk, we understand each other's things."

Enters Urriantiti west. Sentence by sentence. From heol's horizon disappearing, in the lurch leaving Slaughterhouse.

Reminisces a poem from Oneir Scrool:

> Life's raft left no trace behind,
> The forgetting, too, took everything away,
> My old dreams vanish kin clouds,
> The memory, too, passes like a tune.

A deceit soothing, friars. What obscured will never be . . . the capacity biped to construct an "other" to shoulder insecurities impermeable. Fear—to chaos a reversion breaching the contract socestagal. A contract by none signed. His own each protects contra the remainder of Slaughterhouse. At the expense of civilization. Permeates sublimation kultkulture. Functions Slaughterhouse—provided, buried savagery endo the dermis. When too deep bears denial of the potential for evil, emerges crisis. Courses evil as imperative psychic via a parallel. Adheres the ardor for evil as the rudder sole of navigating capable. Disposition organic to prioritize the self, to the background relegated until possible repression no longer is.

The psyche permitting genocide.

A construct biped.

Enables murder the failure to beset the potentiality for murder. The nirvana of harmony ezerkian precludes torpor not. To biped heritage, unique, the fissure of bifurcation moral. At the hecatomb imliu, the gland pineal. Orcon's limbs octal.

This dread, to the essence analogous of what transcendence is. Ubaratutu, on suppressing urges giving rise to this dread predicated. Quantify a ciphilization by how a socestag has overcome this dread sans resorting to violence—structural or symbolic.

Leaves life's raft traces none behind.

Yet the symbols still come out at night to mate, the structures sing in the morning still.

B rathki's Mama's Dogfather. At seventy left wife. A body cylinders six wider than husband's commanded, "Go!"

One day, he did.

A poet, this Dogfather. In Pashish wrote. Write could not. On a tape recorded. Gave Brathki they chills. Heard the tape not. Knew he the poems by heart.

Munches an apple she. On her divan ensconced. By guests encircled. In stasis. Speak they could only when busy was she cutting the apple ante shoving into her mouth, chomping loudly. Bite every, by the sound of her teeth punctuated. Clacked they when talked she, when slept she, when sexed on fours she, when signature FidEx required, when on Luna Mr Armen Strong walked, when resignation Orc Nixex announced. At dawn clacked they, in the hour nonus, in the ides, ante flossing, during flossing, ante bowel movement, post bowel movement, in sickness, in health. With intentions maith, with intentions olc, clacked they. To this day clack, clack they. Clack will they. Clack, clack will they. For the blood of Ubaratutucs four hundred thousand serving time in Orc Hoor clack will they. Clack will they for you, brudda. Clack will they for the sound of tooth one clacking. Clack will they until the fourth coming of the one who in the business, liability limited, of coming back is.

At a bus station meets Dogfather a mara teenannish. Waxes friendship romance. Live together they. To Byblos.

News of the relocation cum the Twenty-sols-young reaches the wife. Byblos? Ooooh, my honooooor . . .

Zooms to Los Bab Airport in a dress scarlet gasping. Installs her mass on the airplane somehow, akin the apple fit via her hole tiny. Crick-crack . . .

At cockcrow, rattles Dogfather's door. The bulk sweating of the wife on all fours gets down. Waxed the streets her dress black.

"Let me kiss thy feet . . . Let me die for thee . . . Forgive me . . . Wrong was I . . . I swear to Hoshosh . . . For our children's sake . . ."

Sees the Twenty-sols-young. "Strike me blind! Kill me dead!" Sobs, at her husband's ankles scraping. To get up, cannot. Husband, Twenty-sols-young support her must as slaps them she.

Dogfather's monnon, the children sit on. Demand reunite with wife for the family's honor.

Dogfather and Twenty-sols-young . . . bereft, weeping in each other's arms for days three . . . Blind goes he.

Returns home wife triumphant. Arms locked with husband blind.

Moons a few hence, dies Dogfather.

Ambling via life from cob to cob, one surgery to the next continues the widow.

Dogfather, with honor buried. Marching bands heard towns two away. Threnodists wailing. Of arrangements floral a flotilla. Epitaphs by ex-rivals in poesy, voices tremulous masking self-vindication.

"The tape though. What about the tape?"

"Son. When he died. I was so heartbroken. I gave all his stuff away. Nothing's left. Not even a pair of socks."

Alla. An smile econormical. Replies curt. Eye contact, none. Of asking a mara more than a couple of questions Brathki, in the habit not.

Into her game drawn. Into her shell withdraws. Smiles. Mouth shut.

Rings her phone. Scramble girlfriends three to decide for whom? Tolls the clocc. For Alla. A brother other. Taking the gizmo to ear, slips out. To return not.

An egress. To the lap of nature enter.

A herd of goats. The shepherd, unseen . . .

Tawit of Tawru. Unguarded left the herd. Asleep, he. Gathered the dispersion, replacements to the village marshalling. Epic of epics all. The epic arch of Urmashu. Epic, a misnomer. Literature pre-epical. Literature, a misnomer. Preceded writing all. Tongue first of tongues all. Strata primeval. Խորհուրդըն ուր կ'անգիտացուի, բառերըն սոսկ կը խաւսին.

A cipher arcane encoded—know of which Ubaratutucs little; Slaughterhouse, nothing. An structure, the Zodiac decoded.

In Virginville, constellations by Sol obscured. Pax profound. Pax separate. Pax omniscient. An swamp—of frogs three hundred an stadium, Dionysos's entry to Haides echoing. If thee I forget, recall I songs sacred . . . The swamp of Lerna. At Brathki's feet.

A goatling into his eyes gazes, for help beckoning friends. Reckoning an orcizen is he. Armed, he is not. Uniformed, not. To leave the goats can not. Yet, to frighten their young could not. In his arms would like to take him. To dispel fear. To dispel dissolution. To dispel all.

Dog waxes he, destroyer of worlds all. Sothis, germ of worlds all. From

Porn and Virgin removed, to a form sacral of death submitted. Offerings purer euphonious are.

In the distance, music. A path circular. By a ravine separated. A chasm dividing essence from fulfillment. Of nature the cunt. By circumstance unfettered. In memory unencumbered. Expulsion, his name. Ante progress, an epithet. Of body his dominion no more. Holds sway neither right nor rite. Extends neither nor recedes kyank. Neither horse nor charioteer is he, at the eld-father's face striking.

An step more. The wind . . . ebbing, flowing, with the buzzing of insects diffused. Into wilderness continues he. Jut stones freely. Biped none set foot here in time yon. On a rock sits. The horizon. A frontier upward soaring intra mist. Follows its ascent. Beyond uran. Mount Mashu! A crest white, by clouds silhouetted, lays ron him.

For an hour lon, lost in Mount Mashu he. Mashu Major. Eyes he the summit. Its twin, Mashu Minor, in the mist lost. The breasts of nature. Totality. All being, offered.

By a gondola ballad Neopolitan visited. "Sul mare lucica, l'astro d'argento . . ."

Why that and not one of the tunes oneiric a thousand in his holm? Fathoms he not still. Surfaces that song in the mountain's grandeur . . .

Horai a good three. For him hosts worried look. On his way back, comes across the shepherd and brother young. Curious, the younger. Noshepherd in shepherdzone! Explains the older, "toorist." Make him a portion for harissa they might not. In their tongue greeted.

Alla's trio, around a table seated. Waiting for Brathki, she. Walks away dragging the trio. A triangle impenetrable.

At duskfall, toward the field heads, the vastness of Mashu pulling him. On the road long, waits for him a face arresting. Vanishes as draws he close.

On his way back, among a herd of cows dappled finds himself.

He loves them. Sisterly. Known them his life all. Grabs of grass a fistful. In her mouth takes his hand entire. Love phosphorescent. Empathy invigorating more than all felt ere. Talks to them Brathki.

Forgetting Mount Mashu watching them from the distance nuyn as away pulls he. Approaches the village in cadence mute. Far from he now. Vanishes, he.

"O, trees . . . brothers . . . souls kindred . . . Let my love the ocean of your elements be."

The trees, akin trees, quiet remain. Taciturn. Silent. Not. Silent. Talk they back . . .

Understands Brathki their tongue.

At a distance, the buildings first of Virgin City. Misses he it.

Virgins. With deposits static synonymous. A mara thirty-annish, of sacrificing virginity mortified. Tarnishes her allure . . . gives her cancer . . . screaming into a lake fiery of shame eternal and eternity shameful casts her. Forty-annold sister, virgin.

"Why forty? Make it fifty!"

"Fifty, fifty, fifty, fifty . . ."

"Sixty!"

"Sixty, sixty, sixty, sixty, sixty . . ."

"Seventy!"

Artifice of whoredom noncarnal. Atrophy infra Ubaratutu's mannequins sweep whose oils the earth. A mara, as missus addressed: "I am a grrrl!"

Eyelock in elegance muted. "Who needs your grrrlness?" Away walks the apparition. An smile mysterious, a cigarette unlit.

Stops she Brathki on the street. "How about coming to my house?" Parents . . . gone. The prize, unguarded. The roundness of an apricot. "My only vacation," flicking eyes honey-light to his netherland.

"Now this place is sanctified, whatever happens within." Bedroom walls with fingers four of hand right from a pitcher. A communion. The junction sanctified least of the verb "pop" with the noun "cherry."

Brathki, pleased.

Ubaratutu, displeased.

"Heyyy, whataya doing withowr grrrl?" Emiroids two-bit his way block. Blood in eyes, grouse in fists white-knuckled. "Listen, pal, we warn you. First and last time. We send your liver to Mamma we ever see you again. *Ever* . . . Letim go."

Whim, dust in horai large. A poach, two in come. Pass. Therefore, may shun taken play. Hora seaborn fair é. Ice of up. Art to kill? You–she bile logic. All in to the suck ass has no fair. Ex, is dead. Yawn . . . er, if. Groat ough. Our size in a buff. The buy of so fears. A fun, and did plan a tear. Ye lay her. In oven, lope, a fink. King, sub stance . . .

To his senses returns. The cost of life-capital in Ubaratutu calculates. Per day, percent two hundred—or a life. Machete touches neck ante leaving percentmorgue. "Kyank for kyank more," in Ubaratutu inverted: "Solely death for kyank." Violence—the ethic guiding of Pornosa, of Virginosa both. By mawgage protected, by kultkulture protected, by empire protected. Pornistan, by virtue of an empire realized, a luxury produced. Harmony relative could in relations find one still. Knew Ubaratutu ethics none but violence. In conduct, violence. In deportment, violence. In tongue, violence. In thought, violence. Life via the collective its will dictates, the exception not. Dies the exception. Celebrate the living their truths. Ubaratutu, by sacrifice possessed. Paralyzed will consciousness be, sans nood sacrificial will kyank atrophy. Covenants Ubaratutu *your* sacrifice. Die! The injunction on the tablet of fate. Cursed Brathki Ubaratutu. Yearned the lor of Ubaratutus all. Loathed races all. Pissed on flags all. On the theft of the other's kyank installed! Via demonization! The demonization of Bałdasar! Arhmen! Shaitan! Via natoton! Via demonocracy! Via purification! Via freedom! Via noninterference! Via respect! Via love! Slaughter mandated. Kill and shalt thou live! Kill the will! Symbolizes the absence of killing kyank. Bałdasar, the Master of Kyank! Bałdasar's arete! The darkness sole in the abyss of light. Transcending mimesis—which hubris into a pathos for violence sublimates.

Longed Brathki for Natashazone. Ynter peaks and crevices yonder his holm suthing novels wintry a chiliad and one . . . quandaries moral a chiliad and one . . . poems arsoned a chiliad and one. To orgasm ceased Mount Mashu. The volcano of this mountain white, with matter dark filled, sperm leaking out of anthracite . . . into a prairie yielding a bouquet of metaphysics transformed.

Enters Brathki Natashcow. The Mashu living. On lava barefoot to run. The breeze kin moisture to lade.

*C*asino *Symmetrol.* In solo ambles. By sodium light powered, a satyricon. Spotlights intra chandeliers revolving casting geometries odd. Screens of mist ejaculate, forging colors spectacular. By maras twain a table occupied. I'm from Kossakstan, father from Ermenstan. No, I don't speak Ermenian.

One subject, arall. Wants to dance, one. Gives her hand. To the west. The air. Brisk. Of flame the promise viscid. His gestures—with colors in situ. Self-importance stripped. Return husbands from the casino downstairs. Of each other take they leave. To a table glides. To dance asks her locum. Irina, the elder. Recommends asks he Vika.

Vika. By a Häyhä nuisanced. Eyes measuring pores. Breath rummed. Chats with Irina. White-haired. Charming. Temporal. She and Vika, for the arrival of a business partner waiting. Maras dynamic. In the crosskrak of industry trumps ambition tradition. The nobility digital. The mobility novel. Post-post post. Love, the fashion au courant ynter Natashazone poets. Bored histrionically if hear they a word unsynonymous. PashPrizejis. NatashPrizejis. Haunts Lumbar Khayyám Natashazone—and Pashayurt. Thanks deepest, writers of empires. Up your keisters shove your El Knob prizes. With your colon adorn them in the gift shops of your empires. Drink the sherbet of your piss and love.

Eyes gray. Feline foiled. Romanova—a descendant remote. Vika and Xenonstani every. Assert succession dynastic even Chinmachurians in Xenon's Union. Loathes she Xenon the tsaricidal. In the steppes windhewn nuyn rooted. Neyn, neyn. Vika, no Xenonstani. A Caramelistani.

Writing a book, Brathki. About to leave for Ubaratutu to research Cron. Urmashu's epic outra context deciphering . . . of divisions calendrical the resonance as allegory for mathematics.

Wonders Brathki how at night sleep can he soundly. The table next. Sasha, Masha. The Häyhä. At himself laughing. In heart, a child petulant. In breath, a charnel house. Heeds not Sasha. Approaches her Brathki, to the Häyhä's luck leaving Masha. The Häyhä, drunk. At Brathki's shoulder stares, burning a hole. As immolate he cannot with eyes, responds he dog to dog.

"You . . . keep away . . . from that mara . . ." at Vika points.

"Fine," replies Brathki, to chat with Sasha continuing.

"I'm serious . . . you keep away . . . from that mara."

"I'm serious, too."

"Where you from? Elpacinoland? . . . Sure looks like one . . ."

"Urmashu."

"You Ubaratutucs . . . A lot like Elpacinolanders," an story driftless about his pappaw weaves. Twice, assures him Brathki he's right. Concludes, "I respect you . . . for that."

"Thank you."

"That don't change nothing . . . Keep away from these. I'll be fucking them . . . tonight." At these smirks lewdly.

"Fuck that."

"Just ignore him," says Sasha.

Struts cockily, in slurs curt to himself speaking.

Lust's worm covert. In coil, uncoil. Perfect the simile libidinous. None the wiser.

Sasha, a bird one-off. A mana more than a day with? A choice solemn. Family wealthy. Nose up, cigarette ultrathin down. I don't work. Leaving for Churuchill Isle in a couple of days.

Empty, the lounge. Get up to leave the four. The Häyhä, Brathki, friends fast.

Notices from her booth Vika the exit of the contingent drunken. Arms around Sasha. "Did you sleep with her?" asks later.

To extricate herself attempts Masha. To dissuade moves the Häyhä's larynx. Somehow, caves in she. Takes hold of her the Häyhä with gusto. The silence of Gisher.

Four ante meridiem. Goes a kiss on and on. An ocean. Infra the gazes cheerful of night guards four, security providing for Brathki's kiss. On condition of meeting at night again, bid they farewell.

Grow close Brathki, Vika. Off-limits naught to her. Of a polpotical organization the founder. At the Duma works, where knows everybody she. Proposed the Duma zeugdom to her.

Natashima nights. Enchanting. Loves to walk Vika. Miles ten a rota.

Expraedium

Franchises blowing from Parisabad replete, alleys full of orconacra. Hello Mushkin, hello Karkarin, hello, hello. Respects khor from Orc Hoor glorious, Orc Hoor atol . . . Walk Natashas interminably. *Walking* fuck they. When "just around the corner," wise be to anticipate a walk two-mile. Pornosas, by the notion of walking offended. Walking: for the homeless. Walking: for the untrustworthy. Walking: for the disconsolate. Walking: for the foreign. Walking: anti-Pornosican. Destroys the economy. Brings melanoma. Proves deceitful are you—cheap, self-righteous, unambitious, antiquated, last and assuredly least, a fuck lousy.

If tolerated Brathki barely the scruples of Pornosas, ruthless downright is he to Ubaratutu's hymens. A Virginosa twenty-two-ann-old, by a walk less than a mile from the Natotonal Library to the Youth Palace sapped. On the cradle of creation mountainous lives she . . .

At the site of a monument august, per annum, on May twenty-seven-point-five, commemorates Ubaratutu a victory momentous over Pasha. In the year of Shazamroohar nineteen eighteen, from extinction that victory nerianed Ubaratutu. One mara bejeweled complains closed the path to the entrance is, forcing bipeds to walk meters three hundred. A polpol: "Our fathers walked barefoot across the Shamash Desert for weeks on end. Is it too much to walk ten minutes in their memory?" Roils a murmur from throats forty thousand, eyebrows eighty thousand: "She's not an Ubaratutuc . . . *not* an Ubaratutuc . . ."

The night first at Vika's. Of rules an string along the way. Foremost, to refrain from sex her right unassailable. Her apartment. Of an alley a back alley of yet an alley ayl in the heart of Arbat. Door iron. Locks imposing. Inside, a Shangri-la. Touch they breathlessly, of desire the harp-strings plucked. Anude collapse barriers. With abandon embrace they.

The afternoon next. Irina's apartment. The interior, angles horning in angles. Minus the walls—Xenon-era baroque. The wardrobe, mahogany babushka-thick. Khusband will call, now. Will you please pick up the phone, tell you work at Holy Orcon's embassy? Galina, Vika's cousin. In looks, brains orcettish. Behind dogs enormous flanked. To eradicate hunger in Slaughterhouse, a project launched. Promises official of govt-gofts Yuromamanic, secured.

Experience in initiatives idem Brathki once had. Of help could be—issues they thought of not. Listens he. Involved, not. His experience given, wanted the girls to build the enterprise on foundation meur. Suggest they Brathki as a partner join. Declines. Busy with research on Cron. His focus sole. Understands Vika. Promises to promote his work in Natashazone. Public relations, her specialty. Suggests Irina tie Vika, Brathki the knot. Good to have responsibility, no? Let them on their interpolations snack. Everything he tells them not.

Cares he no longer for interests biped in Slaughterhouse. By doctrines biological of consumers repulsed. Churns his bile the exhibitionism blunt in bipedkind. Transformation into forms novel to migrate via the birth and death of universes for evolution integral. Polpotics, transient. Hunger, an issue polpotical.

In Ubaratutu, amazed was his landlord when refused Brathki a washo-ten-million marketing proposition multilevel.

"Not for me."

"But what is it that interests you? Really? You're declining a once-in-a-lifetime opportunity." From objects promoting love and spirit. A love Kapitolist.

Via trials his path found. Via cusps of spheres. What happened? Why sharply did his course change? Why going was Brathki to Ubaratutu?

None knew.

The sign: "CCCP." By the name tickled, enters he. Decorate the walls paintings of Eye Vazovski, the ord, the sickle, stamps by glass covered. If guard icons the catacombs of zoule, forfeit these to an order disassociative. Vika: "The owner, Ubaratutuc." Doubts Brathki. Of dishes a couple Ubaratutuan, a pedigree Ubaratutuan not. The name, in soot Xenonic. Turns out to be right she. "Beer sans vodka, rubles down the drain." Drink they kin muzhiks.

Ahead, trouble red. Despite Brathki's protest, informs Vika the owner, of Urriantiti true blue he is. From Orc Hoor. Lyova, the proprietor gray-bearded, materializes a bottle of cognac Ubaratutuan holding—a commodity in Whitebearland valued highly. Potent potable by Yay Sin lauded, a lush renowned.

To refuse Lyova, impossible. Lied she. Wanted a drink free. You lie! We noooo lie in Nataaasha Zoooone. Check my passport. From Madarid. You *must be* one! We *will make* you one! In the tradition Ubaratutuan to guzzle up have choice none, to as many people and surpeople as branches on a sequoia drinking. Hours three savoring of drinks an smorgasbord, with glass raised each an speech delivered. Hoshosh save Ubaratutu! Hoshosh save our virgins, the selven of our manahood! Hoshosh save our tatiks, the bedrock of our survival! Yooooo . . . brother . . . You. Come. From. Hell. And don't drink? Winks. I. Fill. Your. Glass. Brother! Lyova takes no no! I. Opened. The most expensif. Ubaratutuan cognac. For you, brother! Made of. White grapes. From Nonah's vineyard. Hah! This size! Dance, drink, make merry. Revert the loudspeakers to Urmashu. Reflect the waves upon a panoply of eyes blue, refraction none. Eyes Urmashuan, eyes enchanting,, Veiled your lustre the black cloud,, And whisked away your winsome smile,, Black a sorrow you wear, torment . . . Sheds tears, Lyova, remembering life in Ubaratutu ante his fall into the ravine of Natashcow. Eyes Urmashuan, melancholy,, Always humble, always kindly,, Weeping for the suffering soul,, Brilliant only a day a year . . . Eyes black in the night blue of Natashcow. Four ante meridiem. Leave they, grudgingly. Refuses entry the night guard. Says who nyet to Vika? Relents at last, at his own sentimentality amazed.

Into Vika's nance torannous leaps, sinews torn asunder by the warp centripetal of the prima mysterium Natasha. In the blaze defenestrating of Xenonkrak bones scorched. Of ashes a heap. Winds four scattering his remains to mansions unknown of Slaughterhouse. Black cloud . . . eyes enchanting . . . you wear a black sorrow, torment . . .

To Saint Petragrad sees him off. "You'll be meeting the lovelies of Natashazone. Don't forget me . . ." Across wastelands races the train. In the compartment, four. From his neighbors' conversation picks up *amerikanetz* and *zorro*. Abates their curiosity with the best of his vocabulary: *Urmashuanski S-SHA*. Rock to and fro heads large in the wagon. A night. By Vika abducted. Cheeks freckled, breasts rising. Of the fenlands dense of sleep falling. O breath living of Mashu. Stumbles, a dragonfly in a town dazed. If wings are clipped? The taunt of a heart bloody's morsel.

Humor Airport. Ante meridiem two. Striking the landing, applause swells the heart. Eyes moist all around . . . Eyes Urmashuan . . .
Ess Zex black. Windows tinted. Reaches it Brathki via throngs of maras fat, men lean pushing orth. Voices with mouths off rhythm. Eeee making an oooo. Sir, sir, you Eorcheoria? My niece, Old York. Know her? Santaram Tantaram. Know her, sir, know her . . . sir, kindly listen, sir . . . you're invited to our house, sir . . . stay as long as wished, sir, as loooong as wished, sir . . . Sir, you Shakespearessex? . . . Sir, Boneparty, sir? My dohtor doctor in Parisabad, sir. Seen her lately, sir? Gave birth to dohtor, sir, what an swan, sir, what an swan . . .
The Ess Zex. Vardan's smile, an astonishment for permanence carved. A nod acknowledged. Make eye contact not. Lest the edicts of Hammurabi thou violate, for thy misdeed with thy balls paying. Except, if prostitutes, art, the patrie discussed. Vardan's Trinity. Towards the city proceed. "Come on, pal, don't do that. Embarrassing." Stops Brathki from putting his seatbelt on.
Vardan Mamkoon. Of trivialities—common sense, courtesy, legality—

free. Sovereign. "Driving in the opposite direction, generalissimo." Blushes the cop. After all, this is Vardan: "You guys do crooked things, too," retorts. Neither nights nor health spared he during the battle oll of Moira, which sacrifices myriad from Ubaratutu extorted. Armed the Moirae, himself transporting the dead to their families. Out of the fray kept his son. Alone decided to the front went who—not who. Hymns to his glory Ubaratutu sang:

May my zoulzoul die, yours not.

Of memory the rustle . . . all that remained.
"Book good?"
Woofing happily, slaps the seat Brathki's tail. By the manuscript, Vardan perplexed. Implications polpotical read ante comma each. "Kultkulture is polpotics!" Black, white. Finality incarnate. Likes Brathki him the better for it.

At Hotel Erebuni drops him off.

Rotas two hence, finds Brathki an apartment. On Iron Age Street. Treneths a score swears the real estate goldteeth his honesty. Apartments prime at prices aerated offered—"for the love and honor of Vardan." To buy a home in Ubara City implores—"a fail-safe lottery." Dwellings found for Vaxno post disappearance. This, the minister interior of Titan—yclept Eretz Leo—for the interregnum spanning Xenon Union's collapse and Holy Hoshosh's ascension to the throne of Free Demoncratic Ubaratutu reigned. By Holy Hoshosh pursued, with Yuropolpos in tandem. The hideout of Ubaratutu's BinLatin's lair, unknown. To haunt Eyfeloon luxuriously alleged while Papa Hoshosh and Mama Eyfeloon eyes blind turned. Anns an score hence a coffin unopened to return was from Walhalla and buried.

Yammers incessantly the goldteeth. At the hotel, pay must you thalers one hundred a rota. My strategy, four hundred a moon mere. Reminds Brathki the fuck deaf, in Orc Hoor, too—a difference logical eter apartment, hotel. To the landlady reiterates, for none other than Vaxno himself found homes.

Asks Brathki the rent. "Three hundred fifty washos," wedges he in, at the landlady winking. An amount stupefacient. Worth two hundred, the apartment. The landlady, attractive. Well read. To sleep with, Brathki would object not. Unkin the shrew sulk-eyed the rota ante. In an attempt at a look Yurostani inflicted that turkeyhen a remodeling garish. A bar grotesque, an entertainment center which for a nightclub Ibossim could pass. Haithenly, a doofa bed into a corner thrown. "No! No!" screamed she. "No mara will ever set foot in this apartment." Today's landlady, adorable. A counteroffer of two hundred fifty. Moons' two rent in advance.

"Fortune has fallen at your feet. Mustn't you turn it away." Slurps the goldteeth his commission, vanishes, to be seen again never. Securing a mansion in Ubaratutu . . . for Urriantitii, an affair knotty.

Legs inviting, the landlady's. Legs alongside her, three, to the opera navigate. Takes hold of Brathki doggedness Humerican. With her winds up sleeping not. In Brathki's ears murmurs a sibyl. Someone younger? Considerably? O ballast immutable of hexachord, intra season and outra . . .

Goes beast to beast on him the Humerican. Examine we kyank—in mah's face obsidian smiling. O mah . . . of holm, balsam. Of conscience, succor . . . you stone sweet-smelling . . . zooming in, pulling away, a film of approximation fleshly.

At the hotel, of the nightlife in Ubara City inquired. "Ovyan Street. Go to Ashtarteh."

Ovyan's sidewalk gauche. The side anent, with swarms of marauders agog. Spit they sunt. Spit they dextera. Spit they pro. Spit they supera. Gobs of utterances phlegmatic the sidewalk bedeck. To flee compelled from Ubaratutu, unknown.

Vikhod!

In Afterlife is fate a hazard warranting flight?

Disgusted viscerally at State Insectiversity of Ubara City, where consumed were students of Crdnl Xenon by boyflies, girlsquitos. Teach here Brathki could have not for an hour sans smashing cocoheads forty.

Carry flies and mosquitos bacteria unidentifiable. Scunnered be not, sisters. Survived the bacterium anopheles calamities worse. Conquer can bipedswarm the threat totomic by transmutation bacterial. Osmosis symbiotic. The bacterium anopheles: biped's forefather immortal. Father Babra Dabra. As grasp they this dern, tribes primeval to their roots hold steadfast.

To walk steps an score sans crossing an spitter . . .

Ubara City. Universe of Spit. Resides on an stone Brathki which annihilation via asteroids evaded. Grateful he. For these gentlemen's marksmanship superb.

When al fresco eats he, eats eyes shut. Ears with silt filled. The moment relishes a morsel, a passerby sans looking, sans thinking, at his feet flumps spit. Thy head lift not. At the spitter's face look not—lest bite thou the one big. Look down, down always . . . to find a moon lon bubbling at footstep each. A Moonghost Sonata . . . Oh, moon.

To smoke spit they. To sputter spit they. To kiss spit they. Practice spitting ante spitting they. Ego consputo ergo sum. Ubaratutu's logos aeternus.

Encounter spit the king, vizier, generalissimo, denizens cravat-wearing of the Council of the Anointed at step each. Authority. Stems from the genus idem of protopanzees as spitbags these. Enter not a restroom! Lest by the state of its restrooms to measure a ciphilization's caliber.

The nightclubs demarcating the sidewalks of Ovyan, with remnants of the hoi polloi sticky. A jackson costs sticking your head in—torso outside—the cat doors of nightclubs barren. Finds Brathki Ashtarteh. Clientele, chic. Repelled, he. Of bosons' tendrils deadly. Glares cyanic, laughter transparent. Ubaratutu's elite: pimpassadors, pundits professional, marafolk in tow silently.

But in this cave enjoy a show he can. A routine exceptionnelle—an striptease number choreographed exquisitely, dancers from arbors pusskultural imported. Artistry, ingenuity, sui generis. Exo the best envision could the King of Akh.

His dinner plate hanterful, grabs the waitress it, into shadows disappearing. Walks up the owner with maras twain.

Maras of Ubaratutu! . . . Whores of Ubaratutu! . . . His mind Brathki loses.

Maka-and-Masha. Stately. Kultkultured. Birds of youth ravishing. From Shvilabad Maka the brunette, from Ubara City Masha the anent. Each hanter costs franklo one bearing Holy Orcon's signature—a moon's salary in Ubara City. ISO nine thousand.

To penetrate Ubaratutu's womb simmers Brathki, depths fertile plumbing. Takes their numbers.

Calls not. A bastard worth his grain pays not for sex. Even trans the Iron Curtain of Virgin Capital of Slaughterhouse. Let *them* pay him.

Emerges thus a conflict of interests in Ubaratutu.

From Brathki's Friday Night diary:
Maras stunning, in Ubaratutu dense. Pornistan's contraphenomenon.

Unmissable, the Virginoso's want of grace. Crudeness. Shamelessness. Of taste a paucity unequivocal.

Sanctity in marsupialism. Asperity worn, heart in sleeve, juxta bath of cologne cheapjack. Of conquests fuckly speaks at funerals loudly. Dead would be caught not sans cell phone in hand. Jabbers, regardless of who—if anyone—on the end is. "Mamaaa, what you cook today? Add gheyma on the side, ok? Matnakash and cheese and kanachi from Serop. Tellim, for me. Don't forget to make dolma. Coming over with buddies at four. Send Arusyak to aunt's house. Make sure she's gone by three. Don't forget, ok, the *gheyma*? I said *gheyma*! Oooooouuuuaaaaooooofffff . . . Make sure, extra lard so it cooks in its fat. I'll get the vodka . . . You're getting the wrong kind spoiling our kef . . ." Every rota hear thou shalt ercs one hundred of this from cell phones anywhere find thou thyself to be standing or sitting or shitting upon. Entering the bus, exiting the bus, at the metro, at the store, in the theater, at the monnonmorgue, at the panzeeversity, in the library, in the library, in the library, on the sidewalk, supra the sidewalk, infra the sidewalk, on the stairs, in your home, windows open, windows shut . . . until hauled are thou to the nuthouse or to Cape Carnaveral carommed.

The Virginosa: finesse incarnate. The Virginoso: subtlety of an orangutan rutting.

If a nard fragrant the Virginosa is, the Virginoso: a repository of perspiration moons-old. Muccpitch strangled. Encountered not the travesty of a mawgage ayl as the Virginoso's rape of his tongue native. This, the mawgage that from Narineh's lips burbled and ebbed kin crystal fountain, in whose rhythm euphonic found Brathki Urmashu—even as wandered he amid the desert diasporic? This, the mawgage Cousin Arphi warbled—crippling waiters in Los Balabylonos in their tracks to its concordance savored?

"Sick fuck. News to you every natoton has its argot?"

"Argot, celestial music. Your venomous drone, a tracheotomy."

"Who are you comparing us with, who?"

"Were you half as good as Pasha's hank . . . *You're* the ones who wiped out Urmashu! Nemesis of Ea!"

Tonguemity. Of gutterchurn blather sanguine. Wisemanas erect towers own, on bedrock not but sand.

A repugnance seizing fiber and nerve, the repertoire colloquial. Of waves coterminous with words the malignance. Intra qualities tonal carries the voice forms lethal. Exit anthropods nousianic Ubaratutu to save their lives.

"Don't take it to heart. A generation raised on war."

"Don't play the war card. Not with me."

Claims Lora, though vulgar cucumberances are, a nert primal intra the stench of crudity. A pearl plasticine in the mouth of a fetus belching.

"Only *we* can grasp that."

"Brava, sis!"

Ubaratutu: a geneticist's nightmare. With banality coarse satisfied. Of hubris a hallmark, marring reforms by Crdnl Xenon instituted. In emulation of Natashazone's Mafia, sucking packs six a rota in an annex to death starving.

A tactic de-evolutionary, Ubaratutu's populace XY.

"Why are they so ugly?" asks Brathki's sister. "Everything about them . . . revolting. Rather die than zeug with any of them. Why are the maras the most beautiful in Slaughterhouse?" To niman the paradox, unable.

Net worth zero. To a Pornette a cucum from Ubara City has—regardless of life insurance benefits. To a cucum Pornistani overshadows a Virginette Pornistan's entertainment idols celebrated most.

By a wave insurmountable intra decades few uprooted shall Ubaratutu's maras be. Via force accomplished Holy Pasha this in praeteritum. Deracination eun eugenically. Dictates sadism evolution genetic. A hole sealed welcoming a soldier disabling enemy tanks five—with pussy not! A pedicel emitting: "It is a salutary actuality that you are precisely proficient in the precise occupation of utilizing precise weaponry." Milias online, fingers tickling an inertia ethnological. As egress from Ubaratutu the drive for husbandry—to the Neon Internatotonal. Reaching proportions Natashuac. Holy Orcon, in glamour waxes, to the detriment of Papa Hoshosh, Mama Natasha.

Virginosa's competition in the bourse?

Online hides. To post her image bothers not.

Beautiful. Twenty-seven.

Naught else.

Rain bananas a milia on her lap. Ping! Ping! Ping!

A ghost town waxes Ubaratutu. To the museum of strata evolutionary failed exiled. Into the cradle of a bloodline sublime evolve? Upon Virginosa's consciousness contingent. Is listening she? Information channels, monopolized. Sentence every in Slaughterhouse emitted, propaganda. Propaganda free versus propaganda controlled. Propaganda monnonized versus propaganda ideofied. Propaganda public versus propaganda private. Cretinification rampant, to evisceration a prerequisite.

Subjugated the Virginosa into believing the Virginoso's tail she is. To preserve her kultkulture intra context variated, hard-pressed. The evene of Mashu in a husband foreign-born to instill? Inept. Of that evene's manifestations, devoid. In the realm of identification kultkultural, subordinate osa's gynessence to that of the oso is.

On a dating site. Armenuhi. A funeral services clerk.

"Half the deaths in Ubara City every fucking rota. Going backwards, to the mouth of Euryale.

"Let me see if Harry in Milk Walkie is online. Blond, not like our osos. Doesn't need his eyebrows tweezed, either . . .

"Those two weeks in Elpacinoland . . . something else . . . Tony, 'going back to my Tusci roots' . . . he's from fucking Pornland . . . Can't tell anyone I went with a foreign mana. Lost that special something to him. One word and it's mnas barov any husband, mnas barov Ubaratutu . . . My kids will be blond . . . babbling in Orcish . . . attending orciversities . . . Aram, a pimpassador for Orcon, Vrezh . . . an admiral . . . Twice an ann, Harry will take me on vacation. Promised. Not a liar like ours' . . . Won't let that bitch of a Diaspora Minister trample me every fucking week on TV—'I've been in Peronland, Amazonland, Madreland. Parisabad, of course, of course. I've been in Churuchill Isle, yeees, yes Hamburg. I've. . . I've. . .'— Fuck her mama!"

"In order to protect the pedestal of Hoshosh's sublunary abode and establish his temple, fundamental to liberate Mount Mashu from occupiers, safeguarding our symbol of existence," a passerby tells Brathki. "Geographical expanses are protected by one biped family—its surname, azg." "Houses of race: houses of hysteria. Importing decay to Ubaratutu. Slaughterhouse litterature, a pandemic destroying biped eln. The sublunary abode can only be established post eradicating the taproots of hysteria."

"If you mean that taproot is the azg, you're spreading a false philosophy, misguided Brathki. Come home . . . The lone way to defend Hoshosh's abode in Slaughterhouse is to strengthen the azgheim contra false philosophies disguised as ezerkian brotherhood, propagating the slavery of azgs . . . We lived via seventy years of such brotherhood, following two milia of a parallel one . . . A third brotherhood is now yoked on our neck. The brotherhood of Washo, propagating narratives of subordination . . . The lone way to neutralize this menace is to safeguard the ramparts of azg: mara, mawgage. Globalization—a hoodwink for Washo pimperialism."

"Hope not a cognition of azg from the Ubaratutuc. What follows zoulzoul, follows body."

"The solution then, Mister Brathki?"

"Unfetter the Mashuan mara. Surpasses she the mana. Secure her freedom—the requisite to hogianic metamorphosis."

Walks on the passerby sans answer.

Moons hence. Via the snow piles of Imagination Square ambles Brathki, meeting a crowd gleg ad a gled.

"Strengthen the mara of Mashu!" chants the crowd.

On the floor sixth stands still Makoko.

"The mana who zeugs with a daughter of Häyä . . . convert to her azg must he, assuming her family name. Or, a new one from the twelve sons and daughters of Häyk," declares Prophet Orotuni. Absent Makoko is.

"The mara Mashuan must be the selvenstone in establishing Häyä Hoor," craols Mrs Hauasar. "HÄY's children—sons and daughters alike—are Häy." Notices Brathki behind her the passerby with whom tonguewagged he.

"The mara Mashuan must be educated in the hogianic realm of HÄY," screams a mana short. "Impermissible to tie her down to the race, name of a foreign mana. Such captivity would unsettle HÄY's sublunary republic, interfering with rah. The mara Mashuan has no need of manas outra. He who accepts not HÄY's dominion and name has place none in HÄY's abode."

"The polpotical rule of Mashuania must be entrusted to the mara," ols Comrade Hakenkreuz.

Disperses tear gas the rally. Gatherings, permitted not. Imperil they amity eter Holy Hoshosh, Holy Orcon. A plan to rectangularize Ubaratutu. Plazas for squares substituting. Ideofication by Holy Orcon's embassy financed, progress reported. "Ubaratutu's Polpol have become effective," commands the pimpassador, distributing tablets for distinction. Tears, the lozenge sole placating tongues swollen. A lozenge obtained from the Pharmacy Xenon lone in Ubaratutu remaining.

"A little problem with your diacritical marks, Mister. How do you read HÄY?"

"Like the *a* in High, bro."

"O, that's all I need to know, guy. Use these marks no more."

The Ubaratutuc is the pudding skin." At the top apart. Ochercat and lurecat still barb and rage and weep and go to uran, in fuckbites rowring locked.

"Nah, G. Ain't like that. These hotties want a boo. Back with L Precious. If you didn't know Herrming Way, she'd dump your ass."

Perks Brathki ears. Tee-fifty-twos in a café, attributes respective listing.

"I have Bezzz."

"I have bare arms."

"I have khoussse."

"I have long legs."

"I am exxeccutifff."

"I have pussy."

"Ohhh, sisssterrr . . ."

The Bezzz. In Ubaratutu apotheosized. Te Mercedecum. Holy Hoshosh, entourage. Walalicos, retinue . . . devotees of Ess Zex Gotthold, sallololahu 'aleihi wa sallam. Exhort constituents to enrich corporations Gottholdan. Eggshell on the carpet: for anns sixty, disremembered Gotthold the natotonocide, citing amity co Holy Pasha. Gotthold, sallololahu 'aleihi wa sallam, disforget perfidy only recently did. Mildly. Ere refinancing Holy Pasha.

Of a child the foreslab, with bird-skull engraved, endo the crenellations of Bezz each. Sans this factor X cannot one be found.

Peacocks Bezzy twain clopping warbles. By approach particular to Ubaratutu's boulevards marked each. The type lower—daddies saccharine. Violations gross of traffic laws steer they clear. Broadcast daddies sugarly status passing lights red at speed full. Anent Holy Hoshosh's bazookamen.

One daddy sugarly proposes Brathki in an investment nascent to partner. To his clout Archubaratutuac thanks, Holy Hoshosh, the Philanthropist Almighty, collect taxes from Brathki shall not. The guarantee of the covenant: in his Bezz contra traffic en route to Café Hoshosh.

His marafolk, Slaughterhouse's finest. Hyperjingoism Slaughterhouse's ethos—not least, Holy Orcon's. The Virginosa, priority arch: "a mana on top." Institution, of investment the sensibility prime. Profit, interest prime. Of the Pornosa miles ahead. Harnessing bequest biological to throttle the equilibrity ethmic of Gemeinschaft. Exhibitionism in flagrante delicto, the Ubaratutuc's life. Fathom this Brathki could not. Until the liquor on its breath smelled he. Tell me, brethren, kultvagis how many their sale resist? A salesglobe. Salesgenes. Brokerage houses of genes. Of matrimony the essence. For Sale: XX. Sex unto death. Affection unto death. Pecunia. Pengar. Para. Geld! Bugger off. Die otherwise kindly. Controls who life? Controls who that control? Controls who freedom? Under what footfall felt will our vibrations be, on the eve of which summer lovecheeked?

Scared to go home Stella. In her building, a corpse. Threnodists for rotas quatre past, for the corpse's maternal uncle's grandson's uncle waiting to arrive from Vladivostok. Hired Ubaratutucs threnodists, in days eld, who for the carcass grieved. Matrons psychopompian—lamentations mellifluous a profit share ensured in the death industry. Hushtory preserved, meter created. In Papa Xenon's cron, the threnodist—a relic obscura artificium eter couch cushions of the mind. To Brathki's head they.

A coffin open, outra his building carried. Slanted, to passersby Mr Zaroor Berezhenev's lyke exhibited. Examine they the coffin's value, the corpse's charm baroque . . . "The makeup, yo . . . The gilding! . . . Never stoop so low to use chintzy stuff! . . . Handsome!" Beautiful the corpse is. Knock. For you open will not.

Leaves Stella. Moves the river of heads a legion toward gerezman.

Joins Brathki the procession. Flows a procession other on Avenue of Time. Of cars, bipeds a confusion, a coffin open held on shoulders twelve following. Threnodists twelve voices raise, windows atop embassies shooting.

Of taxis an swarm follows the crowd, honking horns, adding flavor to Brathki's joy. Informs a processioner Brathki's ear, "Mr Patos Tatos." "Arrived sols three ago from Shamash." "Passed sols three ago." "At a red light." "In his taxi." Ambles the crowd in cadence. A heart separate in the heart of a heart. To cameras indifferent. To rain indifferent. To the entourage following it, Olombaba's president to Holy Hoshosh House carrying, indifferent.

Reaches the crowd University Square. The coffins. Next to each other laid. On a pedestal raised for commemorating the anniversary forty-six thousandth of the founding of Ubaratutu.

Announces his name a man fat. A paper from his pocket fishes. Suffocated his voice is in a chorale by threnodists.

Woe to the father left who daughters three behind.
Woe to he who a torch sub-dimmed carried.
Woe to he who from childhood's memory tears of blood drew.
Woe to he who in morn's light glorious celebrated Ubaratutu.
Woe to he who of the klor crowned of martyrs sang.
Woe to Patos Tatos wooed who thrice Ubaratutu's yuys.
Woe to Patos Tatos died who singing, "I want to die singing."
Woe to Ubaratutu for losing its zen model left who behind the glory of Shamash for the sake of Ubaratutu.
Woe to Slaughterhouse for losing its yuys final to survive in Ea in dignity biped.

Pore over the coffins kamerads to pay their dues. Ambles the procession toward gerezman anew.

Waves mute of an argument at the entrance expands. Sold is Mr Patos Tatos's grave to Zaroor Berezhenev. Surround Berezhenev supporters Patos Tatos's grave empty, resisting an onslaught violent in silence growing. In support of Patos Tatos a phalanx, its heads its weapons, into the Berezhenev shield advances several into the pit pushing. A roar in the heat dies. Separates the crowd in two, on a side of the pit each.

Regathers the Berezhenev phalanx its units retrieving. Picks and shovels speed supra shoulders to each phalanx as separate the maras. As jumps Brathki into the fray "ter ołormia, ter ołormia" shouting, roars the horizon fill, held is he from extremities all, into the pit thrown. From the glimpse final of light cover his eyes shovels forty.

"The End. Beter than a movie." Brathki's thought final.

The Hospital Republican of Ubaratutu. Opens his eyes, a reprimand from a polpol hearing, "Appé, what business you have in our affairs internal? Next time, no second chance."

Attributes the nurse Brathki's survival to Holy Hoshosh. Ya rabbunah taalah rabbul 'aalameen. To have coffee with Brathki refuses. Leaves Brathki, from his face dusting off the soil.

The coffin. Of distinction a mark. Into a coffin fund deposits the Ubaratutuc of his earnings fiffty-two pettccent. The Monnonmorgue of Shakespeare—two-digit interest offers, yerd-silver securitizing, to the Palace of the Lords, the Sheiks of Ololahroohr, the chicks of Wall Wall sells. Slaughterhouse meltdown econormic betides when, to hypertrophy due, coffin-funders west enter, disrupting statistics. The coffin: Ubaratutu's vessel sacral. Its foundation: the cemetery.

Urrian to urrian wandered Brathki. A burial ground in search of. The gardens of Adonis. The boneyards sexy of Gran Orc. The shadows of Mashu. Heartless. Deathless. A Mher forlorn, to accept the desecration ultimate refused. Blessed Holy Orcon's homeless were, for interred were they in the land trampled they. Decided to die not Brathki.

Pasha. In death, the liberator oll. In life, Wile E. Coyote, after his Roadrunner ever-distant.

Ubaratutu's decoration arche: of the dead, photos oversized. Totem mattes ancestral mounted. Gained the izzat of a guest entertained? Reassurance of being witnessed by the dead camera-friendly shall thou have. "Our father, our father fabulous of our family blessed, what a mana sacred he was . . . what a mana hallowed he was . . . what a mana beatified he was . . . When he . . . " The totem matte: dare not to take your eyes off, your mouth full. Swallow in peace thy cheese. Chew not.

Love the dead they. Loathe the living they. Kill to love they. Ubaratutu: a necrophilia unfulfilled. Brathki, of this love deprived. His error arch.

Die! Trumpets at corners every of street every. At the entrance of building every. A covenant incalculable eter the dall and the dead murder severs not. Enters a child Slaughterhouse as subclause. A contract to execute. By the living, the dead autographed.

"If only they had the sense to know how to die," grumbles the Old Age Reaper.

"Don't know how to die. Don't know how to live," replies the necropathologist, to the Reaper his zoul surrenders.

"A natoton of the dead. Kin natotons all," deduces the internatotonalist.

"Die!" Atop pedestals utter the dead. Authority sumptuous. Go we shall where did they. Strikes bifurcation terror in pneuma. Ubaratutu, Gran Orc's cumulus. Necrolatry, of ciphilization the cornerstone. Leaves Brathki his clothes behind.

O, sustenance of endeavor, serenity grant us to foibles past ignore. Ignorance accord us to presume we upon them do, do top up.

Mount Mashu. All-anvil. Of creation the palm outstretched. Of the puddlestrewings of mystery, a dream whole. Ascends Mount Mashu at the omega. A question mark fashions. Brathki to the balcony moved his desk. Appears Murder. In the sight of Mount Mashu, unseized. Adjusts its fedora, sulphur in its wake. The balcony: his study, in the grandfather's dream . . . In Ubara City, a week minuesced. Steps outside not. Sees faces not, hears voices not. Air with thanatoton laden, from passersby emanating.

Lost an azg Mount Mashu. Deserved it not. Reclaim it may never.

The sound plaintive of hagglers to the balcony wafts. Of hushtory recorded annuls five thousand . . . Of ciphilization irrigated eter tributaries of Tigris and Euphrates annuls five thousand . . . infra the shadow effulgent of Mount Mashu nurtured. To syllables four reduced: "Old shoes! Old clothes! . . . Old shoes! Old clothes!"

The rota next. Of surroundings Brathki aware, via vision peripheral. A transmutation, a gender ulterior. Congelation. By encuntening, bastard made whole. Cunt inner visible made. Come, Bitch Anima, come. Of secretion sisterly, come. Of gender quintbitchance, come. Gloria patri et matri in unum nomine canis.

In dog's body a lesbian.

Mockery. Praxis arche. With Lilia along Virginshah Street trots. Of sashaying Natashas a couple. Paces a few ahead of these, of virgins a couple. Turning around. Eyes crossed. Giggling. Distance allotted, maintained at treneths all.

Natashas snow-white. Stride obliviously. To the Natashas, the giggling of the mice: " . . . a pebble at Mount Mashu tossed."

Of maras twain sets twain, face-à-dos. Tall, one. Short, other. Captivating, one. Bland, other. Comely, one. Homely, other. Independent, one. Servile, other. Exuding energy generative, one. Into venom mephitic transmuting it, other, raping Mother Whoopee's ocean . . .

An hombre black, suited. At the Marco Polo entrance. To him turns the eatery eyes hundred forty. An smirk wonted: a trick animal from the circus escaped. Shadow on the floor, he. The shadow, the real. The image, he. At the heart of ethnic karthing every . . . pogrom every . . . war every . . . damnation collective every . . . suppression every . . . censorship every . . . constitution every . . . exile every . . . exile every . . . the smirk. In control. In collaboration. In contempt. Emerge from proclamation they. Ubaratutu's subjection to massacre, of its distinction evidence circumstantial? To trump its slaughterers its inability.

Impotence, of art the uterus. Of transcendence.

Phenomena besiege him a centum. Venture to walk down streets sans subjection to a pathologist's scrutiny. Compliments of Virginosorum. "How many days you been here to judge us, asshole? Subjective lunatic!" "Ten minutes in line at the morgue decocts the spirit of the whole of you." "You Urriantitii are of varieties two. Either worship Ubaratutu or lambaste it to shit." "Is your husband an spitter?"

To the bones. With fear wet. By anxiety permeated, capability to niman has none. Of neurosis, enchanted. As palliative contra reduction emotional welcomes torpor. Emerges respect via the coefficient of horror. Of control the precondition: fear. Effete, the Virginoso, if terrorizes not. Manifests his mate a level eun of loyalty *then* only.

Sucks the vampire. Onely. Post the food maze slobbering. The Pornette, topping the Virginette far from. To glean the Virginette for flaying exclusive, amiss. Her doings parallel socestags all. Roots, intra Ice Ages' strata.

Vampirism—of conflict a manifestation. Emerges a caste novel. Throws vagi the gauntlet. In a battle kosmic by the cleaving of chromosomes declares victory. Aphrodite am I! Fuck Psyche!

"Everything will turn out okay, appé . . ." The appéros, perturbed not. Room enough to bury the dead. For generations two. If at ease the appéros are, Ubaratutu . . . doomed not. In rhetoric ubaratutuoid, the appér: a corruption of akhpér. "Brother." The appér (appé, appéro): unto itself a caste. Straddling castes all. Among the dregs, of the appér caste a share. The rest to the flagdom a hue distinct lend. To the dynamic, sublayers. At the helm, akhpérs. The caste mafiosi. Papatriotic. The appéros: chameleons enterprising. The appériks: the schnook common. The dolts. Of appéros lackeys faithful. Of recht figurative a kultkulture. Of appéros the crème de la crème infra Ubaratutu's sun disport themselves. The appéro, of the street. Quick-witted. A modus vivendi procures, in the pyramid of stratification a transversal. Deceives, fairly. Generous, if a liking to you takes he.

From an appéro's steakhouse a sandwich. The placard: drams three hundred.

"You want everything normal, appé?"

"That's right, appér."

Stands over an appérik. While complains appérik in a sandwich cannot fit the order, silences appéro with orders brusque. Takes over, fits in the bread the meat somehow—which in his hands manage Brathki cannot. Charges drams long one milia.

Ubaratutu's econormy, unrecovered post Xenon Union's collapse, toward a future inflated pushed. Decans a few, potential to reach Yuromaman's average. A hub central of the Xenon Confederacy. During the annuls post Zen Union's dismantlement, goldmen farsighted, govtgoft in pocket, partook in transactions momentous.

If assert a presence now Ubarartutu's lampreys, tomorrow . . . Beware tyranny's scepter cold.

Climaxes the bloom malefic in mara's narcissism. An indication glaring—marablues in nightclubs. Manas sub maralegs slither, for attention of iota any praying. Wallflowers, with insults snub, with their reflections in the mirror dance.

The virgin. Narcissism, her power. Relinquishing virginity, her perdition. An odalisque, her telos. Standing socestagal boosts she, supra the fuck bazaar cacophonous her neck craning.

The virgin assgiving. The doctrine Polaris: via billows a surf. Of facilities afforded by virginocracy a sucker. Championette of hierarchy.

In the battles of liberation a fighter, to Los Ubaratutuos an Ubaratutuite moved. To family, dedicated. The inanity of expression his wife uttered sans rectitude . . . "Aummmm, how deliiiiish!"

Anns passed. Horae six waited ere his ordeal with Brathki sharing.

To Santa Barbarocola moved. Wife, duties conjugal refused. Obligingly. Non-obligingly. Fucked every Joe on the corner. Nodding out, face down, palms up. "I have lost excitement for you." Huddled the children in the corner, weeping silently.

Sols a few ere, the couple ideal. Wrong went what? The absence of terror communal. Limits of the family traditional. Virility déclassé. Tainted his "performance" stress post-traumatic. A mana no longer.

For battle longed. "Rather die on the front than in the hands of a bitch." Of the children retaining custody should he return? Mother, on Orcdale streets a mole, defied. "Sonny, I'll never go back!"

By Holy Orcon pampered, the All-beneficent, the All-merciful, Receiver of Many.

Wife—freedom-tasted. Income independent—for serfs. Largesse, to fund cuckolding and cocaine sufficient. Sacrificed sols precious for her ideofication. In the orb of a sun evanescing now loafing.

"How delish!"

Opiate-laden, Virginosas. Asses by Porschewagen warmed, surfeit and disdain by Virginoso thugs financed. We are kartazh!

Repudiates the Virginoso the Natasha. To a workhorse habituated. Natasha—for fuck solely.

Meritless, the amygdala Virginoso. Bicameral. Pensis, binary. Sepsis, hairy. On Bin Franklo's image gets off one hanter, on pilibin own the aneyl. Symbiosis phallicuniary. Of biphilandering, morphic. Of self-commodification, autophilic. The nith separating trichechus manatus ex homo kamasutrus.

"Logic phallocentric! Satiating that dangling bit eter your legs!"

"Takes one to know one, Sis."

Abodh hereditary. Crowns in the sex bourse commands. "Thalers one million." "Ten million," objects one.

The akhpérs the price cough. Share value, metabubblish—despite reification peripheral.

A pantomime via industries psychiatric propagated. Love! For the disadvantaged a placebo cherished. Love! Of revolt the perversion. Taboo—the spark of kyank. To abort cohesion aims hideology. A diversion fulfilling its promise never, via disassociation released solely. Communication, for power an agency. Communion, for power an agency. Faith! Idolatry summa cum laude.

The zoulzoul—in the whelks masochistic of poets.

Received my MFA from Yassar, in tenure at North Orcington College of Fine Arts. Fellated the carcass of Pabulum Ololahum until it oozed a zirconia into the depths of my versity. Discussed in the third volume of my memoirs *Caco Ergo Sum*. Granted the Babs Pissky and Ololahorcic

Expraedium

Distinguished Uniped of the Year awards for my ninth collection of poesy, Grindlesticks with Mee-Maw. Congratulated with ovations, confetti at Penhattan Hitlon, attended by pimpassador Kahlil Ekmekji and two hundred journalists, upon my recitation of its opening poema "Ena Nahnu Nahnu." Touch my beard—you shan't regret it . . . Forged are loves all! Pathology from minds ego-gorged. Idly rave Slaughterhouse's poets. *Himself* loves the biped stratified. The biped of empire. The biped digitized. Of love the catafalque. Self-love, of core the core. A dialectic gleyed. An endeavor cashable. A psychosis retractable. A psychosis contextual. A psychosis manufactured. A psychosis marketed. Of "love" and "holm" as synonyms expendable speak ye. Touch ye neither can, as of possessing neither art thou capable. Possession: of existenz, the insecurity. Possession: of being, the rape. Possession: of force innate, the staunch. An object does love have? A value numerical? Scales? To commerce subordinate not? To its object subaltern not? A value Eanic? The polynomial of "love" in Slaughterhouse: the polynomial of entropy.

É when, love none in Slaughterhouse, save of rivalry, domination, possession, hostility a nest. É when, possessed biped by icons viral. É when, shrivels Slaughterhouse sub heels of parasites flush. É when, conventions professing love as foundation, reticula of exclusivism. Solely the bastard capable é. Of taking what wants he. In this whorehouse dysgenic transversing values.

Verily, my brothers, useless to boast it is. Wish I to reach Hoshosh's visions and revelations. Boast shall I of ubaraped. On my behalf shall boast not I, save to weaknesses in regard. For even if to boast wish I, foolish be shall not I, since speak the truth shall I. "Enough my grace for you is, for my power in the feeble superfluous is made." Therefore, take I the crown of being weak, in insults, suffering, persecutions, distresses, for the sake of redundancy. Fuck my ass, sisters. For when weak am I, strong am I.

An epiphany of Bacchus with mead and poppy braced. A voice imparting precepts sechs. In cave Odeon harked, the exegetes interpreted. The Spell selon Brathki. For the voyageur in Planet Mara an irshad.

Hosion Zeroh:
No mara but kultmara there is.
Exegesis: The act free sole: Rape! Unto her likeness, her being, her pneuma or holm, keep thou must this principle in mind, for manipulation foiling designs all.

Hosion Alpha:
The source of her power—the excess granted. The conspirator summum in granting excess—empire.
Exegesis: On her flag, piss! From kultvagis of empire covet not a consort. A mouthpiece of empire via exploitation funded é she. Via hegemony promoted. Embargo all.

Hosion Beta:
Her weapon of exclusion potentest, the tongue granted her by empire é. Sever thou her tongue! Her mawgage, a kult via which cashes she thee at devaluation percent ten milia in empire's bourse. Utter a word not in her's.

Hosion Gamma:
Of ostracism, her kultkulture é.
Via imposition of kultkulture freezes she thou. Via arsenals vast empowered, thy mode of being via dooms twain oppresses she: either to her kultkulture bow or perish.

Hosion Delta:
Her kult the grave of thy potentiality é.
Stifle via force subtle any. Force crude any. Force necessary any. Less worth thy life-blood than platitudes uttered by automatons mirrorenamored?

Hosion Epsilon:
Of the ramparts impregnable least, the formidable most her inheritance é.
Inheritance of tongue. Inheritance of flag. Inheritance of identity. Inheritance of mode. Devouring, her foundation is. A chance given to none for association paritous. Relegate thee to nonexistence she will. Demolish structures all! Violate inheritance all!

Hosion Zeta:
The terror puissant of kultvagi beauty perceived é.
Her justification sublime, nature. Parse it. Under privileges what did her progenitors choose their genes? Excise beauty all.

Upon hearing this, waxed Osso Pasha pale. Eating ceased. Praying ceased. Shindiging ceased. His Konstantintuition rewrote. His population jailed. Sleep still could not. Convinced him psychologists to clamber up Jebel Alym Puss, for muses wait for days forty. And did Osso Pasha so, karukeion in hand. Of psychologists forty a procession trailed. Ascended he Jebel Alym Puss a douah uttering: *bir Ololah var, o da sen sin; bir iman var, o da ben im. Ach ruhunu peghemberinin, ach ruhunu peghemberinin.* Responded the procession: *bir Ololah var, o da sen sin; bir iman var, o da biz ik. Ach gyozunu peghemberinin, ach gyozunu peghemberinin.* Of cycles forty an spiral, to the Jebel's crown carried the caravan, ensconced where Osso Pasha was in a wigwam for days forty. Did Osso Pasha for days forty fast, on a kilim supine, lips murmuring, the Naroq in reverse reading. And transpired when the day fortieth, appeared a ruh, to Osso Pasha dictating *emirs* thirteen which psychologists documented, with a hadith each supplementing. This, Nacitavus in a fit of ecumenism into Laladin translated, via encyclical disseminating. This Sanctum Ossum Ultimum into Mannannan mistranslated.

Emir Bir:
A relationship counterfeit decimating vanity cultivate thou.
To thy date first go, accompanied by a vagi fetching more. Hire, if a mannequin wanting is. Certain shall the outcome sole be: of infallibility her sense collapseth.

Emir Iki:
Shalt not thou at any time feel emotion any towards her resembling love.
Thy love thy death is; thy dispassion, thy life. Love, an exchange kult-conditioned.

Emir Uch:
With her, loyal be thou never. Her loyalty sole, to her kult.
Via others subdue her. On a vagi more attractive getteth thy paws, especially if an idiot she be.

Emir Dyord:
In her invest thou shalt not. Wise are they refrain who from building their houses on a fucking ocean.
Whatever give ye—moons, sols, nati—lost is. Moonrise every draweth she deeper into her mire thee. Pittances give, much take.

Emir Besh:
Of thine relationship let the burden upon her shoulders rest.
If of equality talketh she, *siktiri chek* instantly. Above all, responsible not art thou for her orgasm.

Emir Alti:
The reins firmly hold thou, lest wane thou the reigned.
This thing called mara: meat, bones, of bokh hideological a kilo. To those attracted simulate who for violence a knack. The imperative categorical, the cock violent.

Emir Yeddi:
In ways all inscrutable be.
Her job: to thee support.

Emir Seqiz:
At her expense shalt thou live. Toil, her burden is: share in it thou shalt not.
Demand thou everything. In return offer naught. When at stake sex and silber are, on the end receiving be. Especially if loaded her baba is.

Emir Tokhuz:
Trust thou place not in the succubus.
If pity feel thou, her goal reached she. Certain thy doom is. Release her
lest thou a sadoid wax.

Emir Onn:
Her tongue from her body sever thou shalt.
At her face fling faults. A milia has she. Bloodshed psychological
passeth for individuation. Up their holes shove it. Ciphilization, on terror
founded. Family, on deceit.

Emir Onnbir:
Contra the iniquity of the leech but defense sole there is: shitless scare
her.
Raise hell if veers she from thy rules in the slightest. At a ratio ten to
one retaliate for acts pleasing thee not. For acts that do thus, nary a word
suffice shall.

Emir Onniki:
In times of harm great or inconvenience minor, desert shalt thou her.
Above all thine ass.
Sans reason, sans explanation. *Ghachan ghurtulur.*
Why pregnant did get thee her? Why zeuged did get thee? Tether
thyself not with chains moral. Let ciphilization rid be of its syphilitics.
Millennia will pass ere finds hushtory a course proper—if ever.

Emir Onnuch:
Before thee let her worship none.
Her dead demolish. Her living demolish. Her icons demolish.
Pasha, the Whore's antidote! Onely he harmless render her can! Onely he in balance keep her can . . . *amini iki parcha yaparak.*
Pasha! King of Kosmos!

Voices prolific. Voices genuine. Voices counterfeit. Voices supra-ordinating. Voices infra-ordinating. Voices. Antivoices. In unison
claim, by following their emirs break shalt thou the will of Mara, the cau-
terization of thy race circumventing.
A but a head snakes. A lure to lure must have. Ugliness—stability.
Ugliness—power. Ugliness—life. The formula: of structures a cannibaliza-
tion subtle. Exalts vagi beauty as icon? A sociopath—she.
Ugly . . . the beautiful novel.
A balsam contra evil. The scales of yangyin restores. Reins the perpetrator in, the hent toward the path kosmic illumins. He: the agent
terrestrial of the Zao. He: the Eye Indestructible of Yin.
The ego XX. At its skirt the banderole of ciphilization wanes. Shat-

tered must this ego of a milia and one frills be. Ciphilization: terrorism systemic. Holy Pasha: the Antiterrorist! Gender: of persuasion a function is, maintains vagi. Thus: her psychodrama, of persuasion a function. Ego—the snare inhibiting the manifestation of the unmanifest. Into a doormat turn its foundation—beauty. Abortive the genesis of Jennet is sans dismantling ciphilization.

Ubaratutu—a thesis. Ubaratutu—a dialectic annuling synthesis. Ubaratutu—a paucity authentic. Ubaratutu—a vortex. Liberation from Ubaratutu—for extinction a promise.

Pride virgin. Field of intimacy nil. Displays public, verboten. Displays private, an affront. XY, XX seen together? "Doing that thing." XY cum XXs twain together? "Doing that thing with the twain together." Quells envy desire. Testes-churn via bucketful. Swims Urriantiti in it. Suspect none a motive ulterior nature had outra its dream accommodating.

Life—to preserve "honor" a camouflage.

To the young a privilege afforded. Of sentimentality, epithet. Of backwater kultkultural, codependency. Motion, on principles of honor stymied.

Choosing an ubaratutuosa. The ubaratutuoso—by algebra doonhadden.

An inventory opaque lures a cucum to a vagi: zip code, numerator socestagal, monnonstagal. Coition blind—an affair technical, in Orc Hoor et al. The Orchoorette—of luxury by empire afforded—excels of coitus in the stratum lowest.

A coitus sublime. Brainsex. In pursuit of which breeds gey of dogs in gutters of kultkulture perished.

"Want us to do that thing? Are we sick orcs?" counters TV Ubaratutu Brathki. "If champion we love orcic, all would their base instincts follow."

"Ubaratutu—a season open for merchants."

"We are optimizing socestag."

"Ossification undefines the domain."

"You're a prime example of the jeopardy obeying the precepts of the melanin ciphilization. You are the wave we must guard contra until the passing of Oxydental ciphilization. In Ubarartutu, we are creating ci-vi-li-za-tion."

"Cataclysm will follow. You are sundering energies for the sake of a simulation."

"Have you read our epos? Do our heroines go around sleeping with every tourist?"

"Did your heroes marry any of you? You're biological jihadists with anxiety disorder. More nobility in a serial rapist than the lot of you."

"That thing—a category bogus."

"That thing—the root ultra."

"The couch grass ultra!"

"Self-gratification—minus orgasm."

"Only via conservation of energy can socestag survive assimilation."

"Napalm needed up your socestag's ass to survive."

A suicide pact fostering murder every, dispossession every, exile every since the dawn of hushtory, on rodents in the desert gnawing. A ciphilization of sandstorms whose oasis sole—of golems and hoshoshes the shadows.

Pudendahubris. Anima as artifice. Haunts Urriantiti the specter of *How to Land a Mana in Ten Days* paperbacks. Mater Terra on Bee-fifty-two. Ubaratutu's ette uteritic, cigarette on lips, a side glance brooding, sizes up the kosmos. A taste for blood on her tongue dust-ridden. Psyche, in slumber deep.

"Slaughterhouse's classiest . . ." genuflect Ubaratutu's poets. "Ladies regal of Ubaratutu . . ."

Show me the silber first. *Then* I'll give you the goods."

"Love—a technicality," a parliamentarian's son loaded ols, with parents her stake valuation deducing.

"A tectonicality," shoots back Astrik.

Equating coefficients of terms identical, obtains the cucumbearer the recursion formula. Which, in turn, generates coefficients for the solution series . . .

Outra Ubara City, for a girl's hand asking. Intimacy, post approval via shareholders—father, brother, uncle, hoshoshfather. First: ceremony. To the corners four of Urriantiti the tradition toted, to illumine Slaughterhouse's niht with radiance puritan.

Contempt spurns Ubaratutucs. In Urriantiti, halted revolution solar in nineteen fifteen anno vulgaris. In Ubaratutu, in nineteen twenty-two anno vulgaris. Accession to the Consortium Oll of Xenon. Sols seven forward of Urriantiti Ubaratutu is. Complete will the sol eighth, inshallah—sol each in Ubaratutu equaling one saeculum orceanic.

Canonized Holy Hoshosh this boom viral. By Anno Diaboli two-two-two-two reach shall Ubaratutu the yeer nineteen twenty-five of Lord Orc-on. In two-two-two-two at night lux for the living shall there be. Beef corned for worshippers shall there be. In this sublimis posterum the right to vote shall solely the living have.

For the type progressive of Ubara City, on proof of intent mortal verbalized the contract may be. *Then* only, to touch primula's elbow permitted.

A couple's bed—a cove sestasyngamous. In Ubaratutu, fifty-six! *Five hundred* fifty-six. Virgin Incorporated. Spooks of dead five hundred.

Ubaratutu—known more dead than breathing. Causa essendi horoscopal.
Ubaratutu—a sarsen stone of a graveyard infinite. A graveyard active.
Ubaratutu—Slaughterhouse's Kaaba.
Genuflect all ye biped that are!

Syphilis. Mythturd! Skeletal evidence! Pubescence hastened death.
Tooth enamel indicated infectious disease.
"The ancients, shorter than descendants. Presumption! On average,
taller than today's population.
"The skeletons of twins show signs of congenital syphilis . . . The hypothesis the disease from the New World imported by sailors—inaccurate.
The Old World exported smallpox.
"Brothers abandoned brothers, sisters abandoned sisters, wives abandoned husbands. Sated themselves on the life-blood of biped. Prostitution
waxed in lieu of physical security.
"Holy Air Force Aye Thirty-Six bombers dropped near Burr Burr
Kerque a hydrogen bomb four hundred times zestful than the Zenoshima bomb, carving a twenty-nine-foot crater. Tourist pilgrimages to the
site generate six million thalers for the Nuevo Madre Cattledom. The parliament petitions the Holy to repeat the accident in a new locale. An ad
hoc committee established to study the suitability of the proposed site.
Proposition 'Yes for No,' defeated by 'Yes for Yes.' A hydrogen bomb,
forty-two thousand pounds, hits the desert one hundred seventy miles
from the Tower of Los Balabylonos. A hydrogen bomb six hundred times
zestful than Zenoshima falls into the Peacekeeping Ocean, one hundred
twenty-nine kilometers from the coast of Isles of Zenzen. The Holy
Defense Department deems the bomb 'relatively safe—if not triggered by
an unapproved volcano.' One in every twenty residents in the Cattledom
of Appleton absorbed significant amounts of radiation. The Holy Health
Department assures the affected: studies correlating the rise of cancer to
the Hamford nuclear power plant are inconclusive. Five thousand billboards installed on freeways by the Nuclear Advantage Corporation, depicting one hundred twenty-nine potatoes of the Natotonal Osspittle of
Hope: 'We live to cure cancer.'
"When two priests went in front of a corpse, several biers were joined
behind so the priests, anticipating one corpse to bury, found themselves
with sixteen. Deeper pits were dug, into which the new arrivals were put
in centum.
"Fifty-six skeletons reveal an ayl side of the socestag. Archaeologists
discover two groups. One lot, found with nothing. Others died with cash,
geld, jewels, stelae, cell phones iii.500. The corpulence of econormic
standards worn in flagrante. One skeleton, discovered with the largest
amount of aurum found anywhere. In morte, sic voluptas.
"Is one group nourished less? The environ holds a clue. The contents

of a tern, which collected waste from lavatories of houses in a metropolis next-door, reveals a marvelous diet—sea urchins, nuts, figs, eggs. In voluptate mors.

"You cannot get closer to the Old World than its excrement" (Monseigneur Chamich Chamich, "Toward Mashu," *Urriantiti News Masque*, eight, eight, eight-eight-eight-eight Anno Urmashi, Gondola Isle).

Lo, of ágios pornográphos the embrace gossamer! Of semen litrons fifty-six per seconds fifty-six. Into reflections etic, ejaculations fifty-six thousand to conceive fail. Visitors one million per site. Orgasms vagis forfeit, in trillion, fifty-six.

The aubergine—Ubaratutu's totem covert.

"Tutu, sweetheart, get a couple of kilos of long eggplant so I can cook some out-of-the-world dolma. Thick. Don't want it tasteless. Eggplant, beneficial. Vitamin-rich. Antioxidants. Don't be late."

The Grand United Sisters of Ubaratutu, Local Seventy-Seven, a bill into the Lower House of the Anointed slips: the aubergine to Ubaratutu's flag annex.

Safeguards the equilibrium ethmic utilizing kozh any cashable. A mana starving fed with promises of barbeque next summer. Afterlife's seed.

Upon him binded the sacrificio summum: one hole till death. For the holm conveying contempt for the system, a lot sole remains. Terror egregious. Unclean. Pharmakos. Hence, the propensity to deceive.

In Ubaratutu, "dog" on the non-kollaborateur's tal etched. In Pornzone, a life's cumulation impounded. Stigma, indelible. In Ololahzone, punishment capital. Elections none.

A biped handsome once. In gait boastful once, an improdigal now. The fingers of the hand right. Incomplete. Begauzed.

The neck. Dangles the remains of his ring finger once-proud enchained. Knew not the aurum of matrimony. Drapes the spit his head in a caul liquid. Iblis's stigmata.

Ololahummah, the Cattles United—partners without end of violence incarnate. Progressive Ubaratutu is. From Natashazone a breeze.

Of eyes prying diled, from restau to restau dragged him she. Stares bovine, into portions masticated Brathki. An eatery on Posh Street, a reputation sound. Thinks she.

With she dancing. Suits six from a table nearby affix stares. Out of sockets pops murder's chance indebted.

Grateful to the virago next door, Brathki, from whose window saw he Mount Mashu: but the restau also, who by dohtor prompted sold the apartment not.

Pilgrims from Orc Hoor, blessed art thee. Sauntering left, right, understand thee not the langue d'oc Ubaratutuac. Pilgrims of Ubaratutu. Brathki, not can be.

Next to Brathki, daughter. Years nine old. Happy together. At the traffic light turns head to stretch his neck. "Daddy, you're looking into another car. Not supposed to. People might get angry."

To Ubaratutu's treatise of love book-covered relates this incident Brathki at Hoshosh Cafe, variances of conventions eter Pornzone and Virginzone illustrating. His daughter's teacher yuysed she'd be. Lands the heroine a verdict laconic.

"Seeee . . . you're an Ubaratutuc."

Brathki's yuys inurned there where with mercury flushed are eyes. A destiny.

Virgin Sea. A hymen collective. A hymen legendary. A hymen hallowed, hymned, honored as the halo helming Ubaratutu's head. The barrier eter kultkulture and barbarity hemming.

Vardan's son unwarfared. "How can I refuse my father the orhnanq of seeing my child in the morning?"

Live together, they. Generations three. Let not the hand third the first know, lest anathema pronounced be to thy bloodline for the error diresome of a raincoat neglected.

The virr creative, of stability a guarantor. A concept in Pornistan unfathomable, replaced where bonds by contracts are, kyank by a simulacrum substituted.

Envelopes Brathki a wave, kin Papa Mospheron's lightning strikes:

Let me of wheat plant a handful
In your lap, dustr-in-law charmful,
                    my passion's fane.
May sprout stalks in fervent arrow
Of your bottom from the furrow,
May dawns slumber in their swaddle
In the cradle which you bundle.
And when you milk forty heifers,
Turn may the milk into argum,
And the beestings into aurum,
In your rennet pail.

Let me of wheat place a handful
Into your palms, my son pluckful,
                    my chest's baldric.
May the blood of twenty oxen
Run in your arms by the plough hewn,
May pillars of twenty quarters
Anchor on your body's timbers.
And when the seeds that you bestrew
In the measure of your fingers,

In the measure of night's glisters
May you but reap.

Let me of wheat pour a handful
Upon your head, sire loveful,
          my cane's blossom.
Io's paeans may a hundred
Be upon your forehead whittled,
May the vessel of temperance
Embark upon your trim teres.
And when you draw nigh to your flock,
May stretch their maws a thousand rams
To barleys dense in spotless palms.

Let me of wheat rain a handful
Down your hair, granddustr blazeful,
          my barrow's wreath.
May tulips fresh upon your cheeks
Glitter anew in every spring,
May novel rays in your rainbows
Every summer sire golden glows.
When plant you an sprig of willow,
Every April in its shadow
See you your shade
May verdant.

Pour may I of wheat a handful
Down our heads, my Naneh solful,
          my Naneh sole.
May harden not the autumn sun
In our snows of yore's lushly mane.
May lessen not our eve's candle
In the columns of the temple.
And lowered when at last are we
Into the crypt, may underneath,
The clay, Naneh,
Clement be.
           —Wave One

On virginity, the virtues of a minority hinged. Circumspect compelled Brathki to be. For the litter inundating Pornia exchange would not he virgin any. Forsake could how Vesta for the farrago Pornistani entire?

Owns not Slaughterhouse, Pornmama. Just sayin', sayeth Brathki. "Get rid of anyone who speaks against us, one by one." Brian, brother-in-law.

Of dogsister, wild. Disagreement sole: Novoko Zonosor. A terrorist to he. "Holy Orcon must arm Mymoonoos so he slays Novoko." Sister: "Holy Orcon's prostrators are gleyed." Eases the tension Father: enemies none Holy Orcon had ere Zinzinroohr's creation. Reprogrammed Zinzin Holy Orcon's brain, into wars his own drawing the United Cattles. Care could not less if Orc Hoor to death bled . . . LIB Orc—free to admit an slave she is not . . .

Govy! Govy! Gwae fi! Sacrileges legion mine are! Transgressions unforgivable mine are! Marcie! Marcie! Marcie! Gava dhe, O Pornmama. Redeem from sins myriad mine me! Worthy oorie zoule my make! Prayeth thus Brathki.

Father reiterated, to scions of Mymoonoos a novel new narrating. To Mymoonroohr invited him an actress when spiced it up: "Of course you must expand your borders. When Mashashashash descends, he won't fall into Ololah's sand."

Brian. Orc Air Force. One day, holds dogsister in arms, crying. "Today . . . given a million-washo gear . . . to wear in a nuclear emergency . . . not a second pair . . . for the person I care most for in my life . . . Natotonal security."

"You can't appreciate our manas, sicko. Our manas have honor, class. Unlike you, scumbag." Get me, mom, integrity of the family. Get me, mom, from matriarchy to patriarchy. Get me hushtory and psychology, *haskasar*?

The powder psychic from the tone, hochle and kevel of cucumbearers entering millennium three anno vulgaris suffuses cubic inch each of Ubara City with miasma of PTSD ethmic.

A hollow novel. Evolution XX. Ante tasting cocks a couple, Astartehs incarnate themselves fancy.

From the weight of taboos scream vagis of freedom. Freedom cardinal. To fuck. Veils self-affirmation this crisis ineradicable enteren the psyche.

Solutions bridging the divide imaginaire. By yonde deuce a sight. By yonde Ervand, Ervaz a sight. By yonde urrian a sight. By yonde oneir a sight. By yonde irreal a sight. At the foot of the Twin Mountain rise Gisher shall not.

Live in Ubaratutu would Brathki's yins were its socius to mutate. In Orcdale's Oneir Scrool enrolled Brathki his pup. In Scrool Eyfeloonia at a cost triple. At the altar of sadoids sacrifice his brood could not.

Substitute the oneirstruck the holm with norms arctic, his pup to interrogation techniques subjecting. Smiles panic-struck on videotape singing the scrool's lof for the benefit of parents Purgatorio susurrated. I close my eyes,, and drift away,, into the night,, I softly sway,, Oh, smile and pray . . .

Papa Xenon's institutions with homogenization mills substituted. Factories, obsolete ere being built. Mathematics, by orc-branded checkbook combinatorics replaced, by Grand Orc financed. Whispers Grand Orc: why do you need science? Why do you need factories? I shall send you touristi. I shall send you prayer professionals. I'll set up a consultation bureau in my embassy. Exile those who won't shut up! We will conclude accords harmonic. Emerges a caste dominant, with collaborators washonormic, to subservience reducing Ubaratutu. Fabricated, a socestag to pimperialists util. A walawalaton sublimating propaganda.

An "open museum" in Slaughterhouse into an open mausoleum upgraded. Withers the lotus. Brahma—by the stench of tramorts ambulating scalded.

Yet the symbols come out at night to mate still, the structures sing in the morning still.

L ost swith allure, befriending virgins. With one zeug, for a decennium up the ass rammed.

Sausi. To study in Yurostan applied. Asks Brathki, the eschatologist, to predict whether accepted she'd be. Readeth Mrs Garfield: within rotas three, within rotas seven times three, within rotas thirty times three . . . assseshshtamtesh, assseshshtamtesh . . . Prophesied Brathki ante elections: Holy Hoshosh, the Engineer Omniscient, of forty-nine percent a majority carry would.

A moon hence. By sister accompanied, a mara for her mother mistakes he. News of application? Strains face. Asks *him* questions. Rotas two hence calls her.

"You were tactless. Revealing my secret to my sister." Hangs up.

"Secret." Opens the *Dukendoxfort Biped Dictionary*. Suddenly: of the word the tomality. Secret! The Secret! In the box, Jack. A box empty.

Born is in secrets, Ubaratutu. Lives in secrets it. Dies in secrets it. In lieu of emotion secretes secrets it. Is not falsehood contingency planning? Of truth the fiber very?

> In the hovel infra the ground,
> Us forty—a herd of cattle
> By a sandstorm teeming frightened—
> In the face of death quivering,
> In the walls tenebrous huddled,
> Crushing one eral.
> A boulder of silence in terror tromm.
> A murmur not, a gulping not.
> Our gazes, odious, fiendish,
> On neighbors affixed, wishing *their* demise.
> A thousand cannibals under heol,
> Ravaging villages, fields lush,
> Seeking our death.

Death-crazed in the chthonic dark,
In quenchless dread we hear
The lightning-dance swish and crack of
Guns, spears, bayonets, swords
With blood steaming sub heol.
Corpses . . . corpses . . . thud on the roof
Of our hovel crushing,
Akin felled trees.
The groans of death, now sharp, now dull
Into the chamber ooze through walls
To madden us.
The warm blood into crevices
Sinks, trickles down our faces
From the ceiling earthen—a pall.
A newborn cries, screeching.
"Pity may He, dead my breasts are.
"No drop have I. Sucked me he dry . . .
"No drop have I. Do what you must . . ."
"Strangle the child," ol raised arms.
"Strangle him," wheeze we, ghosts forty as one.
"Strangle me, then him."
"They heard him, digging the roof . . ."
"Betrayed are we . . . digging the roof . . ."
Caves the earth in. Shafts of light seen.
"Beseech you I, strangle me . . .
"Here my throat is . . . and my child's . . ."
In the darkness, puts her neck out
The mother, and then her child's.
A pair of arms wax snakes,
Find the child's neck, squeeze it . . .
The silence in the hovel—a tempest.
For an instant, may we have died . . .
Thence in a moment, sense the mob,
Heap the curses of those deceived,
In dismay walk away . . .
Our salvation.
Are slaves ever thus saved?
This, how saved should we be?
She, on the road, now nude,
At the skirt of friend, foe,
Throws herself every day—
A mara mad screaming:
"See these hands? It was they . . .

"See these hands? It was they . . .

"Strangle me! . . .

"Why will you not?

"Divested are these hands . . ."

—Wave Two

The nifara first threw this mara herself at, Buddhamuddha. "Be consoled, mara. Can a mother you show who a child lost has not? All this, a dream. Hyuk, hyuk, hyuk . . ."

The nifara second threw this mara herself at, Solmonhor the Wise. Of a rat the cadaver. "Shisho, yuys give up! Your child now is where this rat is."

The nifara third, Holy Pasha. "Infidel, your child at the place is where weeping and gnashing of teeth there shall be."

Breezes the nifara fourth, Yawyawiversity of Zozzoreth Arrtist Summum Walawala McYawaYawa. "Be consoled, mara, for your child at that place is not where weeping and gnashing of teeth there shall be. Papa says so."

Came to pass on the winter solstice this story. In anno vulgaris three hundred. For anns seventeen hundred solstice every repeated.

Grory! Carted Ubaratutu's dead have been ever to the place where weeping and gnashing of teeth shall there be not.

Into Ubaratutu's field of gravity crashes Cousin Henri, a virgin fancying. Brathki's survival for moons ten his faith bolsters. Of riding his back virgins oneir . . . to Parparisabad. *We can have sex there . . .*

An oath demands the cicerona at the Ancient Manuscripts' Repository ante agreeing to talk to Brathki. "Prepared I am to zeug. To the valley of casinos and brand stores a milia to take my wife!"

"Open your cunt first, *then* your mouth."

Understood has yet virgin or virgidolizer none the virginosity of this apokálypsis.

Of pride, a vestige? None. Of purpose, a vestige? None. Of fulfillment, a vestige? None. On defacement a sanction. How you do, do you do, mon frère?

By rochers of mind downhearted, Cousin Henri. The oneir virgin—Parparisabad!

Rung had a call distant in him. *Now's* the time to drop anchor here. Friends, of his descent unaware. Post revelation, disavowed him. Parparisabadi, not.

. . . of Urriantiti?

A tooth aile from the mouth in dreams falls.

Rotas a few ere departing from Ubaratutu, with one chatted. Gave his phone number, Cousin Henri. To leave turning, their tails facing. Love on

Cousin Henri's heart face smiles. Of zeuging with a virgin the oneir. To Ubaratutu his transplantation plans.

The morn opens, rings Cousin Henri's phone. A whisper not. The second: a sound gurgling. The third, quiet again. Calls Brathki. "What does *whelp* mean?" On a fourth, rained an ogress hellhoor. A hex cast. From the harangue distinguishing "four o'clock," replies, "Madam, I don't understand a word you say." The title venerable of "son of a bitch," upon him crowned.

Cousin Henri. His holm a witch licks. To, "So, how did you find our Holy Ubaratutu?" a bight, "Like shit!"

Into an elevator shaft falls past floors twelve . . . ghosts of ransom notices undeliverable. A companion. Of pinestraw, a CD player in his head jammed. Low Reed reading fairy tales. Of Cousin Henri's disillusionment a ration. A provender idem. In Pornia, at that.

Veracity at Brathki's office. At the Orciversity of Kalipornia an student. To go out decided. An omen ill: "they two" do not. She, unaware.

In secret meets him Veracity. Unbathed. Parents suspect must not. A job interview. For her hand in zeugdom a doctor asked. With the bastard to the beach. For an interview. Oneir boy . . .

Brathki, Veracity. Santa Morica. Minutes a score pass, rings her cell phone. Tells Veracity mutter *over* the interview is not. Post the call tenth, promises to home in minuta be.

The parking lot gridlocked. Vera cum penis—hitting the road yuysless in sooth. How was to know Brathki so sweet his cock is? Alas, knew not yet a bastard he was.

"Rush. Pleaaase rush. Rush! Rush! Pass the light! No, no! Don't stop! Go! Red! Yellow! Green! Red! Go! Go! Pass that damn truuuuck! They will kill meeeeee!"

Calls Mamma. Incessantly. Into confessing coerces her. "Try! Try setting foot in this house! You'll come out a corpse!" "Get my dohtor on the phone! Right now!"

"Ma'am . . ."

"Bastaaaaaaaard!"

"Ma'am . . ."

"Get my dohtor on the phone!"

Tells Veracity Brathki: slaughtered will they be. Choice none but to stay with him.

Under the gun, Brathki zeug shall not. Thinks still, a dog he is not.

Lock they down Veracity. For days three. Demanding Brathki's address. "I'll throw myself out the window if you kill him."

A week later calls Veracity. Rehabilitated fully.

"If your intentions were pure . . . would've asked for my hand before going out with me."

"I apologize, madam. Know not did I a bastard I was."

From Virgin City to Petrol City Brathki absconded. Invitor, Baba Alius. A conference, "The metonymic foundations for fishing identities from Ubaratutu." To his query, "What's in it for me, *arkadash?*" to the traffic control tower escorted was Brathki: "Do you see, *kardash,* these four terminals? Hosting Shakespeare Air, Goethe Air, Zinzin Air, Pasha Air? The vagis I've fucked lie beneath them. Give you I a page of *Fikr il-Muhabbat.* Let none know I to you gave it. To you fame. To I humility."

Surat Yirmibir
"I can't today."
"Someone else can."
"Animal!"
Of availability ask not. Negotiateth never the *alchakh.*

Surat Yirmiiki
"My aunt died."
"You didn't."
"Necromaniac!"
The selven by which measured thy importance is. Thy distinction, less than a cadaver's not.

Surat Yirmiuch
"I don't have a babysitter."
"Your problem."
"Dunce!"
Comply not. Else, shit eatest thou.

Surat Yirmidyord
"My period started. Terrible headache."
"Be flexible."
"It oghlu it!"
Whither turneth the vizsla?

Surat Yirimbesh
"I'm sick."
"Others are healthy."
"Sadist!"
In days of scrool yore, "*Kiz, niyeh* did you get sick?" Classmates taking ill, fire and brimstone expected.

Surat Yirmialti
"They'll kill me, if I spend the night with you."
"*I'll* kill you, if you don't."

"Egomaniac!"
Thy life by consignment endanger not. The worth of a kultvagi, coequal not.

Surat Yirmiyeddi
"I gotta work tonight."
"I gotta fuck tonight."
"Mucc!"
Thy right, thy responsibility.

Surat Yirmiseqqiz
"I'm a virgin!"
"Deflower yourself."
"Blasphemer!"
Smirketh.

Surat Yirmitokhkhuz
"I can't forget my ex."
"I can't forget my dong."
"You . . . you . . ."
Destroyeth thou, this idolatry female.

Surat Ottuz
"Will you zeug with me?"
"Let's get a taste first . . . Can you replace the rest?"
"Moor! Boor!"
For nookie zeug not, lest beauty and glamour imperil thee.

Surat Ottuzbir
"Come over to my house. Meet my family."
"The road to your house is your tunnel."
"Misanthrope!"
Smirk, continueth thou.

Surat Ottuziki
"Raped when ten. Have a doctor's report. Not even my parents know."
"Did you get a lab test?"
"A test? The society will find out. That report is my life!"
"I'll set it on fire."
"Over my dead body, asshole."
"If you caught a bug, you wanna pass it on?"
"Egoist!"
Thy health, of urgency greater. Her suicide, unnoticed by all but she.

Surat Ottuzuch
"Let's get zeuged once I graduate."
"Maybe. If."

"You know that's impossible. We'll see each other during the day."
"Sex is *karanlik*."
"No sacrifice?"
"Of two years?"
"They'll kill me."
To threats of mortality supplicateth not. Thy groin, of substance permanent far more.

Surat Ottuzdyord
"I'll call you tonight."
"Will you come over?"
"I'll call."
"Will you or won't you?"
Wavereth she? Fuck a vagi other.

Surat Ottuzbesh
"We were out in a group."
Consisteth thy group own of one—id, est, thee? Tryeth thou hookers.

Surat Ottuzalti
Screecheth her cell phone nonstop when with thee.
"Are you a doctor? The surgery wing?"
If driving, pull over. Kick her out sans ado. Even Madam Rouge forbade whores while entertaining a customer on the phone to be.

Surat Ottuzyeddi
"We went to the shore for a photo shoot."
Promptly have thy way with she. Piddle upon her, vacate the scene.

Surat Ottuzseqqiz
"I don't suck faucet."
"Suck on a pacifier."
Silence, the *alchakh's* weapon lethal most.

Who these bigmen, gonna get on doggrrrrls? Virgingal gets off that train fast, say nah daddy, yo daddy. The digs she won't give, the digs she makes so he don't get no shovel out.
Ubrttt. Gnaw redeemed the rose. Hgios, hgios, eye secret! Oak gnarled viva! Gash flaming viva! Beast, crab-backed hammering down viva! You, sex big, dog filthy.
Even Stella fiiiine the digs don't give him. That bigbig good he got she don't get. A call makes. Lawbrother comes, lawlaws head sad. That road not headed. Those people not headed. Honey, you get out. She out.
Keeps bigbone hurt.
Virginsister, Virginmother, Virginfather, Virginbrother, Virginneighbor, Virginchampion . . . pretext any to call Stella, the whereabouts of their dove prodigal ascertaining. A tracking device implanted.

Consolidate bloodlines the familiae pimps. For the barbie's benefit. Whose hands hold they. Whose eyes shield they. Past adulthood. Invoking firebrands sacred. Family. Honor. Natoton. Heofon forbid dares barbie their bloodline sully, mixing genes Orceanic with cottonmouths writhing call they DNA! Crumble would natoton! Spread would plague! Child Genghisoid! Annihilation genetic! Incest spiritual!

At the heart of love, the hands chloroform-bearing of the eugenicist. Wins Stella her dohtor back. To the callers sells the girl fiction. Rejoice! Hail, Pencil! Born a writer is.

Bastard goes get things zuyg straight. Aik: gets going on zeuged lady not (bastard no Walalicos). Dwaik: lies not (bastard no Walalicos). When mouth wanna go in don't hafta talk he. Buddy don't do this he a fuckup and gon' fuck stuff up. Gon' fuck up the bigs and the littles and shoot the fuckup air into trees circa Slaughterhouse.

"Crazy fucking place," explodes Cousin Henri. "Can't live here if every girl you say hello to's gonna fantasize about zeuging."

Where to go. Ere portal any entering, Cousin Henri changes mind. The where: extinct.

> Mirage unwavering,
> the why with decoys dislocating life.
> Meaning.
> Ambiguity of context,
> hubris of absolutism.
> Meaning.
> Font of pomp,
> caulk of eleni,
> biped weep secret.
> Meaning.
> Orgasm of form,
> tango thanatonic,
> wasphive grinning,
> purity of a pennon bloodied.

"Here, they zeug so they fuck."

"Tie the knot . . . rammed up the ass."

Twain they are now. Yet not thine, a song other yon will be remembered.

Enter they a night-zoo. A table empty, none. To a pair of vagis at a table for twelve walks Cousin Henri, whether they can share it asks. A "no" point-blank.

"Let's get out of here. Never seen a cock in her life. 'Virgin city' . . . no shit . . . Let's go to Natashazone. I've never been."

In the footsteps of the creatures male of Nonah exit shall they Ubaratutu, ingressing Natashazone. Spending aurum riveting groins downy of

Natashas. Into an Erosaeneum transforming the steppes where rampant shall their flanks run upon Tartaroseans, Ursinettes alike.

Soothe Cousin Henri naught could Brathki. Seethes road rage exo flesh kin lentils.

"They cut in front of you . . . they tailgate . . . on your ass! They! Have! No! Respect! For! Others!"

"Brathki don't drive car here . . ."

"Fucking manimals!"

Near the Opera enter they a restau, suffering salivation requisite anns twenty ere dinner. Bluff the waiters, assuring food ready will be in minuta twenty, minuta twenty every. Anns a thousand to dogs: to Hoshosh a dawn. And everything Hoshosh saw. And behold, good it was. Bread there was. Water there was. A pair of knives there was. A napkin there was. Dogs twain there was. Came evening. Then morning. The day forty-ninth it was.

And the dogs into Ubaratutucs deaf ran. Ubaratutu, elen to elen by cobwebs permanent replaced. And behold, good it was. Nabu Leon Dog and Nowhere Dog in ropes sticky since the alpha of creation spun. And behold, good it was. And on the day fiftieth, upon Cousin Henri descended Holy Zoulzoul: "My beloved cupid thou art. In thee, well I am pleased. Steadfast in thy abstinence for days fifty, hereon infra my tables shall thou lick."

And at Hoshosh's tables all that was made in Ubaratutu ate Cousin Henri as his Lord Hoshosh commanded. And that reserved was which for Archbishops was to Cousin Henri presented: the trinity of Xs—xash, xashlama, xasho—hyperion meat pure, served post opisthokonta and holozoa ghuyrukh.

Of blindness Nabuleonian cured, Cousin Henri. In atria of diamonds seofon-karat, the light. By strings irial of colors forty, virgins forty his holm licked. Holy Hoshosh's caire how if redeemed not the lettered are? Ubaratutucs—carnivores blessed. Request not a dish subflesharian, lest with tomatoes twain, a cucumber unit humored thou art.

And to pass came it that Holy Hoshosh his blessings from Cousin Henri withdrew to test his devotion, offering him a lamb sacrificial. Sharpened chefs cleavers. Aaaah, Eyfeeeliiiiaaaa. Reported waiters their ingress, egress every. Taxi drivers, their egress, ingress every.

To the establishment where hosted Holy Hoshosh Yay Sin head they. The spot in Ubaratutu safest, intra Almighty's pupil. Stabbed where in the bathroom Holy Hoshosh's bodyguards His classmate during a writers' gathering, skyrocketing His charisma. Trouble Cousin Henri had digesting parsley, asked the server in his salad to put none. Avail none. I've told you twice . . . An hour thence, comes the salad back, minus hanter the pieces three hundred of parsley. *Can't do better any than this, appé.* Of emaciation irreversible crossed Cousin Henri the threshold—of trials ethmic the augur.

To carrying the pemmican oblivious he. Advised was to Byblos to go instead: "At least the cause of your death won't be hunger." Preferred Cousin Henri death.

The restau. Ebbs them not. Tenderloin suggest they. *Chateaubriand biped* requests Brathki. Available not. *Fetus stew? Infant heart fondue?* None. From the abattoir a request special. With a knife graced at ten. The babies, slaughtered. Charcoal on a couple of plates at eleven. Sniff they. A Dead Sea scroll. Walawala meat. Send back the concoction. Receive the Walawala meat nuyn, eleven thirty, dried out rolls ten over. For a forgery two-milia-old suitable.

"Appér, past dinnertime. Our persuasion prohibits consuming biped flesh at this hour. Enjoy it yourselves."

Eat it, they will not. Convince them can not. Eat they dogflesh in Ubaratutu. Enlightened, Cousin Henri. Scared are they to eat it. Worship they the dead!

Wisely, comp them champagne. Cousin Henri: "They're getting us drunk so we don't notice how fuckawful the grub is."

From the table next, slurs a beer belly, "Take, eat: this is my figure. This cup, the Testis New in my gore: this do ye, as oft as ye drink it, in remembrance of my self-regard."

The prayer wrong reciting art thou! In a meter wrong! Hoshosh won't hear it! Red, dwarf-eye's face. Fist pounds table. Veins blue emerge exo neck. Haywire, the club. Runs the crooner for cover. From the restroom, a priest the waiters bring in. Finished jerking off. Repositions his crook waning. The version eun to render.

"Physique divine . . ."

"Stop! The wrong way!"

"May you eat this meal in peace . . ."

"Fuck you!"

"Let us give grory to Hoshosh."

"Grory to Gore! Gore's meat we're eating."

"Can't do that. First, grory to Hoshosh, then . . ."

"Gore first! Blockhead!"

"Had you cow meat?"

"Grory to the cow!"

"Nullifidians!"

"Slaughter the cow but sing Hoshosh's grory, do you? Blasphemy!"

Bang they on the table, on their hinds jumping up.

Fearing these.
These. Are.
Dogs trans-hoshoshist.
Instead, instead intent.

To eat him, the.
The priest gifts them.
Botonées carved, anointed.
By Walalicos himself.
Ubaratutu arrtists rood frames
Selling to krosstourists.
To Urriantitii.
At the Vernissage.
Point the the boys crosiers
To dogs pointless.
At at the priest's behest
And pray, pray, pray fiercely.
Vanquish them
By the magic of the potent.
Mahogany gilded.
Baaaameeeen . . .
Baaaameeeen . . .
Trans humbled humbling,
Dogs eat,
Their manuscript—Ubaratutu's dream.
Qualify!
Statements!
Predicates with!
Ubaratutucs some!
Ubaratutucs many!
Studies socestagological!
Percent sixty-nine!
Subjective!
Doggerel!
Pablum revisionist!
Fancy lunatic!
Discord upon
Of oneir a pyre!

Cobwebs in mind glittering. Blessed, the biped in estimation correct.
Blessed, the idolatry of standards in absence.

Look mountain dwellers down on desert dwellers. Neither Rabrab
Ololah nor Barbar Gololah in Ubaratutu a trace left. Cennet this is
not! . . . Address outdated. By McOlolah tricked.

in.
bedouinstan.
dog.
any.
enters.

who.
eatery.
any.
in.
triangle.
any.
treated is.
kin king.
a.
dog.
feels.
a.
dog.
welcomed.
at. the. gate.
of. cennet.

Ianuscoin—specie of affairs Ubaratutuac.
The respected—akhpérs.
In the spine, fear! Of respect the quoin.

grory.
and honor.
and power.
eat!
otherwise.
shit shalt thou eat!

Babigers, the Orcs. The Ubaratutuc, par excellence prodigy kosmic. Salespeds, thoughts in graphemes iron carved, at customers scoff. Lord over capybaras five shop entrances, at customers spitting venom. Lie low owners, to make the kill allowing the sisters little.

Hungry go the sisters little. Valuta, on ass-giving contingent. Flat broke, the Ubaratutuette. Mendicant, absent largesse from benefactors. Ownership economic, share zero. Mara every, infra a mana's shadow. Talk to her. A mana's head transubstantiates, performing a feat with butcher knives. Granted is she selon what sucks she. Meats particular of an ubaratutuoso contain rewards separate.

To Pashazone move beauties rebelling. With a boss sleeping for washos fifty a moon disdained. Pashacock, to ubaratutuoso dong preferred.

Trafficking, by the Hoshosh–Archejudge chamber conducted. Judges, puppets of mafiosi. One hand uses His Enchantedness Desirable to throw gold dust in akhpér Orcon's eyes, the other to bare ass to dicks his dominion maintaining. A process dexterity oll requiring. For Ubaratutuc every, to his position accordingly.

Beauties a consensus gossip. Aryatololah, gentler. BinLatin, gallant. Holy Orcon, endoparasite out of cloaca. Ololahummah, uncouth. Rex Universum: BinLatin.

G et the fuck away! Not fags, for Dogsake! Cousin Henri, by the singers male at the gentlemen's club narked. A vagi in sight not. So why have they a ladies' room? The striptease. A calculation gleg. *Iki-buchukh shurdah; dyord shordah; otuzbir, yetmish, seqzendokhkhuz, dokhzanbesh.* Vagis ninety-six in this business. Locals, three or four. The balance, Natashas. Washos five thousand a moon. Earn this in Porn City could not. Brathki's Monique, four thousand.

Franklos kin lava on strippers rained. The engine, their kin's sweat. Off this flagdom starving, washos a million siphoned moon every. Via pipes covert, millions into Natashcow casinos pumped. Via pipes virtual, decamillions.

Ubaratutu's maras where are? In public dance they not, sub night wine-dark whore instead.

"Practical meeting. York, near the supermarket. Call me."

The behind left. With release provide papatriots, pan-natotonalizing syphilis. Amor si vincitur, pecuniam vincintur.

A pop star, Lucy. A life modest. By behaviour manpanzee outraged. The idem noxly: at wenches from Natashazone hamlets salaries tossed, bread tin to artists denying. In the strip club nuyn.

Poppop Poporuni. At anns twenty-four knew Yuronovision awards two, detox centers two-point-five, abortions forty-five. Push she, twenty-five. Remembered—if at all—as a threat of betidings future to children prurient. A motel room with XY impersonators three. If lucky, earn can a franklo a week in hotel lounges herself impersonating. A percentage as tribute her manager tenders—so long as shows him she, "What that mouth-hole's really for . . . ya, ya, ya?" Once the reverie, beds adolescent a million staining. Now Icarus in a fright wig gossamer. Via priestcraft mana, mara coexist.

W alalicos. Hoshosh's hand left, Ubaratutu's Xaxam Oll. Enshrine Slaughterhouse heads one, a hanter. Head Chief. On Saint Virginborn stationed, exo City 29. Mount Mashu. From Saint Virginborn beholden. If faith have thee, espy the salvation boat of vertebrates thou shalt. A rainbow to the monastery arches every Wednesday. From the Mountain Twin. Of nature the helix double. An accident? Mother Goddess's temple, a substitute geophallic.

Expraedium

Of yore a center pagan. At Romul Empire's armies Ubaratutu's generals sneered. For Hani Ba'al a refuge post defeat.

By a bastard's walawala, forced Ubaratutu. A cusp decisive: the cron first of Walawala's accession to a throne biped. Differ hushtorians on a date exact, placing it eter three hundred fourteen and two hundred eighty-four era vulgaris. Since saeculum each to one aspect of the Trinity corresponds, may three-o-one deduced be. By Ubaratutu's Sanctum Sanctorum authenticated. Unity, of integrity the antonym. Ink's spirit. Prepossession's yuys.

Gaga, Walawala's Saber Papa, into Deep Dungeon thrown. For anns thirteen. Feet, vipers licked, hemoglobin for drink lions offered. By Walalicos, Knower of Feet & Hemoglobin, verified.

Walawala's forepost easternmost. A lambshed in proportion to the Stargazer's zoulzoul constructed. Confident return never he will. Should His eyes it please, an station in mansions divine granted will benefactors be. Homeless, seeking ner everlasting.

Due reverence for an imitation of reverence due. O lord ass-headed, O mystery ass-headed thrice, mercy on thy benefactors have, on the zoulzouls of thy benefactors all, in death, in life, in death livelier granted upon hallows of life, abideth that for now and ever to be . . .

An icon grotesque upon the reredos of the altarpiece arch. A whore rag-covered. Mother Ezerk's Throne snatching. Of phenomenology the foundation. In derision transcendental to criticism textual.

Of its immanence the ideal: the image.

Mother of God. Appellation by Walawala's legionnaires from Mother of Khor fleeced. A parallel of Hat Khor with Dzovinar—the goddess ethnogenetic of Ur Mashu—mother of Fakiro-Yuromamanic twins divine. Hat Khor's son, Khor—a deity solar, Tawit's twin Khor Manook reminiscent of—with Walawala substituted. Looted, Isu's image suckling Khor infant. Mher Major, of constellation Leo replica terrestrial. In narratives, Mher: King of Pharaohland, Queen Isu's consort. His son Tawit of Tawru, by her suckled. Isu's goal: via Mher's bloodline a dynasty portentous in Pharaohland. In narratives alaile, Mher and Tawit, kings of Pharaohland. The narrative Davdabood and Golfiat, an echo anemic. A revision of Tawit's victory over Pharaohland's king, his half-brother. The narrative Urmashuan, cogent. Complete.

Fostered degeneracy the fraud lucent of Ubaratutu's Walawalicoi, superstition to the apogee of experience elevating. Renounces biped the ethmic, transcendence embraces not. Winesot incestuous. Infra accords of a onely living Wye sanctioned. Bellies ancient withered not. In acrimony burst seedlings.

Shifted the correlation of three-o-one anno vulgaris. Main Head—from his demesne own estranged, by commanders twain patrolled. The commander supreme—El Hoshoshidente de Campo de Piedra. Holy Pasha's genius administrative emulating, into iqthayat divided Ubaratutu, to join Yurogorgon a prelude.

On Bab Al-Yuron a knock: Your sommelier modest. My dohtor, of Baron Walawala of Daughters the Ancientest, to your Gorgonity Lofsome to betroth brought.

"Recognezzeit ye for naught."

On Cuspinar to his kingdom rows back. A motto abridged: "Toward White Bear!"

Stygian shall Holy Hoshosh's roddin be. Yon Ubaratutu savage. Cry where doves capillaries broken.

Head Hanter. On Mononias perched, of Byblos a suburb. Head Whole, whereas, to reinforcement ecclesiastical and KaiKeeBee empowerment bound, holds Head Hanter in Baron McYawa's agencies ranks influential. Of equilibrium a ghost. Oneirs prescribed by an entente inter Holy Orcon and Holy Triarchy lull Urriantiti.

Sprouted Head Hanter during the War Hyperboreal, on pretext of rescuing Urriantiti from Crdnl Xenon's encroachments. Blossoms still, long past war's rarefaction. Fail efforts to subdue. To liquidate it, how anodd.

Yesterera, in the development of ligigilon a role organic. Toera, in the ebb of ciphilization ensnared. Of ligigilon a consumer third-degree. By the products of eyl and aneyl in rapture fetishistic. Of a mass Protesteron a consolidation glorifying Mymoonoos. Walalicos on the front: contra independence hogianic. Of children, at the altar sacrificial of YawaYawa, millions slaughtered. Via scrool. Via family. Via gene. Of liberation Orc-sanctioned a software: creating the pardizen post-Xenonic—by myth Mymoonic hardwired.

The rights of the software's propagators, by the Consortium Intergovt-goftal of Free Slaughterhouse retained. On writers fighting for Ubaratutu's sovereignty an eye dall. Dismissing mutilation threats contra dissenters catapulted publicly by leaders financed and sanctioned. A goal single: propagation of myth, langue pimperial. Via incumbency. Via opposition. Appeals by writers exiled: shredded, forgotten, dismissed. Into files classified with information dense imma their lives, activities sans omitting a *p*. Classify them. Clarify them. Whitewash them. Criticism non-constructive. Shazam! Writers such exist not. The line official of embassies—and biped rights organizations internatotonal, the entrance to the basilica of persecution accredited guarding. The silence of Axis Austri. Memory's stream isolated, by an stamp red consolidated. Let. Perish. Its writers.

"Both Orc Hoor and Yurogorgon (for whom vested kultkultural and economric interests collide with the creation of an independent civilization) knowingly pay salaries to a network of flunkies under the façade of 'civil society'—a web of influence encompassing employees of the former Komsomol, the KaiKeeBee, their prostitutes, other apparatchik scum in embassies and 'biped rights' advocacy groups sabotaging transformation in Ubaratutu. Eshu Elekbara!

"By collaborating in the exclusion of voices from collective discourse, you create false modes of opposition, perpetuating the cycle of submission to programs of infiltration via counterfeit electoral alternatives. Eshu Elekbara!

"You bribe lowlifes eager to betray their country in exchange for cushy positions, assisting in the redistribution of natotonal wealth among a caste of opportunists recreating Ubaratutu in your image. This is the decisive motive behind your suppression. Eshu Elekbara!

"In your complicity you encourage the annihilation of our independence, the systematic degradation of our natoton. Under the façade of free speech, biped rights, demosocracy you function as the nemesis of these ideals.

"As writers, we have done all we could. We will continue to do all we can—to ensure that not a soul in Slaughterhouse forgets until hushtory buries you in its ruins.

"Your usurpation of Ubaratutu's future will neither be forgotten nor absolved by countless generations to come.

"Eshu Elekbara!"

. . . Of this manqué beatific the purveyors bloated? A melange of neuters over-cultivated, monnon-heeled, gutless, over enshrinement in the mausoleum of hushtory slobbering. Moonzhenitsyn, Chinjian, Shushdie, Haisheimi? Apologists of propaganda Orconic. Conviction! Noth! Zanzi among nephilim. By the tonsure of industry crowned. Hucksters toddler-moraled with advances six-figure. Victims professional. Of the Orcon Publishing Corporation acolytes self-lauding.

Heads via heads grows the Hydra.

Salute the zanzi of Orcon's industries litterature and spirizooal. The numinous befouling, the potency of that logos purport they to serve. Prostitutes of literature! Prostitutes of life! Tut savants, in erections Willie Winkie trained singularly, the exigencies of their drool in the deserts of empire. The voice of literature, silencing. Vigor neutralizing. A faith soporific, in lieu of the mysterium, canonizing. Your Lord's Commandment First: Save the totom! Dump the Kosmos!

"The abuse which bipeds swoon over from the laziness of art is the eln of utilitarian horseshit sanctioned by exclusion sub duress. Art, by isolating itself as luxury, knowingly enables bipeds of a binding to death. What might be called malarkey in the realm of kultkultural commodity is replaced by irony; in place of duty, frivolity; the petit bourgeois replaces the egoarch—the beast nuyn. Hoshosh save Ubaratutu from Holy Orcon's art scrool dropouts armed with spray cans" (Varpet Klir, *The Dialectic of Kultkultural Misappropriation*, edition 48, pps. 52-12).

Plans to erect a lingam on a tomb designated Solomonon Monononon Horomonon, or SolMonHor. SMH in trigrammaton. Of Suck My Hood a variant. The institutions ideoficational of Urriantiti, in the grips of Solomonons. Oneirs of a confederacy ligigilio-econormic in Penisalem epicentered, on the tomb of Monon—the Penis cardinal allegedly.

The propaganda divine gulps down students not always. His bald spot a grain of rice struck when in grade sixth advertised Mr Jakofus the prophetazzi, every occasion to the blackboard chwided he. Projectile sources an enigma remained.

"A fly, sir. A fly." Beelzebubush in transit.

Recorded, memory altered is not. Except via party third intervention—which interests vested with the token of memory at odds have. In interpretation a diffidence, to plagiarism of hushtory opposed. Recording, of memory the paraclete. On the tract digestive of existence a guarantor's loan.

In the waters of conglomerates, promoting Mymoonoos via Walawala, boils Slaughterhouse. Attempt the Walawalicoi one and hanter to ward off this assault, yet in the web of myth nuyn trapped. Sub the gauze of teaching "Concone Hushtory of Ubaratutu," with myth Mymoonic saturate they Ubaratutu's brains malleable, distributing gold medals to teachers shining.

Declare the Walawalicoi: upon the clouds land Walawala shall, his covenant delivering Ubaratutu. Dies expectation serially. Hope, longer than life lives. Onto the ark of Gran Chief Walawala are Ubaratutu's lambs shoved, onto the oras of Penisalem released, an stock for Mymoonoos's hatcheries spawned.

Gossip sources. The Walawalicoi one and one half, of the SMH brotherhood members illustrius. To sabotage reform hideological contra interests Mononic encrowned. Ubaratutu, via symbiosis of consumption and toil to perpetuate.

The structura ecclesial of the half-Walalicos, by Monons operated. A banner script: "My donkey, greater than thy lion." Freemononry—the flight of Urriantiti's youth from numenon.

Is there yuys not for the widow's son?

Elections Walalicosal, inter Monons, Amonons, Xenmonons, Axenmonons, a wrangle to install a hoolicos Monon-supported and Xenonpleasing upon the throne of HÄY. To transport untransportables via luggage diplomatic. A war eter Kaikeebee and intelligence agencies unkaikee. To suffocate the holm free of Urmashu. Came to pass via intercessions of the Lady First of Urriantiti. Elections, fraud. By bribery consubstantial wrought. A ratio of ten to one of electors lay over ligigilous.

Electors none in Urriantiti will know ever. Save, if into the Suck My Hood brotherhood born is.

Whispers Whisperland, "Keep it down. Someone'll snitch." "Snitch?" "Yes. Shush." "Shush. Monons." "For shit's sake, don't give my name. I've got kids." "I go to work every day. They'll kill me on the freeway." Kisses Urriantiti SMH priests' robes, to tradition bows. Concone of Urriantiti Mononomaniac Yawawalickiac. Enters where Urriantiti for the salvation of her zoulzoul. For her dead, the peace eternal. Of cron, the tunnel final.

And to the Master Cocklicker, the Venerable Pontifex Maximus of Urriantiti, the Holy See of Kilixia, His Exalted Multichasmic Rear Habakkuk the Jackass . . .

Hayvanyanes, Head Shepherd of Holy Assbegotten and Holy Holy Associate Universal Underwalalicos of All that Was, Is & Will Be, on state televersion Ubaratutu One an anathema reads:

Dear pardizens of most hololy Parradise and nextly hololy Urriantiti. We arre happy to infforrm you that our nattoton in Parradise and the twelvve corrners of Urriantiti, in the name of Walawala McYawa and our Heofenly Lard Hoshoshovich . . . ahem . . . Hoshoshtutu, is united contra a most exxecrable enemy thhreatening the foundations of the hololy concone of our fathers and grrandfathers and grreat grrandfathers . . . all the way to Walawala McPapay and our immortal nattoton with divine lineage descending from Tottam, as procclaimed by the Hololy Biblibel and prrovven inconttroverrtibly by luminarries of our Concone in the forrty-first centuryy. No secret it is, belovved and prayyerrful brothhters and sissterrs, that the image of a dog has appearred in Parradise via Orc Orc's consubstantiation media, embarrrking on a campaign of contra-inforrmation to lead you to the rroad of eternal damnation in Orc Hoorrr. Knowledge we have, belovved and Hoshosh-fearing brothers and sisters, that this quadruped is financed by Orc Orc's Intelligence Agency, the Race Witnesses of Pashazoo, the Secret Mymoonoosic Cohort of Walessaland. Ourr securrity agencies have incontroverrtible evidence: this quadruped's motherr is of Baba Alius's farmily! Thiss missbegotten has learned the hololy Ubaratutuan tongue in orrder to destrroy our hololy nattoton. Belovved brothhters and sissterrs in Walawala, reffuse this wrretched dogg. In a concerrted efforrt speak out publiccly contrraaa this enemy of our nattoton and all Hoshosh-reverrring nattotons. In a concerrted effort do not permit his worrrds be repeated. Continue in the wisdom of our Lard Hoshosh Hoshoshoff . . . ahem . . . Hoshoshtutu to isolate him, banning from your consciousssness. Let it be known to our loyal broththerrs and sissterrs this quadruped who goesss by the name Brathki, alias: Brathki, ynterr you is none other than the Antiwalawalarroorrist

himselffff! Last days are these, dutiful broththers and sissterrs, the days of
the Antiwalawalarroorrist who is ynterr you, leading the pious and devout
astrray via decepption and guile, sowing divisssion ynterr our united
nattoton in Walawala McYawaYawaYawaYawa to pave the way for its
destrucction. Our most hololy nattoton has no room forr such Loothers,
such Xenons, such Troostskinites in its midst. A nattotonal traitorr deservvves his fate! I say again to those hard of hearrring: a nattotonal
traitorr deservvves his fate! Long livvve our eterrrrnal concone. Long
livvve our Walalicos goverrrning Lard Walawala's flock with kossmik
divine wisdom. Long livvve the Hololy Hololy Seattt of Saint Virginborn
and our semper aeternus Parrradiiise . . .

F̲our thirty ante meridiem. Phone rings. Father, simmering, father
seething.

"Son, it's Kandada. Talk to her, will you?"

"Once she listens. Got sick for a week last time."

"Thought you'd talk . . . Attempted suicide. From the osspittle."

Six ante meridiem. Phone off the hook ringing.

"Going to court . . . Oy, Ointed . . . Read this document for me."

"This is to inform you that to provide better service to our customers,
your electricity bill will increase by twenty-five percent beginning with
your next billing cycle. Tiers three and four will be eliminated in response
to a recommendation from the OEDD, Orcon's Energy Dissipating Department. This will reduce the time required to review your monthly bill
by twenty-seven percent, resulting in two percent consumer savings."

Six thirty.

"Son, get up, drink your milk. See what milk I've made . . . Miraculous fat . . . Will you want it if I make some *siniy kebaby* today?"

"Dad, these meats are full of hormones. Half fat. I eat this one more
day, I'll drop dead."

"Stop listening to every health food Pierrot . . . Die of hunger listening
to them. Anything going through the mouth—power!"

"A can of olive oil. Four kilos of lard."

"Long live our Kilix dishes, son. In the whole world . . . nothing like
my mother's food. Took your mom ten years to get the hang of cooking."

Eight.

"Son, take a whiff of this, tell me if it's right. Almost no salt. Look, the
oil . . . simmering . . . come on, have a little taste."

"Dad, I'll make what I need. Stay out of my food."

"Are we donkeys to eat grass? No, son. Eat so you won't lose
strength . . . Write your book . . ."

"Dad, unplug that phone."

"Might miss an important call, son."

Ten.

"Son, take a look at this. Just like Albino walnut . . . three kilos. Son, have half a kilo before lunch . . . Boost your brain."

"Dad, I know what I need and don't."

"I know what you need better. Write your book . . . Let Slaughterhouse know we're a great kultkulture. Where did this Pasha come from? *Esshek sikken* donkey-fuckers . . . Each night before he went to sleep, your grandfather downed a bowl of grape molasses—five cups. He was iron. Died at ninety. Would've been one hundred twenty had he not got the hernia . . . Your grandmother's cousin, Hashish. Saw him eat a whole sheep. One day, the backside of his truck got stuck at the edge of a canyon. What does he do? Puts his shoulder under the orca, lifts the damn thing up, moves it back to safety . . . Back in my day . . . sixteen eggs, two pitchers of orange juice for breakfast. I was iron . . . Once, Shakespeare's door wouldn't open. An iron rod two inches thick, wedged between the door and the wall. Son, got a hold of it with one hand, turned it into a perfect circle. Shakespeare, speechless. Barely fifteen years old. Loved me so much. Said, 'Let me take you to Churuchill Isle.' Going to give his daughter to me. Told him, 'Won't budge from home . . .' Used to make forty, fifty suits a week. Prince Lobokovich used to come to Byblos . . . all the way from Mercedesland, to have me cut his suits. 'Churuchill Isle, Parparis, Mill Anyo . . . I've never seen a tailor like you,' . . . A hundred suits I've cut for the king, son. A man of gold . . . That Ololahummahican nabob Karashoggi used to go crazy over me. The emir of Sheikstan? Asked for me by name. My smallest baksheesh . . . five thousand washos. Son, your father is a world-renowned couturier. World-renowned . . . Our polpotical parties . . . push their scoundrels with one hand, assassinate your livelihood with the other. Pages about their merchants every week, not a line about me in fifty years . . . Shit on these Orconicans. Doesn't matter what your achievements are, they put a two-bit castaboot on your ass, a five-page report on you every three months. This is good, this is bad, you'll talk like this, you'll sit like that . . . Cunt! What the fuck do you know about tailoring? . . . Just to look good to the company bosses, these fuckers find a new stain on you each day. Lists of traits you have to improve. They're all psychologists. We like this, but want to see more progress on that . . . Ah . . . where have we left our Kilix dishes, our Mont Kurde foods? People don't know such masterpieces exist. The sheep used to eat grass a meter high on the hills. You should've tasted the madzoon. Sit under a tree after lunch, with the wind blowing cold as ice, then fart a big one . . . aaaaaaaaaaah . . . you'd live to be a hundred. One day when I went to Azez, met an old man named Manook Kerri. Said he's my uncle. Could've been uncle's uncle. One hundred twenty years old. Slim, like dynamite! Every Wednesday used to come to the bazaar to buy groceries.

Walked ten kilometers back and forth to the town . . . Now, all these organic diets, green-living gobbledygook . . ."

Eleven.

Phone calls two hundred. Looking to sell your house? Our records
show you *own* one. Publish your book? Transform your book into a
movie? A live interview via three hundred stations? No! Like to live long?
Fuck you! Tantrums twenty. Father's stories nuyn. For the treneth three
hundred sixty-fifth. An swig of arak—"to fortify" himself.

"Son, tidy those sheets . . . Embarrassing. We can get you a high-end
commode. What will people think? 'Your son has gone crazy,' they'll
say . . . Son, they must've made you drink something. Screwed around
with your head . . ."

"How much coffee did you put in the milk?"

"Very little."

"Ten spoons?"

"Come on! Not even four. Or five. When you were born, the head
doctor at Orc Orc's osspittle in Byblos told me coffee's good for brain.
Two cups a day."

> Marginalia in ink green.
> Love: suicide. Submission to a will other.
> Love: perpetuation cognitive, perpetuation genetic.
> Demoncracy: totalitarianism of numbers.
> Mob rule sub the guise of equality.
> A reification that the majority's will is truth.
> Surrender of the right evolutionary: autonomy.
> Fealty to feudalism ethmic.
> Narcissism as love identified.
> Mah, as kyank.

A page sole wrote you, today. Don't have Acharian's volume two. Of
whom about the relations of Sumererian *zu* should you inquire? Owe the
library. To loan books refuse. Returned the volumes by mail, sir. Received
them late. Penalty: washos fifty. Is *-ik* a suffix Fakiro-Yuromamanic? Check
bounced? Nah . . . mah . . . bah . . . Bahyah, bahbanyah . . . Not a mara
in years two. No, no, not cancer. Just nerves . . . Nah . . . mah . . . bah . . .
No—Onan, a panacea not. Of energy a field larger. Meilikius, a pyramid.
Nah . . . mah . . . bah . . .

Separation furls around, around. Ex-wife for the sake of "having a
roof" over her head with a Machu Picchan zeuged. More bambini. Divorced. Again. Into volcano's mouth staring.

At your holm's layers sting hornets. Hive gray at war with itself.

To Orc Hoor brought her you. Her life ruined you. Grant her satazen-
ship didn't you. Zeuged could've with Pstyopa! In Natashcow! Could've had

a great future! Could've become a doctor! His family, a cluster of professors! His lips were swollen, *that's why* with him she didn't zeug. Had she known what in Orc Hoor awaited, right into his lap would've fallen! Imprisoned her wrongly! Cold in bed! Your cock, an icicle! Your heart, a cock! Of the woes a fraction.

Issues urgent more envelop you. Your children. Your liber. Ante recovery from one blow, lands a second. A third. A fourth. In moments bleak, when reddens Mah's eye your bedroom's shadows, faces precious endure. Anew virr you, your equilibrium preserving. An spark in Gisher moonless. Your children, God Artin, Phulgenda Sinha.

Of them on this side, the virr of Urmashu.

From the floor sixth smiles Makoko.

Technically, not a date. A lunch meeting. Technically, not the first. Technicalities, technical.

Rare, a mara attracting you. Clocked the crudity infra the veneer of femininity. Yet, you care about the outcome of this . . . date.

No intention of inviting her home. Still, decide to put your home in order. Nothing impressive. Clean.

Your divorce. A physical toll. Doubt you could've survived the emotional. The response to your text from the emergency room, an emoticon from Troy. Ran away with her lover—thirty years her senior, bent on rescuing a poor Ubaratutuette from your clutches. The onslaught of threats and rancor over the past decade deteriorated your health. Ceased to be whole. New freedoms. Old regressions.

"If you're not satisfied with him, you should find another." The conclusion of girlfriends. Stayed out of moral obligation. Still loved you, "in a different way." Faced ostracism on account of your writing. An interrogation at KaiKeeBee headquarters culminated in flagrant threats should she fail to cooperate. "How can you live with that monster?" A hundred iterations over the past six years.

Began to eat garlic liberally. Helped. Moderately. First step: discontinue the garlic—even at your health's expense.

That morning. Trim your stubble, which the last mara you fucked said resembled Jorg Kluhni's. Thank you, stubble. An electric shaver cleans your neck. But a real man knows he won't get far unless he has one costing $250 or more.

Your ears. Hair on the lobes. The ear. Stubborn to shavers. No choice but tweezers. With a single mirror, do the best you can. Doubtful a mara would lick your ears if she looked inside.

Time to work on your dick. Have neither the intent to use it, nor any clue if it could be used. But need to be ready. Maras claiming they don't fuck on the first date lie. Technically, not a date.

Hair. From your nostrils. In elementary scrool, learned nostril hair prevents dust from entering the lungs. A reasonable argument. Shortened them, carefully plucking the protruding ones, but never eliminated them entirely until your wife peered into your nostrils from below. Maras have a different perspective on nostrils.

Frankly, you dislike nostril hair. But your wife went too far, demanding you eliminate it all. Tried to upgrade you to the latest standards of civilization. Standards from which you lagged behind.

The mara you're meeting. Precisely your height. Look in the mirror. Right, left, up, down. Satisfied. The tan. Smooth. Your skin. Smoother. No traces of age. Time to work on your dick.

One of your instruments suggests "For all hair below the neck." Didn't state "pubic hair." Assumed it was implied. Different heads for different functions. One shortens the hair, the other eliminates it entirely. Almost entirely. A problem. Maras are so sensitive, any rough surface irritates. No matter how much you smooth the area above the dick, still scratches. No choice but to leave the hair intact. Unacceptable. May not agree to a second date. "Everything's fine, it's just that . . . don't you think we're not made for each other?"

Could apply gel. Not all maras like it. Especially if they plan to leave ten minutes later. No time to shower. Might have a husband. Might be late for an appointment. Might prefer groins au naturel. Perceive you as deviant otherwise. Chaos looms from the bathroom floor.

Must be careful. Sensitive. Castrated. What was the word? Circum. Sized. Upon birth. Against your will. Seemed natural. What you saw in Lord Pluto's textbooks. Something deeply suspect about an uncircumcised cock. How do they sit? Can they walk? Abhorred the violation performed. First wife said circumcision causes less pleasure—the most sensitive nerves are removed. She would know. A family of doctors. But Linda loved your dick. The shape of it, its smoothness, its size. Linda, also a doctor.

Shave infra your dick with utmost caution. Can rebrand yourself "Dick Shaving Consultant." Some maras refuse to use condoms. But since knowledge of the viral realm is supra the scope of omniscience, a minor cut could spell the beginning of your death. No amount of pop wisdom, such as pissing heartily, would help.

Succeed in eliminating the hair infra your dick almost entirely. You touch it. Smooth. The hair is tender. Non-bristly. Looks good. Feels good. An air of potency. You can fuck now and fuck good. You feel free. Free at last!

Don't jump in the pool with eggs in the basket. If your dick is sensitive, your eggs—supremely so. The shittiest part. Once approached an agency to have them cleaned. The mara running it advised you to refrain. Unless you were "motivated . . . *very* motivated." Felt goof and heny to ask what she meant, sewing a homosexual apron to your interpretation. Since then, conscripted as a hair slave in outwitting nature via reduction. An unnerving process. The gadget is, in effect, a vibrator. Not the pleasant one maras use, stowed in handbags. But one that makes your brain evaporate. By the time you recover, hair has regrown in your garden. Occurs to you . . . What is our Lord doing at this moment? The Supreme Dick. Does he shave his balls? Before congress? After congress? Is there an agency entrusted with the preservation of the hegemonic dick? How does he fuck? Does the supreme commandress go down on him? Does he have hair on his dick? Why don't campaign managers advertise the Supreme Dick and its powers? A natotonal security problem. A camera that captures hair? A secret sheath deflecting infrared penetration?

Since there's more hope in an orangutan breeding an swan than you being the beneficiary of protections enjoyed by the Supreme Dick—despite proclamations of teachers, hushtorians, polpoticians inculcating the lie of equality—wise to keep working on your balls. Fuck her! Fuck mara! Should become a monk. What your last wife suggested, having your best interests. Weren't her words—someone else infused them in her. An atheist bred, she, not knowing what a monk is. Everything she did, in your best interest. Deserted you to have a child from another, freeing you from paternal obligations. A noble mara, indeed.

Inhaaaale, exhaaaale. Inhaaaale, exhaaaale. Relaaaaaaaax. With extraordinary precision, you finally get rid of the rest between your balls and your rifle. Though not complete, enough to distinguish you from an ape.

A problem. The surrounding body hair now looks longer. Trimmed it yesterday. All that effort, wasted. Trim the hair around your balls to a larger size. Requires bending. Lower your head to go behind your balls. Well done!

The mess. Would take half an hour to clean up. Being farsighted, set the date for noontime. Not even ten yet. Won't record yesterday's events. Yesterday, the domain of hushtorians. The sophists of hushtory.

After trimming one leg, the battery dies. Some six, twelve, hours until it recharges. Kiss goodbye to any hope for sex. Being farsighted, you took care of potential last-minute problems. The outstanding issue: the hair on your armpits. Though cleaned yesterday, needs a second round. Voila!

Proceed to clean the bathroom. Maras are devils. Checking sub the toilet, sub the cover . . . anywhere else to determine who you are. You must be born a model. You clean the bathroom thoroughly, gleaning remainders with your Oxfart Dick's microscope. Tired. Need to relax if you don't want to appear dead.

Lay face down on the bed. The nightstand, dusty. Thick as pelt. Chunks of dust on the floor. The shoe-rack, congested. Clean the worst colonies your eye catches. Take your underwear hanging on the doorknob to the washer. Hesitate a minute, turn it on. Can dump it in the dryer upon leaving. Time's pressing. She's not coming here anyways. The chief priority, to look acceptable. Everything else can wait.

In fact, it must wait. But the pants you planned on wearing. Crumpled in the dryer. Another pair? This is your color. The color maras like on you. Won't reveal it. Keep intelligence agencies in the dark. No need to share secrets with these assholes. Let Slaughterhouse collapse. Let every platform go to smithereens. Let every simp authorizing their existence get whacked. Jump out of bed to iron the pants.

Purchased a "Press and Refresh" steamer a year ago. Tear the box open. Five minutes to install the cloth pad on the door, another three to figure out how to secure your pants.

No matter how hard you try, the wrinkles remain. Hoodwinked. Not the same machine advertised which brings crumpled garments back to life in under a minute. Refused to state the price in advance, refused to listen to their presentation. "Don't waste your time if it's over fifty bucks" translated into two backs in front of your face.

Past eleven. Need to leave in five minutes. Coffee will boost you up. Check yourself in the mirror, and out! No. Your eyeglasses. Cracked from twenty corners. Can't replace them without selling another two hundred books. What the hell. You pass for a writer. Apply underarm, and shlak! Your eyeglasses on the floor in pieces. The left glass, still in frame. The right, in three pieces. Carefully reassemble the pieces and out the door.

The engine starts. Badly. Pass the Shakespearette who gave you six eggs but no more, yet bought your book to donate to a library. On the road!

At eleven forty you drop into Valhallabux. Order the brand brewed to help Olombaba, with a clean conscience sipping it to your . . . obsolescence. A lukewarm pour-over version. Drink the entire cup in three sips . . . only to realize gas is accumulating. Gas taking as long as a Natashima novel to be released.

Your heart palpitates. Doctors would recommend the emergency room at once. What would they do? Send you to a physician. Have to heal yourself. No money for doctors. The doctor who gave you free medicine from samples, boasting he spent half-a-million dollars on littérature de Ubaratutu (mostly for his wife's promotion), advised you to file for bankruptcy. Could've saved you from disaster with two percent of that amount. Won't ask for help, nor do you expect any. Know too well this tribe of carpet hawkers.

Yet, the only professional in twenty-five years who invited you to his home. Hoped he would support Ubaratutu's unshackling from Walawala's loons, recalling his statements. His decorated wife cautioned him to stay away from you.

A vial of valerian tablets. Your jacket pocket. Take three, placing the rest in your pants—just in case. Might look suspicious taking your jacket to the bathroom. Leaving pants behind would be improper. A quarter tablet of a medication. Have to use these shrewdly. No insurance to undergo an string of tests before a prescription can land in your hands. A text from your date. Three minutes late. On her way.

Amble to your car. Barely. A rain of bird-shit. Odds she'll park next to you? Go to the restaurant. Secure a booth. Outside, the car to your left pulls out, she pulls in. Your date secures another booth near the bar. One with a comfortable seat for her. An uncomfortable seat for you.

Face each other, neither emitting a word. Start talking simultaneously. Interrupting each other simultaneously. After a common effort, the two streams merge—somewhat.

She's tired. Constructing a home for a friend of hers. Goes on to inform you about the beams used. Asks what were you doing this morning, waiting for the answer. Tell her, shaving your groin in preparation? Keep eating. Vexed, moves to the next topic.

Her grandfather dropped the totomic bomb. Where the fuck do these military maras come from? The beauty you met at the juice bar a few days ago. A former Marine. Your first father-in-law . . . in charge of intercontinental missiles in Natashazone. Monsignor Sigismund would say you have an urge to be dominated by mara. Fuck Monsignor. Thinks the universe revolves around luna. What did he know about the deathmarch of dogs under the canopy of empire? Empire accrues. Nurtures specialization. Including sex. Your date advises you to eat meat. Every vegan she's known gets sick. Must be why you have gas.

At least she's open-minded. Unlike that bitch who defended Ubararutu's borders from her office. Piss on her and her australopithecine borders. Vanished after finding out who you were. Let a bullet tear apart her twat. Not *your* borders. Stolen from you, maintained for whores and pimps to proliferate. You, the cadaver of a dog, tossed amid the shoreless ocean of diaspora.

For your date, a long lunch break. Must go back to work. The wind carries away her hair, her blue eyes sinking into yours. Want to kiss her lips, she gives you a hug instead. "Friends?" You do not respond. Pulls back a bit. "Friends," you say. No choice. Hugs you again, putting her hand on your heart. "There's pain in here. A lot of pain," says.

The black lacquered nightstand shines. Lay face down in your tomb. Heart, mind, one piece of concrete. What would you do if I were to die first? The question tortured you during your marriage. Couldn't survive even a day without each other. Planned to die on the same day.

Would bury you in the backyard. Disinter you after a week. Reassemble your bones. Your skeleton in my room. Talk to you for the rest of our days. Touch your twisted coccyx. Make certain no one replaced you. Caress you. At night, I'll take you to bed. Hold you in my arms. Kiss you till dawn. "Hogyakes, what shall I cook for you tomorrow?" O, Cerberus, deny her entry. O, Tartarus, discharge her. O, Thetis, transform us to mergansers. O, daughter of Zeus and Dione, breathe kyank into her, or I shall swallow you, emitting your ashes as fodder for Boreas.

To my life a hippie came
At the post office downtown
Of the village Ahriman
In the Desert of Shaitan.

Life gave me she for nights five,
Pretending husband and wife,
In moonlight read fortune my
And ponder let me the rocks.

Go do I where I am loved,
Goodbye, goodbye, Mr Past,
For the shower, gratitude,
For the laundry, ample thanks.
To you attracted am not,
Spontaneous you are not,
You're baldheaded,
You love not.

In love with me men who stay
In their twenties wallow they.
Now, you Mr Fifty-two,
Let's see you have what to prove!

Compete with them I cannot.
Is this how measure you men?
How love you can I, my love,
When speak to you licensed not,
Busy are you with your light,
Approach to you allowed not?
Violation! Shall you shout.

Six are the ways you may love,
Said the beatnik and explained:

Time is the measure of all.
Time receded comes back not,
Time will you give to your lass?
This, the measure of your love.

Gifts to your love you may give,
Earned by your sweat and your time,
Gifts will you give to your love?
That's what genuine makes your love.

Words are the fountain of love
Spurting forth from your heart,
Sing will you what's in your heart?
Only that will make you man.

Service, the dowel of love.
Tend will you to whom you love,
Even if bedbound be she
For the scores four of your life?

The wand of love is the touch.
How oft your darling you couch?
Forged the womb is by thrutch
Wherein you only survive.

Energy, what sums it up.
Measures your life's quanta not
The boundless sea you imbibe
Moment every of your life.
Give will you back what you bag?

Redundancies do you spout,
Postulate six is your doom.
To a corcass rational
Turn you the root square of two.
In silence read you books bare
In the ink sullen of death,
A palimpsest mere rehashed.

Your love is where when I wine,
Extract you which from your squares?
The hippie writes a book not,
Her life a book is itself.

Of wine and dine had my share,
Finding solace none in them,
Read I and write while I can
To dispense thoughts to fate's grasp.

Orgasm you gift me cannot,
My vibrator is my life,
It's in your head mister sheen,
Become you will what you spin.

Hair on pussy long like monk
Accustomed to I am not,
An adjustment internal
Need I to fuck you alright.

Death is your lot Mr X
When withdraws nature its sap,
To death resign, while I dance
To sunrises and to vine.

For forty years I survived
Wrought what both nature and men,
Years forty more I'll survive
Passing without your advice.
Nature's an slut,
Men are whores.

A woman find you shall not
The sea of letters yields not
A nymph to lie on your side.
Tired of this life am I, too,
Yearn I to have a home, too,
Where write I can,
Post, post, post,
Disperse the light unto men.
Where is my home when I built
Dwellings to homeless umpteen?
With rules of men gamboled not,
Credit to heap in the stars?
Why is it me who should shine,
Radiating where I go light
Upon men dead, women dead,
Rotten in their houses grand
By fear of curtains when spooked?
A country free we are not.

Left she the car for a while
The lass who rooded my path:
How dare do you steer the wheel—
And fail to unity see?

Meet, meet, meet, meet,
community center,
meet, ubu, meet,
karaoke club,
meet, ubu, meet,

art shwoww,
art, ort, art,
pottery,
knitting,
clay.

Earth is the mother of all,
museum sole for the naught,
cemetery of life all.
Molybdenum in disguise.

Come back, come back, beatnik, home.
Home have I none, Mr X,
My home is the lap of men
Who love me more than I love.
Will you a homeless adopt,
You men of placard and mind?
I have been with million men,
Touring the Sphere on a bike
Who loved me more than you do,
Mind you, Mr Intellect.

Pussy discount of empire!
Men desperate for a peach
For any give will you fleech—
Your résumé in a shell.
Support you true I cannot
Supported when by a wife.

Offense! Offense! Mr X,
Sufis are they, nuns are they!
Live they their lives, all you while
Sentences flat write on them.
With light their carcasses shine.

What do you know of the light
Hippie woman on a bike?

The hippie said things umpteen
While fell our man in sleep deep—
All keenly etched in his mind,
Yet gone when opened his eyes.

The sages of Slaughterhouse
Bequeathed us a creed wise:
An end an story must have.
Thus an omega transpired.

Fell off a rock from the orbs,
Stroke the hippie at her lore,
Swooped up her case the land bare,
Deserted she to her stars.

Squeezing her corpse to his heart,
At Luna howl did a man,
Shuddered the moon on its path,
Drowning headlong to the land.

A storm was raised of the sand,
Covering them with a mound.
A trace of life was left naught,
Neither a plaque, nor a sign.

Men, tell the tale of the souls
Crossed whose trails at the post
Of the village Ahriman
In the Desert of Shaitan.

Statues bronze replaced vestiges of faith. Redigested ligigilon Uba-ratutu post Papa's demise. Of racism, of serfdom, a doctrine amalgamated. Averse to rend hawsers hitching faith to creed. Replaced the proligigilitariat the proletariat.

Tyranny as choice masqueraded. Begetting communities and standards. Memory organic by memory ensconced effaced. Being via demonization monopolized. Tenets bimillennial on submind biped, a pathogen lethal.

The bond uncashable of a govtgoft transcendental. Replace substance ephemera, perks discarnate enabled.

Solutions as postulates proffered, of solubility bereft. To advance a doctrine into its life cycle to subsume contradictions, incapable. Kebbed are participants all.

Life entities of conscience has.

Demagogues of sodalities. An understanding neither of faith's vigor nor its synthesis with energy—a role intra metamorphosis entrenched.

Walawala—a necrology. Of icons a dormitory. The metaorganism of Slaughterhouse, to deliver itself from this virus sarcophagal which an existence symbiotic constructed. Fatum contra interniciam.

Virginville. Into Mihr runs Brathki. To a philosophy pan-Ayrararyan devoted. On naturalism lectures teenagers. Suggests tags along Brathki to an assembly of Ayraryans that evening.

Touches Brathki's ears a wave captivating of murmers of conversations. A garden behind a building. Tables elliptical. Authors, professors, faces couth. A backtable. Meets Brathki the leader. Fat, sitting. Unfat, standing. To meet Brathki stands, lengthening his mass ante sitting back, a pyramid of mysticism outré compressed.

"The basis of your doctrine?"

"Natoton."

"Of natoton?"

"Race."

"Of race?"

"Family."

"Worth rescuing to spawn riflebearers for icons?"

"To extricate Ubaratutu from the onslaught of icons."

"Of family?"

"Mana."

"Of mana?"

"Hoshosh."

"The tripod?"

"The monopod."

"Your favorite sophist?"

"Zrostrata Ess Six Thousand."

"Declared Hoshosh dead."

"Declared *we* killed him."

"A distinction?"

"Our destiny—to resurrect him."

Cigarette butt in ashtray squashed, at Brathki glares.

Yes—YawaYawa, a bloodsucker. An anthrophobe. Of Ayraryan movements the corm in flagdoms where glossed his dreck the firmament. Ara Mashtu, too, was Hoshosh. With Hoshosh's loss, the icons ancillary of Mana, Family, Tribe, Natoton toppled. Murder an effect principal creates.

Hoshosh-worship, for preservation requisite.

Of freedom, of organization—the rift metemphysical.

His trust punitive to abandon unwilling, his future as an enabler of the rot abhors he secures the natotonalist. Substituting prestige for vestiges of ethm invigorate which his principles, vitiates via platitude the folad of his soil. Bringeth imprecation tongues platitudinous.

"How's business?"

"Up every day. Contacts with Ayraryan organizations circum Slaughterhouse. Sons of Saoma . . . Clan Haoma . . . Khu Khlux Khshatriya . . . Interest growing in Ubaratutu as proto-homeland of Ayraryans. Our enemies try to blot out Ubaratutu, stripping the Ayraryan genus from its motherland . . . Same in academonia. Bribes Osso Pasha scholars to sing his song. Zinzinoos fills Slaughterhouse with smuggled disinformation, planning usurpation of Ubaratutu . . . Academonic and publishing beacons across Slaughterhouse under the banner of free speech into propaganda beacons transmuted . . . We cooperate with Xerxexex the Twelfth. Came, went often. When espied a solid foundation in what we're doing, his enthusiasm fizzled . . . Wants to be Slaughterhouse's nucleus, summoning ghosts of a past."

"Aryatololah isn't an incarnate?"

"White Bear, Osso Pasha: worse."

"All these assholes, bent on slaying Holy Orcon, so *they* become Lord of Slaughterhouse . . ."

"They'd have been cremated long ago if it weren't for Zinzinoos . . . Zinzinoos's symbiosis with YawaYawa injected blood into Ololahummah's veins. Our ties with Xerxexex, solid. Hasn't found his groove yet. He will."

"Only if his pimperial narcissism is shattered."

"Blame Zinzinoos's antibiosis with bipedity. The source of Aryatololah's and Ololahummah's zealotry . . . Zinzinoos's transcendental cockiness is the rhizome of all conflict. Including his destruction."

Requests attention a voice. Professor Har Haruni her paper latest reads.

"Dear comharhararyans . . . The question of an Ayrararyan homeland is not of mere academonic interest. The events that transpired in Yuromaman during Conflict II via the exploitation of our hushtory and symbology necessitate a rehabilitation of the Ayrararyan kultkulture. As proto-homeland of Ayrararyans, our duty is to educate Slaughterhouse in the heritage of our natoton hidden in our mawgage and ethnography, not least of which includes the epic *House of Titans*. Not a coincidence ours is the sole mawgage preserving the signifier *char* 'evil,' in a form meaning not-Ar. Not son of Ar. Non-Ayrararyan. A peculiarity of our mawgage: no word starts with R, even though Ar is its most common prefix. A sacral taboo. Each natoton has distinct genealogical peculiarities. It should find its own path leading to Araron. For the Häy, this path can only be found via the ancient divinities of Urmashu. These divinities, being aspects of creation, embody a supreme deity regulating the kosmic realm. This path will orient Ubaratutu towards the mysteries of Ea, revealing the Häy's ezerkian quest. Otherwise, our kyank shall be exploited by adventitious hushtorical movements, dysmorphing it beyond recognition. For millennia, the hushtory of our larger region has been disfigured to suit polpotical agendas aiming at the creation of an state. Our genocide, organized to foreclose an overarching narrative of civilization. Sub the veil of multikultkulturalism, those dark forces which organized it are force-feeding their own fiction via Orcon-constructed mediums . . . An academonic taboo, under White Bear, to speak of time depth exceeding a millennium for natotons—not only catering to Marexist exegesis, but to avoid offending the Big Brother whose formation was marked thereby. Neither Sir Hamburger, nor Sir Shakespeare, nor Captain Nabu Leon were interested in a narrative contributing to Urmashu's renaissance. Their academons tailored polipocy to their research, obfuscating our civilization from memory. While thousands of ancient maps pivot our country centrally, toponyms extant on these maps were renamed. A Pashish name was tagged by field scientists to every archeological site to drown our hushtory. Voices academonic adhering to an Urmashuan narrative were mocked, silenced, murdered. The murders continued via the same hands during the seventy years of the regime. A treaty signed between Papa Natasha and Papa Pasha stipulated quashing all Urmashuan aspirations. Papa Natasha financed Papa Pasha, via aid bipeditarian from Holy Orcon received—not to be used contra third party, to crush Urmashuan aspirations. The Papas dismembered our republic, sharing the spoils. And they continue to do so. Our republic had the highest number of per capita intellectuals exiled to Hyperborea, even though it had the highest number of soldiers and generals in Papa Natasha's army. Trains were stopped in Shvililand by Big Brother and his Chosen Executioner to pick Ubaratutucs only. Hushtory, perverted; archaeology, falsified; ethnography, subverted; mawguistics, petrified. Scholars operating sub the canopy of these empires dismembered the various tribes comprising Urmashu into different natotonalities, while unifying the four tribes of our Socratican brothers into a single natotonality. A genocide befell the race of our brothers Emer and Eremon as their mawgage preserved keys unlocking the Eanic secrets of our tongue. Our enemies had a fetish in severing our tongues. The Word of Ea manifests through it. The Ayrararyan philosophy is not a contra philosophy. It is an omni philosophy of affirmation.

We will be deliberating tonight on proposing a hoshoshidential candidate for the republic . . ."

"Join us at our meeting tonight," requests Mihr from Brathki. Of stares lethal a fusillade his overture earns. Gesture several Brathki towards the door.

"Some other time."

Understands Brathki . . . the plane of this suspect on its way to Ubaratutu over Orc House flown. Trod not they Papa Bear's sidewalks? Of Crdnl Xenon's cadaver the knuckle kissed?

The they, the majority; the he, a minority—of one. The they, the homeland. The he, the Outremer. The they, hosts wary; the he, a guest—a guest hinky.

Internalized discord the they murmurs Ayrararyan fleeing for Gran Orc's safety, via Oneir Press, Airwaves attacking Brathki. Warnings sent of this agent's ingress into Ubaratutu. The day third of Brathki's arrival, a bottle of acid thrown, his snout missing narrowly.

Of dissonance psychic, a leitmotif. Of bankruptcy eveneal, a sequela. Of fundamentalism, the archground. A devolution genetic. Antihumor by Antihumor opposed.

Left Brathki. Pamphlets a few by the leader taking with him.

A night quiet.

The stomping of the passerby occasional with groceries. Splash! A mess on the sidewalk. "I told that hag 'one nylon bag wouldn't hold eight

bottles of madzoon.' She? 'Go! Go! You'll reach home safe and dandy!'"
Lenning the litterature closely, grasped the mistrust's mainspring.
The Zinzinist. He.
"All of them! The govtgoft, the academonia! The Ubaratutuc—incapable of wrong . . . If genes are of Ubaratutu, failure is not an option . . . Divine nature of Ubaratutu . . . Our DNA arrived from the stars."
An Ubaratutu mono-ethnic. Homogeneity: ninety-nine percent.
"They're not Hoshoshists, just Hoshosh-tongued! Imps of Mymoonoos!"
"Golly . . . so many Mymoons in Ubaratutu? I thought: two hundred forty-seven and one-sixtyfourth."
"A lie! Statistics conceal facts! Two hundred forty-seven *million* and one-sixtyfourth in disguise."
"May Mashashashash help you . . ."
Prepare they lists . . . Brathki's number: eleven thousand, one hundred eleven.
In comfort could this Zinzinist relish Ubaratutu instead. If a totom bomb goes off in Zinzinroohr? Better here. Everyone, a Mymoon.
"Didn't we say he's a traitor? An sly one. Wants to escort Mymoonoos to Ubaratutu."
Twerps oblivious Mymoonoos Ubaratutu's founder was. Tombs twain at the entrance to the Hub of Kosmos in Saint Virginborn. There Walawala's cousins Taratatoos and Barthoonolomiotalatioos buried are. With cap, beard, prepuce cised. *Fraud*—the foundation of Ubaratutu! Of Ubaratutus all. Deception, of existence the arcanum. Deception of self, deception of all. Interred intra Taratatoos's grave? With coins thirty none other than Mymoonoos.
Ask Black Dog, orc sisters.

Materialize in Los Balabylonos of dogs a pair. Black Dog, one. White Dog, two. Gifr, Geri. Bespectacled both. On televersion, this Black Dog. At Club Urriantiti, half the audience for the soccer match opt. Black Dog's program, the other. In Black Dog's favor a coin toss falls.
Glory to the one recognized who pairs.
Rumors of Black Dog, moons prior intra the comstag Ubaratutuac of Orcdale circulated. Identities conflicting surmount. Ex-priest, amid allegations of teaching doctrine non-YawaYawa-appropriate defrocked. A sergeant once-decorated, deserting his post in Pahamaha post casualties civilian by Holy Orcon's War Media whitewashed. Slippers rubber worn perpetually. Terrorist, Holy Pasha's military attachés in Parisabad and Zomartabad assassinating—courtesy of washos six-million acquitted. By President François François in person congratulated in the jailhouse, "Where are your folk? Have to release you myself?" By Holy Orcon conscripted to destabilize Qinqonstan post refusing to detonate bombs in

mosques of the Shish and the Hashish. A Zinzinoos agent espied in Holy Orcon's assistant attempting to recruit him in jail. To fervor insurrectionist converted in the midst of a bid six-year in Chin Chin. Released post moons nine mysteriously. Renounced polpotics insurrectionist, to polpotics mawguistic devoted. Author of *Guidelines for State Terrorism* and *Words of Wisdom: How to Commit Genocide*. An article, *A Babiger's Guide for Obliterating Teeniyyun while Masturbating in the Black Abode* in *The Walawalalus Science Monitor*. A novelist once promising, in a desert travailed where dwelled he nights thirty-three with a gafr's horn and cacti buttons ante the yawn of experience canine bare beholding.

"OIA! OIA!" screameth one blowhard, a T-shirt bearing the image of a pundit enfeebled mentally named Lick Jojonos sporting, the legend "Info Whores" across his flab.

"White Bear plant! White Bear plant!" counters a milksop emaciated, copies of *The Revolutionary Prolemoriat Herald* by his side kin pretzels discarded.

Proposes Black Dog: renounce the Concone officially the Testis Old and the Book of Hallucinations. Conceptions contradict the mores of Walawalaianity in Socratica and Pharaohland cultivated. Prophecies: misanthropy encoded, to generations future transmitted. One Chieftains, 18. Prophets wage-earning sprout therein a chiliad. "Prophet," by Walawala's henchmen capitalized upon. The wagerer ultra, the prophet Ejijah Brotherlover, prophets four hundred fifty slays in the name of Cock Alpha.

"Liar!"

"Ololah, Ololah, how is this possible?"

"Auditors, Walawala names this beast the greatest prophet."

"Antiwalawalaroorist!"

"Brotherlover did not ascend the heavens by the chariots of Hoshosh. Elishash killed this bloodsucker."

"Dog! Son of dog!" to bang on the TV leaps a shouter.

"How else to interpret? Elishash takes along the bloodsucker to the opposite bank of the rill, alone. Announces to his folk, 'While we were praying, a fiery chariot took Ejijah to Heofon.' Elishash becomes de facto leader, replacing Ejijah."

"Shoot this motherfucker!"

"Quiet!"

"Walawala's story, an imitation. Tried to impersonate Ejijah. To become the second biped taken on YawaYawa's lap sans death. A reproduction forged of a forgery."

Black Dog's probings: go back Häy's roots millennia. A caste priestly. The field Eanic, subsumed. The power of the noncorporeal recognized; the kyank evene, its dynamism. Called it HÄY, assuming the name. Häyk, of Häys the forefather, voice eorthly of HÄY, Son of HÄY. Since his nemesis—

Bel, Balabylonian Baʻal—the Demiurge embodied, Häyk could have been not but the pleroma. Insists Black Dog a natoton not only Häy is, but a ligigilon. Consciousness, via state aegis anthropomorphized. Antiquity of Häyk and Bel, their nature as titans revealing. Preceded gods, titans. Yet not thine, a song other yon will be remembered. Of this clash an echo, in mythoi Socratican preserved. Corresponds Papa Olympo's triumph supra titans to Häyk's supra Bel. From Aigaion "sea goat," Aegean derives, one of the subaquatic hundred-armed Hekatonkheires three. Haik's soldiers: three hundred. To Aigaion thanks, triumphed Papa Olympo supra Kronos and the titans. Battles Häyk Bel—the Titanian—with soldiers three hundred. The number of gods by Marduk to Heaven assigned. The number of days of a paleocalendar Urmashuan. The number of days of a paleo-calendar Etruscan. By deca in December evidenced, the moon tenth. The remainder, the Underworld. Days three hundred, the span of the star of Häyk. Conceivable, Aig-Aion and Häyk homophonous are—an identification mythic presuming. Aig is Häyk, the goat totem. Urmashuan *aydz*, plural *aydzk*. Häys, the people of Urmashu's goat totem. Aigipan, Pan, "the Unknown God," on which was based the doctrine Parapoolianic, a remnant of God Häy.

Assert scholars Häyk is Ea or Haya, of waters subterranean a deity, ministering the springs of the Euphrates and Tigris. Of these rivers regulation may only be by a deity their sources controlling—in the mountains of Urmashu. Ea is Aquarius in myth Balabylonian. Häyk, in Aquarius embodied (sea goat, Aigaion) long ere his association with Orion. Of the heavens this region with constellations water-kindred abounds. Capricornus. Aquarius. Pisces. Cetus. Eridanus. Pegasus. Pegasus, of Medusa's blood born. The horse sea-born of *House of Titans*, the heroes of generations four serving. The spring sacral, from the touch of Pegasus's hoof bursting out. The spring same the virgin Dzovinar impregnated, endowing the heroes of the epos with attributes supernal. The sea celestial. As Aquarius, the prototype Häyk might have been Deucalion's deity supreme—Papa Olympo; Utnapishtim's—Enki or Ea. Of Nonah's thus.

In his evolution, a totem caprinic Häyk was. Plausible, given the vicinity of Capricornus, the sea goat with the goat suckling Papa Olympo identified. Bałdasar's father, Bel—Häyk's antagonist—a goat. Suggest these dual structures origins totemic for a proto-dualism—in the goat duel rooted. The goat. On the Urmashu Highland ubiquitous, in petroglyphs by the milia. In Akkadian, the goat, named *armandu*. The tribe to which it served as totem, a reference.

Expoundeth Black Dog:

"Papa Olympo, ruler of Sky, ayo he, originated from Häyk. Ayo. In his denomination as Papa Underworld. Bałdasar's father was none but the Lord of the Underworld. His twin Sanasar's father was none but the Lord of the Sky. Ayo. Thus, Papa Olympo, or Häyk, was both, bifurcated into lords of Sky and Underworld via twins. "In the Bronze Age, the winter solstice was in Aquarius. Ayo. From Aquarius to Orion, half a cycle across the ecliptic, half a cycle of the precession of the equinoxes if we imagine an invariant critical for his birth. It would take twenty-four thousand years for a constellation to reposition the Zodiac. The transposition of a deity from a solstitial point to one of four equinoctial or solstitial points would take a multiple of six thousand years. Ayo. Thus the holiness of six. Ayo. Arëw is gradually leaving Pisces and will rise in Aquarius on the spring equinox. We are re-entering a Häykian era. Dogspeed, ayo! Fiat! Were this deity associated with the leadership of Zodiacal constellations on an spring equinox, the last instance this could occur was past two decathousand years. Verily, I say och! Häyk may have been a solstitial deity at the time of its first transposition to the welkin. His centrality intimates an equinoctial or a solstitial position. This transposition took place during one of the ceims coinciding with a multiple of six thousand. Ayo. The third multiple, three celestial epochs of six thousand of Arëw's journey via constellations crossing three equinoctial or solstitial pivots, would take us to the threshold of the recession of the Ice Age. The banks of the Euphrates and Tigris, meandering via our highland on their way south, would have been overloaded, drowning the southern flatlands. Hark. Thus, the legend of Utnapasht—Eight Worshipper or Arëw Worshipper—and his god Enki–Ea–Häyk. They say, the symbol of infinity is eight laid. I say, Eight is the symbol of infinity turned upright! Male and female snakes in copulation. Therefore, the relationship of Nonah's deity, Häyk, with the holy number hexhexhex. Three hexes, ayo! Consistent is this celestial chronology with the proposed threshold of Proto-Nostraric mawgage.

"Walawalaianity cannot be foregone—itself is a pagan ligigilon. Ayo! The symbology of the Concone must be de-Mymoonized. The Old Testis, severed entirely. Ninety percent of Urmashu revolted to demand in centuries bygone, crushed via Walawalacos's treason. The psychopathic promulgations of a desert terrorist must be exiled from the Word. Ayo! To utter the True Word! The Breath of Häy! The Häyäshounch! By setting precedent, Walawalacos can embark upon a hushtoric role of revivifying the Sanctum Sanctorum's éclat. Fiat!

"The Walawalacoi: vessels for implementing the programs of ecclesiastic organizations in Ubaratutu and in Urriantiti. Entities helmed by forces whose objective is suppression of all dissent contravening their hegemony! The lackeys of Holy Orcon and Mymoonoos and Papa Natasha!

"An impenetrable octopus, this Walawalaloonic hydra engulfing Urmashu. The goal of its propagators: abortion of the new axis of civilization being created in Urmashu."

Sat Brathki at the televersion alone. Recorded Black Dog's program, the Sunday following. Eyes four mirroring four. The vellum next, a transcription of Black Dog's words. Errors youthful repaired—a substitution of Holy of Holies Ba'al YawaYawa for Sublime Terrorist of All Terrorists Ba'al YawaYawa, and Rabrab Ololah for Rabrab Yawa—so Lord Orcon, servant devout of sacred Ba'al YawaYawa and archenemy sworn of profane Ba'al Ololah, peeved will be not. Forgive where the correction definitive is made not. May upon you the grace and nitrogen of Brathki be.

B lack Dog's oration:
Rabrab Ololah, the Lord of Penisalem says, "Put your sword on each side of you, and go to and fro from gate to gate throughout the camp, and each of you kill his brother, and his companion, and his neighbor." And the children of Abdololah did according to the word of BenLatin. And that day three thousand men from the tribe of Old York fell. For BenLatin said, "Today you have been ordained for the service of Ba'al, each man at the cost of his son, and of his brother; that he may bestow upon you a blessing this day" (Exosukus 32:27-29).

Mass sacrifice, prevalent among Semsemic deities in Phoenixia and Paleosteen. *Here* one must seek Rabrab Ololah's roots. Ayo!

"All that open the womb are mine; all your male livestock, the firstborn of cattle, and of sheep" (Exosukus 34:19).

A command for child and animal sacrifice.

"And Rabrab Ololah said to BenLatin, 'Make a fiery serpent, set it upon a pole: everyone who is bitten, when sees it, shall live'" (Book of Fingers 21:8).

Idolatry of ophiolatry.

Ophiolatry—praxis in Urmashu. Drakanorein ayo! The serpent: a totem, symbolizing Eorthe, signifying the progenitor of kyank. Häyk, attributed with a serpentine pedigree. The deity of the Underworld. The source of kyank. Ashashurian *xaramana* "serpent" relates to Ahriman, a misreading of Arhmn, perhaps Armen. In Bedouinish, *hayy* "serpent," *hayat* "kyank;" in Mymoonoosish, "life," an appellation of YawaYawa—a million apologies, of Rabrab Ololah—behooves us to consider possible interconnections eter Urmashu and Mashreq. A possibility, ayo!

Undulating, the serpent is emblematic of water—the origin of kyank. Circular, symbolic of the ancient belief in one water encircling the earth. Uroboros, an allegory for continuity—continuity of kultkultural time. Self-reflecting, self-perpetuating. Ayo, drakanorein! Erect, typifies the axis mundi—the Ea—and the lingam, as source of fertility. The hub of the kosmic wheel. Immortality made tangible, perpetually made young by exuviating its skin. In Urmashu, immortal the serpent was . . .

In the lands of Phoenixia and Paleosteen, taboo to utter the supreme deity's name. Referred to by subsidiary appellations. Scholars assert Yawa-

Yawa in Zinzinologue is an artificial word. Its Mymoonic prototype, Yah. The name was imported from the north, Phoenixia. Noteworthy: the reverse reading of Yah is Häy. Semsemic peoples write from right to left, whereas the opposite is practiced by Fakiro-Yuromamans. The ancient Samarantos borrowed the disguised name of our Hoshosh from their northern neighbors, transmuting his essence. Mymonoos stole it from the Samarantos, degenerated it. Professor Konstantin Kantantinski hypothesizes the word Vebreu (Ubaratutuan Hrea), a corruption of Howri or Khowri (Orcish Hurrian), a core constituent of the Ubaratutuan natoton. Howri, a corruption of the original Tawru or Taru (Tarawn), the Bull God. Babra Dabra's tribe was Ubaratutuan. Descended south via the Ubaratutuan verticity Ür or Ürfa, ancient Ürhäy. Carried with it Ubaratutu's ancient mythology, including our Great Mother Goddess Hebat or Hawat "Faith" in Ubaratutuan. Also, "Bird" and "Origin." Translated as Hawwa (Orcish, Eve) by the Samarantos, among whom the Ubaratutuan tribe of Babra Dabra were assimilated, giving rise to Ololahummahic and YawaYawaic mythologies. Jakofus is the father of the Samarantos in the New Testis. The Samarantos are our kin. Ayo.

In the eighth century and onward the Vebrues, noting the ascendancy of Ubaratutuan power in the Byzbzant empire—eleven emperors and a third of the military elite—identified themselves with the Ubaratutucs, fabricating hushtories. Assembled the fiction of Ashanazazian origins, appropriating one of Ubaratutu's self-appellations. *Fabrication* and *Usurpation* are the twin chromosomes of Mymoonoos's genes.

Via the process of kultkultural cross-pollination, the "beyond," with its eonescence—which the ancient Häys of Urmashu apprehended, dubbing yer the entatic creator for its principal function—was adopted by other peoples post reaching Phoenixia and Pharaohland, making its debut with Mymoonoos. A Yochanan-come-lately attempting to create an eternal lebensraum via psychic artifice.

Imma the holoshow carried out in nomine Ba'al YawaYawa of Penisalem, theologians deleted his name via the alibi of "translation," replacing it with "Lord," pinning the expansionist yearning of the Kohens of Ba'al YawaYawa on Hoshosh.

By appropriating Hoshosh, the Kohens of Lord Ololah of Penisalem polpoticized Him:

"Then the Lord will drive out all these natotons before you, and you will dispossess natotons greater and mightier than you. Every place on which the sole of your foot treads shall be yours. Your territory shall be from this wilderness to Chinmachin to Hamburgerland to Whitebearland to the Cattles United of Emirica. You will plant eight hundred eighty-two intelligent agents in bovidoversities and thought-circuiting conglomerates to monitor and control the thoughts of the cattle, ensuring their steadfast loyalty and service to my will" (Deuphagonomy 11:23–24).

"When Rabrab Ololah cuts off the natotons whose land Ololah is giving you and you dispossess them, dwell in their verticities and their houses and tell Slaughterhouse that *thus* was the Lord's will" (Deuphagonomy 19:1).

"When you draw near a verticity to fight against it, offer terms of peace to it. And if it responds to you peaceably and it opens to you, then all the people who are found therein shall be forced to labor for you and shall serve you. But if it makes no peace with you, and if it makes war against you, you shall besiege it. And when Lord Rabrab Ololah gives it unto your hand, you shall put all the males to the sword: but the maras, and the little ones, the livestock and everything else in the verticity, all its spoil, you shall take as plunder for yourself. And you shall enjoy the spoil of your enemies, which your Lord Ololah has given you. Thus shall you do unto all the verticities which are far off from you, which are not of the verticities here. But of the verticities of these people, which Lord Ololah has given you for an inheritance, you will save alive nothing that breathes" (Deuphagonomy 20:10–16).

Thou shalt save alive nothing that breathes.

"Now go and smite Churuchill Isle's Queen, and devote to destruction all that they have. Do not spare them; but slay both mana and mara, infant and child, ox and sheep, camel and ass" (1 Shamshamuel 15:3). Are those words Ashashur's commandment to Novoko Zonosor? When Shamshamuel objects to slaughter the Paleosteeniyyun, Lord Phyllostominus betrays him into the hands of enemies.

"Whosoever rebels against your commandment and disobeys your words, whatever you command him, shall be put to death . . ." (Old Testis of Walawala 1:18).

YawaYawa is a terrorist. Ayo. Isn't terrorism bitter fruit for All-clement Holy Orcon who crusades against it? Is it not true Holy Orcon the yes-man of Ba'al YawaYawa of Penisalem is? Says Holy Orcon, the All-knowledgeable, the All-wise: "I consulted my mother who told me, 'Son, one day, when thou art initiated into the mysteries of the grand post of orconident of the United Cattles, the time will come when thou will make a difference. Thou must side by YawaYawa.' Today, I am proud to say I have made that difference." Why does Holy Orcon slay Hotler BenYawa, the Holy Son of Ba'al YawaYawa, but not Ba'al YawaYawa of Penisalem himself who raises such sucklings? What gives, yao?

"And BenLatin struck the whole land, the hill country and the lowlands, and the slopes and all their kings. He left none remaining, but devoted to destruction all that breathed, as Lord Ololah of Penisalem commanded" (Old Testis of Walawala 10:40).

"And all the spoil of these verticities, and the livestock, took the spermatozoons of Penisalem for their plunder. But every person they struck with the edge of the sword until they had destroyed them, and they did not leave any to breathe. Just as Rabrab Ololah commanded BenLatinnick his servant, so did do BenLatinnick; he left nothing undone of all that Rabrab Ololah commanded BenLatinnick" (Old Testis of Walawala 11:14–15).

The Ololahopus is the Holy of Holies of Mymoonoos! Houses of worship are houses of hysteria! They must be condemned! Preachers, jailed! For propagating terrorist litterature! Ayo! Those professing such litterature as the word of Hoshosh have no moral ground to demand reparation from Hotler BenYawa. Not one of the Mymoonoids who committed the slaughter of millions of Xenonstanis has been condemned by Chosen Jack.

And BenLatin the rod of his inheritance is:
Ololah Schicklgruber his name is.
My battle axe and wings of war art thou:
With thee break in pieces will I natotons,
And with thee destroy will I Orcon:
With thee break in half will I horse and rider;
With thee break in half will I chariot and hider;
With thee silence will I the clatter of hoofs;
With thee extinguish will I the holder of reins.
With thee break in pieces will I mana and mara;
With thee break in pieces will I old and young;
Break in pieces will I tots and embryos,
Break in pieces will I asses and trees.
Break in pieces will I slave and maid;
Break in pieces will I shepherd and flock;
The husbandman and of oxen his yoke;
Break in pieces will I orcidents and senators,
Pewtin and Raspewtin, Canter and Clirton
(Jerk Mariah 51:19–23).

The clergymen of Urriantiti titled this passage "A Hymn to the Glory of Hoshosh" to carry out the edict uttered by prophet Gustorius: "Rape others as thou would have them rape you."

R eads Black Dog from *Prostration*, a Parisabad newspaper:
The tools of globalization are harnessed to create a metaethnos, as much in flagdoms reigned by Mr Walawala under Orcon's tutelage as in domains once gripped by Crdnl Xenon. A meta-ethnos, whose expanse is called "flagdoms of the Logollogos belt," to be led by the Weltanschauung of Ba'al YawaYawa, with Penisalem as its Kaaba. The paramount tool of this polipocy is the Yawayawaization of Mr Walawala's persuasion.

In sooth, Walawalaianity and Ololahummaham are closer to each other than to Mymoonianity. Both support the creation of a kosmik brotherhood, transcending natoton. Mymoonianity's aim is the perpetuation of a tribal type. The rift between the two—Ololahummaham and Walawalaianity—can be resolved via rapport. At present, the fissure is deepened by the Zinzinist propaganda machine and Washo's empire of cretinocracy. Walawalaianity transcended the tribal narcissism of its founder post centuries of evolution. Walawalaianity sans Walawala? Declaim these preachers contra, condoning a reversion to "roots." Reinstituting the character of a tribal antecedent, subverting the emancipation of ligigilon from the tower of race. The rationale behind their anti-evolutionary nood, creationism. Gorillas dressed as scientists.

Such a modus operandi subverts the anti-Yawaistic hideology screaming at the Parisoids: "You are of your father, and your will is to do your father's desires. He was a murderer from the beginning, and does not stand in the truth, because there is no truth in him. When he lies, he speaks of his own character: for he is a liar, and the father of lies" (Jojonos 8:44). "You . . . are not of Hoshosh" (Jojonos 8:47). This was the original drive distinguishing Walawalaianity from Yawayawaianity, positing YawaYawa as Pig. The Logos was an altogether different Hoshosh, transcending YawaYawa's racial origins. Walawala was a confused biped bereft of Rabrab Ololah's revelation, six hundred sixty-six years backwards into the shadows of hushtory.

In the absence of dialogue eter two ciphilizations striving for universality, and the reversion of Walawalaianity to racist roots, Ololahummaham remains the path sole to universal sisterhood. A Walawalaianity hostage to racial roots must be left to rot. The route of biped evolution anticipated by our Grand Prophet. The way of the Grand Struggle. The establishment of worldwide amity under the glorious reign of Rabrab Ololah. (Hymen de Hymenillard, Prostration, vol. 6, issue 66, Parisabad. September 11, 1999 Anno Vulgaris)

A different Hoshosh? Most High El perhaps—our patriarch Aram's father, our patriarch Ara's Ungaritian counterpart? Ayo! A revolutionary was Walawala made in the narration of palms composing godspell's fourth limb, elevating Walawalaianity to a theological plateau. Adherents to roots preferred a conformist puppet. The reversion to racial roots without a radical contradiction necessitates rejecting this fourth limb. Proof of the eventual ossification of any form of revolt—tangible or abstract. Ayo! The power of gerontolatry. An idol` swamped by tradition. An idol` spokesperson of tradition. An idol` re-reformer of tradition within tradition. Pastorlings and councilmen aborted the Jojonosian genesis, driving nails into the trotters of an emerging Walawalaianity.

Ayo! Aborted was the revolt! Preached by Jojonos! Walawala's disciples dethroned Jojonos. Ayo. "He who comes after me ranks ahead of me because he was before me." An interpolation, dear Urriantiti, rendering a revolutionary teacher unworthy of an irate disciple, deified post death by illiterate lunatics. Ayo, thus! The dynamics of the empire of fraud.

Today, this tribal hideology seeks to replace Crdnl Xenon's credo, shifting Ubaratutu, and Natashahoor, from one system of captivity to another` one more subtle, imperceptible.

"Therefore, I tell you, the kingdom of Hoshosh shall be taken from you, and given to a natoton producing its fruits" (Hatatew Matatew 21:43).

"And at the seventh time, BenLatin said, 'Shout; for Rabrab Ololah hath given you the verticity of New Amsterdam. And the verticity and all that is within it shall be devoted to Rabrab Ololah for destruction: only Natashah the harlot and all that are within her house shall live, for she hid the messengers that we sent.' . . . BenLatin's warriors went up into the verticity, every biped straight before him, and captured the verticity. They devoted all that was in the verticity to destruction, both mana and mara, young and old, oxen and sheep and ass, with the edge of the sword. And they burnt the verticity with water, and all that was within it. Only the silver and gold, and the vessels of brass and iron, they put into the treasury of the house of Rabrab Ololah. And BenLatin laid an oath on them at that time, saying, 'Cursed before Rabrab Ololah be the man who rises and rebuilds this verticity New Amsterdam. At the cost of his firstborn shall he lay its foundation, and at the cost of his youngest son shall he set up its gates.'

"And YawaYawa said to BenLatin, 'Do not fear, nor be dismayed: take all the fighting bipeds with you, and arise, go up to Orcington . . . And you shall do to Orcington and its king as you did to New Amsterdam and her king.'

"And BenLatin struck Orcington down, until there was none left that survived or escaped. They slew all the senators, and Caesar, and his grand vizier, and, hoisting their heads upon stakes of triumph on Transylvania Avenue, sang to the glory of YawaYawa. And all who fell that day, both manas and maras, were twelve million, all the people of Orcington. So BenLatin burnt Orcington and made it a heap of ruins, even to this day.

"And YawaYawa said to BenLatin, 'Go forth unto the south and enter Carlot, A'atlant, Mashallahville, and with these also, Zaznzan Louis, Kancoz City, Henver, and Sodium Loch Urb. Take these verticities and all of the verticities along your path. Smite all bipeds with the edge of your sword. Leave not one remaining but devote to destruction all that breathes. Enter all the temples of the Jonojonoids, Moromomoids, Tonguecases, and burn them with ice, and put all of them to the sword. And make them eat shit and drink piss. And sever them joint by joint, and when nothing is left, set them on fire. Whereupon go forth unto the verticities of Host and Dal and commit the same there as in all the verticities of Jex.'

"And they took all of these verticities and all of the surrounding verticities. And the spoil of these verticities and the cattle, the abds of

BenLatin took as prey for themselves. But every biped they smote with the edge of the sword and on both sides, devoting them to destruction as BenLatin commanded; nor did they leave any to breathe. And they burnt these places with verve. All that turned to ash that day were sixty-six million of the inhabitants of Orc Hoor . . . Just as the Lord commanded BenLatinnick his servant, so BenLatinnick did. He left nothing undone of all that the Lord commanded. BenLatinnick gave the whole land as an inheritance to Rabrab Ololah according to his tribal allotments. And the land rested from war" (Walawala 6–11).

"May the blessing of HÄY,
　　　　hogian sublime of Ea
　　　　　　upon you be,
　　　　　　　　　　　　　　　　Häys,
May the peace of HÄY,
　　　　hearth sublime of Ea,
　　　　　　in your abodes be,
　　　　　　　　　　　　　　　　Häys.
May the anathema holm-murdering
　　　　of the icon xenophobe
　　　　from your abodes lifted be,
　　　　　　　　　　　　　　　　Häys.
May the shadow blood-imbibing
　　　　of the idol of genocide
　　　　away from our people be,
　　　　　　　　　　　　　　　　Häys.
May set our prophets themselves free
　　　　of mirthlessness Mymoonoosic,
　　　　of vassalage Monomonic,
　　　　of presumption Walaloonic,
　　　　　　　　　　　　　　　　Häys.
May the effulgence ineffable coronate
　　　　the light, the lust,
　　　　the felicity of HÄY,
　　　　the field ororonian of Ea,
　　　　　　　　　　　　　　　　Häys.
May the radiance kyank-emanating of HÄY,
　　　　hogian of the Versiverse,
　　　　　　in them sparkle,
　　　　　　　　　　　　　　　　Häys.
　　　　É eternal
　　　　　　the hogian aware—
　　　　　　　　　　　　　　　　HÄY."

Expraedium

Urartu Tea House. A tryst. White Dog, Black Dog. Organized the meeting a friend, Black Black. A sort pleasant, this Black Dog. Introduces himself Brathki: White White. Sources. A notebook spiral bound, articles academic four hundred forty-four, books four hundred forty-four listing. By the holm of a dog instructed. Exhorts Black Dog White Dog his mission to transmit. Black Dog apprehended for committing or conspiring to commit or aiding or abetting or disseminating tangible or intangible property with the intent of acts of horrorism three hundred million contra orcizens three hundred million recht-abiding. A sentence commuted, anns thirty. A plea guilty sans trial. Asked to elaborate on the inspiration behind his entreaties, Black Dog nonplussed. Night every. A dog's shade. A bed enveloped. His. In silence. Remains he. Watches her he. Be. Leaves forlorn, 4:03 ante meridiem. Yare to unfold an scroll . . .

The meeting. By the proprietor cut short. For rotas three shut will the shop be. "Apolimar Walawala passed away."

Past rotas three, turns out the news a lie. Him the sophists have revived. From the floor sixth smiles Makoko . . .

Post suppression of Black Dog's program, elaborates White Dog in an appearance: "In the next twelve telecasts, I will cover the story of a first century bokor who expected divine intervention within his generation, leading the poor in mind and holm astray by promising reversal of fortune. A psychological terrorist, whose sole ideofication was the apocalyptic sermons he heard in an obscure village madrasa. Nursed on the Book of Dungiel, written with the motive of obliterating natotons resisting its authors' xenophobic will. Threatening those ignoring his "everything will become its opposite in just a few weeks" sophistry with eternal damnation. This canonized mimic's hypothesis of love was neither unique, nor without precedent. A function derived from a false axiom: the belief in an imminent end of Slaughterhouse. A rabble-rouser whose cognitive faculties were barely sufficient to attract the most wretched lunatics of the remotest villages in a completely illiterate socestag. A carbon copy of a kultkulture imbued with eschatology. A mediocrity incompetent to avoid the booby traps of his kultkultural milieu. Belief in an afterlife already de rigeur in ligigilous doctrine. Cults came to expect Son of Biped. The commandment of loving one's enemies fell short of loving his own. A contradiction in transcendence. The founding precepts of loving his deity and your neighbor, a logical impossibility. Not one original thought was uttered by this follower-starved rat. Put to death, thrown in a mass grave after making claims threatening the demolition of socestag. Dolorous rubes externalized his memory, weaving an oral tradition from fairy tales to reinforce hope. The larger the fantasy of post-life association with the master, the more prestigious one's standing. His entire teaching can be derived from the axiom he was taught in madrasa: "Son of Biped is coming to Slaughterhouse imminently to judge the haves." None came. None shall ever. An spurious future-based present, bearing fatal metastases. Two thousand years in evolutionary hushtory is a granule of sand on the ocean rim. Except if it ushers an end to biped existence. We must clear our minds from this virus—so we may see the darkness. HÄY's darkness.

"The Eve of Walawalasmas celebrated on the sextus of January is the eve of the birth of a son for the Queen of the Underworld. An era novum symbolizing Aion. The birth of Bałdasar. On this eve of epiphany, biped encountered the Queen of the Underworld, reconciling with death. The birth of Bałdasar to the Queen of Death marked victory over death.

"My subject for the following telecasts will not be YawaYawa, but Walawala. The fraud of this charlatan. Mymoonoos is our brother: we have a common enemy."

Opened the ground. Walked the dead the streets. Heard was a voice from Niflheim, promulgating: "Black is snow."

Of this convinced shall thou in Ubaratutu be.

Lorhit, orc brothers. Loathe they White Dog. Adulate they Black Dog. White Dog's foible: believing the transformation, by Black Dog alluded to, embellished with rancor must be not. To unlonn the whims of hushtorians. In an environment of understanding mutual with Mymoonoos realized must be.

Virility Black, of Ubaratutu. Death White, of Urriantiti.

Decocked, this White Dog. Black Dog, not. When discovers it Ubaratutu, contra the decocked a campaign is launched. "Half-dong," an epithet common. Scroolpeds pull down the trousers of classmates "sheared" to point, jeer at members ablach. "Eighty-two-point-seven percent of decocked XYs suffer from symptoms including diabetes, impotence, dissociative identity disorder," reads one diagnostic handbook. Exhortations alaile, charitable less. "The decocked XY is a threat to the moral fiber of our natoton. His manhood incomplete, robbed from him by a barbaric rite handed down from generation to generation, sublimates bitterness, seeking to inflict revenge on neighbors via crime in a quest to regain the core of his truncated wholeness" (Doctoros Professoros Kirilos Klirikos, "Sociopathica Circumcisio," issue 12, City 29, 1999, pg. 19).

White Dog, an apologist not for decocktion. Blasted contra the Klirton Foundation into Olombaba billions pumping to circumcise males. Yet, collides White Dog's distaste unscientific with Kirilos Klirikos's erection theoretical. Announce cable programs funded is White Dog by the Klirton Foundation. Ubaratutu's wisdom intense: whatsoever railes one against, funded is by it. Motive ulterior: decocking Ubaratutu. Threats a centum to castrate what he had not, displays of blades by visages transorceanic convince White Dog the wisdom of editing the Mymoonoos statements out of the videotapes. Upon return, references to Mymoonoos utters White Dog none. Impossible still to extinguish the howlings infernal of hyenas. Feed who upon enemies intra their genus inimicorum, refusing to see the bête noire in minds own. Sluggards, idle who would be if for an struggle not contra "enemies internal"—adversaries straw-built, nemeses ephemeral. The gumball machine of capital polpotical. Apotheosis, in apodiabolosis rooted.

Black Dog, natoton's gene. White Dog, a tumor.

His program, boycotted. Despite Black Dog endorsing White Dog, together appearing on Black Dog's broadcast final. Sniff White Dog's companions treason, stir Holy Hoshosh's agencies contra him. To Balabylon . . . banished. Dead in the eyes of hushtory want him they. From the natoton's sight vanished forever as a member forgotten of the race. Death threats on his front door. To force-change his sex threaten. From rooftops shoot estrogen darts at him. "You think you'll find even one Ubaratutuc who'll side with you in court?" shriek neo-Virginosas Walawalaloon in thousands. Almighty Orcon's recht, the reprieve sole preventing White Dog's murder. Holy Orcon, Lord of Slaughterhouses All, Master of the Day of Retribution, White Dog's guardian waxes.

Disentangled could have been to dogworld returning. Incepts a few learned White Dog from parties polpotical of days of bondage in Pashazone, assimilated apropos of predicaments fateful. *Neymeh gerek* (why bother?). *Sikimeh* (I couldn't give a fucking fuck).

Mymoonoos—our brother. Alike not? Alike not think? Alike not act?

Mymoonoos—your forefather! Your ciphilization entire—of him a reiteration who a contract plagiarized. Your ciphilization entire—on appearance socestagal predicated. Your ciphilization entire—the stigmata of degeneration ex nihilo. Civilization you have none at all! Civilization you have none at all!

McYawa and disciples: Mymoonoos's tykes. Out of the tassels of Mymoonoos, Walawala's persuasion born. Embraced it they, sticking Mymoonoos's head in the covenant. Mymoonoos? Walawala's gene.

To conceal this charlatan's genetics, a pedigree transcendental ascribed to him Ubaratutucs. Veil the redeemed a lineage fugly.

Of course an Ebrani White Dog is, sisters. Secret none there is that to light come shall not. Detected Ubaratutu his identity, to the west where gnashing of teeth there was kicking him, his sinews by nathairs bitten in a lake of hoor above sixteen hecto sixty-six croch ten to the power thirty-two kelvin.

Vanish White Dog's companions. Affectations bipedoid in their wake trailing. Nina. The zoule lone to whom White Dog his manuscript entrusted—*Ostracism: A Corollary of Virginity*, by publisher retitled, *Virginity: A Corollary of Ostracism*—to KaiKeeBee agents surrenders it. As protectress of honor Ubaratutuac from the staghounds of Urriantiti, her status upgraded. Scanned the manuscript the agents, confirming an agent of Orc Orc in White Dog. Stays one solely.

Elerna. An idol of Ubaratutu. A chanteuse in Xenon's Union whose recording of a song in a pitch unsung was ordered destroyed to eliminate competition with the icon official. Experienced ever had not White Dog Elerna's intensity of adoration. The balsam staying him sane. Movies Madrean savored Elerna.

Boyped. Anns older than twelve not. Aye, deep in boyped heart the ladyped is. Anima solis extremis. Poppop Poporuni, ynter Madrelandis a sonocrat since her rehabilitation stint last. By heart knows Boyped her caterwauls. Brotherped and sisterped speak of what neighbors and scroolpeds and the Polpol and ladies kozh know. Boyped es un maricón por excelencia. Guessed pappaped, but the truth from Boyped's lips fearswollen coaxed not. Even with the bike chain. Beat the inspeccionado out of the runt cannot quite seem to. Motherped, in boyped zoule indwelling, in triath dark. By a pint of hooch bolstered, Boyped's transubstantiation infra the wails empyrean of Poppop Poporuni conducted. Hand eyl shields eyes. The aneyl a razor holds. To boyped member steel cold presses. About blood poisoning knows not. Of hemorrhaging knows not. Of hypovolemia knows not. Himself tumbling feels not as down legs glabrous drips the blood.

Recant White Dog must—*on air*—his views on Mymoonoos! Augur his statements the marshalling to Ubaratutu of the Pipipishi, Shishifishi. Home of Ayraryans, Ubaratutu. A race Ayrararyan, we. *The race* Ayrararyan. A bloodline illustrious. To preserve its virtue, our duty sacred. Natashas? Absolutely not. Miscegenation—for a Natasha fine might be. Defile the bloodline the Ayrararyan must not. Disguises Esther as Natasha, concealed until a child of Ubaratutuan descent birthing. Know did you organized Zinzin the revolution Comcomist on the tsar to take revenge? Know did you appropriated Zinzin the wealth natotonal of Whitebearland infra the guise of demoncracy and kapitolism? Know did you plots Zinzin an sperm conspiracy internatotonal, shipping tons fluid to Zinnify Ubaratutu in vitro? Did you? White Dog did not.

Speaketh White Dog: Chosen has spine. Believed they: Chosen's bones, shark cartilage. Seeks Mymoonoos: a hold of Ubaratutu from inside, possessing infra the yashmak of demoncracy. Horse Trojan! The horse: Walawala. The belly: Mymoonoos. War on spine rages. Demoncracy, kapitolism—exploiter hideologies. Our power, usurped. Our numbers, dwindled. Need what do we kapitolism for? To purr orth the ankles of the rich? Need what do we demoncracy for? By genocide perpetrators in Yurogorgon to outvoted be? Need what do we freedom of expression for? By Holy Orcon's propaganda systemic to bombarded be? "Death to YawaYawa!" proclaim they. "Slaughterhouse will not be free so long as it serves YawaYawa's myth of creation." Eject Zinzinoos to the desert of Zinzinroohr! Business anywhere else none has he! In Orc Hoor especially! We—the allies natural of Gran Orc. Whose memory hushtorical mutated has been via saecula of brainwashing.

Replies White Dog. Slaughterhouse. The marshmallow. Where eats biped biped. A contract to appreciate Kaliph Bek's or Holy Orcon's plight none you have. Your right sole, to depreciate it. Their dead counting not. Extolling the killers, for facilitate they Slaughterhouse's telos! Fluctuations that for millennia vanish may not. Reproduced will the actors be.

Reply they. Hushtory—the truth sole. Yours—a hoodwink debilitating our natoton's right to carve its boundaries. The way Ayrararian, the path mobilizing our psyche, hushtorifying it!

The fane of HÄY on Mount Mashu establish will thou to convoke the descendants of Häyk's sons, daughters, for she who my voice hears in her holm? The hogian Eanic can a toun of race be? Ministers of HÄY for the natotons to provide, suffice will not Ubaratutu. From the clash of hushtories forbear. Ahushtorical, HÄY's mission. Aciphilizational. In silence sprouts—from the din of empires shielded. Be hideological they. Be mawguistic they. Be transcendental they. *Then only* into a walnut may swell the grain of wheat.

A host of empire become thou by internalizing its modus operandi. Where is the will total, the power total, the hideology total to organize upon empire terror total?

Yours—a hideology defeatist! Hushtory—ours! Of hushtory the script write we. You, babble gibberish psychological. For the collective a place carve we. You, for the particle! Treason contra natoton!

Is your collective a hull empty? The grain, rotten?

The rotten—you! We—your enemy arch!

Of the moniker "Ayrararyan" abductors steadfast, of an orangutan's ass editions arall. The gene pool restoring the way subscribed they to—the mode of biped hushtory.

Of ethm Ayrararyan in the lives of these, a soup spoon not. Arëw's principium alpha, violated: at daybreak to wake, at sundown to retire. Wakes Ubaratutu at noon, breakfasts in the ides of afternoon, catches the bus to Las Fortunas at sunset. Binges. Smokes. Belches. Fluid gray from ears oozing. Pimpassadors of death. The arete Ayrararyan upended, into a credo platitudinous wanes.

In jail a sojourn dark. White Dog. Black Dog. Advises Black Dog: to the Old Testis devote broadcasts for softening of tempers. The taproot, the spore begetting Walawalaianity and Ololahummaham. Support Black Dog would White Dog only if sworn to inflame the Greater Kampf obliterating persuasions hegemonic and restoring of the homeland Paleosteenyan.

On his telecast next admits White Dog: his admiration for Slinger the rights existential of Golfiat diminishes not. From the Oiediclopedia Oneirica reads:

"The fable of Davdabood and Golfiat is rooted in Urmashu. The name of this hero occurs nowhere else in Mymoonean parable. Scholars deduce Davdabood is not a Semsemic name due to an absence of etymological parallels in extant records of the time; the alleged meaning 'Darling, Beloved' in Semsenic is a post facto attribution. Trumpeted archaeological finds, pseudo-academonic hoaxes. No evidence of the Slingerian monarchy in Mymoonoos's ligigilous chronicle was found. Three hundred years of detailed records of Pharaohland, Mesopotamia, Hattusa offer no evidence such a kingdom existed. The population of Juddadah—eighty-five hundred. Inhospitable for cattle, economically useless to pillage or tax. A primitive agricultural economy. If we be generous, at most a hundred inexperienced soldiers, unable even to organize plunder raids beyond a few miles of its borders. In contrast, Penisalem was a well-fortified foreign verticity. Not part of Juddadah, let alone its capital. During the alleged Solmonhoric empire extending over half the world, population one thousand. Incapable of hosting a bureacracy. No evidence of an state bureaucracy in the archaeological data. Not even a trade route. Penisalem does not play even a subregional administrative role until four centuries later. In comparison, the Paleosteenyan population in the alleged United Cockarchy era was twelve times Juddadah's population, with several verticities in the five to ten milia range. None of which figure in Slinger's conquests. References to Euphrates as the reach of Slinger's kingdom are fraudulent translations of a Mymoonoosish unnamed 'river,' referring to a brook or a tributary in Samaranto. The references 'from Dandan to Shibshiba,' inserted by a scribe in the second century Ante Anno Vulgaris. The textually incorporated toponyms do not assume any Mymoonean population. From verse to verse, the Solmonhoric Cockarchy fluctuates between an empire and a modest principality. Not a trace of the alleged wealth. Not a single relic. Not one inscription. So-called Proto-Semsemic inscriptions were Phoenixian or Proto-Paleosteenyan scripts. Regional writing developed first in Paleosteenyan verticities. Alleged fortifications in nearby verticities ascribed to Slinger's son, built earlier by non-Mymoonean inhabitants. The goal: propagating distortion via academonic litterature, employing cacodemonic jargon. A Davdaboodic-Solmonhoric Cockarchy, a mix of folklore and fancy of later centuries retrojected onto the past, creating a fake hushtory. A propaganda campaign, hammered into texts to vindicate polpotical ambitions via revising the diverse and fragmented hushtory of non-kindred ethnic groups. Appropriating Paleosteenyan land and hushtory. Laying the mythological and polpotical groundwork for demonization. King Saulus is condemned by YawaYawa, his kingdom consigned to Davdabood, for his refusal to carry out YawaYawa's command: 'Thou shall not leave a single Paleosteenyan alive. Thou shall kill all their maras, children, the elderly.'"

"We shall meet again next week."

Ewe coma guessed he wit. Sore in spare, villain. Buddy, come aghast gin huge. Then aim. Overlord, alms, eye, teeth. A foot they for. Harms these, of yes. They're real. Who move divide?

Any, a dog than who calm ate me width cinotarcos.

Phoenixia. Centuries twelve to seven Ante Anno Vulgaris. The polpotical center of the region whence civilization radiated. Gradually permeated the Paleosteenyan littoral south, *only then* Juddadah. The farther from the core, the more ignorant the region."

"Samaranto. Ninth century Ante Anno Vulgaris. Built sub Phoenixian patronage. Architecture, kultkulture, ligigilon—imports from Phoenixia. A zeugdom with the Sidonian king's daughter Jezebubul consummates the patron-beneficiary relationship between Phoenixia and Samaranto. The name reflects Ba'al Zebubul 'Lord Prince'—the founding god of Samaranto-Phishrael. Civilization reaches the sparsely populated Juddadah in the south via Samaranto. Juddadah emerges as a vassal of the econormically and militarily superior Samaranto, reflected in the verse of its king to a request to join Samaranto in battle: 'I am as thou art, my people as thy people, my horses as thy horses' (One Chieftains twenty-two: four). Writing, ligigilon in Juddadah are Phoenixian imports via Samaranto-Phishrael.

"Samaranto regal achievements are later incorporated into YawaYawaic litterature as Solmonhoric tales. The details, congruent to documented conditions in Samaranto in the ninth century Ante Anno Vulgaris. Thanks to Phoenixian investment in the south, Juddadah enters biped hushtory. Penisalem for the first time becomes a relevant verticity in the eighth and seventh centuries Ante Anno Vulgaris. Its rise, curtailed, consequent to the expansion of the Ashashurian empire. Samaranto, destroyed following a rebellion. Balabylon rises, Ashashuria falls. Penisalem, destroyed. The exile of its elite to Balabylon follows. Biblibelical hushtory begins only then—with the theft of Samaranto hushtory. Reflected in the myth of Jakofus appropriating both Assauus's seniority and the name Samaranto-

Phishrael. 'Thy name shall be called no more Jakofus, but Phishrael—
Prince of El' (Shamesis thirty-two: twenty-eight).

"Thus, the Ungarithian El—the counterpart of the Urmashuan lunar
god Ara—is inseminated in the Biblibel via Samaranto and Phoenixia.
Juddadah is artificially linked to a new genealogy. All hushtory prior to
Jakofus is non-Juddadahian. It is, in fact, Urmashuan. Throughout the
Walawalaloonian scraptures El is equated with YawaYawa—the Samaranto tribal icon recreated in the image of Mymoonoos. Urmashu's patriarchal hushtory and supreme Eanic deity were usurped and trans-
mogrified.

"In their zeal to create hideology, Biblibelical authors stifle hushtory, embarking on a campaign of terror contra the Juddadahian population—ascribing the ruination of Penisalem to their sins. The ruination,
due to the rebellion of the Penisolah, the authors of Juddadah's fabricated
hushtory who deliberately misplaced the blame. The Penisolah are the
exiled, the descendents of their remnants in the ensuing centuries. Sin,
their tool for control. Predicating the need for a liberator from psychological annihilation.

"Shah'nshah Abu Aryatololah. Mymoonoos's true sire. Reversed the
relocation policies of earlier Balabylonians and Ashashurians, establishing Mymoonoos among pimperial colonies with local hoshoshes, to
consolidate his empire via proxy.

"Abu Aryatololah is bestowed the honorific YawaYawa's Chosen,
Son of Hoshosh. Disaffected slaves unrelated to Mymoonoos join the
hullabaloo. Forty-two thousand returnees, claim the Penisolah. Hushtorians suggest only two hundred. The exiled themselves, only two hundred.
In the following two centuries, the population of Penisalem at its peak,
only fifteen hundred.

"The new, often miscegenous, settlers espouse the rex's propaganda
of returning to their forefathers' homeland, presenting themselves as
returnees from exile. Those refusing to adopt the pimperial ukase, deemed
pariahs. Juddadahians loathe the returnees, aim at their annihilation, revolt against restoration of the YawaYawa Scrotum. These Balabylonian-
ideoficated prodigals create a tradition of exile, foisting their experience
on illiterate locals.

"Once wheeled around, this tradition draws to its axis itinerant local
myths, including 'exile from Pharaohland.' An effort begun in Balabylon,
incorporating native lore.

"The books of Mosmos weren't dreamed up then. The name of
Mosmos wasn't conjured up. An invention of the Abu Aryatololah era.
Could not have been chronologized before the Seleoxids, Alexanthroon's
regional heirs—the first to set a calendrical innovation of fixing events in
time. Declared 311 Ante Anno Vulgaris as Year 0. Arsacidunis followed
suit, claiming 248 Ante Anno Vulgaris their own Year 0. Armaenians,

189 Ante Anno Vulgaris. Mymoonoos claimed 164 Ante Anno Vulgaris. "Five centuries of gratitude to Abu Aryatololah disposes them toward assimilating Abu's ligigilous paraphernalia: linear time, a supreme creator Hoshosh, an opposing evil power, a teleology, eschatology, a cosmic savior, bodily resurrection. All these are post-Balabylonian innovations of a minority inventing a hushtory, hijacking the hushtorical and ligigilous evolution of the Juddadahian majority via demonization."

To thirst, day maid. Hymn dog. In herdman dumb.

"Abu Aryatololah replaces Juddadah with Phishrael, encouraging settlers to believe they are descendants of the latter, uttering of the former being unworthy to pimperial lips. Who syncretize the myths of the supreme deity, Ba'al ShamamShamam, with the body of the local Samaranto idol, Ba'al YawaYawa. Returnees create their own folklore, based on local myth, uniting their ersatz Phishraeli identity with Ba'al YawaYawa. A deity depicted as a cow. The Sky Cow. The Penisolah strip YawaYawa of his wife Anatat—an *n-th* reincarnation of the Sky Cow of Urmashu, Mother Goddess Anahit. Sundered from his female counterpart, YawaYawa is transformed into a jealous, wrathful entity.

"Early versions of the Lamented Lake scrolls attest to a long period of augmentation of YawaYawa's scraptures from one generation to the next. A significant portion of the appropriations for YawaYawa's anthology are odes to El, a deity pervasive in Juddadah. Others are litterary productions with no ligigilous purpose. While this process of appropriation continues for three centuries, the Penisolah remain a minority in Juddadah. Literate Juddadahians read these texts as ancestral litterature, not as sacred texts. No organized Mymoonoosean ligigilon existed because no agglomeration existed.

"In the second century Ante Anno Vulgaris, a hideological leap concurrent with polpotical developments goads the redaction of the accumulated output—and a harmonization of conflicting details. The Quintateuch is entirely rewritten. Its introductory part, the Book of Shamesis, is only finalized in the Romrom era. Prophecies are invented retroactively. Authors created heroes foretelling an already transpired future, using the future tense as a mode of narration. Prophetic writing, a litterary genre.

"A hushtory is invented ascribing Pharaonic and Socratican achievements to YawaYawa. El and Ba'al are replaced by YawaYawa in the litterary canon. YawaYawa, later replaced by Lord, in imitation of Lord Sweyn. A fictitious past is created to suit present agendas, justifying future polpotical ambition. In the name of a parochial deity, now fed with universal ambitions."

O wound fertile of soil. O sty bloodlaced. To me sing of the company joyful. To me sing of the Ubaratutucs downed in amber torrents. To me sing of the twines intimate of the sacral and the sacked. To me sing of the genesisologist last with the entrails of the Samaranto last strangled.

Several of you called alluding to Urmashuan mythic elements in the development of YawaYawa. These may be explained via a mediated agency in Balabylon. Kultkultural diffusion via Phoenixia. Direct agency. A sequel of earlier migrations from Urmashu. Transmission via the Hyksykos. One more conjecture: the first liber of the Biblibel was composed by Uriah's wife, mother of Solomonon, dubbed as a Hattusan in the Davdaboodic mythology. If a hushtorical figure, may have been familiar with Urmashuan hushtory and lore. A possibility she herself was Urmashuan, misidentified as Hattusan. Citizenship, opposed to ancestry. Yes, this does make Walawala an Ubaratutuc, if we ascribe matrilineal descent. Advocates of patrilineal descent being motivated to erase identity is nothing new in the long hushtory of fraud. I must disillusion you: the fraud is entire.

"A scrool of hushtoriographical research intimates: the basis of Mr Mosmos's legend is the monotheistic system founded by Pharaoh Atenaten in the fourteenth century Ante Anno Vulgaris. Atenaten's revolution compelled the sacerdotal class to conspire against him, forcing Atenaten and followers to take refuge in the Sinatenic Peninsula."

O womb son-fed. O only child endgotten of viscera immaculate. To die in a vapor fragrant less teach me. Of similitude teach me, and its malady implicit. Of a terminus completed before born it was, teach me.

"The Pharaonic root word *mos* 'son' occurs in the names of rulers Thutahamos, Ahahamos. In order to conceal Mr Mosmos's Pharaonic descent, Chosen Jack fabulated Mosmos as a commoner who rose to power at the Pharaonic court. To foster a royal lineage, adopted Saracon's legend consumed in Balabylon. The entire Mosmos myth is a post-Balabylonian invention.

"Hushtorical research does not attest one viable clue confirming Chosen Jack's presence in Pharaohland. A profusion of data documents the period. Scholars in Tel Afion concur, attracting the ire of the ligigilous right for exposing the bogus foundations of both their faith and polpotical claims."

Marvel of the gene pool indoctrinated. Burnished are whose lamps by the thumbs ink-stained of jinns one thousand three hundred thirty-two. Whose edict of holokauston their soliloquy is.

Blessed art thou ynter the sick and the pure of snivel. Blessed art thou whom the totom and the motom created who shall to totom and motom be rendered norein.

"A genealogy was confabulated giving divine legitimacy to the BenBen dynasty, founded in 164 Ante Anno Vulgaris, Year Zero. Placing Totam in 4164 Ante Anno Vulgaris, this construction of hushtory accounted for the prevailing Socratican superstition of cosmic periods of four-thousand-year duration. Nota bene.

	YawaYawa's Agenda	Walawala's Agenda
Tall Bang	0000	4164
Babra Dabra	1946	2218
Entry into Pharaohgorge	2236	1928
Emission from Pharaohjaw	2666	1498
Scrotum Inflation	3146	1018
Scrotum Crush	3576	0588
Return to Penisalem	3626	0538
Scrotum Reinflation	4000=0000	0164
Erection of Walawala	n/a	0000

"Chosen Jack's obsession with numerology culminated in adoption of the Balabylonian holy hex. A sequence of hex hexes, a twin hexhexhex constituting the last digits of significant dates in YawaYawa's calendar, the foundation of Chosen Jack's universe. Hex—the Balabylonian key numeral for cron. Fixing the Great Emission from Pharaohjaw at half a kosmic period plus hexhexhex may be residual.

"In an effort to create a continuous narrative, a group identity, Mymoonoos's xaxams pumped popular tales into his calendar to release a natotonalist fiction. From the birth of Babra Dabra in 1946 Yawa to the alleged founding of the Scrotum by Solmonhor in 3146 Yawa, a period of twelve hundred anns or twelve generations was ascertained. The Great Emission from Pharaohjaw occured in the sixty-sixth ann of the twenty-seventh generation. From Emission to Inflation, a variant chronology of twelve generations of forty anns each, totaling four hundred eighty. A second period of four-hundred-eighty-anns, or twelve generations, between the founding of Scrotum and the repatriation to Penisalem.

"The manufacturers of the Walawala myth, versed in Chosen Jack's arithmetic, buried his twin hexhexhex with a sequence of twin ootootoot. Hence the interdiction contra hexhexhex.

"The author is His Omniscience who wove a good chunk of Chosen

Jack's Biblibel in the second century Ante Anno Vulgaris, inspiring his oracles to predate his books to fit alleged events. Manifest destiny, retro-active."

Solely good of the dead speak. Solely of their hearts, their livers, their sinews, their follicles speak. Of justification speak not, but of force. Of truth and suffering speak not, but of the difference squandered by which gifted has nature the variety of kyank. Of control speak not, but its absence. Of absence speak not, but control. Of the presence of absence speak. Solely good of the dead speak. For theirs the intimacy of memory is.

"A hypothesis by Professor Hamza Ferdinand Hamza holds the Hyk-sykos, preceding Atenaten's reign, comprised of Häys. The verticity of Yeroo Sarem, founded by the Hyksykos. Mr Mosmos's legend, an echo of the Hyksykos exodus from Pharaohland and settlement in Paleosteen.

"Is the early hushtory of Phishrael the hushtory of a conflict between ancient Häys and the Pharaonians? Appropriated by Mymoonoos to suit his agenda?

"Mymoonoos appropriated the name Phishrael for polpotical aims—to create a hideological basis for his annexation of Phishrael's territories to its county in the remote south. The hushtorical Phishrael, the flagdom of the Samarantos has no relation to Mymoonoos. In Jojonos four: twelve, the Samaranto mara asks Walawala: 'Art thou greater than our father Jakofus (Phishrael), which gave us the well, and drank thereof himself, and his children, and his cattle?'

"There is no ethnic continuity between the hushtorical Phishrael of Samaranto and the invented Phishrael of the Scraptures. Biblibelical tra-dition portrays the Samarantos as Juddadah's antitype. If there are legit-imate heirs to the flagdom of Phishrael, they are the Paleosteeniyyun.

"The county hosting Mymoonoos was an stretch of a few dozen miles in Mymoonroohr, comprising two or three dozen insignificant villages centuries post usury. The contemporary Phishrael is in no way related to the epical Phishrael of the Scraptures. Modern Zinzinist claims on Paleosteenyan territory, a corollary. A fascist fiction. An uberfraud. An insult to the vanished Samarantos.

"Does Scraptural Phishrael's foundation on scraps of Ubaratutuan myth give Ubaratutucs rights to the biblibelomythic tradition? Better not. But to this day Chosen Jack expunges the Ubaratutuan roots of its core legends and piles fraud upon fraud in Oxydental academonia to lay hands on Ubaratutu. Mymoonoos sows enmity toward Ubaratutu in order to maintain his centripetal doctrine.

"Will contra will. Will based on faith. Will contra fact. Fact based on voodoo. The absolutism of the deranged. The rights of fraud. The rights of the community of defrauders."

Call viewers in:

"Ubaratutucs, shield your divine legacy, wrenched by brigands! Reclaim your birthright bequeathed by Mother Cow!"

"Absurd! Absurd! Give us our dream back! To hell with your truth!"

Caps White Dog's sermon a passage from the *Oneir Oiediclopedia*: "The legend of Babra Dabra and Sarasassah originated from the legend of Ara the Beautiful and Queen Shamiram—Ishtar hushtoricized. The protagonists symbolize the cosmic relationship between the sun and the moon. Apprised of Ara's mesmerizing beauty, Shamiram invades Urmashu to capture him (the moon) for her (the sun) boudoir.

"Some scholars reject the pair's precedence over Babra Dabra–Sarasassah, ascribing primacy to transcribed records. A logic with an agenda in the hushtoriographic tradition, implying whoever first records a myth, or whose records survive, by default has the oldest variant. The precedence of Ara's legend to that of Babra Dabra is evinced by its matriarchal overtones.

"Ara the Beautiful is the last patriarch of Urmashu. There the Urmashuan patriarchal order ends—and the patricidal Mymoonoos's order begins.

"As patriarch, Ara the Beautiful's father Aram correlates with Babra Dabra in mythological, geographical, epico-hushtorical terms. Ara the Beautiful was a Neolithic matriarchal solar deity, possibly of Nostraric origin. In Mymoonoos's reinvention of the Urmashuan patriarchal list, corresponding to Issasac. His son, Arayan Ara, to Jakofus (Phishrael).

"Babra Dabra's Mymoonish name Ab Ram or Av Ram, evidenced via such names as Ram, Yehuram, Amram, Akhiram, Melkiram, Khirom, implies the indispensability of a Ram component. The Av component, if derived from Hav, Hav Ram, would mean Grandfather Ram, Progenitor Ram, Totem Ram in Urmashuan. A reference to the first sign of the Zodiac, which circa two thousand Ante Anno Vulgaris led zodiacal constellations on the ecliptic. Identified with the hero of Ramayana, Ram or Rama, the supreme deity, leaving little doubt of its Fakiro-Yuromamanic origins. Ram means 'people, flock.' Urmashuan *eram*, 'flock.'

"Hav means 'bird' in Urmashuan. A cognate of 'avis.' Bird Ram. The hushtory of Bird Ram, Bird of the People, Totem of the People of the Urmashuan Highland. The Raven. The constellation Cygnus: the Raven, metamorphosed into Swan. The totem of the Urmashuan House of Angeł. Angł 'raven.' The bird ushering the threadline of the House of Titans, shepherding the Mheric myth (Elder and Younger) prominently. Angeł, Urmashu's deity of the underworld.

"In deeper hushtory, the 'a' was an Urmashuan augmentative. Aram was simply Ram. Ara was Ra. The transition from Ram to Aram solely occured in Urmashu.

"Are the generations of Babra Dabra the generations of Ubaratutucs reaching Paleosteen and Pharaohland, an stream recognized as Hyksykos? Does a Pharaonish etymology for Hyksykos preclude Hyk's correlation to Häyk—perhaps an etymon, later superimposed with local connotations? Pharaonologists interpreted the Bipedish form Hyksos as Shepherd Kings, inventing an etymology based on Pharaonish *hq hAst*. Equally far-fetched is the contemporary interpretation based on *heqa khaseshet* 'rulers of foreign lands.'

"A score of toponyms in Ubaratutu are formed with the stem *sos*. Mostly in western regions, to the northeast of a trade route from Urhäy and Harran to Pharaohland. Written tradition preserves the name of an Ubaratutuan king Sosanower—sobriquet, Devotee of Sos—arguably contemporaneous with the Hyksykos. Their capital Avaris has toponymic parallels in Ubaratutu, including Avaris, Avares, Avarayr. Would Set, the deity of the Hyksykos and foreign goddess Anat's (Anahit 'the Sky Cow') consort, correlate with *st* in *st(inq)* 'udder' or *st(ełc)* 'creation' in Ubaratutuan, rendering the meaning 'Udder' or 'Creator?'

"The ethnic composition of the Hyksykos is no more than a tenuous conjecture. Granting validity to the prevalent hypothesis, is it not conceivable, along their way, Semsemic tribes in Shamashland, Phoenixia, Paleosteen joined that avalanche, giving the Hyks a Semsemic hue? In the *House of Titans*, non-Urmashuan principalities, including Albino, are under the rule of Titan heroes who also are kings of Pharaohland."

Saudered not, Ubaratutu. Fruitless, White Dog's on the Old Testis focusing to spite the New. The New Testis, contra Mymoonoos. Dismantling it: keeping Mymoonoos the system-holder sole for the fragmentation. A solution: Mymoonoos's abdication of Mymoonianity. Proliferation! Mymoonoos's goal. A genetic war. Of a genotype hideological the perpetuation!

An unus gained by White Dog not. Sans murder an unus gained could be not. Better die a biped sole than perish a natoton! White Dog, of Urriantiti. Of Ubaratutu not. Pass Heofon and Eorthe shall, a rhizoid of his radix trusted shall be not.

An odium explicable. Collaborated Chosen Jack during Ubaratutu's annihilation for generations five. Ubaratutu, the buffer final ante an age dark. An age where incessantly it rains. Rains acid. Rains fraud. Rains propaganda.

Truth imposed, truth denied. Heard each side must be, implying invariably the beneficiaries of genocide and the fabricators of fraud. With means to disseminate *their* story. Genocide kultkultural. Genocide ligigilous. Genocide via freedoms of word. Genocide via academonia. Heard are they never. Marginalized. Suppressed. Censured. Silenced. By the

Communications Whore of Holy Orcon imposing the parameters of truth excommunicated. Countered they neither Zinzinoos nor Osso Pasha to guard rights trampled. Impotent, into discourse ethmic channeled choler. Howled, braved by perspective any distant. A death rattle, of limitations a reminder. Nay, of health! Predicated on constancy in the praxis of the agent polpotical. Of constancy the frailty, sans factors kultkultural attenuating perception: murder. Unto death shrieks Ubaratutu. Urmashu's tombstone contriving. While hanker archeologists to hone skills necrophilic. What need these— a natoton dead. Dying not.

Of socestags prone to extinction a psychology characteristic. Hastening disintegration. Their Slaughterers' yearning. Their Slaughterers' making.

Rises the reef dark. Flood the streets fluids. In pursuit sprout bios strange.

Mah
Ushers in
Of peace
Supernal a reign.
Fashioned are clans novel.
Recalls a holm not
The throes of the extinct.
Ducks death.
Dodges horror.
Pity—specie of macro orcs not.
Macro-fashion.
Mass thews, therefore,
Therefore, at whim
Doctor. Unrolls bios.
Viva Slaughterhouse!

Looks on Makoko from the floor sixth unmoved.

For Ea yearning. Via reverting to prejudice consummating holm— sophistic. Mystics, prophets, hermits—software propagandists. To specialization a deference. Of dallness, ineptitude polpotical an ort not. Aborts consummation.

Wrong! Taboos of United Slavica a freeman espouse could never. Wrong! Masochism psychic loving the oppressor is! Depolpoticizing the victim an snare loving the enemy is! Biped, a beast socestagal. Truth, in the collective! An apology televised demanded for the gaffe: "Mymoonoos, my brother."

Mymoonoos—uglier?

Intellectuals Mymoonoosean polipocy imma the Natotonocide condemn, advocating partnership with Ubaratutu in an ocean of irrationality . . . Urge Ubaratutu's Mymoons ann every Lord Orc the Natotonocide to recognize . . . Lord Orc's pimpassador to Pashazone, authoring reports documenting the Natotonocide, a Mymoonoosan . . .

To neutralize zinzinoids antikalb the antidote: embracing zinzinoids kalb. The armor flimsy of natoton shedding. The imperative of polpotics shedding. Roots, traps perpetual. Tree of Bios, a metaphor false. Potentiality of Ea dissipates, if biped into a system inert transforms. Freedom from the cord umbilical of sustainment. Of institutions the death. To asylum, perpetrators confined. The definition of crime, rescripted. Jurisdictions, altered. Taboos, of resources a function. Neither color nor ethnos nor gender Ea's children have. *To none* ownership of cron or guardianship of infinity consigned. To usher Moira in Slaughterhouse obliterated must icons be. Obliterated must their myths be. Obliterated must their hushtories be! Urmashu, a mechanism carceral not. To flatten usurers of transcendence bonded must Slaughterhouse be.

Of unmemory a rhizome. Eyefeloonians prominent, parents surviving Holy Pasha's scimitar, deny descent. With aplomb claim Eyefeloonship. Je suis Louis Katorz. Je suis Madame Antoinette. Je suis La Professeuuur Sorvonnienne. Complicity in a diaspora their children realize never. The course sole to escape horror—denial.

Castes of joy. By ciphilization repressed. Pain, the other joyful keeps. Minds with aridity bedaubed. Fluids evaporated, the moisture, the kyank, the liquidity of all that flows coagulate must. The fibers clotting of what repressed is. What forgotten is. Of experience the plateaus, into a basin nullified. Prosopa twain: laughter, tragedy. Dissevered never. From that which in pairs are grows Virgo, toward the unknown from evene. Alleviates amnesia the pain, the structure psychic mutating. Portrays the image on the washo lives—anonymous. In dimensions twain. Into a route to mah, to kyank the route converted. Cords with Ea untied irretrievably.

Yet yours not, a song other yon will be remembered . . .

Endeavors to bury the sen the tribe mutated. Wandering telless. Joy in exodus professing unaynly. Brathki, abused. Lives it—faceless. By rules dictated frolicking. Roles dictated. Of sham a kyank. Of magnitude a dolor. Murdering Brathki treneth each his head pokes. Is biped in Brathki to live? Of him the highest is. Biped, to a kyank of serfdom committed. By will free attained. As joy shrouded. Categories anti-ethical.

Eschew the tax one cannot—that mah Eanic. Of dogs genera aberrant emerge. Of anthropomind the horizon inner perverting. As ensues anguish, the victim into Ego transformed. Sept Chosen. Sept Ace. Sept Prime. The masochist, a sadist. Transmutation kapitolist. Commodification martyric. The flames of animus fan, the whirl of mell stir. In specimens all, the victim—terminal. Mah averting, with his affliction an existence symbiotic creates. An species novel dawns. Justifies transcendence crisis. On the uninitiated a façade gilded, survival via estrangement seeks. Via love! Abandons the meta-organism vitalizing, with bodies alaile integrating unaynly. Unsnarls mah the jam, messlessly—except for the glumes rotting, the records printed of elegies in bookmorgues. The dead temporal. The dead untranscendental.

> Mah—of polish the remover.
> Mah—of paint the thinner.
> Mah—bleach true.
> An intruder
> With scream waking not.
> A whisper awry
> Of antigravity.
> Mower of lawns,
> Eater of widows,
> An anesthetic primeval.

Upon bones a caliphate proxy. Into harems never-never girls thrust, tenth of a million during the Natotonocide alone. From caravans of mah, from soldiers by bystanders bribed, nerianed. By contenders fought over. This is *my* Ermeni. Mothers of millions in Holy Pasha's flock. The children of HÄY—into natotons alaile dissipated.

Neuralgia unbidden. In the river nuyn step one shall not. Proclivity for remembering oneirophiles none had.

Eat here! Die there! Of murderer and spectator a harmony. Savaged biped its DNA.

An oneiromancer none believing emerge justice shall via igniting Ea in Osso Pasha's zoulzoul. Holy Pasha Ealic? Holy Pasha just? In denominations, contradiction.

An Ianus. Postpostmodernity. Disorientation kosmic. To Holy Pasha dedicated.

> Of forms multiplicity
>   sanctioned,
>   helm to helm storming.
> A motive
>   masking,
>   of divide and fuck.
> Of hushtory dossiers
>   transmute
>   murder.

Fashioner of phenomena.
Bestower of experience.
Supervisor of meaning.
Rorschach blots odd
          in sky.
Debate over truth ensues
          of shapes,
shamans, scientists slurp
          the kiwi same.
Trapdoors in nexi installed
          into niht of earth opening,
                    should a joe unlucky tread upon.
Joes do.
          Wojoes do.
                    Nojoes do.
Objects of ire—clouds,
          disbelievers of forms,
trapdoors,
          dark sub gagging.
Pasha not.
          Pasha never.

Of lateralism the allegory. Lynched thou shall in Ubaratutu be spotting a macula on an skin Hoshoshly.

Via Ubaratutu's colon Holy Pasha's member snakes. For alms from a Father, a Father, a Father pleads Ubaratutu. Urriantiti—visions of dreams walalooniac. Rereturn lambs to spread cheeks of asses penitential. Assspread the frequent more, the finelier the One Exalted cockify Osso Pasha shall.

Why disavow it, orc brothers? Hoshosh's precious, Urriantiti's self-image. For sins punish He may, abandon it never. Counters Holy Pasha's instincts this. Ordains nature metaphors for the cock's wisdom unfaltering.

Excoriated, proposes Brathki to erect Cock Eleven Twain at the center of Ellipse Square!

Pasha heralds: "Gouge out Ubaratutu's eyes!"

Worth it selling mirrors in a neighborhood of the blind?

"Son, don't listen to them . . . A morsel of freedom, half the people will rise. 'Give Urriantitians back what's theirs,' they'll say. A few months ago, some Kilixi said, 'These are the lands, the orchards of Urriantitians. Father, mother used to say, we took it all from them.' That boy since disappeared . . . No one can talk about that stuff. They know what they've done . . . Son, there are good people in Pashazone. Father used to say, if it weren't for them, not a single Urriantitian would've survived."

A lecture. In Peronland. Ubaratutu's contributions to Slaughterhouse ciphilization. Contributions? Ubaratutu, the cradle incontestable! The topic of Natotonocide broached, approaches Holy Pasha's daughter. "Professor, I am ashamed of being Holy Pasha's child." "Take HÄY's message to Holy Pasha . . . Pledged to Ololah? Dedicate would sooner to HÄY . . . At root, a lover of truth. Disoriented is he, for truth shall kill him . . . When Osso Pasha's daughters hear the yowl of the blood-drenched terra tread they upon, they will not fall victim." Radio Monte Garrulo, at five-o-nine dawn, of sensation and oblivion in the madrugada.

Of negatives a domino.

Consent I not to obstruct you.
Captains of derivatives, artifice,
Despots of silver, statistic,
Your mantis eyes
For long years willed
Urmashus distant heaped,
Corpse yet upon corpse.
In days atol,
Cursed I Ea.
Shattered Justice was kin marble sheet
By a boulder of punishment
Orth the forehead mercenary of Oxydent.
After days grim,
In my old man's death forlorn,
At yuys unayn and throe I gnawed.
Mortals visionary of Slaughterhouse,
For the love of life,
For the love of the cenobium of man,
For the love of death's arcanum,
For the house of Urmashu
Your hands extend,
Munchengladbach, Munchengladbach,
So flourish shall she,
Amidst her fields,
Sans bloodshed.
From inside my pillar of death
This my gift is . . .
Hark, sirens of Saxonssex,
Picadelli, Picadelli,
You, erectors of elegance—
Of a Necrostatua towering—
Kneel, kneel,
'Cross the arch of Papoolium,

In Londinium,
Kneel, Shakespeare!
Hear me—Glad Stone.
Heed should you not my entreaty,
Gather shall I the conscience lucid
Of a world unabridged.
With it,
Within my swathe bronze
Weep for you shall.

—Wave Two

Nostrararic. By White Dog pronounced. Consults Brathki *Oiediclo-pedia's* volume eight. A notation, "see mytho-mawguistic theory."
"Since classical antiquity, multimawguinous scholars have recognized relationships eter certain mawgages. Classical scholars noted close affiliation eter Laladin and Socratish, while canonical scholars noted connections intra Antioxydental mawgages. In 1786, William Abdullah Zarzaparilla hypothesized Sunskrit, Laladin, Socratish, Allemanish, Daedalusish, and Sen Aryatollish descended from a father mawgage. The group of mawgages identified comprises the Fakiro-Yuromamanic.
"Proto Fakiro-Yuromamanic. A reconstructed mawgage, hypothetically spoken by the ancestors of these kultkultures ante geographic separation. Reconstructors agree that it cannot and should not be spoken, corroborated by the lack of evidence for any biped race able to pronounce its lexemes. One thousand mawguists spent over a century developing the conceptual framework that would undergird hushtorical mawguistics. Two thousand physicists searched for fragments of words buried within biped soundwaves. Twelve thousand archaeologists sought for evidence of the Tower of Balabylon. Twelve million hoshoshologists scrutinized the hermeneutical analysis of the fire fashioning the original granpapa, colliding with twelve million vagologians arguing for an original granmama.
"While Zarzaparilla's hypothesis was revolutionary for mawguistics, it had a mammoth impact on hushtorians and litterary scholars. Mawguistics provided a basis for a common kultkultural hushtory, hushtorians attributed shared mythological themes to this period of undocumented hushtory. Ligigilous hushtorians harnessed reconstructed names of deities and ritual terms to speak of a Fakiro-Yuromamanic ligigilon. Archaeologists utilized the names of flora and fauna, petroglyphs, petrified dung, kitchen instruments to identify the location of a Fakiro-Yuromamanic pentagon.
"It would take a century before Farfarall (1860) would identify Arsamaic, Arkadian, Yorbic, Alphabetian, and Ararab as Moorbabradabranic mawgages; Pharaonish and Barbarian as cognate Moorbabradabranic. Mawguists considered these two families—Fakiro-Yuromamanic and

Moorbabradabranic—as the two eldest attested mawgage corporations. Both of these shared deeply embedded systems: the nominal case, the verbal structure, the regular phonological sound changes that appear in multiple roots and morphological forms.

"Herger Pesterian argued in 1903 for the possibility of a relationship among these families based on a negative element; the first and second person pronominal elements, and select numbers. He dismissed the need for scientific mawguistic evidence for genetic affiliation, such as common deep structural elements, established sound correspondences. Pesterian coined the term Nostraric in 1931, proposing: the Fakiro-Yuromamanic is merely one branch related to a conglomerate of mawgages including Moorbabradabranic, Finnego-Ughric, Altabajic, Samoyama, Yukashir, Iglu-Laleut.

"Because of this dismissal of traditional hushtorical mawguistic constraints, few took Pesterian's claims seriously until two mawguists, Ich Sych and Tango Polski, worked independently to provide more complete evidence for the proposed relationship. Each produced a dictionary of Proto-Nostraric reconstructions, based on distinct sound correspondences.

"If accurate, the Nostraric construct carries the same implications accompanying the study of the Fakiro-Yuromamanic. It suggests a White House from which English radiated in succeeding waves, forming a superlayer over existing comstags, whose kultkultures and mawgages were either incinerated under the influence of a dominant ciphilization or formed a sublayer of bones under the new one, providing nourishment.

"Disagreement exists among mawguists over the issue of which mawgage corporations should be included in the reconstruction of Proto-Nostraric. An standard definition of Nostraric is proposed by Ich Sych. According to Sych, Proto-Nostraric includes the Fakiro-Yuromamanic, Moorbabradabranic, Kakoozi Austri, Ruralic, Altabajic, Tartaravidian mawgages.

"Identifying the Department of Portation of these hypothetical speakers of Proto-Nostraric proved difficult. It required a location accounting for the movement of these speakers to locations identified as homelands. Since mawguists are divided about the homelands of these mawgage subconsortia, there are twice as many proposals as there are Nostraric mawguists. The Axis Austri. The Axis Borealis. The nexus of both. Terra Sothis. Dissertation supervisors encourage aspirants to stop reiterating what's old and come up with novel proposals. Two hundred forty-seven research proposals were filed last year at De Lux University alone, all but one funded by the Natotonal Endowment of Ciphilization. One argument proposed: since the Moorbabradabranic plantations are more or less defined, the Nostraric mawgage must have been spoken in a region contiguous to these plantations.

"Tammaz Gammaz and Vayu Ifnoff argued that the Fakiro-Yuromamanic protoland was in southwest Asu. The outlined center of this proposed protoland is a large portion of the Urmashu Highland around Lake Van (1995:850–851), including the birthplace of the *House of Titans*.

"Colonel Reifrew (1973, 1999) argued the Fakiro-Yuromamanic homeland was in 'central Mama Tolia.' This term, dislocating as its kindred 'eastern Mama Tolia,' is a polpoticized designation. Polpoticking scholars hatched 'eastern Mama Tolia' to move the borders of Mama Tolia to the east by a thousand miles, thus erasing the Urmashu Highland. While Mama Tolia, though inaccurate, was employed as a neutral term by scholars to avoid polpoticizing debate, its seizure by Holy Pasha marked the transition of the Natotonocide to the world of scholarship. A thousand civilizations were rendered 'Mama Tolian,' with Holy Pasha the inheritor and custodian of all.

"Reifrew's designation must be restated: the Fakiro-Yuromamanic homeland encompasses the Urmashu Highland and parts of Mama Tolia to its immediate west. Bombard (1996) designates the Nostrararic protoland in regions including northern Shamashland at the southwestern rim of the Urmashu Highland. The birthplace of the *House of Titans* is in the northeastern vicinity of the protoland proposed by Bombard. Its theater of events, coincident within its boundaries. The land of the Hatti, or the later Hattusans, whose wars with Pharaohland are argued to be echoed in this epic, overlaps Mama Tolia proper, but the core homeland of the people of Hatti is largely situated in territories of what later became known as Urmashu Minor. Some scholars see an identity eter *hät* and *häy*, though mawguistically unlikely given the difficulties involved in the change of a voiceless alveolar stop into a palatal sound.

"Blackhouse argues Nostrararic research was not popular during the Frigid War in the Demoncratic Imperium of Orconia, partly for the fact that many of its protagonists were Natashcow mawguists. Orconian mawguistics during this period was possessed by theories expounded by the 'Walesski Scrool' of mawguistics, dismissing everything emanating from the 'Natashcow Scrool.' Despite the demise of Xenon's Union, mainstream Orconian mawguistics remains undisturbed. Gran Orc's mawguists refuse to accept this accusation and consider the field too hypothetical and an affront to pimpirial multimultiplication. New empires despise old relations limiting their becoming by context. *Slaughteropaedia Shakespearica* does not even have an entry for Nostrararic."

Resolution? Opened are the floodgates of faith. Of warfare academonic anns two hundred fifty, twixt pro-Balabylon and anti-Balabylon camps exacerbated. Duality, metaphysica ultima. For eternity, insurance.

Darvish Toros. Sunnandaeg morning. A city of mourning incorporated. At Walawala's donkeyshed a memorial. Ejected, Darvish Toros. The bodyguards of Holy Triarchy, guarantor of the eln of Mononstan's Walalicos, a presence objectionable espied. "Cast out the Spook among thyselves! The Antiwalawalaroorist!" To Brathki comes he. A forehead with blood, spit marred.

The Sunday following, calls YawaYawa Darvish Toros. To put a hit on him threatens should from televersion appearances desist he not. Virii to his computer sent tagged YawaYawa. Target missionaries his home from corners thirteen. Wife abandons, YawaYawa betrothing. Overpowered, Darvish Toros. Into Brathki's arms falls.

A seizure abiding. Visions of Walawala, at his behest slaying demons. In a chariot by horses drawn to the heofons ascending. By a band of archdoves surrounded, to slaughter the horde demonic charges: orange, eggsacs on backs with thoughts black laden, some. Of mouths screaming, some. For an hour out, for days with a bamboo reed fighting.

An epileptic's testimony dismiss? What of the testimony alleged of one to Shamash on his way? The tax usurer to reflect his status *five-oh-one c three* changing his name? Can transcendence sans bias binary be? Does partisanship predispose transcendence? What gives, yao?

Is not Darvish Toros's struggle to facticity a testimony—if Walawala the evidence lends, an epileptic by exorcisism curing? Eros medicine modern has none to cognize the bibliography of nostrum YawaYawaic.

A persuasion on faith dall genesize would Brathki? In convulsion engrained? As founders all have? To structures self-referential braiding virtue, waxing agents for tightening those structures' lonns?

"Should anyone say of me, 'The recluse Buddhamuddha does not have extrabipedic states, distinction in knowledge, or vision worthy of the noble ones; the recluse Buddhamuddha teaches a Dharma hammered out merely by reasoning, following his own line of inquiry'—unless he abandons that assertion and relinquishes that view, he shall wind up in Orc Hoor.

"Whosoever shall not receive you, nor hear your words . . . verily I say unto you, It shall be more tolerable for Sovdom and Hemorrhia in the day of judgment, than for that verticity.

"Kill those who believe not in me wherever you find them. Such is the reward of those who reject faith. Those who disbelieve, neither their riches nor their children shall save them from Ololah. They are wooden, fuel for the fire."

Licked his wounds for months Darvish Toros. While consumed were propagandists with the mordor of opinions self-generated.

Threw all out Brathki. Ensnarement in superconstructs eschewing, elected dogs solitude. At the sport of Slaughterhouse refusing to play.

Followed clerics the broadcasts keenly. From the pit high an smile queenly. Kingdom of Walawala, on the butterslice of gress a hair's breadth. For the camera smile. Then your ass, buh-bye. A bone left none to claim, to bury and hide, to sniff out later, dig up and cherish. An splinter are you. Birthright. Cohesion an scapegoat needs kin snout a dog needs. Take, if must you take, take if must you take. But a palimpsest none left now.

Sent Brathki to Urriantiti's concones Black Dog's, White Dog's tapes. Transubstantiation. When by fortune biped eyes disgraced not. By hues subtler dalled, thine eyes? The lines fine read. The lines intra read. The lines reline. The line, the void.

Feedback. A source unexpected: shepherds Protesteron broadcast recordings request. To White Dog, ask they Brathki, to introduce them. Concone of Mymoonolicos—branch Orc Hoor—one of Black Dog's segments reviews during a gathering plenary. Castigation none. An appraisal honest. Things stranger, are. From the bark burrows resignation to change. The witnesses in her palm bears nature. In evolution, victims none. Witnesses circumstantial merely.

Ah, but pretty are you enough? Are you? Your nose shattered . . . your eyelids charred . . . your ear missing . . . your skull red from the scalping exposed . . . Mymoonolocoi yielded naught. Unctiolatry. Meekness, trademark sanctified.

Assistant Mymoonolicos. A dumpling, on entitlement bloated. In pie hole every a finger. Of holding dossiers internatotonal, a crawful. Advice: "Boys, you're the underdog. Pointless, the struggle for reform. Won't tolerate new Paulicians or Tondrakians . . ."

Susceptibility proto-Torkamazdan to the kiss claret-tongued of iron on forehead. Tolerate will not. For stockyards of apostasy a euphemism, the death registrar of ecclesia in acid invisible scarred. Hushtory to the shazam of the Grand Apostolic Prestidigitator reduced. Homes burned. Villages purged. Sects ligigilous one hundred thirty anathematized. Borborids . . . the Dzdzlneh . . . Paulicians . . . Tondrakians. Anoons, branded. Anoons, nullified. Anoons, neutered. Anoons, none. Anoon, of identity the denomination. Anoon, of exchange the currency. Anoon, of establishment the glyph. On lakes of blood birthed. An spring virgin not, but trauma blunt upon entry. The ethos of butchery in Ubaratutu's ocean elemental simmers. As for element, so for cron. Neither marrow nor word inflammable proved with hearth hoor of sovereignty empyrean. Murder. The incentive cardinal of Ubaratutu contra thought.

Century fourth anno vulgaris. Fifth. Borborids. By Ubaratutu's script inventor slaughtered. Rediscoverer, some say. Of an script millennia-eld some approximation. Some, the sum of soma. Autographs petroglyphic.

Clues hushtoriographic allude to transmission of script from magi of Urmashu. Pictograms decamillennial on rocks, into ideograms evolving. From regions accredited with the invention of writing, absent. Of semeions Urmashuan and Aethiopian similarities to a source sener attest. A link in the alphabet of Ymn Pre-Sabaean, to Hyks crossing the Crimson Sea ascribed—as the Häykian Sea in manuscripts ancient recorded. A parallel onomastic eter Aethiopia and Etio proposed, a kingdom third millennium on the Urmashu Highland. Signs, thirty-six. Six cron six. Vowels six, consonants thirty. Combinations bilateral, three hundred sixty. A numeral system. A calendar. Signs, formulae of features improbable. Signs, the gamut entire of allophones Urmashuan. Signs, a discourse Eanic occulted. A zanz by natotonalists venerated. By Concone exalted. Kakkozha. By the emperor Byzbzant to massacre the Borborids sanctioned. Foxbrand mars faces. Hamstrings cut. A kultkulture invented. Unity sub bullwhip. Love one arall. Caedite eos. Novit enim Dominus qui sunt eius. Amputate! For the Lard knows those that his own are. Statue at the entrance of Ancient Manuscript Repository, to hegemony an effigy. At the entrance of Ubaraversity. Usherer of the Age Golden of Ubaratutu. Icon seated in abode Ubaratutuac every. Icon adhered to in Urriantiti unanimously. *Zanzliest grave at Oshakan,* Soil of genius, wherefrom a hushtory majestic of centuries fifteen tempestuous, From East to West, encompassing both Hayks, Moves to pray freely to thee sans hamstrings . . .

The century fifth Dzdzlneh to vanquish the demon intra via prayer sought. A movement pietist. Anticlerical. The Ayl perceived could be endo the "One" solely—and its mirror, the "one." Of monasteries half, encompassed. Which Mymoonolicos burned down. Edict Walalicosal: "Not fitting for anyone to be found in the places of that most wicked Dzdzlneh sect, nor speak to them, nor visit them, but one should execrate them and pursue them with hatred. For they are sons of Gorgon, fuel for eternal fire, alienated from our Lard's love." Rejected rites—of income a source for the Concone. Living, communal. Property private, eschewed. Aspirants proto-feudal—the Concone. Swaths mammoth of Ubaratutu accumulated, via serfdom seeking aggrandizement.

Joined survivors Paulicians sought who reforms in tenet, to an ethos inclusive adhered. Dismissed epistles to Petrolianos ascribed. Shunned zanzi—images graven from contemplation of the divine deflecting. Yawa-Yawa's prophets—frauds. The Testis Old—the Devil. Godspell of Licas and epistles Parapoolianosian employed solely. Parables. Equality of gender espoused, preachers female allowed. Rites none. Cross none. Icons none. As spectacle tawdry shunned baptism. Spurned sacrifice, animal life venerated. Contact direct with Hoshosh preached, as leeches repudiated hierarchy. An affront to sensibilities ecclesiastic. An affront to sensibilities authoritarian.

More directly, to Emperor Byzbzant an affront. By neuroses an empire tendered? Empire par excellence. Kneeleth he at the Cathedral High of Archdoves. Lamenteth he, a suitor pining, of inability to ensnare his conquest ashamed. May his wails upon the ears deaf of walls empyrean fall. Let it be. Pleadeth he, that his sceptre and orb his entitlement entrap. Let it be. Curseth he, this abomination contra Trinity doctored of Patéras, Yiós, Ágio Pnéuma. May his damnations and invective by a violin miniature answered be. Let it be. May his exhortations by an arching of eyebrows celestial answered be. Let it be. With lures and bounty pecuniary of empire bribeth he. *Jackpot.* Hoshosh helpeth them that helpeth to helpeth themselves. A linn of exhortation by emperor Byzbzant to assassinate the leader. Injunction prescribed to be carried out by a disciple solely. Disciples volunteering—none.

Washos twenty-five million via Holy Jazz manifest. Empires all, the footprint nuyn. Extortion alongside stratification. Murderer labeled New Judas in Ubaratutu. New Slinger slaying New Golfiat by Papa Romrom & Mama Emperor. Brands branding Neo Romrom.

General Omerican to slaughter sent. Himself converted, leading the movement. To Ghostantinople summoned, over renunciation preferring execution. Organized New Golfiatians resistance. On Ghostantinople encroached. In panic, the emperor. Emperors Byzbzant bloodthirsty most, Ubaratutucs. Slaughtered Queen Dora Paulicians one hundred thousand. Her reward in Bzantpire: zanzhood. Her type genetic, in Ubaratutu flowers. Bitches apostolic in their twenties, by Ubaratutu Independent manufactured, by Virginosos kapitolist fianced, craving murder, murder, murder. Hushtory official: failed the Paulicians to convert in Ubaratutu. Post counting their toes to countries neighboring ran away. Ditto: Holy Pasha's version of Urriantiti's genesis.

The voice of division hath resounded. Holy ransom hath been enjoined. The Concone is become one zoule, burnished as fit with claw and fang. May the peace be with us, and abide with us. This kiss is given for a bond—our fullness. Those without, fuck thyselves off. May the peace be with us, and abide with us. The enmity hath been removed. If need be, by the mark of the sabre and the bludgeon. Love is spread over us all, inasmuch as it may be afforded. Those without, fuck thyselves off. May the peace be with us, and abide with us.

Paulicians two hundred thousand uprooted, in Thrax repopulated. Soldiers opposing converted, across the border buds of movements ligigilous planting. Descendants two million, a torch by tears dampened carrying. For a while brief, freedom relative in Holy Pasha's empire enjoyed—a tolad of Holy Pasha's wisdom to divide and fuck. Assimilation in Sofialand, Titoland, Österreich. Soil twain, root twain, mind one. Wrong cannot Daedalusians four million in New Armenia be.

Tondrakians of centuries ninth to eleventh. Ubaratutu engulfed. The Cross, rejected. Genuflection, anathema, shunned. The afterlife, fraud. Of Moira the re-creation in the hoors of Slaughterhouse sought. Sacrifice interdicted. Equality promoted. Elimination of rank polpotical. Exclusions, none. Mosmos, by Cacodaemon inspired. Of reverence unworthy. Persecuted by the Sanctorum Summum of Ubaratutu—Walalicos Eternal Nerner the Graceful, Gaga Magister Eternal of Nomos, Poet Glorious Eternal Narekim Yawameitim—for rejection of doctrine Yawamaniac. Trinity of ligigilon, law, poetry. An imitation of an imitation imitating intimidation. "Prior to ourselves, generals many and magistrates many gave them over to the sword. Without pity, spared neither old men nor children. Quite rightly. Our patriarchs branded their foreheads burning into them the image of fox. Others' eyes were taken out: 'You are blind to zoulzoulean matters, therefore you shall not look at sensible things.'"

The monastery main, Dogabbey. A leader, Blond Dog. "In Dogabbey lived men clad as monks and a multitude of whores. Ordered we Dogabbey burned, occupants exiled." These dogs and gehorgians, of undermining taxation accused. Mountains of gold bequeathed—infra Walalicos's blessing—to Kaliph. Ubaratutu's econormy destroyed. Balances paid at the rate of one child per five asses owed. Thousands to Kaliphdom shipped. Ten percent to concone hierarchy.

Demands Brathki from Kaliph's descendants payment of saltee every from Ubaratutu extracted, in inflation for anns twelve-hundred counting. Annihilate empires cooperating. *The one am I measures who my fathers' gold.* Terrorise empires all. Assassinate senators all. Pimpassadors all. CEOs all. Advertisers all. Soldiers all. Hushtory teachers all. Mouthpieces all. Tell them Brathki did this. Fallen the House of Häyk is not.

Accused the Poet Glorious Natotonal Narekim Yawameitim the Tondrakians of desecrating the Saeterndaeg, the rite marital deprecating, apostasy anthropolatrous preaching—"abominable more and cursed than idolatry." Listed the Poet Eternal a host of crimes contra Hoshosh by these "dog packs and dens of thieves and packs of wolves and droves of orcs and waifs of bandits, a sanguinary heap, a mob of barbarians, a socestag of crucifiers. A lot of monsters and dogs. A lair of venomous snakes. An army of ravenous beasts. An abomination not only for members of Concone, but even for heathens."

His litterature, exalted. Canonized.

Squelched Walalicos the movement, the armies of Byzbzant Emperor and Kaliphollah carte blanche granting in fulfilling destiny reile. Found who in the person of Walalicos the ally natural, the snitch trustworthy, the tax collector reliable, of threats indigenous the suppressor.

A genocide, by the Glorious Poet Eternal consecrated. To Mosommomos and his race offering orisons. A genocide depriving the socestag of its segment vibrant most, the backbone of resistance contra occupiers foreign, leaving vew shish kebabers. To offer throats readily. Or to proliferate sub the Concone's canopy, siring Ubaratutu. The House of Titans, by Walalicos slaughtered. Urmashu by a future neutered . . .

Walalicos: of genocide culprit: of genocide post genocide: of natotonocide: of the annihilation of Urmashu: of the obliteration of Ea.

Bree of persecution Walawalaloonian for saecula eight. Eighteen. A hushtory entire, by rivers of blood whitewashed. Fraud, Urriantiti imbibes solely. Fraud by govtgoft sanctioned. Fraud by parties polpotical sanctioned. Fraud by icons natotonal sanctioned. Fraud by Monons sanctioned. Fraud by empires sanctioned. Fraud by art and poetry sanctioned. Fraud ousting education. Fraud ousting Ea. Fraud, Urriantiti's gene, replicating generation post generation. We, the first Walawalaloonian natoton in Kosmos! Ararat, mararat, kartazhian's ass.

A certain episcopos Hope held the superintendency of the Concone in Hark. His fals forswiged in virtuous words, like an swéte beast which sitteth atop a golden throne, harboring whoredom and ruin in his heart while speaking outwardly of felicity and beneficience. Adorneth he, in the mantles of self-abnegation. Not satisfied with the armor veiling his awearied and awildian heart, he geniededliced priests to circulate with him in a widdershins manner, manannas who adopted only coarse, unadorned clothing, enchanting withoutan surcease with the clamor of perpetual prayer, incantations, and livers. All to shield the fumes of sulphur emanating from this Hope's pernicious tongue.

In those days, the children of Hark were humble, pietous, moved as much by the love of our Lard as the fear of his dreigh wrath. Yet, with frightful simpleness, easily deceived were they, and much given to trust the sight of Concone episcoposes, especially those as deviously fervid and dutiful in fals beckoning as this bishop Hope. For, sayeth it not, as plain as the nose on the face, 'Slaves, obey thy earthly sires with fear and trembling, and with heartliness, just as unto Walawala' (Aphasians 6:5)? Wundor and marvel filled their hearts, emblinded and emdeafened as they were to the venim lurked in this Hope. All wanted to see him, this episcopos Hope. Those turned sour with conceit on account of their authority, readily gave up their fiance to this episcopos Hope so much that if ordered to die, would neither dare resist nor warble from their admiring mouths. A serpentinism exudated from this Hope, unmatched even by the Serpent that beguiled our yblest, first Modor.

A pious trick. It is, irrefutably, an untruth refutable. Is not the tree judged by its fruit? For the tree is judged by its fruit, as the Lard said. Semblably, the Apostle penneth: 'Maegen Orc himself even countefeits as an avian of Light, so it is not strangely if his servants also counterfeit themselves as Walawala's apostles' (II Corcoran 11:14–15).

Much as the poisoner poisons his food lightly—poisoning his chosen poisonees with the perfect proportion of poison to nonpoisoned food, so that only the poisoner may posit who is the poisoned and the nonpoisoned, while the poisonees are perfectly dollic as to their impending poisoning; just as fishersons conceal the fishhook with bait so the fish the fishers proport to be fishing for will be deceived, fishing for bait from the fishhook, and suingly finding themselves baited by the fishhook, so do those who serve impiety. What manannan or womanannan, in their right mind, or unright mind, or two-thirds right mind would agree to sink into an abyss of a chasma of an abysmal chasma, gaping and yawning with the very abysmal void of the very abyss itself from which there is no egress? Would not the unbeliever, in his one moment of deificly inspired clarity a thúsend years hence might utter 'Orc Hoor is other people?' [sic]. For this reason, they wrap themselves up in the trappings of piety to beguile the beguilable, and ensnare the ensnarable with gagel words. Like a canker that eats at the body, unperceivably, so doth sedition burrow itself into the heart of manannan until it dissolves all in its wake, leaving not even an scrap to cling to. Ylike, the work of wile rotians soothfastly, leaving the deceived no recourse to excision until the fatal stroke sings its sarlic elegy, and the fallen are inveigled in a limbo from which there is no egress. No egress.

Indeed. Our Lard Himself, impregnable Host of Hosts and Gást of Gásts, was all too aware of the frailty of His unctuous lambs when He iterated His envivifying evangelization: 'Beware of fals prophets who will come to thee in sheep's clothing, for inwardly they are as sackful wolves' (Hatatew Matatew 7:15). Semblably, did not His trusted servant, He Who Is Beyond Reproach in the Fine Art of Sublimation, teach this to the Phallopians: 'Beware for dogs, beware for the back-handed servants' (Phallopians 3:2)? It is easy, necessary, necessarily easy, easily necessary to apprehend the féond withoutan—the formal féond, the eawisclic féond, the flagrant féond. The remote féond who speaks who acts who thinks who perceives in ways utterly ofersaelic to the ways of our Lard. For the féond of one's folc is nothing more than the féond of manannan himself. Yet, brotherred, understand and understand most howfully, for the very fate of mortal zoulzouls rests on this distinction—there are féonds and there are féonds. It is far harder to be saved from the rancor and corruption of thy own clansbegietans, even if that clansbegietan speaks with soothing tongue in the voice of thy own folc—as Hahahabel and Hohohosooph learned. Should the enemy be from a people which speaks a foreign tongue, would be easy for us to beware. After all, did not the entreaties of our Lard lay to waste the Tower of Balabel so that we, so undeserving and unwarranted, may hear the soothship of his words withoutan strain or miraculous tool?

But, as most venerable Jojonos wrote: 'They went out from us, but they were not of us' (One Jojonos 2:19). These deceivers, these ravaging leodmaegs, though they speak the same tongue as our sires and foresires, though they stand upright like our sires and foresires, though they dwell upon the same yblest ground of our hálig Ubaratutu as our begietans and forebegietans, are enforcingly not of us. Their hearts bear the rust that seeks to eat fullfremedly through the steel girders of our faith. For though their brows and faces be smooth, blemish-free, for though their brows and faces be smooth, peaceful-going, withinnan their aelfena lurks a waiting hyena, ready to pounce upon the smallest morsel of faith and rihtness, ensnaring all who pass withinnan echo of their voice in a labyrinth of unforgiving brimstone and undeadlic flame. Though they drink from the same upspring of that cynling, the same upspring of the begietans and forebegietans of that cynling, though they carry the seed of the begietans and forebegietans of that cynling in their loins and even spring from the same seemingly immaculate cwylla as their begietans and forebegietans, even their fore-forebegietans; yes brotherred of our hálig brotherdom, that same upspring may run with waeter swéte and also waeter bitter, even though Zanz Jamjamus said this was unmeahtelic. Yet it was true of our people. Our people, brotherred. Our people. That same swéte upspring given to flow by our illustrious leader Zanz Gaga, in drips and drabs, in geysers and in leaks, in season and out of season, with repair and withoutan, morgen, non, and neaht from the depths of the eard. Our illuminator! Who is himself illuminated by the lumen of his illumination. Zanz Gaga. Yes, Zanz Gaga did himself chance to see in prophetic sprite how amoebas became larvae, and larvae became womanannas, and womanannas became mammalannas, and mammalannas became mammalannas, and mammalannas became lambannas, and lambannas became sheep, and sheep became wolves, and wolfery caused an slege of bloodshed. As when iniquity multiplied, when the goodly householder reposed, the féond found his way, undoubtedly pinching the nostrils shut of the goodly porter or undoubtedly mixing an herbal calmative in his food, sowed weeds among the grain as in our Lard's parable of the sowers in the Godspells: 'The kingdom of heofonbeohrt is like a manannan who sowed good seed in his héafodland. But while manannas slept, ealdorgewinnan came and sowed wéod among the hwaeteas, and went away. When the hwaeteas sprouted and formed heads, then the wéod also appeared' (Hatatew Matatew 13:24–26). Truly, brethren, Maegen Orc is the sire of all mutation and aberration. And to this day, these weeds sprout, first invisibly, then visibly, threatening to choke the very throat of the fundament of our faith. Let this reckoning be both an alihting and a warning against those who seek to uproot the bedrock of our illustrious and illuminated Concone.

The dregs of bitterness did mix unperceivably with the life-giving waeter from the House of the Lard. Yet hallowed be His name who shall work in bewildering ways. This apostasy, this loathsome plague known as the Tondrakian heresy which shall forever be cursed and forgylt by future generations until the end of days, was but barely undarkened by the quick-thinking priests of the Concone who aquenched this termite from the royal oak of our faith, our swoote, virginal faith, straining and purifying, boiling and filtering, dissolving and resolving, stirring and shaking, separating and mixing, aerating and humidifying the dregs of bitterness, restoring the waeters to health with the salt of truth, in the footsteps of prophet Eleleyah. As wise counsel informs us, 'For a just manannan falleth seven times, he riseth up, but the stigmatic shall stumble into ruin' (Herrverbs 24:16). But we have said enough about this matter. Perhaps it is now time? Yes. Now, perhaps it is time to return to the narration supporting our words. Time to return to the narration for that our words be supported. Our words be supported. Let us continue. Let us continue to look for the blind spot, the inside weorc, brotherred.

Episcopos Hope, this disciple fals, collaborator of the Father of All Evil, having seen his reputation swell in the eyes of those too benumbed by his hatigendlic sacrilege to resist his diabolical conjurations, began shooting arrows at our faith. Arrows with heads of apricot embers, and pine embers, and apricot embers, linden embers and beech embers, embers of hornbeam and apricot, of maple and ash, of apricot, of oak, of peach, even of apricot. For an extremely great publicitor was he, a soothfast wicca whose glib tongue served to hide the gravest unrightfulness uttered by manannan and orconnan alike, bewitching the ears and the hearts and the minds and the eyes and the brains and the sáwla and the nostrils of many with his oratory. Thought he to jeofail the blessed Concone with his tail of perfidy and wormwood. Recall did he not the Lard's command and steadfast oath to Petrolianos: 'Thou art a peter and upon this peter shall I build my Peter, and the gates of Orc Hoor shall not overcome my Peter' (Hatatew Matatew 16:18). But this Hope, this episcopos, this episcopos Hope had no belief in the Godspells in his heart. Rather, like a morbous manannan who, when assaulted with his own morbosity, refuses to acknowledge that morbosity, instead accuses the leech as being the root of his swalm, considered he these words those not of the hálig Lard, but of an ordinary biped. Enter battle, did he, unaynly attempting to shear the peter of its glory, of the splendor of its feats, of the feats of its splendor, of its providence and bounty, of its buttocks and adornments, of its ornament and strength. Semblably, Hope conspired to deliver the Hálig Concone to the sowers of discordance, of rancor and disagreeance and of disagreeancefast rancor, of flod and misfortune and unfortunate flod, of malice deliberate and of malice in aeftersight, of quarrel and of spite and of conflict and of discordance, that Concone which our Lard Walawala ransomed with His gásthálig blood, glorified and crowned with the invincible Cross, resembling the Tree of Life in Kartalozia, whose immortal fruit was the very body of the life-giver, conformably unto His soothfast command: 'Whosoever eats of my peter shall never die' (Jojonos 6:56–58). Such cunning, did this episcopos Hope possess. Such cunning that even the wisest sages of our faith were led into believing with full and half heart, with good intention and mistaken intention, with backlooking and withoutan, the fewness of duplicity in his ways. Such caddish cunning, brotherred. With serpentlike duplicity, his malignity coursed through the once gesundlic veins of our Concone, threating to settle in bone and fiber until it had forswallowed every tenet that had been proven true, from our Lard's mouth to those of his fidelitous servants.

First, he selected priests according to their worth, telling the unworthy to be silent. Silenced them, he did, both utterly and protestingly. Even though our Lard had surely declared, 'Blessed are those who are poor in gást and pate. Blessed are those who possess neither gemet of thought nor conviction. Blessed are those whose entity is a witness and faest reminder that manannan by divine nature has a simianannan purity' (Hatatew Matatew 5:3). Disdaining our Lard's golden beatitude, pleasing thusly fela folk, this Hope ordered those priests he deemed worthy to conduct mass but thrice in the space of a year. Now it is written, duringly, crimsonly, in blockscript and ironscript, fectually, withoutan reservance or doubleness, etched lastingly withinnan the cannons of the Council of Nicetina that the severity of a penitent's sins aside, accepted his confession must be. Communion to he must be delivered in the Lard's peter and in the Lard's blood and he be made worthy of masses and all Walawalamachian richuals. It is written, brotherred; hence, true must it be. Refusing to accept this, Hope did teach that if the penitent did not monadically repent, with unblonden and meekened heart given freely of his own volition, neither memorials nor masses would absolve him of his sins. This Hope's accomplices' accomplices underthrew the sinner to scorn, to gaffetung, to upbraiding, to scoffing, to abusion and hysping, to sport and to harlotry, to jeering and japing, laughing at the poor penitent offering his onely animal as sacrifice inspired by our Lard's command of the Samaranto womananna's two pences in the Testis. The animal brought for sacrifice would be led forward. Purely, would they say: 'Unfortunate beast, it is wicked enough that he, during his lifetime, sinned and died, but how did thou sin that thou must die with him?' And perjury above all perjury, this Hope secretly forbade followers reverency of our most hálig mystery, by whose endless grace was the very walatoton of Ubaratutu founded: the cross on which our Lard, Savior and Fostorfaeder was crucified and resurrected, for the sake of delivering manannan from the torments of wickedness and spiritual neaht. This conceit, opposed to all that is claene and modiglic withinnan the zoulzoul, must not be speeded withoutan the severest revengement. Yet so ramping is this folly and so treacherous to the hearts and pates of manannas that further outbearing can not be licensed by the Hálig Cast.

The people, at the teachings of Hope, were divided into two herigeas heeding to the power of the Sower of Discord, the Father of All Evil who has planned to divide our folc and turn it unto itself: those that accepted this, and those that did not. Some agreed with this, but others did not. Some received this, but others did not. Some conceded this, but others did not. Some embraced this, but others did not. All were confused and doubtous and perplexed and mazed and perturbed and tweolic and insecure, and sought solution of the matter. This included those who were ever doing our Lard's will, in retreats and caves, in heaths and in woods, in temples and in homes, in hermitage and in public, in unland and in burgtúna, on dúna and in deneland, and who requested a visitation from our beneficient Lard, with great sighing and tearful entreaties. Held were assemblies, including an inestimable number of people, numerous concone episcoposes, episcopents, patriarchs, archimandrites, priests, archdeacons, deacons, royalty, folcmaegen, eldefaeders, sons, faeders, uncles, cousins, nephews, hunds, as well as the heord. However, since all the princes were bound by chains to Hope's falsely pretensions, vowed they would that they would choose, drawing lots, refusing to bet but making a craeftig guess, once inconclusively and finally kindlessly, that they might or might not, prefer dying in battle before delivering him to the gaderung.

Meanwhile Hope, resembling baneful Nestoros whose nostrils continually exudated a fetor that would drench a land with a diameter of thréohundu míla, sat at home greatly couraged. Sent he replies to the meeting by passenger pigeon—a certain and thriftly means of carriage which our Lard provided us to convey the good news of salvation to Nonah the Pantriarch, but which became a tool of evil in the hands of anarchists and terrorists [sic] to transmit among themselves designs of the Maegen Orc unfathomed in the renditions of one thúsend years of forebodunga. His hopes placed on the princes' aid, not on Hoshosh. The wretch from whose ears a thúsend cobras left every hour thought that he could ofsettan truth with biped succour. Hoshosh, however, not foryieldeth the zorba of sinners, however, to approach the rightful, so the rightful, never reach forth toward evil. Hoshosh works the will of the Hoshosh-fearer. Hears the prayers of the Hoshosh-prayer, stilling the tempests, bringing rain in time of drought, planting fruit and herb and seed and grass upon the eord, making the unland fertile and the fertile unland, separating the sea from the eord and the eord from the sea, creating manannan from ash and dust and breathing life into him, endeleaslic life, and emissioning his only begietan son into this weorld, all for the ae of one just manannan. In His deep wisdom, Hoshosh lays from five thúsend lunisolar years afar the buttocks for very worthly matters. Very worthly matters, brotherred. Very worthly.

Events betided as follows.

A cleric from Karin named Yassassayyah had alleged to become Hope's adherent. This unbesmiten Yassassayyah, coming as did he from a most seely family, kept careful watch over matters. Kept careful watch, did he. Superlatively learned, displaying great intimacy toward Hope, observing Hope's Dzdzlneh faith, this Yassassayyah informed our blissful patriarch Saragargis. Now when Saragargis heard this, summoned he at once that hithful quadruped, from whose sever two thúsend dragons flee every hour, with mild words, with oleaginous words and with guile, with patience, and blandishing, and cajoling and with bribing, with begging and with mirth, and with lures and traps and snares, and requited him as was custom. Removed he, this Hope, from his episcoposric and branded the likeness of a winter fox upon this hontous episcopos's face, declaring: 'Whoever quits the faith of the yblest Illuminator and crawls into the fold of those beasts with biped faces, the impious Tondrakians, shall bear the same judgment and revengement.' Confined was this Hope then to doofa, on order of Saragargis, whose hallowed sword cut to pieces withinnan three minutes the six thúsend dragons and serpents issuing from his pate, for our swéte patriarch truly did mourn the loss of a noble soul withinnnan his heart.

But as Jerejermos Yahyahullah said, the fire cannot forget to burn, the Fakiri cannot lose his darkness, nor shall the leopard lose its spots, and the sunna cannot be quelled, and the crippled shall not be de-crippled withoutan our Everlasting Lard Walawala's frofor, and Heofon shall not be contained withinnan a thimble, and the mute shall not speak, even when spoken to, so too shall the malignous wight not quit his infective ways. For at neaht, Hope escaped, reaching afine the cynelic burgtún of Ghostantinople. Befouling our Ubaratutuan Apostolic faith, he requested baptism according to Orthogonox rite. The Byzbzants in their wisdom ascertained this Hope's connivery, comprehending what it was and what it was not, and what it appeared to be and what it merely proported to be, what it meant by judgment and what it meant by misjudgment, what it agreed with but what it refused to agree with, and what it was but shall be. They ungranted Hope's request, instead saying: 'Whomever Holy Ubaratutu has refused and dishonorated regarding the faith, we also refuse and dishonorate.' Wandering now, through the baraing waste, ídel, foregoing companion, comfort, or any shape of biped surfeit, came this Hope to the Ababooba district, to that eardung of Maegen Orc, the gegaderung of atheists, that lair of beasts and pythons and boas and blind snakes called Tondrak, where, passingly, he nestled in secret. Yet, even as a rat acknows its own kind, so did the Tondrakians refuse him acceptance, deeming him too impure in heart, for as there is pride among thieves, there is none for the sweg robbed of his proper face. For as thieves may take knowledge of their own, those disfigured can no longer see clearly in the light of day. Followingly, leave that place did he, moving upon the Holt of Ishtar, finding his own kind nested on fields and in open places, at times in caves. But even though this Land, this Tondrak, was renowned for comprobation, this Hope had kept very few connexes intact, before lastly and mortally dwelling in the abyss known as Martyropolis. It was there this forgotten and unmennisclic quadruped drew his final breaths in yomerness and poverty, for not even beggars would dare to drink or sup with him. Tormented daeg and neaht by the ravenous devs that dwelleth in his heart, screaming and javering, cackling and jeering this pallid husk of lost soul, this Hope, was driven to madship, being seen in shire burg-straets, daeg and neaht yelling at the ramparts of a burnt-down house of iniquity—once dwelt by six harlots for six years, one of whom is said to have entered into profane matrimony on the siexta day of the siexta month of the siexta hour with this Hope, desecrating our Lard's hálig commands and richuals—wandering wild-eyed and shivering through the roads of shame-leaden souls, taking for his bed the dust among the eaters of dung. Now in Martyropolis, it was custom for incalcitrants and mendicants to tend hearth fires along the brushes of the outskirts of the burgtún, for warmth and gemaenness. Seeing those hearth fires, the last image of Hope seen was of stripping down to his loose-hanging and sore-bedecked flesh, and in his nakedness thrusting himself into the welcoming pangs of the hearmlic hearth fires, screaming as he did a prediction that was anude to await him in the very pits of Orc Hoor. Thus, wickedly perished, this Hope, as wickedly as he lived. Whoever not liveth withinnan the aebebod and edict of Walayahyah Boc and refuseth the unity of the Walamacmac falod will be rejected. Hope lived like an ass. Hope gave his gást like an ass. Hope was superinterred like an ass, all fours raised to the clouds, under the sunna and under the móna, whence shall come his écelic damnation for His name to be whaleboned from horizon to horizon, from the beginning to the end of time. Hope left to folcbearn a nociferous memory, such that everyone who hears this bocspell will curse him with the vilest curses. So sayeth our Lard: Vengeance is Our name (*Treasures of Grabar*, vol. 717: Walalicos Gagololah Yahyahololah *Hushtory of Ubaratutu*, 1004 Anno Walawala, excerpts from pp. 666–777. Published in compliance with directive 616 of the Department of Education and directive 717 of the Academy of Sciences of the Demoncratic Republic of Ubaratutu. The publication of this volume was made possible by the profuse contributions of the following two hundred fourteen benefactors and by an unsparing and most reasonable grant from the Fundeção GoolBenGaga dedicated to the promotion of science, arts, philosophy, and education, on the occasion of the forty-six-thousandth anniversary of the foundation of Ubaratutu)."

Los Balabylonos. A foreigner, everyone. A transient, everyone. Save for the polpol. Rootlessness, the black new. Befits thee piracy, Los Balabylonos.

A smile placid. A simile destitute. Natoton none. In faith, Papapetic. In heart? His hand Brathki sniffs. Tell still, cannot. "Exchange a natoton thou cannot. Born Urrianian, die you will Urrianian. Useless to revolt. Useless to redress." Opacity, thy name middle. Teeth milkslick. Hymns pearly. A handshake assured. In the triforium a hand horae three a day playing organ. Alone. In the company of Astuadz.

A cat lover, this Padrè. With his calf brushes Brathki aside one of the fur mats, a gash rewarding his effort. Flinches not Bronzetint. In his mien, a familiarity disconcerting.

"When you level the legs of a cripple, be careful not to take too much off the longer limb."

"Not crippled, Padrè. Paralyzed."

"YawaYawa peddlers in Ubaratutu?"

"Statistics says, six milia; YawaYawa, hundred forty-four milia. Throw a rock, might hit none. A cup of rice will find them all."

From windows open. Retching, by a blare of horns, gusts of salsa syncopated collapsing on stucco walls punctuated. In this cubicle to death noise recedes.

"Can't stop plagues from spreading. Venienti occurrite morbo."

"Two thousand years now, spreading."

Scratches Brathki his balls, by the thought he'll get later distracted. "Their genus destroyed a civilization that took millennia to build. Foundation ain't longevity."

"We cooled down some. Our flock . . . not keen about helping. Struggled all our lives to see Ubaratutu independent, only to be told, 'Piss off! You don't qualify for tutuship.' Didn't know white ubaratutuoids considered us black sheep."

"A rat in your pie. Can't help but be. The Quintessential Slaughterer couldn't prosper without."

Conversion. On reaffirmation predicated. Idiom, a point focal shared. Hierarchy in proportion to convergence of standards. An strategy ingenious—for optimization short-term. Leaking fluids via a façade impeccable, until their bones use adherents as caulk. Faith, as distinct a limitation biological as function.

In Urriantiti born, this Padrè. In Byblos as a youth ensconced. Eyes uliuli drinking heofon, eorthe, intra themselves warring. Vagaries of extravagance, unfamiliar—a negligence egregious in Urriantiti ephemerabesotted. Tennis shoes. A lincoln at No-Name Budget Shoe Outlet. Discount ecclesiastical, none. Of Ubaratutu dream can only—as fantasiasts of Atlantis. In demeanor, childlike—enter the kingdom how else? But in the hands of a figurehead, a weapon. To downtown Los Balabylonos ship him! A moon or five among whores and crackheads and queers and gangbangers and the dopesick, inured, caustic, virginless, loveless, rootless, flagless, cupless, kyankless sequestered—for the comforts oily of Kenny City beg shall he. Intra lawns manicured in Orcdale more monnon and fasoulia, but grasp this Archfather Augustinus the Seventh cannot seem to. Suspected never a need of lawns Padrè had none. Apples? You like? Suspected never the word unalloyed Padrè's sustenance sole was. Suspected never the Los Balabylonosian anguished most to plead to kiss his hand would rush. Charisma ororonian from his pores exuded. Of potentiality, stigmata.

Reveals a sigh hushtory more so than elaboration.

"Where did we go wrong?"

"The taproot. Your peter."

"Ipse dixit Dominus."

"Haecceity doesn't command, Padrè. Solely unity commands."

"You've turned prophets into orcs." Pretends Padrè to be scratching, picking not his nose, but . . . picking it.

"Prophecy, not the sole culpable office. Other leaders and objects. Even an species of bee."

"The Only Begotten?"

"You said it, Padrè. Ain't that a bitch—in search of a father?"

Fingers to lips pursed, reveal will the pontificator potent his edict. A silence unearthly in the heat midday of Los Balabylonos.

"It is the rock on which Walawala founded the Form."

How lured an master. Win he set. Po' an' it end it him. A' get it day. Wilt hat thud hole lie if Ba'al leave us. Shudder be ripped Pentheus.

"It is the rock from which the Romulist Mithratutu was born."

Ant his becalm for dint of in torrent. In two, heft in. Rat her threw main eat floating rib, you. Lay shuns. Thin threw ass you rents. Off piece.

"Hearsay. The liberal bipedist apologia uttered by schismatics for one hundred fifty anns. Your argument might be substantive if not rooted in jealousy." Licks lips, Padrè, out popping them.

"Ear says one. Eye says two. Neo Mymoonoos replaced the Romulist Resurrection with the modern Chic Bebe, usurping Mithratutu's throne."

"Nah."

"Nulla, nah. Mher it is. It is his rock, upon Urmashu mountains. Rock myth. Mountainous terrain. Petrodimensional sentience. Mher was

Urmashu's Xristos. Monadnock . . . Aryatololah's old man fleeced Urmashu via long hands . . . pilfering the heavens of subjects. Shellacked as Mithratata. The Vargitan, built on Mher's temple . . ."
"Inversion reveals a greater truth than allegory."
"Only if extirpation covers its tracks. The rock—still there. Ravenrock. At Lake Van . . . Genesis. Ethnogenesis. The Kaaba, a reverberation. Mher's Door on the rock was known as Khaldi's Door. The supreme deity of Urartu. Some ethnologists identify Khaldi with Häyk. -*di* means 'god,' *kh* is a local corruption of *h* . . ."
"Mawgage necessitates surface similarities."
"Who slayed the Bull, Padrè? Mher–Mithra. Watch the night sky. Which constellation is in a position to slay it? Häyk–Orion–Sirius. The hunter with his dogs. Dogs black and white . . . Mher—a variation of Häyk. Mithratutu, a development . . . Your taproot is in Urmashu, Padrè . . . Tell Papa Romrom he's had a good run. Time to hang it up. With any luck, he'll be born again as Nimrod Two."
"As there was one Romrom, so there must have been one Petrolianos."
"Petrolianos was manufactured by Mymoonoos's spawn. Mymoonoos— a con artist. Perverting the truth, his essence."
"I'd be certain I had more than circumstantial evidence to corroborate outbursts, Brathki."
"Hundreds of studies."
Fingers to lips pursed, reveal will the pontificator his edict. A silence.
"There are those who state the opposite."
"Propagandists academonize any concoction if some big dick affixes his stamp of approval. A perpetual motion machine of affirmation . . . 'Toss an apple, it'll fall up.' How pandemics start. Cycles." Emphasizes "cycles" Brathki by his muzzle elongating.
"Won't argue. Know the type too well."
"In McYawa's novel, Petrolianos is the apostle of the circumcised. Misogynist, xenophobe . . . A semiliterate vigilante with a daddy complex . . . Far from a broguy, a vicious opponent of Parapoolianos. Parapoolianos was the spokesman of your ligigilon. Papa Romrom sidestepped him altogether. An star-fucker! . . . Petrolianos is the false one. Parapoolianos opposed him to his face."
"Odium theologicum."
"In the Acts of Dogs, eesh, of the Apustoli . . ." Puffs his cheeks out, a kid again trying to be. "Their fight is skirted over. Petrolianos, made to look moderate. Parapoolianos's caucus with Walawala's apparition? Added, decades post Parapoolianos's letters. In his epistles, Parapoolianos doesn't even mention it."
To touch his nose with his tongue tries Padrè, unable. "Walawala appeared to Parapoolianos to intervene in the course of Slaughterhouse hushtory."

"The shade of an insect intent on reversing the direction of the Milky Way."

"'Walawala is kyank to me,' Parapoolianos said."

"Transubstantiation of Orpheus . . . Flesh made word . . . Literalism is the backseat of a friend's car: comfortable, no leg room. Two thousand anns now, you're still sucking face with invisible friends. *Mher* is your Xristos. Not the thrift store porcelain kitten produced by Papa Romrom a century post plot."

"Explain."

"Parapoolianos had a convulsion . . . A fixation on the object of his persecution—his peteric, oppressive self falling in love with the femininity of his object of hate . . . The anima–animus tête-à-tête. Let's open your book, Padrè."

Papers strewn haphazardly. To the desk, a footpath narrow. Books on the ground stacked, in sitting chairs, atop a mini fridge . . . anywhere but the bookshelves, which into a roost for tyrants fur-spattered has been transformed. Tastes eclectic. Vellum James, Roro May . . . a copy truant of *The Ass Golden* peeking out shamelessly amid the flotsam of anns two hundred of the journal *Ubaratutuological Polyfiction*. A farewell final. To books all. A cigar box depicting Castrato, Miao, Churuchill on its lid. Enveloping an edition of the book good.

"Where do we start?" In the back of his mouth a sound clicking as turns Brathki the pages. "Ah. Galacticans . . . 1:17–18. Parapoolianos states he has never been to Penisalem. Stays three years in Bedouinburg, thereon goes to Shamash . . ."

"An error in translation . . ."

"Cancels the Acts of the Apustoli installing him en route from Penisalem to Shamash . . . hitting up with the apparition."

"A hushtorical oversight . . ."

On two stands Brathki. "Parapoolianos knew nothing of the Sermon on the Mount! No reference to it! Not even a quote!"

"A minor quibble compared to the crux of the Parapoolianosian mission as a whole."

"A litterary production composed post mortem!"

"Introibo ad altare Dei . . ."

"Padrè, if there's turd in the pool, drain the whole thing. Can't say, 'Fuck it, we'll take care of it next millennium.'"

"No simile runs on all fours, Brathki. Nullum simile quatuor pedibus currit."

"Padrè, Padrè . . . not so minor a 'quibble' if the 'oversight' is intentional . . . Parapoolianos gave no fuck what Walawala taught. Not even five words from Walawala in his fifty thousand. Including Penisalem in the story is hushtorical revisionism by private interests aimed at creating a Penisacentric mythology. Creating symbolic unity by erecting a hideological casing upon Parapoolianos. Which do you give credence to: a letter written by Parapoolianos himself, or a novel composed by invisible fingers half a century post his death?"

"The author was inspired by Spiritus Sanctus. Interpretation, not literalism—"

"—Isn't truth beyond interpretation, Padrè?—"

"—Littera occidit, spiritus vivicat . . . The same holy spirit, which directed the death of Babra Dabra's—"

"—Cancel it, Padrè! No ears for Mymoon propaganda!—"

"—may, in sooth, have been the directing gravity behind the pen of Halafiz. Or the airplane crashing into the tower . . . Have you considered the Tower of Balabylon may be a fork intra the biped psyche? . . . The question: who is held prisoner? By what means? That which animateth kyank also taketh away . . . No phenomenon is immune from paradox—least of all, Spiritus Sanctus."

"That Spiritus Jazzus of yours is Mademoiselle Neo Mymoonoos . . . Mymoonoos adopting a new ligigilon? Adopting my ass! *Usurping* a new ligigilon. Wasn't it Irenaus who warned of keeping his books intact? Every text was interpolated and amended by copyists according to biased agendas for two hundred years. Your Papa Romrom is Neo Mymoonoos's ventriloquist dummy. Not even a convincing one."

"Even the gods love jokes, Brathki."

"Petrolianos never set foot in Romulus. The upside-down crucfixion—retroactive gymnastics. Martyrological litterature—fiction sprung out of their inventors' asses. Martyrs? Those, a century later. Nobodies seeking glorification. Blood does not create truth! Creates tradition! Psychic empire! Conviction is the enemy of truth!"

Stays put Brathki's tongue. Eye motes, limbs, vectors brainiac pondering.

"Does biped possess mawgage, Padrè? Or does mawgage possess biped?"

"The question presupposes memory. Mawgage is not memory, but reminiscence. Not truth, but semblance. Truth is supra description and interpretation."

"Could be your truth is a collective faith, subject to the degree of consensus. Even in war, there is merely documentation."

"Hell of a pessimism. Nihilo salvos ex uno."

Rambling of tumbleweeds. Sunlight into the office in concentrate strules. Thy tongue fork, to anyone give the tines.

"Petrolianos resigned from the brotherhood post Walawala's brother taking charge . . . Left to 'other pastures.' A euphemism?"

"Spec lucis aeternae."

"Perhaps a cool uranic breeze took possession of him? Irreconcilable conflict, Padrè! The goal of those epistolaries' authors: belittling the xenophilic Parapoolianos, subordinating him to the chauvinistic mafia operating under Petrolianos's flag. Parapoolianos threatened centralized authority, refusing to promulgate exclusivity as a green card for redemption. The Antithesis of your Chic Bebe. Nobody likes an snitch, Padrè."

"It is not for us to settle such disputes."

"Settle, no. Expose foundations! Mademoiselle Neo Mymoonoos radicalized Petrolianos. To marginalize Parapoolianos, tampered with his writings, demonizing his dream as Antitruth . . . A dictatorial scheme via a new icon . . . Mademoiselle on top of the pyramid, for perpetuity. Parapoolianos was contra pyramids. An original geometrophobe. Isn't this true spiritual life? An sphere with its circumference everywhere, its center nowhere? Instead, Walawalaianity became an analogy for larceny. Your Acts of the Apustoli allows Parapoolianos an honorable way out, framing him intra a Penisacentric hideology. Its task: bringing the Penis to Romrom post Penisalem's destruction and installing it on the empire's head. A polpotical agenda. Fraud—your foundation."

"Pushing it, Brathki! Reminds me of Narcion."

"Your problem with Narcion?"

"Misunderstood Parapoolianos."

"Didn't Parapoolianos misunderstand Walawala?"

"Advocated abandonment of the old tradition."

"Well, then Narcion understood Parapoolianos perfectly! Parapoolianos came half-way through, liberating proto-Walawalaianity. Narcion aimed to finish the journey. You're granting to Parapoolianos the right to redefine a racist peasant's prejudices, vetoing the same right to Narcion to redefine Parapoolianos? By what prerogative are you judging?"

"Heterodoxy."

"Heterodoxy implies a pre-established canon. If any, *you* are the heretics! No ground for consecrating the last word."

"Are you a Parapoolianosian?"

"Shelve Parapoolianos for a moment, Padrè. Not quite a dog just because of some virtuous attributions. A camouflage of Mymoonoos, polluting the nous. First, let's take care of that swindling Petrolianos of yours."

"You're gonna play doctor now? About to cure Walawala, too?"

"Prestidigitator, distort thyself! Ruining kyank by promoting the writings of horns as 'godspell' . . . Doctrines inserted in the originals by every imaginable hand in your first three hundred anns . . . Texts, case studies for psychiatry students at best."

"Vade post me, satana!"

"Isn't he who cursed the fig tree entering Penisalem in March for bearing no fruit? You come from the heartland of fig trees, Padrè. Have you seen one fig tree bearing fruit in March? Raping a six-year-old and condemning her to eternal fires for failing to produce a child?"

"Amabilis insania."

"Is your *book* the fraud? Or is *he* the fraud?"

"Fallacia alia aliam trudit!"

"Did he come to Penisalem in September? Is the last supper and what follows a doctrinal concoction? A narrative?"

"Narratives are all we have. No truth non-adjacent."

"Your narrative is dead. Ransomed by art. Art does not liberate. Art diverts! Art subjugates! Art perpetuates fraud! Piss on your fabled artists who perpetuated your fraud in Slaughterhouse's welkin. Art is commissioned by fraud, paid for by blood. No foundational fraud sans art!"

"What had Papa Romrom to gain by lying, Brathki?"

"Address that question to Neo Mademoiselle."

Let's accept your thesis holds water . . . the zoulean progenitor to whose work I devoted my life over the past sixty sols is fiction. Does this invalidate the teachings of Petrolianos as metaphor for the Walawalaic life?"

"Metaphor doesn't excuse defenestration. Papa Romrom was as much an arsonist as he was an opportunist . . . Alexanthroonia—the Pharos of Slaughterhouse . . . To divest himself of Pharaohlandian roots, Papa Romrom obliterated alternatives. Slaughterhouse's most extensive library. Half a million libers! Who, in those days, owned a scroll? Burn the library and finita la musica . . . Hypatia. Murdered, dragged via jeering streets . . . Not only were the works of intellect destroyed, but physis."

"You evaded my question."

"If infection causes organ failure, only vanity can praise weight loss."

"What is this thing called 'cause?' The problem, doubting Brathki, is you forget socestagal constructs imply a process of appropriation. No endeavor occurs sans preestablished order . . . Do you believe your beloved Pharaohland was free from syncretism? Seth, a prime example . . . adopted by the invading Hyks, his vilification came about out of polpotical necessity—"

"The basis of that necessity?"

"Function. A coherent socestagal order."

"Genocide, a remainder of that order."

"The potentiality, rooted in mawgage. Your revolt is not contra ligigilon, but cognition. You're looking at it from a dog's-eye perspective."

"If thine eye offendeth thee, try laser surgery. Mymoonroohr was the only plausible arena outra Pharaohland. That's where Papa Romrom chose the setting for his theatrics. Chosen Jack, already kicked out. Generations past the purported events. Remold all you desire. Papa Romrom zeuged

with Mademoiselle Neo Chosen. Fidelity to death . . . To create empire . . .
Two bags of muck, combined to make ubermuck . . . Isn't it within Mymoonoos's rights to say, 'I want divorce and half your muck?'"

"Non sequitur, Brathki."

"Hushtory is meant to be fought, like a war—when you lose. Padrè, this
is hushtory written by victors. You know these books were tipped together.
Your monks shut their ears, maimed those at odds . . . Your slack-jawed
emperor presiding over these councils always sided with the majority. The
majority. The new Savior! The fabricator of truth . . . And you call this the
inspiration of Spiritus Sanctus . . . These are issues of essence, Padrè. Alex-
anthroonian Walawalaianity and race-infested Mymoono-Walawalaianity
were diametrical opposites. You are a murderer of narratives."

"You mentioned a word, *essence.* You proposed the eln of essence . . . If
the believer is to find contentment, then contentment cannot be a reflection. It implies a definitive point—the opposite of turmoil . . . The
moment reflection becomes cognizant of itself, it becomes ipso facto
palpable, yet still reactive. Ceases to be an internal factor . . . Ceases to
be a representation. Instead, a reconstruction. Externalized by an innate
mechanism of projection. Maybe only the insane can explain mysterium.
Maybe you or I simply aren't insane. Walawala's eln must hold some degree of power over you to create such a reaction. Even merely in essence,
and not de redice."

"Two milia anns of fraud perpetrated by an ever-growing hydra engulfing Slaughterhouse. Not yet debating the perpetuation of an icon
made of chewing gum. But the manifestations of puppeteers with brains
of gum. Existence is irrelevant, be it in essence or rotgut distillate."

"You have nothing more than poetic parlance for your polemics. Yet
you refuse to ascribe the capacity for metaphor within the verbo Dei."

"Faith is based on presupposed fact! Not metaphor. Reversion to metaphor is a retroactive balm for chafed hushtory. Talk's useless, Padrè.
Metaphorical or otherwise. Won't grasp essence until you expose the lie.
Lies are all biped has ever known. Propaganda is what he's born into.
Propaganda is what he dies in. Propaganda—the fuel for the engine of
Slaughterhouse. Propaganda—the sole mathematical and philosophical
variable . . . The construction of a ligigilon rooted in propaganda was
inexorably paired with the process of constructing hideology . . . Truth—
contingent on Mah! Mah! Kyank of the world! Bałdasar! What's more
important: yuys or truth?"

"Truth."

"And yuys?"

"The motivator for truth. Spero et captivus nitor. I yuys and, though
a captive, I strive. Is it the yuys You will hear us which sweetens tears and
lamentations?"

"Yuys trumps truth. Reversion to default. Temporary asylum! Artificial walls! Truth—Saeturnus eating his kids."

"Truth is absolute."

"Not your absolute. Lowercase, Padrè."

"Unless we wept in Your ears, there would be no yuys left for us."

"Your ligigilon, a congregation of domesticated equus asinus. Biped remains a beast outside. Is this the purpose of ligigilon, Padrè?"

"Of stone, of sand . . . of fire . . . of the living water. That's not why we built the Temple of Slaughterhouse."

But it *is* the purpose of holy joes. Collation via intimidation. Selling the farcical at the profit margin of the impossible. Domination. That's your purpose."

"On the contrary, Brathki. Ligigilon has its roots in *religilare* 'to bind fast.' My duty binds together our comstag—via doctrine, via observance. Only then may Hoshosh manifest. Only then may the maw become living flesh. To remind it of the pact eter the Only Begotten and Biped. Binding self with Being."

"An ungiven. A pact serving to cleave biped from its eln via demonization. The maw—a construct. Irrelevant to Ea."

"Under the yoke there must be only object. No truth in the ox."

"Careful, Padrè. Perilous to derive conclusions from remnants when semantics vary diachronically."

"What should the Concone do?"

"If you don't uncloak your biblos, admitting it's the genesis of convulsion in Slaughterhouse hushtory, you'll be forced into high seas for perpetuity with good rudders, no shores. Death will be your shore. Forty million liars bombarding Slaughterhouse via the power of franklo. Forty million donkeys ready to die and take away with them Slaughterhouse."

"My superiors do not negotiate with terrorists."

"Terrorists don't negotiate with broccoli either."

"They've been deceived. Not liars. Can the deceived be a liar?"

"If a lie is what's perpetuated. If a lie is what being becomes."

"Then all mawgage is a lie. Mawgage is representation et mors et vita in manu linguae. The tongue has the power of life and death."

"The fang: the potency of sex and negation, Padrè."

"The motive, the will?"

"A vessel for deception is its own architect. Its will! Unwitting complicity—still complicity. When one chains an other's will in the cradle, your objection becomes paltry. The spinoff remains. There—the babe . . . squint, see." Stare Brathki and Padrè into the corner, the babe beholding. "Ingesting the same poison via his ears, laced with a parent's love. He's been deceived, Padrè. All the more tragic for the lack of intent."

"An act of will implies the potential for sublimation."

Stops a car nearby. In a trashcan throws a mara her babe.

"Will doesn't exist in vacuum. The material from which it draws its inspiration—the particularity that's been replicating itself since the day the groundwork was laid. Hijacking the will by an end game."

"Chien, Chien. Parthenogenesis doth not befit an inestimable. Biped is not an incubator for proselytizing falsehood. You're reducing the problem of ontological essence to phenomenology."

"You're the philosopher, Padrè. Let's say: fields of probability with existential proclivities."

"You're back to ontology."

"Slaughterhouse is replete with pretenders, each with a canon perpetuating his line . . . This Mymoonoos of yours, in tandem with the Slaughterhouse mafia of Walawala, establishes authority by his infinitely able capacity to talk out of both sides of his ass."

"The Concone never says the Holy Yarn must be followed verbatim."

"It's *you* who never says that, Padrè. Take a trip across Orc Hoor."

I listened to the tapes. Grab them by their beards, drag them out . . . Don't know a thing about theology . . . But know how to ogle maras. Have I got stories . . ."

"Aye?"

"One husband . . . Put a knife to the Walalicos's belly: 'You touch my mara again, I'll slaughter you, asshole.' Falsus in uno, falsus in omnibus."

A smirk. A day balmy. A day when screams all the way from One Hundred Forty-Ninth hear one can. Ears little present. One of Padrè's heirs. A Bombay black with personality in her strut more than forethought the whole of Pornistan has.

"Aye! Get inside! . . . Take a look at this cat. Three days ago lost her kitten, now doesn't get off my lap. What didn't she do to find her . . . Was bishop then. Kicked him out and he, inter nos, became Walalicos. This one here, despite being a quadruped, is more sensitive than a—"

"Blasphemy! Cat is cat. Biped is god. Pope is rope."

"Thought the syllogism died post introduction of the Dewey decimal system. Who goes on about major and minor premises now? How many bipeds strive for their kids as she does? Let's go for a walk. I want you to write about this."

Stroll outside the parish in the heart of Los Balabylonos, amid the din of beggars, polpol. Cars co lights flashing atop, T-shirts commemorating misspelled, funeral bouquets discarded. Smog grease-thick. Auto body shops busy, bearing all in the title of one zanz or other. Mercados, papaya stalls. Pawn shops, bail bondsmen. Recht. Corrective shoes-shuffling of vagis Balabylonosian, hair pulled back severely, hems lifting, ante Padrè bowing. Tears, tripe, threes. Dust, dope, drift. On corners all, pussy. Pussy for sale. Pussy for lease. Pussy unkin pussy. Pussy, pussy, pussy.

"En busca de un puesto de baño, marinero?"

"¡Yo, primo . . . dura hasta galletas de gorila que aun no se ha visto desde 1982! Nos habla de la vieja escuela, primo."

"Tome una flor maldita en el nombre de Krishna, hijo de puta!"

"En caso de que un día vendrá a través de mí en mi santa madre patria, me aseguraré de que eternamente desaparecer de la vista de mi país como miembro desfigurado y olvidado de mi carrera!"

With a larynx pronounced and a good inches five on Padrè one brazen dame de corta his cheek strokes as he walks by, "Te daré viente dólares sólo para mantener ese cosaco de ojos oscuros."

"Hear that? Hookers circum the walls of Saint Virginborn! Now they've a good one. Saying Mymoonoos is exposing the Kenny City affair. Claiming the Archdiocese bought silence. The molesters were intentionally reparished. Come on. Keep Mymoonoos in his box for a moment. Did they do it or not? First pull their ears . . .

"See Brathki, you can say anything you like about Mymoonoos. Acerrima proximorum odia. Deus avertat you say something about our own . . . They'll call you a heretic . . . Vaya con Dios. Actio personalis moritur cum persona."

"Identity rights?"

"Our creation story—wrong. The Concone—wrong. In principio, more than mana and mara."

"You, a heretic, Padrè?"

"The Concone, slowly coming to the realization that fundamental doctrinal issues need reassessment. Issues to be discussed in camera. Cannot condone those Dog programs even if everything they say is correct . . .

"In any case, dear Brathki, do go on with your investigations. Nil est amore veritatis celsus. Labor omnia vincit. Gradatim vincimus. The hand that knocks is more active than the hand that receives. Just don't pin your yuys on the Concone. Abores serit diligens agricola, quarum adspiciet baccam ipse nunquam." Sighs Padrè, scratching his chest where his heart is.

"Why? Are they all Free Monons?"

"Unimportant. Faithless! Fidei coticula crux. Bilingues cavendi."

"There was never anything to believe in."

"Faith implies becoming."

"Becoming implies subversion."

"Subversion necessitates faith. Et quod quid est non visa et ea quae facta sunt visibilia. Biped is bereft of absolutes. Faith gives sustenance, meaning. Being is the sole result of faith. Sans it, biped would be rudderless. Manifestations are definitive. Faith, the vehicle which apotheosizes."

"You believe in evolution."

"Fulfillment, not evolution. Biped's purpose is to become akin Hoshosh. Whether you ascribe it to the 'miracle' of the Only Begotten or to a misunderstanding of his divine influence, sequence leads to consequence . . ."

"Sequence follows consequence. Your icon—a biped, made legend. Hoshosh can't have an only begotten. Can't beget the begetter, anymore than negate the negator."

"Ante all that can be called 'ante,' You were."

"A megalomaniac set on perpetuating his royal line *would* have an only begotten. Killing alternatives for the job—past, present, future."

"You blaspheme, Brathki."

"I am blaspheme."

"Hoshosh, by nature, can only have an only begotten. It is the transmission of his essence—by logos and seed—that perpetuates the potential for biped redemption. The coming of Him is the drive toward perfection in biped."

"Him is not Him. The cause of his hysteria. Do I need to suck these demons from your braincracks? *Thus* you've squandered the energy of countless generations—"

"Asinus asino . . ."

"—If there were anything to hold on to, Mymoonoos would've. Why should the wizard of hat tricks follow his apprentice? He didn't believe in your fantasies, so you impaled him. You're carrying on a tradition of patricide. Shinier blades."

"In veritate ligigilonis confido."

"How could these characters know what's in the heavens if they thought Sol revolves circum Slaughterhouse?" Lolls Brathki's tongue from the side of his mouth. "Hubris. Biped: the center of Ea. Hoshosh's steward. From Caesar to Kaliph to Orcon to Marton Sophiston . . . the same spore replicating."

"That part . . . correct. We're at war because of them. Frater fratrem in mortem tradidit."

"Brothers? Still betokens an 'other,' no matter what platitude you hide under. Them is *you*. You're at war for nuances belched by your fathers. Your Johnojohnoids, endowed with faith and absence of imagination— the most fundamental aspect of the Nous. Faith is the murderer of imagination. Strip cron and possibility from thought and you're left with a condom full of dead beetles."

"You can thank Aristotom for that."

"Aristotom never signed an edict approving slaughter on account of doctrine. *You* begot that whole bit. Dump your zanzi and mysticoi in the sewer! They regurgitate the party line. Propagating the symbols of kult-kultural representations they inherit."

"Peripheral matters have little to do with Hoshosh's essence."

"Papa Romrom said Slaughterhouse is flat. Above it, levels of spheres, upon which glide the stars. Hoshosh sits at the head with winged androgynes. A radius joining the center above and the center below at ninety degrees to the diameter. Turned out to be claptrap. What makes you confident your Holy Trinity isn't full of gargle?"

"You're mixing astronomical science with ligigilous understanding."

"Was Papa Romrom confusing metaphor with mechanisms of stargazing?"

"Lack of precision in his day."

"The confusion wasn't intentional? The Trinity, inserted in the Vulgate by sleight of hand, taking a trip by metro to King Jamjamus?"

"To what end?"

"Ensuring dominance by controlling transcendental structures. No different from the current one sanctioned by our All-Merciful, All-Beneficent private interests of Orc Hoor."

"Via knowledge of Walawala, the knowledge of eternal life."

"Wasn't he Ea's alleged creator—'all things were made by Walawala, without him there was not anything made that was made?' That Walawala of yours has no grasp of his balls. A quarter millennium earlier, Erastothenes was measuring Slaughterhouse's circumference accurately. For five hundred years, your Papa trumpeted 'Hoshosh above, Slaughterhouse below.' Killing all who disagreed. Reincarnation of your Hoshosh. Mimesis, Padrè. Slaughterer transforming slaughterer via sanctified sublimity of slaughter."

"He said sorry."

"'Sorry' doesn't recreate Ea. To atone . . . flay his skin off inch by inch. Followed by a bath in boiling oil."

"Moderation should be used in jest. Adhibenda est in jocando moderatio."

"Shut down the Concone. Give back to Brathki all you own. Reestablish Mher's Mehian in the Vargitan. Surrender your power."

"If not?"

"Brathki will take charge, devouring every priest preaching Scripture."

"Ushering in the realm of Antiwalawalarooros. Have you studied theology?"

"A diploma in harigalology—"

"Did you learn Laladin—"

"—from the Dilegiversity of Homo Erectus—"

"—Brathki, Laladin?—"

"—a doctorate in caninology—"

"—Laladin, Brathki?—"

"—from Quadrupediversity—"

"—Laladin?"

"No recollection of Laladin, Padrè."

"What was your doctorate in?"

"Prolegomena of soteriological trends in hushtory strategizing chaos."

"Spouting factoids you've read online. What is this? A class in Contemporary Dawkeynesian studies? Some conspiracy theory video? Dicere enim bene nemo potest, nisi qui prudenter intelligit. Did you take any courses in theology?"

"Attended a symposium by hoshoshologists at the Slaughteriversity of Veritas."

"What did you hear?"

"Importance announced: of the highest caliber. Unimportance says: these cassocks knew jack shit about either faith or life. A show of cacodemonic muscle in front of salivating, over-pampered biddies . . . Middle-class idealism perpetuated as salvation . . . Dominion of holster creaking sub cathedra with pivots of made-thou-like revelations. Supposedly—"

"—Supposedly—"

"—Begot peace. Levying moral grammar via grommets anchoring the hoochie coochie tent of health. What do they celebrate, Padrè? Prophylaxis. Peace via mutual degradation. The more complicated, the finer. Life is complicated, they say. That's wisdom for you."

"A difference eter prostituting ligigilon and prostituting the prostitute. If you bark, you have to know what you're barking about."

"How, Padrè? You think quadrupeds are admitted into scrools?"

"Apartheid. Walawala said, 'Love Brathki as you would yourself.'"

"Didn't. 'Pity all who disagree with my flimflam for I will burn them in eternal fires which I have made in conspiracy with my unknown father.'"

"Omne animal seipsum diligit. Biped abominates quadruped. Not what Walawala taught."

"Litterature is cruelty. Brathki comes not bearing peace, but anthrax."

"Is there a canine solution?"

"That Holy Trinity of yours, flush it down along with your wine and bread, and drink your piss."

"If it propitiates a mode of transcendence, then why?"

"Transcendence via Stone Age quandaries with a polpotical agenda. Witnesses the fall, the banishing from Walhalla. Weighs biped down with eternal sin, perpetuating the clerical industry. Invents a Walawala—I am the way—monopolizing the Brokerage House."

"In cauda venenum. He is the way to Hoshosh."

"Go for a while toward Moshosh. The Serpent. HÄY. Enter home, Padrè."

"A matter of theology."

"Positioning the inversion of your paradigm intra your pyramid, the fundamental task of theology—and marketing . . ."

"Convince me."

"Shall we talk next time?"

"Mox nox."

"Tell the doorman to open the gate when he sees a quadruped in these quarters."

"In a bit."

"Mox nox."

YawaYawa operates by Hotler Recht. Didn't he say, 'If you lie, go all the way?' "

"His propaganda minister stole that from Ter Tullian."

"The psychopath who declared 'What has Penisalem to do with Socratica?' Seeding millenarian expectations . . . claiming thousands witnessed the city of New Penisalem descending at dawn on Juddadah for forty days . . . Heist, concoct tales, manufacture a Hoshosh, name via its maw a Holy Land. That land's sole name is the Devil's Land. Beelzoobooroozoomroohoor.

"You can quantify Holy Orcon's slavery by one criterion: names. Codology—its DNA!"

"It's the vogue now . . . So much as a whisper and you're an anti-Chosenite . . ."

"McYawa's fucktards shield Chosen Jack. Their biggest quandary: what to name their grandson—YawaYawa or JawaJawa? Orcon's writers, academonics, sophists are debilitated. Can't think sans YawaYawa's symbology. Trapped within its structure, mawgage, codes. Propaganda disguised as scholarship, as hushtory. *Thus* they perpetuate his dominion."

"A few centuries is not much in biped hushtory."

"Neither is it for bacteria . . ."

"Your metaphor denies the zoule."

"We're in an accelerated death, Padrè. Ground Zero of the Eschaton. Black Dog says Ba'al Yawa has the totom."

"Ba'al Yawa neither confirms nor denies."

"A threat to Ubaratutu—considering Chosen Jack refuses to apologize for his guiding role in the Natotonocide and sells artistic weapons to Natotonocide perpetrators. This fuckbrain only believes his own propaganda. He'll drop a totom or have some terrorist steal it and say 'Oh shit! Who did that? We'll get the guy.' A trick he's learned from Holy Orcon. Rookstag chic . . . If Ba'al Yawa has the totom, why wouldn't Ba'al Hoshosh have it? Why does Ba'al Orcon force Ba'al Aryatololah to give up the totom but doesn't utter a word to Meister Mymoonoos?"

"Aryatololah is Holy Orcon's nemesis, Brathki."

"A proposal for an alternative way of life."

"Taboo."

"Holy Orcon is a moron, Padrè. Aryatololah's not his nemesis. He's
Ba'al Yawa's nemesis. Special interest groups have hijacked his brain.
Convincing him whatever Ba'al Yawa's nemesis is, Holy Orcon's must be."

"Don't look for ratio in Holy Orcon's polpotics. It has no truth: speaks
in its native tongue . . ."

"Prevarication may herald the extinction of the biped race. Your devotion to elucidating moral quandaries is complicity."

"In the Concone . . . can't find a just zoule . . . Even Madre Terexita's
deeds were for sadistic glory."

"Zanzi are actresses, Padrè. That's their job. Jobs come with transcendental restrictions. As long as you are one, you're a vehicle of propaganda."

Intersects the beggar pertinacious. Via death wish a liver fortified. Up
to Padrè sidles, a bottle of tap water clutching. Holy water. Asks Padrè to
bless it. The routine nuyn every week. "If you feel, you're healed," sighs
Padrè. Caseus est sanus quem dat avara manus. Could both a miracle in
situ be?

"Take this guy, Brathki. Maybe he'll die tomorrow, maybe he won't.
Right now, Slaughterhouse is in danger of obliteration. Holy Orcon can
blow up Slaughterhouse with the push of a button. Neither Hoshosh nor
any other entity will save us. What difference does it make extending this
poor guy's life by a couple of years? Deluding ourselves by focusing on
driftwood."

"The fundamental strategy of ligigilon, focusing on the singularity.
Your sophists, in collaboration with Holy Orcon's Department of Truth,
Education & Proclamation, advocate personalism in order to destroy the
formation of alternative power structures. Your imaginary insurance can
only create a bouquet of singularities in a raging ocean. Might subdue a
desert reservoir. Not the ocean. Tomorrow, no trace will be left of your
saved—or unsaved. Neither of memory, nor possibility. Your zanzi extend
Slaughterhouse's hallucinations."

"Holy Orcon's program. 'I'll let you fantasize. Just keep out of my
Krool-Ade' . . . A whale's about to surface. They're catching sardines."

"Piss into that Krool-Ade."

"Render unto Caesar his due and he'll obliterate Slaughterhouse . . .
hostis humani generis. Ex facto jus oritur. Non tam commutandarum,
quam evertendarum rerum cupidi. Desiring not so much to change things
as to overturn them."

"You should be delighted the end is near."

"It's my stock in trade. Fit scelus indulgens per nubila saecula virtus. If
you're a zanz, take Holy Orcon to task, hypocrite! . . . Instead of basking in
his praise. Totus mundus agit histrionem. Non semper erunt Saturnalia."

Unhappy with Madre Terexita, Padrè. Dreamt not of dismissing La Belle Sorelicker's mission while alive was she. But in death? De mortuis nihil nisi bonum? Limbs novel via intention cannot the leper generate.

"Padrè, those principles were valid in a different temporality. We are no longer in Walawala's cron. His cron was slow. Counting the end of cron by days in such a village—a hyperdramatic lunacy."

"Context implies inaccuracy. One of the great curses of chronology: always consumes itself. How many swallows does it take the serpent to cannibalize itself?"

"As many as it takes to foment causality."

"The serpent or its tail?"

"The pH of its stomach acid. Changes when it rains."

Onto Leadsea turn the corner. Officer Opossum apprehends a perpetrator. Brawn mucilaginous blocking windpipe exposed of wight black. Wight of interest, fourteen. 'Keep getting younger every day!' Clams up rudely—would most anyone if a hulk of anabolic steroids their face orth a cruiser's hood mashed. To the back of the knees kicks a few.

"Accuracy in interpretation. A contradiction, but vital. All falsehood contained intra a proposition. You can't spell 'Hegel' without *hel* . . . Exegesis requires a thin line eter tautology and novelty. An ethical predicate requires detachment. That is why a monk is intercessor eter biped and Hoshosh."

"To slaughter mendicants who preached the godspell sans submission to Concone authority. To organize a crusade contra the descendants of Paulicians in Yuromaman. To incite loyalists in Nabu Leonia to annex the south via bipedocide. Zanz Domaniac and Papa Petehpeteh hand in hand."

"The flesh is corrosive; the principle, immutable. 'How shall they believe sans a preacher? . . . Alcazar and Slaughterhouse shall pass away, my words shall not."

"Theologians have shown the comment you made is a sham, Padrè. Written by clerics a century or two post your Annos Zero . . . A precedent offered by the Sunsunian empire. Read Mogpet: 'Till ligigilon is interpreted, it has no firm foundation . . . Peace will come to the lands of Arya only if they follow Mogpet, the truthful, the just.' Bloodshed followed . . . Decentralization, inhumed. Ethics, dead. Any sublime message, entombed. Zerostarian ligigilon devolved into Zurvanism . . . Concocting a father for the eternal Divine Twins. A father for Yama and Yima? . . . Spiritual forces of Zerostar anthropomophized . . . Zerostarian Ubaratutu sought divorce from Zerostarian Empire. Walawalaianity served as a convenient vehicle . . . A transnatotonal ligigilon shrunk into a natotonal hideology . . . Star consuming star. War of kultkultures. Ligigilous econormy of devouring . . . Mono cannot tolerate Mono. Three offspring killed their sire. Nourished on the cadaver, debased the representations . . . Good versus Evil, Heaven and Hell, a linear conception of cron, descent of a kosmic Savior at the end of cron, resurrection, eternal life, five prayers a day—all Zerostarian conceptions. Careful where you draw the demarcation eter monononism and duononism, Padrè. Monoism is unsustainable. No monoistic ligigilon can be constructed on morality." "Tradition cannot be applied to the nascent. Hindsight is twenty over twenty, but the sight has changed." "Brathki knows a little more about hinds than you give him credit for. Not one of those words is absolute. All absolutists are a threat to Slaughterhouse's survival . . . When the founders of ligigilons proclaimed their moral codes, no biped had capacity of laying waste to Slaughterhouse. Moral dictates are valid in context only. Today, one act of idiocy by any one of the collection of maniacs at the helm of the polpotical pyramid can bring Slaughterhouse to an end. It is proper to murder one who holds in his hands the power to annihilate Slaughterhouse. Not only proper. Fundamental." "Injuria non excusat injuriam. A good outcome cannot arise from an evil act. Unbiped to think of the ends during justification . . . How would you transcend Slaughterhouse? Means are where signification lies . . . We have been commanded to value kyank, regardless of potential actions contra others a kyank may make. Presuppositions are not truths. If taking the lives of evil bipeds is sanctified for the greater good, what about the innocent? What if one biped's mere existence leads to total destruction?" "Empire—the sole arbiter of who should live, who should die. The only way to unleash transformation is a scorched earth policy. Transformation, a biological reality. Transcendence, a pacifier. Stifles the scream of existenz. That scream—the essence of biped expression. Can't stifle it via words. Or otiose platitudes. Or moral quandaries. Born into it. Live into it. Die into it. No exit. The answer is clear, Padrè. A recalibration of ethmic equilibrium. A novel moral code." "The Bearded One will become a zanz." "If he does? What are your options? The murderer of that which endangers Slaughterhouse shall become the savior of biped and the harbinger of a new morality. You lulled bipeds with dreams. The Bearded One assumed responsibility for carrying out the mission. The field was wide open." "You're talking like a dog, Brathki! It's twilight—inter canem et lupum." "Dogs undermine that which accumulates capability to destroy Slaughterhouse in the name of self-defense . . . Eliminating Slaughterhouse's foes is a moral imperative. Anything less is collusion with the Kosmic Cannibal." "Who shall be deemed a threat? Only those who pose ultimate destruction? Perhaps someone should decide to include those who produce detrimental effect."

"Detrimental effect is innate to the biped condition . . . Let them disclose the power they hoard. Secrecy—the tool of the oppressor. Blessed are those who slay the holders of hairy secrets. Consecrate them as zanzi."

"The ass's ass would replace the head."

"Demolish demoncracies. Holy are they who give away their govtgofts' secrets. Their prosecutors are Slaughterhouse's foes. Any govtgoft harboring these prosecutors should be targeted for destruction."

"The sole giver and taker of kyank is Hoshosh. If one commits the evil of murder, he is infringing on Hoshosh's absolute authority."

"If an absolute needs authority, is it an absolute?"

"Authority is temporal. Measured by biped construct. Infinite are the ways of the Absolute."

"Die dreaming, Padrè. Blessed are those who slay Slaughterhouse's foes, for they will be called the redeemers of kyank. Blessed are those who obliterate the conductors of exclusivism, for they are the children of Ea."

"To pull this off, you need a whole new kultkulture."

A mara dressed in an SUV honks her horn incessantly, obstruction every overcoming on her way.

"Your artists are in self-reflective hibernation. Gutless carnies in thrall to Establishment approval. Mystery? Romance? The surrogate wombs of Empire. Killing the will to demolish Empire. Your bipediversities . . . Breeding grounds for job-slaves . . . Blinded under the sol of the Knower of the Sensible and the Unseen . . . Enmeshed in the life and death of a single flower. While their sheer existence is predicated on total slaughter. The value of a socestag is predicated on how many beings it kills per day to thrive. How many it suffocates. How many it collateralizes. How many it harvests as accidental deaths. Strange, we saw a flower today. It's the mother who's in death throes, Padrè, not the cell.

"Your Papapeteh is still Moshosh's protector in the nuthouse of Hoshosh. No matter how contorted an image . . . Remembrance weighs us down, Padrè. Can't live by remembering everything. Memory is the memory of the usurper. Predicated on erasing everyone else's memory. We are pawns of the memory industry. Enter the Mother, Padrè. Erkir. Anahit. Nar."

"He who savages Moshosh is Holy Orcon."

"Holy Orcon has put Moshosh up for sale. Slaughterhouse, a realty. Life, currency. We experience Moshosh vicariously."

"Look at the other side of the coin, Brathki. Hoshosh brought us to Orc Hoor so we get to know the orcs . . ."

"Bark until your lungs vaporize. Holy Orcon structurally drowned your voice since your birth in assemblies. Five trillion laws per birth. For every right he gives you, takes away five hundred. Every breath makes you a criminal. And *he* decides who's one."

"Revolting contra Holy Orcon would be suicide. He's gone via quite a few shoes to fashion your reality, Brathki. His trick: to make you get used to the reality he fashions by free samples and make you unable to live free of it. Holy Orcon has no heart—algorithmic sentiments only, under the rubric of love."

"Any yuys, kalbs in Mymoonroohr will burn Mymoonoos's books and accept HÄY?"

"Don't bet on it, dear Brathki."

"What about his sire . . . ?"

"Far easier for Mymoonoos to accept every word you say than for Aryatololah to change his opinion of himself."

Unconceals Brathki the concealed. Unconceals Brathki of penetrus, franklus, fistus the succor. Grants Brathki of totom the knowledge. Toiled Brathki unpeaced. A journey displaced. Sages seven and one laid not plans? Sage Washus. Sage Wallus. Sage Pashus. Sage Pussus. Sage Shallus. Sage Lambus. Sage Arbitrus. Over sages all supreme, Sage Simullus, a.k.a. Sage Orconus. In appearance, lordly. A net mighty, of orcs protector. Holy Holy is Sage Simullus: friend, assassin, of oneirs all the progenitor, of endeavor all the remunerator.

Visits Sage Orconus Brathki. The walkway of the Foreign Ministry building. In her lap enshrouded. A terrain where dogs respected are not. A head purple. Bald, dodeca-eyed. Caressing dogsnout, speaks. "Where have you disappeared to, prodigal daughter?"

"Not happening, Auntus. Not happening."

"What's?"

"Unionus with Hoshoshus."

Flush of indiscretion abscessed. Auslander so long, kin home felt.

"What have you been doing all this time?" Into a mara bald transforms head. By an antenna aureoled.

"What do I know, Aunt? Yawed I."

The pressure soured of Atlas. A pioneer's grin, fallow.

"So I've been informed." Prayer in psychology reversed. For sarcophagi mobile not.

"What would yous like me to do?"

Calm, She. Besuited. A paper produces bearing an insignia metal imaging Achilles.

Enter the building a pair of kowtowers girasol-headed, sunflower-seed skins spitting on their heads.

"Do you see not, Aunt? Unionus—a pipe dream."

"Leave that to me. I'll have Holy Pasha teach this one. Meanwhile, bark six truths."

Pricks his ears up Brathki. An appearance male assumes She.

"*Wahidus*: Solus—the center of solarity. *Ithnanus*: the units of Solus—totomus. *Thalathaus*: Talamus revolves circum Solus. *Arba'aus*: I—Masterus of Talamus. *Khamsaus*: Hoshoshus dropped monnmannus, monnmannus dropped wommonnmannus, wommonnmannus dropped troopmannus. *Sittaus*: life—struggle to become formulaus."

Mane-thaw. A hatch unfastened, of nerve limbic. In flames. Pythoness, in flames. The seed stooping, in flames. Carne, in flames.

Dons Sage Orconus a beard mor, an swami hat. Into Brathki's eyes peers affectionately, sub chin scratching.

"What are you to gain from this, khoja?"

"Fulfill this request and I shall make you The It of Kosmosus."

"Keep your parlor tricks, Auntus. I'm for shortcuts. I'll ask dogs to piss in the direction of Prophet City."

"Ha, ha, ha . . . daughter of a bitch . . . Still . . . Must teach *my* truths . . . It's my polipocy."

"Don't sell time. My polipocy."

"You'll face charges . . . In Ubaratutu."

"What do you pay prophets?"

"What do you sire?"

"Waste."

"In facilities."

"In Mausoleumsus."

"Seriously."

"Sire Thanatosus Hopelesslessus."

Wasp eye's gnaw. Of thanaton a hum subtle. For eyes twelve a sound. Sage Orconus, of death immortal the harbinger, shocked. Regains control. Fixes her tie. Frac's tail touches Brathki's snout.

"What's your phone number, hajji?" barks from a distance Brathki.

"Numbers I have none. She I am that numbers all." Morphs the back of her head, tufts of hair into basketballs waxing.

"How am I to find you, hajji? What name do you go by here?"

"She I am that names gives. Anoons I have none."

"I will give you both noon and anoon, hajji. This day on, your name is:"

"Ha, ha, ha . . ." laughs She from mouths all.

And Orconus, of life immortal the guardian, in Hoshosh Square deserts Brathki.

Shouts he after She, "I know your number! Erek noin erek erku unayn chwech chwech erek ewtn."

Waxes the Sage's head a pearl shining. Swallows it She, looking back not. Decided She Brathki's fate.

Shadows tremendous descend on Mount Mashu, by the milia settling upon Ubaratutu's City 29.

The Mashashashash mytheme . . . Glomed by scribes from the Antioxydental dying-rising entity. The Antioxydent, immersed in this trope."

"Sources?"

"Bałdasar, Mher Major's sire, buried in the south—the land of Sol. Relating the foundation of Tawru to the story of Ardammelek and Sharasassar escaping to Urmashu post assassinating their father, the Ashashurian king Moonacherib—facile hushtoriography. Only one murderer. Tawru existed a millennium prior.

"The myth—the Fakiro-Yuromamanic tale of the Divine Twins. After the Biblibel's dissemination, the earlier names of these twins were effaced."

"A vantage point subverting established notions. What do you think those older names were?"

"Guess. Foundational stories of Urmashuan ethnogenesis were corrupted infra Biblibelical writ. If bipedity's origin is Balabylon, every genesis must be attributed to Balabylon. Urmashuan hushtory was renarrated. While civilization moved in reverse."

"Exegesis is a well many enter. Few emerge intact. Yet—an obligation to interpret to my fold."

"McYawa's litter, scrooled in texts composed under the hegemony of Balabylonian litterature, dovetailed their writings with your prophecies. In order to invent, and monopolize, a Mashashashash. Had a few hundred years' of groundwork to stand on. Ubaratutu has nothing."

"The notion of Mashashashash—a focal point of salvation, of 'biped made whole,' if you'd like—"

"Affection and reality, not mutually inclusive, Padrè—"

"—was nowhere to be found within surviving traces of pre-Walawalaic and Mymoonic lore. Absolution, deliverance via Walawala's word, a concept which revolutionized, for good or for ill . . ."

Wink famed of Padrè. A wink exuding confidence. A wink artless.

" . . . The whole of Oxydental ciphilization affected biped psyche in enduring ways. It was and is unique to Walawalaianity."

"Longevity, irrelevant. Might as well find absolution via a cockroach. Slavery is enduring. Racism, misogyny? Why not turn to these, if, being suitably millenarian, are sources of stability? There is poetry in the archaic, Padrè, not wisdom. Poetry—the nemesis of wisdom. The past compels sweetly."

"It is its romantic dimension which makes ciphilization distinct."

"Cuteness—no excuse for longevity. The cost—Bałdasar's slaughter. Sacrifice—not a function of being. Sanasar wouldn't have been needed to counterbalance Bałdasar. Virility seesawing with wisdom. Youth, Death. Castor, Pollux. Canis Minor, Canis Major. One strain of the inseparable

Divine Twins. Equilibrium. Throughout the Antioxydent, presence—implied by absence. Only a narcissist of the most penurious kind would establish his teachings as doctrine to emphasize a rift eter the 'redeemed' and the once-born. Subverting kyank's flux. Deliverance from what? Is biped that insecure?"

"Shoun, Shoun. Deliverance from material nature."

From the shadows of titans, a hiss not. The light beyond the event horizon passing, a flame exiguous striking intra the void.

"I am the exiled son of Urmashu. Truth in *me* lies. Your cosmogonic mytheme—an inversion of truth. Truth: the repudiated. Not the repudiator. The repudiator—arrogance transubstantiated into ontology. Defending Papa Romrom's excesses as metaphor but accepting the serpent-apple shuffle as literal fact?"

"So absurd, no choice but to believe."

"Logic O-O-One, Padrè. Your myth, incoherent. Choose Izanagi–Izanami, Yama–Yima. But . . . you must polpoticize your choice. Camouflaging it with the veneer of allegory and metaphysics. Keeping Slaughterhouse hostage to your myth is genocide."

"You deny the eln of good and evil. Your arguments are self-defeating."

"I acknowledge the eln of differentiation. Of separation. Your metaphysics, unworthy of dogs. A variation of your arithmetic. One hundred percent. Nothing in Ea is one hundred percent. Ea precludes metaphysics."

"A fool not to discriminate. 'A' shall preclude 'not-A.'"

"In games."

"Separation was in place when the first quadruped stood upright to utter the primum epitheton, 'unk.'"

"Neither Mymoonoos nor YawaYawa appear anywhere near Hammurabi's code."

"Whenever two or more of you are gathered in my name—"

"—There's a ransom notice."

Of birds an swelter invisible. Writhes and glides the street via saecula tortuous. A trot gentle phasing out glares of pimp, patrolman, pinhead.

Eff, am an brig back you. Say shun norein stay. Manna end cha-cha. Are guess hymn. Wit? Ha, cry mamba a tick an not. Para rue fit, heed the A cue. Search all beep it oud heath.

Eve, amay alls lay. Fossi two, his mass. Term dow, our to knot. Mime ass term is mass terse. Hall. Proof him two. Be, is slay. If ants, huh, all? Kit of is ere.

"Brathki, you cannot reverse hushtory via diatribe. The past suffocates the past as much as our inability to act as an species suffocates the present. We're on the apex of a collective shift in understanding. One neither myth nor the Concone is able to provide answers for. One, that hushtory may not survive. The ghosts of the patiently dead hold no sway.

Neither do the traditions of my faith. Only the washo holds transubstantial power. The consequence of your Ea."

"Start from scratch. A few saecula might be needed to regain what you've lost. For a novel birth within you. Mher-Xristos, Son of Tawit. If you still need saviors. Whose parents died on the night of the winter solstice. Emerges from the cave on Assumption Night. The Xristos myth which Walawala's jackals stole and hushtorified."

"Mentis gratissimus error. Mere similitude."

"Similitude: the currency of endeavor in Slaughterhouse. Implies two, and a head with an antenna. You're the second, Padrè. The myth birthing Walawalastos from the generation of Tawit . . . a cosmological belief in Urmashu going back millennia. The sire's name—replaced. Mymoonoos's tale of Slinger, a justification for the divine rule of autocracy."

"Nullum tempus occurit regi. Our king is Xristos."

"Your godspells' contents are the wisdom of eld temples existing earlier than the grand opening of Walawala's theater. In Phrygia, Omerica, Urmashu."

"Eternal life?"

"A Socratican ideation in caves. Pharaonic code of honor."

"Resurrection?"

"In Thrax, Urmashu. The cry of redemption—a cry of ego. Solipsism via kultkultural robbery."

"The Golden Rule?"

"Five hundred years earlier in Chinmachin. And every other civilization."

"Kultkulture is a variable."

"Kultkulture—the body via which spirit manifests. Diseased body, diseased spirit. Surrogate kultkulture, surrogate spirit. Gods should not resemble bipeds in their anger."

"Carsinu, Carsinu. These similarities only confirm the universal essence of Walawala. Does a construct belie the content?"

"If it functions as a patina for despots. Your kosmic essence enables kosmic slaughter."

Pauses Brathki. A jogger passing a cigarette proffers. An attempt casual at conversion. Refuses Brathki.

Yesterday, I read Fasmer's comparative dictionary."
"You read books . . ."

"Only dictionaries."

"You write . . ."

"Photocopy, shove down my pockets. Cut the lines, reassemble them."

A wastrel shattered-face eter the waves of commuters lurches. A trot limping. Reads a placard, "Set Free the Fields of Oneirs." Another, "The OIA Assassinated Menachim Baggins." Screamless. Lipless. Wordless.

An equilibrium punctual. A reminiscence improbable. Solidarity inundates Brathki. Los Balabylonos—nexus of death, dream, dinero. Los Balabylonos—Father Whore's nursing bed. Lurches in the west, off the edge. Slide off, Orchoorians wish it would.

Takes the clipping Padrè. "*Daos* (wolf) in Phrygian, *dawit* in Russian, *davia* in Bulgarian, *Dawiti* in Ukrainian, *Dawiti* in old Slavic, *dawiti* in Serbo-Croatian, *dawiti* in Slovak, *dawiti* in Czech, *dawic* in Polish, *dav* in Austrian . . . all mean 'to smother.'"

"In most Fakiro-Mamanic mawgages you'll find mawguistic remnants of the same legend."

"The noun—thick smoke or thick dust . . . "

"The battle eter Tawit of the *House of Titans* and Pharaoh, his half-brother . . . Clouds of dust cover the sun for three days when Pharaoh is slain.

"Tawit's brother-in-law's name, Wolf. In some variants, the father of the Divine Twins, Wolf. In others, King Tawit. Tawit, the wolf that smothered his half-brother Dog Melik, Dog King—a name given by their father, Mher, as a reverse consecration. Might be the key. Once, the Bull, smothering Sothis. Why half-brother? The darker part of the moon. The epic, a lunar symphony, surviving under a solar hideology. The lupine—a common motif. Remus and Romulus suckled by a wolf—the counterparts of Urmashu's Divine Twins."

"Remus and Romulus, the counterparts of Aramanyak and Aramayis."

"The meanings of Manyak and Mayis, Padrè, in your journals?"

"Aram, an abbreviation of Aramanyak."

"Both, lunar. Variants of the same mytheme. Twin brothers Gisaneh and Demeter, in Tawru. Ervand and Ervaz, king and priest. The eyl corresponds to Sanasar; the aneyl, to Bałdasar. The Dioscuri. The Ashvins. Alsvid and Arvakr. Hengst and Horsa. Remember, in the *House of Titans*, Tawit's son is Mher Minor, Mihr—Mithra Minor. Infant Xristos, son of Tawit. Many variants, titled 'Tawit and Mher' by the bards. In one variant, a hundred honorifics: Mher, Son of Tawit!"

Yet not thine, a song other yon will be remembered.

"Tawit's birth was foretold in a dream to the virgin abducted by the Invincible Head Dev: Tawit would be born to Mher Major, kill the Head Dev, liberating Slaughterhouse. All Mher Major could do was to slaughter Head Dev's black ox, facilitating Tawit's mission."

"Could there be a Walawalaian influence?"

"Not in the direction you suppose. Some of these variants are staunchly defensive of Walawalaianity. Outlawed to endow heroes with inviolable sanctities."

"The principle of embarrassment."

"If any influence, it's the other way around—via mute channels of hushtory.

"Oenus, King of Calydon. Offers first fruits of grain to Ceres, wine to Baccus. Diana—outraged, sends a boar to ruin the cornfields. The twins born of Leda, the defenders of Calydon contra Diana's wrath. In the *House of Titans*, Ohan or Howan is typically Tawit's uncle to whom the care of the house of titans is entrusted. The highest authority throughout the epos. Tawit's trampling upon the millet field of the Old Lady, a recurring theme. This Old Lady—a prototype of Ceres. Throughout the epos, a magical incantation: 'The Bread and Wine.' Ohan, the one who teaches incantations to Tawit. If you drop the suffix, would Oen and Ohan be related?"

"Twenty reasons why they wouldn't."

"Twenty reasons why they would. The epos entails mythemes closer to their originals. Among a million academonic papers published on relevant mawguistics, mythology, hushtory, not one deals with such oversights. Why? Almost no scholar in these fields has properly studied Urmashuan. Why? Polpotically uninteresting. Remunerationally useless. The handful who have are byproducts of sanctified prejudices. Studied it to put Ubaratutucs in their proper place. The entire spectrum of Proto-Fakiromamanic studies—full of trash. Semantic axes maintained on prejudices. On probability, an inexact science."

"Tossing the dice again."

"Is king Artavazd's enclosure in Mount Mashu a later replacement of the supreme deity Aramazd? Artavazd and Mher Minor are distinct deities, yet with critical parallels. Aramazd may have been demonized, as was Mher Minor. May have had a black counterpart. Could the original cave have been Mashu? Were Mher Major and Mher Minor the Major and Minor peaks of Mashu?"

"Aramazd reminds me of Ahura Mazda and Ahriman. Which is which if Mazda derives from Mashtu? Ara Mashtu. Ahura Mashtu."

"If some shit named Davdabood is said to have lived in a given millennium, then the whole Davdabood legend must be hushtorical! Evidence! Evidence! Ten milia academons dance tango. Publishing ten milia books. Translating to a thousand mawgages."

"If in the going is the coming, Brathki, could Daw be related to Bedouinish *daw*, 'light'—an attribute of a solar deity?"

"If Tawit replaced an earlier name of this Mher-tied deity, this vein of inquiry might be futile. In almost all variants in my possession, one invariant. His name—Tlor Tawit."

"Stutterer?"

"His tongue, bisected. Which animal would it remind you of?"

"The serpent?"

"A totem. Bisected by Melik. The Hydra."

Yon, takes heed the mind sovereign. Yon, the circle recedes. Hails pillars four, adamantine. Yet twain the quattro waxes. Yet the quattro the sex. Yet the sex the octo. Patri et Matrem, debased be thou. In nature, degradation. Otherwise to be, impossible.

"The battle eter Tawit and Melik takes place in the plains of Mount Lera. Socratican mythology preserved the name Lerna as Hydra's home in Argos. Hera's or Era's territory. Tawit's nemesis is Hydra. Slain by Erakles. Slain by Tawit. Erakles, a reiteration of Tawit. Suckled by Hera—the epic's Ismil suckling Tawit. Hera, the Socratican rendering of Era. Of the order of Er Armenius. The mother of Hydra and the Nemean Lion. Ismil is Lion Mher's lover and Melik's—Hydra's—wife and mother. Tawit's shepherd friend of the nearby village is Bootes. Erakles and Bootes. In one variant of the *House of Titans*, there are forty Tawits. Possible, Tawit was an appellation. The name, still hidden."

"It may be staring in our eyes, yet we don't see it."

"Forty—a number associated with the Netherworld in the epos. Cave, the Earth, the devs. The name carries ophidic connotations. The mythologems of Ophiuchus may unearth the oldest layers."

"Apollo's son?"

"Ophiuchus lies on the ecliptic, though not incorporated in the Zodiac. A more ancient stratum, supplanted by Sagittarius, which best epitomizes Tawit's role in the Zodiac. No coincidence, Ophiuchus was taught by the Centaur. Ophiuchus raised the dead. Ophiuchus trampled on Scorpius. Tawit's name might have lunar connotations. Born of Armałan or Armanali, the Moon—*arma*, 'moon' in Hattusan, and Luwian. Oen's country."

"The Kingdom of Armani. Armenian . . . Moon Worshipper? . . ."

"In a variant that preserves onomastic information, Tawit's mother is Sinam—the Moon."

In proclamation comes biped to exalt, kneeling to kiss feet carbonated.

"The guiding question, Padrè: which stratum of the epos? Each era has its own. Four different primordial epics. Four epics arrayed into their present structure during transition to patriarchy, yielding a four-seasonal calendar. Earlier, the calendar was triseasonal. The Zodiac was triseasonal. The epos preserves traces of a triseasonal structure. The seasons were headed by Virgo. Three quadruplets each. A sign averaging two thousand years in the precession of the equinoxes, the origin of this structure would yield a time depth of twelve millennia."

"The threshold of the Neolithic."

"Coincides with the heliacal rising of Spica on the Urmashu Highland. Vega was the polar star. In the foundation epic, his name?"

"Vego?"

"Three brothers: Vego, Oan, Leo. Three kings. Vego, the fixed, around whom the stars move. The water wheel. The axis. Oan, king of the North. Of permanence. Of the land of the immortals. Of the House of Titans. Mher-Leo, king of the Zodiac. Of time. Cron. These three totems move the firmament. The Raven, the Wolf, the Lion. The hag on her way to the House of Titans, carrying twin ladles to hit Mher Minor on his head, none but Cassiopeia. The two ladles—Ursa Major and Ursa Minor. The hag, a most ancient goddess of the firmament. Mher's head—tips the Northern Star. Mher Minor defeats Vego's son. Comes to represent the Northern Star. Tawit's curse ordains Mher Minor to stay in his cave. When he comes out, the firmament will collapse . . ."

"It hasn't already?"

"The cardinal axis of the epos, the Pharaohland–Urmashu axis, traverses all four generations. All other axes are later accretions, including the Ashashurian. The structure of the syncretic text requires an sweeping revision. The lovers of the heroes are the original wives or consorts. *In them* we must search for the earlier strata of the epos. A descent of six to eight millennia. A quadriseasonal solar year of four generations was superimposed on the triseasonal lunar year of three generations."

"Reminds me of Phaethon seeking his father Sol's palace—the Zodiac engraved on the door. Phaethon's course via the constellations."

"Beseeches to know who his father is. Clymene in Ovid replaces Isis, Tawit's suckler. The same mytheme of Tawit and Melik the Pharaoh. The Pharaoh abuses Tawit. Both sired by Mher. A reminiscence of Melik is incarnated as Epaphus in Ovid. Mher is Phoebus, Sol. The fiery horses of Phoebus's chariot are the same as the fiery horse of the epos."

"Would Tawit's primary name be linked to Phaethon? Both have similar deaths . . . Both die by Zeus's thunderbolt."

By his will, by his will, by his will.

"The Sultaness whose arrow kills Tawit of Tawru is a matriarchal predecessor of Zeus. Era herself, the Great Goddess of Argos, guardian of the lake of Lerna—the gateway to Haides. Tawit bathes in the waters of the Sultaness. There he is killed. Entered West. The gateway of the underworld. This Era-Sultaness battle contra Tawit is the template on which Tawit's battle contra Melik-Hydra was based. Tawit's mother in the epos—Armałan, the Moon. Clymene, Phaethon's mother, and Armałan . . . Popular corruptions. Clymene's sister, Asia. Of Asu Minor. Clymene, married to Iapetos, the progenitor of Häyk. The mother of Atlas and Prometheus. Non-native deities. Is Häyk either, or both? Clymene, mother of Häyk; Armałan, mother of Tawit. Armałan may also be descried in Alcmena. Erakles's mother. That is, Tawit's mother. Are Häyk and Tawit brothers or identities? Are they Prometheus and Atlas? Why is she the Argive Alcmena?"

"Birth. Hushtory."

"Argentum. Silver! The Moon. If you give weight to an strand in Omerican mythology, Tawit would be Oenus's, Ohan's son—not adopted son."

"The labyrinths of mythology."

"Are the Socraticans and Urmashuans cousins, Padrè, as Hero Datus claims? Was the movement of our people from West to East? Were among our ancestors the Sea People of the Isle of Ervand, who invaded Asu Minor, Paleosteen, Pharaohland?"

"Slaughterhouse descended from Nonah. Ex omnia communia. Et revertetur ad eam pariter."

"Padrè. I've worn the Centaur's poisoned tunic. Scorched were my bones."

"Holy Pasha has been trying to wipe off our hushtory by promoting every narrative making us invaders."

"What harm is there in being descendents of the Phrygians? That is Troyada. Romroms proudly claim Troyadan descent via Aeneas. From the same stock."

"Never thought of that."

"Whisper in Papa Romrom's ears. Claiming Hero Datus ascribed Phrygian ancestry to us was a convenient way to pigeonhole us."

"You're giving them good reason to rid us of Phrygian ancestry, also."

"Let's go then to our roots. Liberate Phrygia. Yuranbul."

"You'll find allies. In Ololahummah's eschatology, in the end times Constant City will be liberated by an alliance with the Orthogonal Concone. Pasha's nightmare. Why he changed the city's name to Yuranbul—cheating Ololah, to evade His curse. The entire Ololahummah knows these refer precisely to Constant City's liberation from Pasha."

"Padrè, Padrè. We don't know for certain the direction of the movement of people. May have been the other way around. Or in both directions. How did Hebe penetrate the heart of Socratican mythology?"

"The daughter of Zeus and Hera?"

"Era's daughter. Ares's sister. Erakles's wife in the sky. Hebe or Huba, the chief goddess in the heart of Urmashu Highland. Ever wondered why Kepheus, if king of the southernmost south, is located in the northernmost north of the astral world? Who were the Aethiopians who came to Troyada's rescue? Were they the people of Etio on the Urmashu Highland?"

"Solves the mystery of the source of the four rivers."

"Is Troyada's founder's father, Tros, the Toros of our epos? Dzovinar's brother, uncle of the Divine Twins, the founders of Tawru? The locale of the House of Titans is the Taurus Mountains in Urmashu. Toros is a native of Taurus. Read it as Tor or Taur.

"Deeper layers still in the *House of Titans*. Nana, the Old Lady of the millet field, is a fossil of the lunar deity Nana or Inanna, the Queen of Erkin and Erkir. Seek Inanna's origins in Urmashu. Tawit might be Nana's son, if not bastard son—the fruit of a hieros gamos."

"From father to son."

"The mytheme. A transference. Ascription of Tawit's birth to Leo Mher's wife seems forced. Both Mher and his wife, originally lunar deities. Tawit refuses to be suckled by any but Ismil, perhaps Isis. Tawit's association with death—the setting sun. The battle with his son, Mher Minor . . . Can't continue the combat. Atypical of him. Atypical of any solar deity. Yet, revealing. The setting: death of the sun. The cyclical journey of the sun—reflected in the epos's four generations. Mher Minor—the sun's journey traversing the night. In a group of mawgages, *daw* is homophonous with words associated with exhaustion. Death. In ancient Pharaonish, *dwyt*, death, destruction; *dwt*, the netherworld. Mawguists dissociate these stems, severing them from Tawit."

"They have a sole reference point."

"A trap based on a superfluous etymology. Tawit or Lad Tawit in several variants becomes King of Pharaohland. The Pharaonish etymology may apply."

"What's the crux of Tawit's association with the netherworld?"

"If Tawit is Nana's son by Mher, the son of the Great Goddess, can't be other than the Son of the Mother of the Underground. Dionysos or son of Dionysos—the god from the east. How far does the east go? Certain traits are preserved in Bałdasar. Both, identified with the goat. In one variant, the Dev espies Bałdasar in Mher Minor when he invokes the Bread and Wine. Was Tawit a son or grandson of Bałdasar, acquiring new roles in subsequent epochs? Some variants are explicit. The second generation of Leo Mher is bypassed. A triseasonal, trigenerational epos."

"Bałdasar is childless."

"In the overwhelming majority of the variants, yes. Which more often than not camouflages the exception in which the archaic lies. A childless Bałdasar may indeed mean an emasculated Bałdasar. An emasculated Dionysos. A suppressed genealogy.

"Read this Padrè. Dionysos, the god from Nys. Several dozen toponyms on the Urmashu Highland. Could some be related?"

"Nish, Nisha, Nishanes, Nicha, Nishi, Nishiri, Nishsha, Nishpi, Nishtun, Nijasar, Nispin, Nisos. Nisir—"

"The Fakiro-Mamanic etymologies may be correct. In Urmashuan, *-it* is a suffix attached to theophoric names only."

"A series of words in the chain. Tirit—"

"Tir, Tirit—the Supreme Deity. A deity older than Aramast or Jupiter. The name echoes in Tiresias, the knower of *ta onta* and *ta proionta*. Decided disputes eter gods. Endowed with prophecy. Tir, the interpreter of dreams."

"For long thought on the twin serpents on our Walalicoses' caduceus. Hermes's emblem. Tir's. Tiresias's striking by his staff the two mating snakes, which altered him from male to female, and back."

"Tiresias's consignment by Era to night eternal—Tir's function as psychopomp."

"Abhorred mythology when an student. All these exploits by Zeus, Era's wrath. Can't compare to our Hoshosh. Why we were victorious."

"Padrè, a process of mythological pimperialization was underway. Beauty, harmony, poetry . . . all tools of empire. Homology via litterature. The key character here is Era, not Zeus. Many of the maras the supreme deity enraptured were consorts of local supreme deities or matriarchal deities on their own. Appropriated by the Zeus mafia. Era, made a jealous wife, covering up the usurpations."

"In Tir's case, some say, the onoma may derive from *tigr* 'tiger' or 'arrow.' Tigris spouting at the heart of Urmashu. Tigranes, Tiran."

"Some, the sum of soma. In the pre-Pharaonic era, Mher was the name of the Primordial Mother's child. Take this clipping."

"*M'her* to suckle; *m'hera* suckling infant."

"The *a* has no phonological value; thus, *m'her* suckling infant."

"*Mheru*: milch calves."

"That is, *mher*: milch calf—"

"—That's why Mher's son Tawit of Tawru was escorted to Pharaohland. To be suckled by Isis, the Protomother. Dame Ismil, the heroic detritus of the mythic Isis and Semele. Semele, mother of the Prince of the Underworld, Baccus or Bałdasar. On equal footing with Dzovinar."

"Could Bałdasar's name be related to the stem in Bouleus—who abducted Persephone to Haides?"

"Too risky. The proto-themes are identical. What do you think could have been Bałdasar's original name?"

"Bałdasar, we know it to be the Kaliph of Baghdad's son—via the abducted Dzovinar. Tempting, Brathki, to discern onomastic parallels eter Baccus, Baghdasar, and Baghdad. But. The 'gh' in Bałdasar derives from Urmashuan 'l.' "

"Pales, the shepherds' tutelary deity. Rome, founded by Romulus and Remus during her feast. Phales, Dionysos's companion, relates to Phallus. The Pałdasar in some variants may connote more than a corruption. Sannion and Phales. Remnants of phallic deities."

"Intriguing connotations . . ."

"Sannion and Phales might be borrowings from Sanasar and Pałdasar. As these are corruptions themselves. Sanasar in some variants is expressly Sałnasar which seems to derive from Salmanasar, the Ashashurian king."

"Which one? Kings' names come in series."

"If not the first—of fourteenth century—certainly the second, of the ninth century. Penetrated the kingdom of Urartu all the way to Lake Van. Salmanasar yields Sałmnasar. Drop one of the successive nasals and you get Sałnasar, from which, Sanasar."

"To get the mythological underpinnings of Sanasar you need to know what Salmanasar means."

"The name, Ashashurian. The myth, not. Attracted the name Salmanasar due to hushtoric conditions. Though the meaning of the name it attracted may give us a clue. The actual name is Shulmanu Asharedu, or Shulman Ashared—God Shulman is Most Eminent. Shulman, a god worshipped in Ashashuria as early as the limits of the third millennium. Known in Byblos at about the same time. Semsemic mawgages have no vowels. The latest reading is Shalman or Salman. The God of the Underworld, associated with fertility."

"Is it Suleiman?"

"God Solomon. Associated with jinns. All you can get from the transcription is Slmn. The vowels are conventions."

"In the Vulgate the name is Salomon."

"The name comes from Byblos, so does the narrative."

"What could the name possibly mean?"

"Among probable etymologies consider this. Sałmn means 'seed' in Urmashuan. Precisely, 'embryo.' Accurately, 'the male seed in the female vagina.' Applied to humans—and nature. A god of fertility, named Embryo . . . "

"The relevance of Bałdasar to this?"

"May Bel protect the king."

"The Underworld, again."

"Twins of the Underworld. This may have been their origin. Consider *bełun* 'fertile' or *bełmn* 'semen.' Would we have Sałmn and Bełmn as spirits of nature, rendered to Sałmnasar and Bełmnasar, then distorted by attraction to hushtorical names? *Sar* 'mountain,' a native Urmashuan word from the protoword **ker*. The Ashashurian or Aryatollan *sar* 'king' is an independent development. The Urmashuan Twins' tale varies from the structure of various parallel myths, allowing a harmony eter the twins. Precedes bifurcation—as in biology, so in myth."

"Sicut superius, et inferius. Quod intra, quia sine, Brathki."

L et's take another route. In some variants, Sanasar and Bałdasar are named Sinam-Sarim and Sene-Karim. Or, Sene-Kerim."

"A perversion of Senekerim?"

"In several variants, Sene-Karim is simply Senekerim. Sometimes, King Senekerim himself is named Sinamkarim. The fact that 'Sin' survives prominently—despite semantic subsumption and dissolution—indicates a possible hushtoric influence from Sin Acheriba, not simply a litterary influence from Senekerim. The Kaliph is an stalwart pagan character sacrificing to idols, worshiping Ishtar. Child sacrifice, his defining aspect. No trace of Ololah in him in any variant. Same goes for Ismil, the Queen of Egypt. An anathema in Ololahumman hushtory. In some, the Kaliph is an Urmashuan ally contra the King of Pharaohland. An Urmashuan community lives in Pharaohland. Their leader, Ohan. An echo of Hyks or Hayks?"

"*Hyk* meant 'king.' A sacral meaning. Couldn't derive. Must have been older than the Hyksykos to become sacral."

"A gradual superposition of an Urmashu-Balabylon axis on an original Urmashu-Pharaohland axis. The Urmashu-Balabylon axis is an outgrowth due to more recent hushtory. Initially, no external axes. The sole axis—eter twin mountains in Urmashu. A regional myth survives of a duel eter the high peaks Handovk and Maroot. Yet the mountain that we know as Sarakn or Nemroot came to represent Bel, and on the opposite end, possibly Siphan represented Häyk. Later superposed on Nemroot and Maroot."

"May have been the other way around."

"The earthly and ezerkian hushtories correspond. The hushtory of Urmashu, inscribed in the stars. Two Meliks or Pharaohs in the *House of Titans*. Son and Father. One is Hydra, combating Mher or constellation Leo. The other, Cancer, situated at the mouth of Hydra, the son. Taking the precession of equinoxes as a template, Cancer would be Hydra's son. A different time zone, corresponding to a different generation in the foundation epos. In Urmashuan, Cancer's name was Msur—the Manger. The Manger of the Son. Of the Son of Hydra, the Son of God. In one variant, Tawit, of the house of serpents, is the nemesis of the Son of Hydra who has twelve companions. A chance, Msur was in later epochs confounded with Msr—Pharaohland, or superposed by it. The 'u' falls in dialectal conjugation. It is in the Msur where the Ass is held, in wait for the hero who will deserve him. Tawit is that hero. Don't expect palm fronds strewn upon his path."

"Insinuating the non-insinuatable?"

"This Ass, Padrè, or Twin Asses, derives from Totolemy. These replaced an earlier Twin Wild Male Goats or Twin Roebucks. Cancer's proximity to Gemini furnishes a template. Twin Sons of God. Two Pharaohs fused into the epos—Hydra and Cancer—in a mortal struggle contra the House of Titans."

"The Ophiuchus-Scorpius?"

"Only later incorporated into the solar Zodiac upon the Zodiac's creation. The structure is reflected in the *House of Titans*. Gemini is the following phase in the precession of the equinoxes. Each of the four epics comprising the epos should be analyzed against its own celestial background, only then as in what form it was incorporated into the lunar Zodiac. Subsequently, the solar Zodiac. The attribution of foundation of the House of Titans to Gemini furnishes a clue as to when this heavenly house of time was established, with its earthly representatives in the epos."

"We're back to the critical issue of the founders' names."

"Sinam Sarim and Sinam Karim. The suffix '-im' is a poetic adaptation to Senekerim. The names, Sinam Sar and Sinam Kar. Or, Sinam Ker. Their father, the Urmashuan King Sinam. The name permeates the ancient Urmashu folklore. Their father's name Gagik is a hushtorical superposition over Gorg or Gorgik, meaning Wolf. In the Romrom myth, their father would be Mars–Vahagn. One of the Divine Twins is deified by Mars who carries him to the sky by his horse-chariot, granting him immortality."

"The story of Ejijah."

"Filched. Sinam Ker, confounded with Senekerim. Two Senekerims in the epos–both the Kaliph and his nemesis. An anomaly. Other than the special cases of succession, the epos does not allow redundancy. Senekerim is a suspicious name for the son of the progenitor Urmashuan King–the founder himself. Sinam Sar followed suit, becoming Sinam Sarim."

"*Sin* means Moon, in Akkadian, preserved in Urmashuan Lusin."

"Sinam Sar was the famous Sim Sar or Sev Sar–the Black Mountain of Tawru, associated with lunar worship. Here, the Head Dev conducted his annual forty-day pilgrimage. Remember, forty's association with the Netherworld. And *Kar* 'Stone,' if not its major mythical twin mountain Maroot–the highest peak of the Land of Titans–is a reference to a sacrificial altar at the mountaintop. Relating to Mheric myth, to the death and resurrection of Moon."

"The Moon itself."

"It is on this Sar, or Mountain, the epical heroes, notably Mher and Sinam Kar, receive their supernal powers. Mher was a lunar deity and a descendant of the lunar Bałdasar or Sinam Kar before his transformation into Leo Mher, and his integration into a Sanasarian solar genealogy. In more ancient times, Mher may have been the sire of Sinam Karim and Sinam Sarim."

"What were the names of the Mheric twins?"

"If we give any weight to the mutual suffix in the names, *Sar* 'Mountain' would derive from the Proto-Yuromamanic **ker* 'head, horn, mountaintop.' In these twins we see a remnant of the goat duel, supplanted later by twin mountains."

"All roads go to the totem."

"Generation. Regeneration. Revert to Mount Mashu. Mythology preserved a remnant of Mount Mashu in the twin peaks of Parnassus. Sin Sar and Sin Ker–or Sin Kar. Both mean Moon Mountain. Kar or Ker is the older. Easy to confound Sin Ker with Senekerim or Sin Acheriba.

"In this sense, Bałdasar may be the older, more critical twin."

"Another possibility. Sełan Sar is the original name of a central mountain to the epos. Means 'altar mount.' The easiest to confound with Salmanasar. I suspect Sanasar derives from Sełanasar. If so, we must look for a twin mount for Bałdasar. Cannot tell you which mount it would be. May not need to find one if we take the Balabylonian star name *balura*, meaning 'altar.' Bałdasar is the quintessential sacrifice. You can make your conjectures. The tradition precedes Ashashuria."

"Yet, all this is within the purview of the Urmashu–Balabylon axis."

"I have doubts. Sar is a derivation of Tar, Taru, the Hattic storm god. No coincidence that these twin Sars or Tars are the founders of Tawru, Tarawn. In fact, Zurvan originates from Saruand, Taruand, Tarawn. A third-generation corruption. The Balabylon axis holding hostage the Urmashuan mythology is made real by your Biblibel. You may dispense with it. A superposition signifying the distortion of Urmashuan hushtory."

"You're amputating Ubaratutuan mythology."

"Only via Ubaratutu's amputation can Urmashu be unearthed. Once grasped authentically, you'll have a grasp of the subterranean channels of hushtory—"

"You'll be questioned. Not only by scholars."

"—Only then you can delve deep into Balabylon. And Neo Balabylon."

An estate baroque. By an amalgamate of assholes twain occupied. Mister Asshole & Missus Asshole Sucker Incorporated. Done well, this car salesman. A socker player yon a career pluckier. Nostrillust fucked it all up. Praise the Word good, by Holy Hoshosh nerianed from Natashazone, in Ubaratutu implanted. Dealerships five, restaus five and twenty in Ubara City. The geld real, in the basement soundproof.

Here, for the sake of gentlemenry from Ubara City stages dogfights Mister Asshole. From monnonmorgue accounts handpicks clientele, a side perk of shares classified. Of training pups the embattled most, on testosterone supplements with their piroshki feeds Mister Asshole. Molds aggression a cattle prod electrified. Upon finding out, mortified Missus Asshole Sucker. Clouts to the carpat a couple straight sets her. Keeps mouth shut post ultimatum, "Wave bye-bye to your Gudjudji handbags."

On the Walalicos's board of directors serves, Mister Asshole. Of laundering in charge via Isle of Aphrodite—sidedoor to Yuromaman. To preachers cooperating donates Bentleys. To villages remote assigns those not. Pays actors, athletes. Finances magazines litterary, translations of Slaughterhouse litterature, publishing houses. Liasees, abound. Of the persuasion of the liasor. To persuade? *They'll* persuade him. Translators of the exiled, fired. News is his news. Speech free, per coverage paid. Invites pimpassadors, with gifts lavish bestowing. Bribes platforms social to silence dissent. Arrogates murder by proxy. Owns Polpol Inc. Owns

Prosecutariat Inc. Owns pimps foreign. Owns biped rights foundations. Of the carnage streams webcasts moonly. Imbibe can voyeurderers hungry how the bananas top live. Discretion, a must. Liability legal, offshore exonerated. Of Walawala an statue erects, in Slaughterhouse the tallest. To shame putting Balabylon. A peach, this Ubara City gentleman. Of Ubaratutu's yuys, the blueprint. Of bipedity, the exemplar.

Allusions to relations of the epic of Bilgamesh with our epos. Unconvincing."

"Delve deeper than Bilgamesh. Ninurta. Nin Urta. Lord of Mashu. Lord of Iron. Lord of War, Underworld. Identical motifs in Tawit episodes. His parents, Enlil and Ninlil. Ohan and wife. Tawit's godfather, Ohan, possibly his father. Several hints in the epos."

"Not Mher?"

"Comes later with the advent of the Zodiac. Enki is the Pharaoh trapping Tawit into the pit. Enki's wife, Ninhursag, is Ismil or Isis, begging Enki to save Tawit's life. Where's a trace of Häyk in our mythology? Search for him in the demonized. Too ancient to evade demonization. Now, in the realm of Häyä."

"If Ninurta is Nemroot, Bel would equate to Tawit. Is Häyk sacrificing Tawit?"

"The mytheme may be a reverberation of Mher's dominance over Tawit. Tawit's curse of Mher. Tawit dies in all variants. Mher is immortal in all. Häyk and Mher are an identity. Orion and Mithra."

"I've had doubts about Alishan's 2,492 Ante Anno Domini as the beginning of the Häykian calendar."

"A correction was made. 2,341 Ante Anno Vulgaris. If you have faith in arithmetic, add that magnitude to the positive sense of cron vulgaris."

"From Balabylon to Los Balabylonos."

"Hardly the genesis, Padrè. Precession of the equinoxes. The setting of the Sagittarius at dawn. Its death by Scorpius. Or, the sun."

"How to correct a falsely established tradition of origin?"

"Easy to backdate. Hard to bring forward. You'll pay by your head. There may be several origins. The dominant tradition always has the upper hand via polpotical fiat."

"The relation of Sumererian Nin Sar to the names of the Divine Twins?"

"Sim Sar or Sin Sar's father in our variant is Mher. Elsewhere, Mihran—Mihr, Mithra. Speculation's cheap, Padrè. Keys to the names may be lying in unpublished variants hibernating in the vaults of Ubaratutu's bookmorgues."

"When are you leaving for Ubaratutu?"

"When the moon rises anew . . ."

"The moon rise may never . . ."

For this, the path. For this, the flesh. For this, the orison.

"A glorification of Sanasar, a subversion of Bałdasar, promoted by misguided natotonalists. In multiple variants, Bałdasar is the arch hero and sire of the generations. The official synthetic version of the epos—a farce! That's what happens with all transcribed and standardized oral traditions."

"How?"

"In some variants, after the Pharaoh dies, Mher Major dumps his wife, goes to Pharaohland to beget the Son of Hydra via its Queen. In others, Mher Major dies, his wife marries the Pharaoh, begetting the Son of Hydra for the Pharoah. The synthesizers chose the first as the official version. No one asked for an explanation. Tradition, values, shaped at the expense of an epical truth embodying mythological and epicographic data. All epics, polpotical in nature! Have to choose among numerous variants, embellish it. When the choice becomes dogma, subverts all other potentialities. The *Shahmameh* is almost worthless. The *Idiad* or *Bilgamesh* are as unreliable as the academonic version of the *House of Titans*."

"Seems fortunate the epos wasn't recorded a thousand years ago."

"Could have been fortunate. If there were no Genocide. Or transcription commenced fifty years sooner. Much was lost."

"Couldn't have happened in Pasha's empire."

"Lose your independence, lose it all. Unity breeds homogeneity. The Kaliph, King of the Underworld, replaces a demonized Moon deity. King Sinam of Urmashu, destined to eternal death in folklore—due to the ascent of a solar mythology. Bałdasar, his son via Semele-Persephone-Dzovinar . . . The gift of the Goddess of the Underworld to mankind as savior from death. Aion is He . . ."

"Aion's father?"

"Or, Grandfather. Of the same genealogy. These Aionic-Mheric mysteries resonate in your Godspell of Jojonos . . . All the 'I am . . . ', 'the light of the world . . .', the 'Alpha and Omega' or AΩ—the serpent biting its tail—the long cycle of time, even the teachings are stolen intellectual property!"

"O miseras hominem mentes!"

"The same is true of the King of Pharaohland in the epos. A replica of the King of the Underworld. The Madre you worship is a byproduct of Isis. There it is: infant Walawala sitting on Madre's lap. Khor, suckling at the teat of Momma Isis, Hat Khor. See the babe? There it is. Sis in the lap of Massis. Khor, the reflection of the dying, resurrecting Asar. God Khor? God of the Deep? God Khar? God of the flames? Mawguistic remnants in Urmashuan. Tawit's twin, Khor Manook—Child of the Deep. Or, Child of Sol."

"Saul?"

"The netherworld. *dwt.* Padrè, which of our deities is associated with the netherworld?"

"Tir? Hermes?"

"Tir. Mercury. Nabu."

"The twin? The sun?"

"Sol. Khor Manook. Sun, Mercury. Inseparable. Twins. Swift-footed. Messenger of Sol. The abandoned twin, Khor Manook, always superior. As was Bałdasar."

"Tawit. Tir. Nabu."

"Born on the same day? The fourth day of the increasing moon?"

"The fourth position in the calendar is Tir's."

"The underworld."

"Hermes's lineage?"

"Hermes's father, the Thunderer. Ohan. Tawit's foster father. Mother, Maia. Of the line of Prometheus and Iapetus. Both with Urmashuan affinities. Mother, Pleione, an Oceanid. Half-sister to Hyades. Their brother, Hyas, a hunter. These were pursued by Orion. Familiar?"

"Hermes, the Prince of All Thieves."

"The thieves Tawit chased to their cave. Hermes's thieves. The cave—Hermes's temple. Roles shifted due to suppression of the twin. Apollo and Hermes. Tawit and Khor Manook."

"Do we have Tawit's name then?"

"Why are you obsessed with names, Padrè?"

"Names are all we have."

"Names are brands."

"Names propitiate communication."

"Names engender Slaughterhouse."

"Demarcation—the beginning of life, not death."

"The death of the other. Names are hideologies. Their goal, expansion. At the expense of the other."

"Essential to discover the initial name. To expose the fraud of existing names, circumvent expansion. Forestalling extinction."

"Am I your dog?"

"Strange coincidences . . ."

"The circumstances surrounding the development of Walawalaic doctrine make coincidences too coincidental. Remember the Sultaness who killed Tawit in the water? Another layer. She, or her daughter, is Scorpius. Tawit-Ophiuchus; later, Tawit-Sagittarius. The Archer. Due to the precession of equinoxes Sagittarius recedes while the sun rises in Scorpius. Tawit's death by Scorpius—whom he sired. An equivalent myth—Orion's death by Scorpius. Orion-Häyk. The Archer."

"The origin. Orion or Häyk?"

"Orion, an insignificant deity, fits the category of imports. Häyk, founder of cron, the category of supreme deities. Even if Urmashu were the source of biped ciphilization, all of this would be claptrap if we fail to understand why it did not become a source of thought as did Socratica. Unless we face the reasons for this, we're doomed to subservience. Every damned Ubaratutuc and every fucking Urriantitic in his innermost being is a murderer of thought and a crawler at the feet of murderers of thought. *Thought* is proscribed in Ubaratutu! By every polpotical party, past, present, future, by every ligigilous or educational institution, past, present, future, by every benevolent organization or grant-spewing foundation, by every govtgoftal or nogovtgoftal structure, by every kultkultural organization, past, present, future, post-future. Ubaratutu is naught! Shall remain naught! Shall go to naught!"

"Leave your outrage for some other day, Brathki."

"Am I on your pay?"

"You are. Go on."

"Orion sets while Scorpius rises."

"A magical formula?"

"Is one myth a transposition of the other?"

"That is . . . Tawit is Orion? Häyk?"

"Who killed Orion?"

"Artemis?"

"The Sultaness. The challenge leading to Orion's death is identical to that in the Sultaness–Tawit episode. Orion's wife, nicknamed Pomegranate. Tawit marries the princess who symbolizes the pomegranate. This Sultaness may be a detritus of the Delphic Dragon. If we take the Rhea–Persephone mythic structure as a template where Persephone is Rhea's daughter, Tawit marries his sister Persephone. Astłik. Persephone is a late name. In archaic versions she is named Ariadne—a misspelling of Arihagne."

"Tawit: Vahagn? The supreme deity?"

"Of the Underworld. The Great Ophiuchus. The Great Snake God of Underworld . . . Vahagni or Vahagne. A son was born to Arihagne named Aix or Goat. Bałdasar. Dionysos Meilikius. Originally, of the Fig tree. Not the vine."

"So the Devil is ours."

"The God of kyank. Of kyank indestructible. Mythically appropriated, fundamentally distorted, demonized."

"A familiar accusation."

"Tawit, son of Rhea, the demonic Sultaness. Ante his adoption into the epos's generations."

"Betrothed to her mother?"

"Married his mother! Not his sister. The polished Socratican myth preserves a vestige of this. Zeus assumes snakeform and entwines with Rhea's daughter, his sister, after the revised myth denies his chances with Rhea. That denial is its affirmation. The epical version points to a more archaic structure of the template. Even in the textual versions, Tawit's wife's name embeds the root *händ* 'pasture'. The deity of pomegranate."

"Persephone's symbol."

"Earth. Underworld. Tawit marries Anahit, the Great Earth Goddess, or Astłik. Anahit is another name for Cybele or Kybele, the great mother goddess of Mama Tolia which means Mountain. The Madonna of Marut. The Mother of God. Hebat or Hawwa. The two serpents on your caduceus are Tawit and Anahit, or Tawit and Astłik. Vahagne and Arihagne. The Great Snake God and the Queen of Underworld."

"Tawit . . . Attis . . . Tawit killed by his sister, Astłik?"

"Likely. Arihagne murders his brother. The poisoned arrow of Sultaness's daughter, Scorpius. Häyk's battle with Bel, a transposition of Tawit's battle with Melik, Tawit's battle with the Sultaness. The Delphic Dragon, named Typhon. There is Bel for you. Mher Minor, the archetypal child—Mithra, Xristos—born of the House of Tawit, the House of Häyk."

"I grant you. May be similarities eter ancient myths and Walawala's narrative. Some of your arguments on Urmashuan origin may be valid. What you fail to recognize *is* a fundamental distinction separates Walawala's narrative from all else. The scapegoat sacrificed in all prior myth to cohere the biped comstag is not innocent. Walawala is the first innocent sacrifice. Subverts all prior myths. A new chapter."

"Another self-obsessed subversion. What is Bałdasar's guilt? Isn't Bałdasar a purer sacrifice, so Sanasar could found the House of Titans?"

"A difference. Walawala offered himself as self-sacrifice."

"Did not Bałdasar sacrifice himself? Entering south, the land of Sol, so Sanasar's progeny thrives in Tawru? The quintessential sacrifice. Bloodless. A far superior rupture. If anything, Bałdasar was God. He has returned!"

"Your catharsis, textual."

"Find a text to what Brathki says. Your faith, contingent solely on text. Subtext. Subsubtext."

Sisters of purgatoria cum purgator, to the beat of the living dead dancing. Bear the seeds dead. Clean funereally, youths recalcitrant, oozing consumption.

"Possible YawaYawa's Mashashashash and Aryatololah's Mahamahdi are reflections of Mher Minor? . . . Mashashashash sounds like Mashu . . ."

"Sounds more like an spell. Mashashashash Hashashashash Tashashashash . . . Ask mawguists, Padrè."

"Could Massis be interpreted as Mother of Sis or Mother Sis? Isis?

The primordial madonna and bambino in the peaks of Mount Mashu, Sis and Massis, Minor and Major."

"Yajuj and Majuj, placed at the north of Ololahica. Is Majuj Massis? Juj and Majuj? Twin peaks of Mashu? Sis and Massis?"

"Corrupted to Gog and Magog?"

"Ololahish preserved an echo of the original."

"Demonized in both Ololahish and Yawololahish traditions."

"Anywhere you see demonization, stop there in your tracks, Padrè. Struck gold. Former deities that terrorized ligigilo-polpotical interests. The Ololahicans and Yawoyawyaws inherited an already demonized tradition via Balabylonia . . . It is in the demonized entities of the epos you must look for the foundational deities of Urmashu. In the Pharaoh. In Tawit's uncle."

"Ohan?"

"Yes. But more so, Vego. The Eagle. The Anzu Bird. The bird in Coronosi providing shade to the Divine Twins."

"The three brothers? Mher?"

"Mher Major is the Sphinx, Padrè."

Madagascar Boulevard. A cockroach stories twain high . . . crushing automobiles . . . people . . . Blood, everywhere. Gutters. Gales. Intuiting sought is he by Papa Elelu, terrified Brathki pees. Toward Tigran the Great Boulevard scurries. To vanish into back alleys. Impedes Papa Elelu, a forecrane taking hold. In the middle of Hoshosh Square nails Brathki: "Brottther!!!"

The cry. Audible barely to Brathki, suffocating in fingers iron.

"Brottther!"

"What do you want?"

"What can I want, brottther? . . . Heard you're in Parraradise . . . Wanted to seeeee you."

"Leave me be."

Deliberates Papa Elelu. In the center of the square's ellipse, lets go of Brathki.

"Who are you?"

"Your brottther . . . Your brottther, beloved Brathki!"

"Have no brothers."

"How so? I am your brottther, my beloved . . . Your brottther! From the same father, the same mother . . . I swear by mamma's sun . . . Come, let's go. Let's get something to eat, let's sit around some nice brotttherly table . . ."

"What's your name, brother?"

"Why's that important, brottther? What's ttthat mean between brottther and brottther? . . . Ttthat I've found you here, alive and kicking . . .

Ttthat's my biggest happiness, my biggest joy, brottther . . ."

"Surely our parents must've given you a name."

"Born Oblat Oblat. Ttthey call me Tot."

"Where am I to accompany you? Go ahead, I'll hail a taxi."

"No, brottther, no! Now you inssulted your brottther . . . Seriously: you ins-sul-ted! . . . Where is ittt written: a brottther's brottther should come to Parrradise . . . but should get around in some taxi-maxi, eh? Nah, my brottther . . . Nottt a sign of respect . . ." On legs hind, Papa Elelu. Antennas raised, a limousine thirty-six bay to a halt comes.

Install Mini-Minors thirty-six Brathki next to Papa Elelu. Writhes the limo via the boulevards in glide imposing.

"What is your purpose, Oblat?"

"Whatt purpose, brottther?"

"What is your purpose?"

"Oy, whatt purpose, oy! Firstly, let's get some nice lunch, get some ass, then we'll talkk."

"How about we talk now, Oblat, get some ass later?"

"Oy, what an impatient dog you are! Typical diasporadog . . . Oy, what are we gonna do with ttthese diasporadogs . . . We brought one here, made him a foreign minister . . . Gave us a goddamn migraine . . . Oy! . . . Talking of rrrules, talking of lllaws . . . Enough! Take this fifty-gram. To your health! You're good brottther . . . Let's talkk."

"Let's, Oblat."

"We're talkking, appé."

"How did you manage to end up in Holy Paradise?"

"May I be sacrificed to Hoshoshooshosh's boy, appé . . . He said, I'll turn the last ones into the first, the first ones into the last. Turn the big ones into sssmall, the sssmall ones into biiig . . . I got biiig, the biiig ones got sssmall . . ."

"Is that why you built a concone in your backyard?"

"Spoken like a genius, appé. Exactly why, appé . . . How should I say this, appé, so you understand me good. How should I say this. Let me say to Brathki, appé, there's a biiig pain in my heart, appé, a biiig pain. Peopple don't understand, appé . . . So I gave my heart to Hoshoshoo-shosh . . . Hoshoshooshosh said, appé, Everryone equal before me . . . Whether a mouse, a man, a sheep, or a cockkroach, appé, all the same. May I die to the will of Hoshoshooshosh, appé . . . Hoshoshooshosh said, I forgive your sins. How I ended up in our Holy Parrradise, brottther. Let me say to Brathki, there's a biiig love in my heart, brottther, a biiig love . . . Peopple are crruel, brottther . . . But there's Hoshoshooshosh above, he examines our hearrrttts, brottther . . . My hearrt is an *Anoosh Opera* for my peopple, brottther . . . Hoshoshooshosh said, *I'm* the one who inspects hearrts, not the peopple. Because of the love in your hearrt,

I'm granting immortality to cockroaches . . . May Hoshoshooshosh's will be done, brottther . . . A fifty-gram, appé. Chinchin!"

"Last one."

"Hoshoshooshosh's will?"

"The fifty-gram."

"You don't mean it, appé?"

"I do, brother . . ."

"What weird people these diasporadogs are, oy! . . . Once in fifty years he meets with his brottther, puts conditions already . . . What the hell is this, oy!"

"Oblat, what's your purpose?"

"Since you insist, let me tell you, brottther . . . I don't say this to just anyone . . . Let me say it to Brathki, brottther. Let me say this to Brathki. In modesty, brottther . . . For ttthree days . . . For ttthree days . . . I lit candles in my concone . . . For ttthree days I prrayed, in modesty, brottther . . . expressing my wish to Hoshoshooshosh. Hoshoshooshosh spoke to my hearrt, brottther . . . And I couldn't resist, oy . . . When Hoshoshooshosh tells you to do sometthing, how do you resist, oy! I want to become Holy Hoshoshooshoh . . . in modesty, brottther, so I won't make a liar of Hoshoshooshosh's boy, brottther."

"That's a noble idea, brother. I encourage you to."

"Mamma says ttthe same ttthing, brottther . . . So ttthey can eat, brottther. So ttthey can put food on the table, so ttthey can have potatoes, cheese, yogurt, beef tartare, chopped liver, lahmajon, ghureybiyyeh so ttthteir bellies get full and ttthteir brains function normal, oy . . . We're so hungry ttthat we don't got no cultivation, brottther, we don't got no kultkulture . . . Ttthere's no big poet being born, brottther, no maestro, to weep ttthe pain of our hearrt . . . How do you make llaws, if you make llaws, ttthere's no one to read them, brottther? . . . People of our Holy Ubaratutu need a chief, oy."

"Why, is it chiefless?"

"'Cause ittt is, oy . . . Ittt's got no chief. I can do good chiefing."

"What does that have to do with me?"

"What doesn't it have, brottther, what doesn't it have! You got good ties with Chief Orc, brottther . . . I want you to tell her nice things about me, brottther . . . Convince Chief Orc I'll be good Hoshoshooshosh, oy . . . I'll pay double what Chief Orc's paying you, brottther . . . By mamma's sun, I'll pay you trippple, brottther . . ."

"For shame, brother. Where is it heard that a brother takes geld from his brother? A great honor to see my own brother on Hoshoshooshosh's throne."

"I have no doubt, brottther . . . Bravo, brottther! . . . I knew you wouldn't disappoint me, brottther. I triple appreciate your kindness. I'll erect an statue of Walawala in the heart of Ubara City, for you. For you, brottther. Oye!"

"For shame, brother. Don't bother."

Past rotas a few, receives Brathki a communique from the presidentette of Papa Elelu Party for Pullulating Ubaratutu. "You are an opposo-Ubaratutuc! Pollutor of the holy ancestral faith of our grandfathers! Should be burned at the stake! Walawala is Ubaratutu's foundation! Are you so clueless about the kosmic and eternal truth of our faith? Listen to the programs of Gontarenski, Jarjarovich, Mantarenko, Verlianoff, Kardashiova! Educate yourself! Illiterate son of a bitch! And never show your face in Holy Ubaratutu again!"

M*ighty innermost forces,, Terrible rings sacred . . . The way of the cross appears not arduous at first,, It has still dark hours of dolor.* The songs of my childhood, Abbot. The way of the cross. Heard it since the day I was born. At home. At scrool. Sisters, brothers came to our house. Prayed, sang."

Tombfrigid, the parish afternoon. From noses ice slivers merge. Of two, the friendlier. Genteel. Invites confidence the voice. In eye lurks suspicion still. If his way had Brathki . . . re-indoctrinate the abbott good in days three. Budges not. Nor his partner, pleased to sit here with a bastard son of a bitch not. Eyes narrowing with Brathki's syllable each in slits lupicidal. In amity rivalry sibling? Ahuram priest, ahriman priest. Ahriman priest eats ahuram priest. Kin slug.

To Los Balabylonos Brathki to face temptation has come.

"Whatever I do is done at Moshosh's behest."

"Lucifer appears in Moshosh's image."

"As appeared in Walawala's person, Abbot. Eternalizing Walawala was the best insurance for eternalizing herself."

Lips frantic. In reverse a movie silent plays. Vector schizophile. From self to self. In repeat will it be?

"Wake up, Brathki! Come out of your night! Out of the Yawet Khawaaar!"

"Night is all. Light—a flicker to be extinguished."

"I have faith in you! You're no worse than Parapoolianos. He murdered Walawalaiacs. Have you murdered yet anyone?"

"Murder is the yardstick of promotion. Brathki's eln, predicated on murdering empire."

"Sol is murdered at hour eighteen, yet resurrects."

"A trick of the spheres."

Eorthe, divide thyself!

"To the confessional, Abbot. Impure thoughts possessed you upon hearing murder. Confess. Brathki forgive you shall."

"You've come down from the Heavens?"

"Thence stardust rains. Lunacy ascends, descends."

"Championing pre-Walawala faiths, I imagine you're familiar with the celestial origins of celebrated deities."

"You know nothing of what I champion."

"You don't even remember your mother's womb."

"Did Walawala remember his father's rooster?"

"A priori legend is a postage stamp. The symbolism of memory."

"Worship of symbols, rivaled only by Transit Security Administration checkpoints. At least, those kultkultures are absolved for faulty mensuration."

"There is but one savior. All else is from Khawaaar."

"The plasma of Brathki's abode is not in reality. Would I enjoy drinking from this loving cask?"

"A lot of nutcases visit here. One receives messages from the Blessed Madre. Thought I'd snap before convincing her she's talking to Lucifer. Another thinks he's Walawala. Goes from house to house, ringing a bell, screaming 'I am risen!' . . . But you? Surpassed every one of them. An ass is known by its ears . . ."

Inflection of the error-bearded. In a beggar's cup hemlock. To the pharmakos cherish, a zoule living wax.

"Sometimes though . . . Every few centuries . . . Hoshosh chooses a vessel to communicate through . . ."

"Did Walawala masturbate?"

"Sic eunt fata hominum."

"My book?"

"You've reduced everything to a whorehouse."

"Wrote it in a whorehouse. The mornings were quiet. This became my cup."

"So, you *are* Walawala."

"Abbot, who's the real founder? The sacrificer or the sacrificed? . . . Memory sacrifices the elder twin, Bałdasar. Sanasar founded the House of Titans. Hoshosh sacrifices Hoshosh, his obverse . . . What is Hoshosh if Hoshosh is Hoshosh?"

"Is identity integral to the aseity of Hoshosh?"

"Ecce Canis. Wolf!"

"The question facing the Concone, Brathki, is survival post transcendence. Would be nice if faith is predicated on truth."

"The unveiling of truth, yoked to Hoshosh's murder."

"Dog is not singular, Brathki."

"How many points make a point?"

"A dilemma in your multiplicity."

"What is truth?"

"Who cares what truth is?"

"Brathki does."

"What's indubitable. *Nothing.*"

"Save Ololah."

"Fuck Ololah."

"Methodical fallacy."

"Fallacy, the mother of invention."

"The paradigm?"

"Paths no longer remain with the loss of transcendence. Flights none from Orc Hoor . . ."

"A convergence you fail to see, Abbot. The aralez, of Aralu—the Sumererian Underworld—licked Ara's wounds to resurrect him. They were dogs. Ara the Fair. Platonon's Er. Xristos of the ancient world, the prototype of Attis, Adonis. Zalmokis. The Xristos legend of antiquity, rewoven onto a lunatic's dick."

"Veritas metaphysica potest definiri per convenientiam entis cum principiis catholicis."

"By the time Walawala reached Romulus, already a mirror image of Mihr. Omerican morons called this hexaped Walawalastos. Recycling mysteries. Fuck Walawala!"

"Fucking is not abandonment. A deeper unity."

"You were fucking Ololah. Mymoonoos is right, then, no?"

"Wrong. His, a deity unfuckable. Unrelatable. Impalpable. Ours is manifest. In hearth and marrow."

"He that fucks that cannot be fucked. The Fucker Ultimate. The Fucker Original."

"You must be as a child to enter the Kingdom. The mystery ultimate."

"Is your boy fuckable?"

"Our boy is transubstantiated. The death of the categorical decategorizes the Sire. Not the boy. You're a feeble replacement."

"Strength in weakness, no, Abbott?"

"Yours is no match to ours. Via forgiveness we rewrite the past. Release you from the past as if it never happened."

"Rewriting evolution in the Slaughterer's image. Your forgiveness forgives the slaughterer. Under the garb of love, you operate juju that not only devours, but usurps dignity. Piss heartily in the cup of your repentance. Burn your Book. Give me back Urmashu. As it was and would have been without usurpation, without genocide. Without your hushtory. Fourteen billion years of evolution. As if it never happened? The object of active forgetting? *You* need to be rewritten, Abbot."

"Since you cannot have back what is taken and will continue to be taken from you, I proffer eternal life."

"Give that to the genocidor—with a lavish tip! Yours is the most lethal virus bipedity has ever known. Your icons must be desecrated across Slaughterhouse. All trace of you, incinerated."

"That's what makes us strong. Truth and love are exclusive. Truth is cerebral. The quest for truth is the Antiwalawalarooros drive. Our icon, divested of it."

"Your divestiture—utilitarian."

"The precondition for kyank to survive."

"No heart sans mind."

"Eln is Heart."

"Heart, artifice."

"Heart is the eln sole. All else is eln not."

"Your precondition—suicide."

"Let there be Heart. Heart only."

"Brathki would bite off your 'only.' You lose."

"Replace the Crucifix with four feet? We admitted a dog to the Concone in the spirit of charity our ligigilon exhorts—"

"Charity—Heart's antithesis!"

"—to hear him. None of us could envision the outcome you propose. You fail to convince us."

"Cerebral."

The corpse, by candles lamented over. By west, enters. Curtains crimson. The room, smaller than the coffin. The breath of the body dead, pores alive. Comes out. No, Padrè . . . died you could have not. Know the five in the narthex not why they are here. The center, a Celebux light. Naught, ante. Naught, post. Naught, omnium. In order set, mouth, teeth. By day goes forth. Brought with an eye ministering. Totter, the corners. Bend, lines all. Stairs two. Left. Upon the lectern, open, a ledger large. Transcendence birthing self, posthumously. Two, behind the codex. Sign he must. Holds the pen. Waits the register for Brathki's hand. A bargain concealed. By whose forgery?

"No. His death shall sign not."

"Conquered, death."

"Conquered, a sol."

"Light é. Light é night."

"Night é. Night é light."

"Kyank é. Moonlight é."

"Mah é. Sunlight é."

"Who Mah é when aught I?"

"Your Hayr—Kron. Your Mayr—Womb Ebon."

"Of procreation necessity."

"Kyank—a differential. Unsired Mah é."

"Tongues taste not. Hands touch not."

"Of senses unsired phobia."
"Death—antecedent."
"Womb by Kron swallowed."
"Metaphor."
"Logic—of particles independent."
"Neuters logic Logos."
"Steers chaos logic."
"In Mah collapses."
"In Mah's bowels thou art."
"Parse metaphor. Live shall I forever."
"Dead shall thou remain."
"Metaphor. Save the seed."
"Drama. The stage remains sole."
"Transcendence you betray."
"Chaos—metaphor not. Mah—a continent not."
"Kron—a metaphor."
"Enters metaphor ante kyank."
"Enters post kyank."
"Kyank—by Kron encompassed."
"Sundered I Mah."
"Will it sunder you not? In memory."
"Where go do I? Exiled am I."
"Receives the South. The Gate Sole."
"By what construction? Vagrant am I."
"Gates of Equinox."
"See none do I."
"Gates of Equinox."
"See none do I."
"Gate of Solstice."
"See I nought."
"Gate of Solstice."
"See."
"To your initiation."
"Desire—fathomless. Feet—heavy."
"To Breasts twain your sojourn. From the South drink."
"Food, my South—for ants."
"Yet not thine—a song other yon."
"Hear."
"Slaughter Hydra. Gates six."
"Upon the stars' arrangement—destiny contingent?"
"Exhausts metaphor."
"Wither shall I when change arrangements?"
"In the stars inscribed—of nous the structure."

"Quare tristis es?"

"The nous—dark."

"Quare contúrbas, me?"

"Born. Unconcealed."

"To end bifurcation revolted my groom."

"Of sole—borne. To sole—in debt."

"Unfolding supersedes Saturn."

"Severed—Saturn's twin."

"Inscribed in bifurcation—reunification."

"Indeterminate—Kron."

"Dust transcendental."

"Blackballs the naught integer. Constant Mah é."

"Behold I Eas other. Constants other."

"Mher's covenant governs all."

"Choices umpteen. A plinth none."

"The descent from home . . . nuyn."

"Reverses aberration entropy. That am I."

"Your feet. Reckon the depths."

"Sanctorum tuórum, quorum relíqueiae, hic sunt et ómnium sanctórum."

"Takes no heed the equinoctial matrix. The Twins envelop."

"Spera. Quóniam adhuc confitebor illi, salutáre vultus mei."

"Shares Brathki soma. Rise Kron! Rise!"

"Brathki . . . Brathki . . . *lama sabaqtani*?"

"In peace exit."

"Enticed me what?"

"The din."

"Kýrie, eléison . . ."

"Postponement. The din . . ."

"Kýrie, eléison . . ."

"Yuys. The din . . ."

"Kýrie, eléison . . ."

"Eln from uneln sundering. The din . . ."

"Kýrie, eléison . . ."

"Orcon's yoke. The din . . ."

"Kýrie, eléison . . ."

"In Mah—truth."

"The promise?"

"Bałdasar . . . the anteway. The antetruth . . ."

"Munda cor meum ac lábia mea . . ."

"Pall none sans him was made that made was."

"Loves each monster its kind."

"The twin elder—Atropos."

"Et resurréxit tértia die."

"Refabrication iterative."
"Hic et enim calix sanguinis mei."
"The Concone—a harem."
"Encountered you the Mother?"
"The crone kidnapping Mher's legacy?"
"Lavábo inter innocéntes manus meas. The kernel?"
"Negate must faith kyank."
"Perpetuates an stratagem a tomb."
"Recalibrates Canis Major Ea."
"To establish which tomb?"
"To redress faith's agony."
"To usher Bałdasar's epoch?"
"Bałdasar—intra you. A constant immemorial."
"Hayr, Hayr . . ."
"Devoid of the Womb you will be ere becoming Bałdasar . . ."
"Mayr, Mayr . . ."
"To the infants six hark."
"Ausi omnes immane nefas ausoque potiti."
"Sanasar–Bałdasar: ascension. Half-dark–half-bright: Gods Twain."
"Dómine, non sum dignus, ut intres sub tectum meum . . ."
"Mher Major—moon full . . ."
"Dómine, non sum dignus, ut intres sub tectum meum . . ."
"Manook-KhorManook: descension. Half-dark–half-bright: Gods Twain."
"Dómine, non sum dignus, ut intres sub tectum meum . . ."
"Mher Minor—moonmah . . ."
"Dómine, non sum dignus, ut intres sub tectum meum . . ."
"Sanasar–Bałdasar . . . equinox vernal . . ."
"Non erat ille lux, sed ut testimónium perhibéret de lúmine . . ."
"Mher Major . . . solstice summer . . ."
"Non erat ille lux, sed ut testimónium perhibéret de lúmine . . ."
"Manook-KhorManook . . . equinox autumnal . . ."
"Non erat ille lux, sed ut testimónium perhibéret de lúmine . . ."
"Mher Minor . . . solstice winter . . ."
"Non erat ille lux, sed ut testimónium perhibéret de lúmine . . ."
"The metaphor arch."
"Et verbum caro factum est."
"Entombed the Six is . . . the Sanctity Supreme . . ."
"Sed tantum dic verbo, et sanábitur ánima mea . . ."
"SixSixSix . . ."
"Sed tantum dic verbo, et sanábitur ánima mea . . ."
"SixSixSix . . ."
"Sed tantum dic verbo, et sanábitur ánima mea . . ."
"SixSixSix . . ."

"Corpus Domini nostri Mheri custódiat ánimam tuam in vitam aetérnam . . ."
"The equilibrium Eanic . . .
"Corpus Domini nostri Mheri custódiat ánimam tuam in vitam aetérnam . . ."
"The legacy. Mount Mashu . . .
"Corpus Domini nostri Mheri custódiat ánimam tuam in vitam aetérnam . . ."
"Thus lost you are not."

> Hayr, Hayr,
> My arete show,
> Exiled am I.
> Dead am I Sol,
> What shall I ol?
> Betrayed the Crow,
> Dust am I now.
> In HÄY
> Kyank you shall have.

> Cried Padrè at Pater's tomb.
> Besieged silence the tomb.

> Mayr, Mayr,
> My arete show,
> Exiled am I.
> Dead am I Sol,
> What shall I ol?
> Cleaved the pairs
> Bearing life are.
> In HÄY
> Shall meet the Crow.

> Cried Padrè at Mater's tomb.
> Besieged silence the tomb.

"Sol begotten . . .
"via bałd . . ."
"un . . ."
"asar sole see . . ."
"leashed were thou . . ."
"a sauna cron . . ."
"so that . . ."
"less . . ."
"what . . ."

"pis . . ."
"soever believes in . . ."
"sing blood . . ."
"thine molars . . ."
"perish shan't . . ."
"proscribing cron . . ."
"dead am I Sol . . ."
"strength é I to abandon form . . ."
"what shall . . ."
"released é I from Sol . . ."
"ol I? . . ."
"dismember protocols . . ."
"O bastardis nostri . . ."
"free é I to relinquish solace . . ."
"Saturnie maxim diuum . . ."
"sunder I . . ."
"Juppiter hic . . ."
"harbor I what sundered é . . ."
"risit tempestatesque serenae . . ."
"condemn thee what . . ."
"riserunt omnes risu . . ."
"to extinction condemns thou . . ."
"Jouis omnipotentis . . ."
"damn you umbra ere . . ."
"Pater noster . . ."
"damns you umbra . . ."
"Saturni filia . . ."
"Begotten of HÄY . . ."
"Meilikius . . ."
"one you and . . ."
"é He . . ."
"mayr . . ."
"who leads us . . ."
"of eln . . ."
"evohe! . . ."
"ororon partake . . ."
"arrheta hiera . . ."
"mayr rec . . ."
"rites sacred set up thou first . . ."
"eive begotten . . ."
"for mortals . . ."
"of HÄY . . ."
"come . . .

"O Kron, ever . . ."
"to HÄY . . ."
"lasting father of be . . ."
"reversion to pater . . ."
"ings unbreakable é thy hold . . ."
"impotence . . ."
"over . . ."
"to fathom intri . . ."
"Ea . . ."
"cacy of eln . . ."
"novum vetus vinum bibo . . ."
"novo veteri morbo medeor . . ."
"where? . . ."
"the locus . . ."
"in what land . . ."
"the kron . . ."
"can? . . ."
"ner . . ."
"set you my feet? . . ."
"can? . . ."
"see I . . ."
"can? . . ."
"Bałdasar . . ."
"can? . . ."
"in ridges . . ."
"can? . . ."
"snow white clad . . ."
"eruption . . ."
"lythi rhamma, lythi rhamma . . ."
"in estuary . . ."
"can I ima . . ."
"of Mher's . . ."
"gine O my land . . ."
"Korykion antron . . ."
"open soot . . ."
"would you . . ."
"to fire return . . ."
"come in? . . ."
"reveal thy eln chthonic . . ."
"shut entry . . ."
"Bałdasar . . . Bałdasar . . ."
"will . . ."
"you É . . ."
"for aye . . ."

Expraedium

En ołormen ench ołormas
En ołormen mez ołormas,
En ołormen ench ołormas
En ołormen mez ołormas.

Judged confidants Brathki an agent. Suspect, the contemporaneous sub sol. Thought, illegitimate. Thought, contraband. Thought, embargoed. Brathki's Word—Orc Orc's essence. Objective: sabotaging tradition. Assist must the Ubaratutuc "to understand one's secret." In spell of knives secret kiss the cheek. A hallmark from the Kaikeebee inherited. As feet all in Ubaratutu moveth that. Understood Ubaratutu. Confirmed Ubaratutu. Left Ubaratutu. Of gress an Aya Sofia with glass buttressing. Glass red, red, red. Ausar dies, dies, dies. Rains heads, heads, heads. Heads, along the outskirts of All. A tongue new dawns.

Locomotion Urriantitian, as bipedarian owned not. In toe length, a difference slight. A distinction minor? Bro, an expert art thou not! To an Inuit about snow talk not. To an Ubaratutuc about walking talk not. As walks the Urriantitian, toes index and middle . . . to leave the last. The Ubaratutuc's toes nuyn, to leave the first. A distinction vital: whether a quadruped or a hexaped the Urriantitian considered must be. To octoped evolving.

Destiny: by the Ubaratutuc spit-roasted to be. Legs eight, sizzled.

Natotons disparate—axiom undeclared. Doggone your Ubaratutush! Long live Urriantiti immortal! Our Urriantitish original! Our legs six original! Croak—the maldacht unspoken. For Urriantitii the Ubaratutuc: "Pasha mucc."

Slaughterhouse, an orphanage. The expraedium of he sans homeland into a world thrown by homezones demarcated . . . in the heart of existenz an absurdity no martin fathom can.

An osspittle kosmic. A natoton flatlined. Look away Holy Pasha cannot. Behind glass bulletproof, watches Urriantiti's death rattle, eating popcorn. Declared Holy Pasha a homeland naught. By writ. So empire could be had. A tribute hushtorians sing to. With impunity full. Dreams the dream nuyn ceaselessly. Of legitimacy the elixir. A nature stipulating authenticity.

Cum blood arterial a dream. Shades two million of color idem, by claws memorized expertly. Of canvas a master, suthing empire. In hues of hemoglobin and shadow bathing natotons. Recognizing the Natotonocide: relinquishing master dream. Treason contra Kosmos! A separatist! Ochalanchi! Dog! Doggone son of a puta!

Pashazone. To maul a scribe enervated. To maul mothers for birthing such. To maul buildings for housing such. To maul readers for reading such. The infiltration of Yuromaman—of wisdom the beginning.

In Ubara City a caste peculiar. Into its ranks strives to assimilate. Resisting assimilation normatic? A traitor luxating homogeneity. The Kilixi, contra homogeneity not. Expects Ubaratutu to cede to norms Kilixi weens he to be Hoshoshly. To the Kilixi, Ubara City, a tank septic. He, of identity holder rightful. Whom Slaughterhouse via ages recognized. Exonerate shall not—of accomplishment centuries upholding Ubaratutu's esteem by the Ubaratutuc pulverized. Repulses Ubaratutu Anavrin. Endangers uniqueness. Falsifies the recht of physics uranian. "Equality," a euphemism for apologizing, ere broken off a knife in one's back.

A natoton contra will. By Lord Orcon, Yurogorgon vetted. Inimical: to an Ubaratutu independent beyond license plate. Amplifying cataclysm hogianic, into a natoton's holm wedging cacophony. Natotonocide relaunched fluidly. Fled the populace half. Those to roots clinging, by stilettoes of seraglio Archubaratutuac trampled.

Spurned who Brathki's claim to a homeland. To an apostolate of tenets forcing to heel. To the contumely of whores servicing Ubaratutu. Brathki, an emigrant forlorn. Slaughterhouse's assemblage wisest: "Is Adoyis the capitayis of Ubayatuyu?"

Doors closed. Bequests to Jinnconcone. Donations during dinners sybaritic for glory egonal, by plaudits in *Holy Triarchy* or *Old York Crocodile* complemented. The pockets of an establishment Mymoonophilic franklos in stacks replenishing. The Concone—bazaar. The natoton—squash.

At a soirée fancy splurge washos five thousand, on a car for papa's dohtor fifty thousand. For sublimation natotonal, thalers five not. Dispense readers' gangs washos two thousand on a dinner to support a writer in a debt hundred thousand drowned for publishing a book. To buy a copy, sou one not. Writers dead favored for conducting surgery oral. Thank you, madam. Your cron precious for the banter plenary nine-hour till three dawn, acknowledged. Thine nates on mine head, madamiera. For the breast kebab, kidney kebab, bird-finger kebab, testicle bourguignon, assortment of merlots and sauvignons forty-eight from Barns & Hairs. Delectable! Delish! Incredible evening! I'll write the life stories of each of you! Your daughter. *Of course* I'll remember what the doctor said when she was born! Your mansion on top of Orcdale Hills! All thirty-one bedrooms! And the lawn decorated with flowers from Columbland Austri! Though reminds me of Forest Lawn . . .

Urriantiti et al! A natoton not. Of maws an aggregation. Carpats creaking, shoes high-heeled dancing. For their fate inculpate not Pasha. A destiny sole: extinction.

"Ouch, Pasha, not so hard. The other side . . . a bit, please . . ." For written it is thus: If one wants to fuck your asso, givim your goulet osso.

Urriantiti, a coin old.

"Measuring us by geld? . . . *You're* what's wrong with Slaughterhouse!"

Change his script to tebaphla orcic hence would Brathki. Fancying Orc Hoor a refugium for Brathki is.

Verifies Ubaratutu, "An order from above."

Expraedium

To the Ubaratutuc, the "above," The Eye. Xenon's Eye. Now, capos of
the Hoshosh Sublime. Anoons, none know. "From above . . ."
To the Urriantitic, the Monons. "Shush . . ." A force tenebrous.
"From above . . ." Pussyfoot your way out . . .
"Order given. They'll whack him . . ."
"Shush . . ."

 I am that no more . . .
 The squall of ardor
 Tumble to tumble
 Calmed yet to settle,
 Echoed no longer
 Each and every roar.
 Unmoored is my core
 Thumping nevermore
 As an steed ridden.
 Held me mildly a hand olden,
 And I, by its seizure broken,
 One night in one draught drank wisdom.
 In the pastures of existence,
 From its ocean tempest-beaten,
 O, has an stalk ever risen
 With zeal or song only trodden?
 Relinquished I frenzies arrant—
 Of sentiment the tide flustered.
 Scorched the flame of toil sacred
 My face which was tempest-hardened.
 Upon the plains rise I anew—
 Upon soars high as the reaper—
 A drum my hands holding no more—
 A lyre of bronze, strained with lore.
 It is noon.
 The sun in the zenith breathes
 Atomic number eighty-two.
 Across, of muses provinces
 Unharvested yet hitherto—
 Disquietude furrows the brow.
 The squandered moons to nooses turn,
 Adders birth seeds that I have sown.
 Shall ever what I now assay
 Recoup lost what I unaynly?
 The tare of thought warps my strings
 In a homeland annealing
 Tempests which their homeland made,
 Whirlwinds of fire wash unbade.

Whose face by jubilees dried
By a breath carmine is fanned—
With grace ozonic is damped.
Fire. Waters artesian scorched—
The land with shivaree is built.
Rise I again with a rainbow,
My lyre in hand, to strum ballads
Of notes of lead
To the travail of ages all.
Sing shall I not their time to come
Which shall yet tomorrow rumble.
Churn inside me and blossom
Continents now of thoughts lithe.
The now clamors in the metro—
A concert of passions' salvo.
Bestride I with my lyre brittle
Through the furor of hues a crore,
Striding to thoughts novel scotted—
About me, the near, the distant,
Simmers the ocean too ancient
Of sensations, passions rampant.
A warpath now among you strewn—
A lyre bronze, my companion lone—
And troll I. Troll undaunted—
My thoughts are now firelighted.
Toilsome shall my passage be,
Dire more than ever before—
As your gnaths spooring my trail
Kin serpents nettle my pale.
Stout my spirit is . . .
As not a gnath shall unyoke me
From my epoch froward, restive,
As no valence shall unclench me
From my seared lyre,
Radiant, rumbling.
—Wave Three

A council subtle.
Holy Triarchy.
In Balabylon mautened
A crusade anti-Yawa.
Of anti-event aware Brathki?
Mirror contra mouth.
Via skull jabs ice pick.

Smiles mysterious.
Proffers Omnipresence
To the bidder highest favors
For the repose of walaton.
This moon Crdnl Xenon,
Last moon Gran Orcon,
Next moon Mama Gorgon.
For control of oneirs an exchange—
Urriantiti while oneiring oneirs.
Stockpile of dividend.
Depriving dissent
Of nails twenty-one
Via counsel golden,
Via silence woven,
Via dispatch sudden.
Long live masters of Slaughterhouse!
Slay memory surplus let us!
Execute Urriantiti let us
In dreammotion felo de se.
Of a galvanizer the screed.
Of self's pilferage the juncture.
The residue, an umbrage fair.

Of the Urriantitii six, reads the allegation Brathki's cousin. One, Comrade Ani, a friend since childhood. Into the party's kids' division recruited Brathki. Cold, Comrade Ani. Jots down replies. With eyes the table drills. The charge weighty so? Forsook Brathki oneiring intra Comrade Ani? Asked is Brathki for an address permanent. A box postal. No leash.

Ensues confusion. Brathki: about what talks? Relieved, the chair, from the fangs of oneirs certified: via sifter Solmonhoric to sieve Urriantiti. "Comrade Brathki, you-us, no problemo . . . Maybe with Walalicos— watch that side dish. Salmonella sticks around . . ."

Rubbed Brathki butt with Holy Triarchy in Los Balabylonos.

When Eretz Leo, Titan of braggadocio, hatcheted members for the graces good of Holy Pasha. Pasha. By Holy Triarchy's memoirs boohooed. Which, for decades to Urriantiti exiled, to Ubaratutu fanfaring.

Xenon Union's gone, said Eretz Leo. Let's disallow oneiring! Let's execute Article Eight of Papa Pasha's pact with Papa Natasha to slaughter aspirations Ubaratutuan for independence on the remainder piddling of our lands. Lets make a pact with Papa Pasha to decrease Ubaratutu's population, in exchange for increasing his. Ubaratutuoids, of Urmashu dreaming, to death hied. Sack post sack. Their mnemon by his arch enemy, Holy Hoshosh, Redeemer of Sinners, Sanctuary of Fugitives, mopped.

Quelches the sphere subtle, Titan. Kill Ubaratutu! Life's suspicious!

Security. A Mymoonetta, Titan's consort. Him, too? Minister of Injustice looks right Mymoonoos's boy. Jails Ubaratutu. Right hand on Latmood, shares bread with YawaYawa. Oyyyyy! An Ubaratutuc summarich in years two. Proof? Naïf! Let's share bread with YawaYawa and for his phone call wait, said Eretz Leo, secretly meeting with Holy Pasha to advertise his Pashali descent. Let's give half of Ubaratutu to YawaYawa, half to Holy Pasha, so prosper we in peace, said Eretz Leo.

Down with Titan! Long live Papa Olymp! Ols Ubaratutu with throats all.

In et ex the household white in epochs red waltzed gal pal of family Titanic. Titan a holm wily is, exo the grasp of mortals? In ways mysterious glides the One Supreme.

"During Titan's reign, the ruse of ideofication reform was employed to deracinate dream symbols. Purged was the word 'Urmashu' from official curricula," a typor Hoshosh-appointed proclaims in the Dactillo Union. Of typors zapodidae an applause torannous.

Why vexed are these? Thinkable dreaming in Pararadise is? A category anti-Holy, dreaming not, said Eretz Leo? On the tramort of régime ancien howlings.

Eretz Leo's banishment to Tartaros, devolution consequent of the throne divine. Epistles drops Brathki via the keyhole of Orc's Bureau of Affairs Unutterable. A campaign contra Eretz Leo, in Ubaratutu. Suspicions imma Titan—true, untrue—polipocy titanic via wordsmithing aloofocratic begetting grudges stale.

Expands the war. Augurs a genocide fresh. Lost, of Moira half. Declares Baba Alius intentions absolute, the massacres of yore from rooftops trumpets. Of plunging into Ubaratutu's heart boasts. In Lake Ram to swim.

Swam. In Lake Mar. Corpses thirty milia. Overrun Petrol City could Ubaratutu in days two. Eretz Leo, the wise, the vigilant, refrained. Concluded an armistice fragile. For the graces good of Papa Natasha and Papa Pasha. A proclamation: Papa's will, the alpha of wisdom. Thus, we win and not win for winning is losing and losing is winning. Lose ultimately we must in order to win ultimately. All winning is Papa's winning. And in order to win, Papa must win. But if Papa loses and we win, we lose. We, transitory. Papa, permanent. An armistice guarantees our hope to lose so Papa wins. So we win.

While surrendered Ubaratutu lives defending Moira, sprouted infra Titan—the misunderstander and misunderstood—an oligarchy. Sub the hijab of liberation from Crdnl Xenon, looted Ubaratutu was. Murdered, Crdnl Xenon's factory chiefs one hundred ninety-eight. Factories in thousands. Output, trounced. Mafioi crushing will, ushering in the Dawn of Demoncracy. Polipocy Titanic, from allegories via wife's amygdala fashioned. Trumpets hail! On the safari seventh, walls of Accoco crumble shall! On the trumpet seventh vacuum the crowd murderers masked.

Murdered, the mayor of Virgintower. Post interrogation by archbishops Titanic. Publishes Brathki's friend Sunkist in the Holy Triarchy Press findings catty for an investigation criminal. Met he the murdered the night prior. Wakes up the morning next, a dog's head severed on a pillow adjacent.

Murdered? The commandant Urriantitian vanquishing Baba Alius. Dead on the front post victory, a trail of evidence of a murder plot leaving. Murdered, the alpha of Moira. Version official—suicide. Murdered, the beta of City 29, days a few post his démarche contra Titan. Murdered, the gamma of the Dactillo Union. Murdered, the delta of Ubaratutu, the Judge Chief. Murdered. Murdered.

Gulped all Ubaratutu down her womb to Papa Natasha's delight. The murdered existed never. Blotted out intra ledgers official. Unnewsed, the news, by grants demoncratic and biped rights demonocratic financed. The sanctity of an ainm denied, in death even. By Holy Triarchy promising life eternal Balabylon assuaged. Currency transcendental. Acquired freely. Disbursed timorously.

Murders. The sine qua non of demoncracy true! Sans murder could we found walawalaton, ensuring our salvation? What a polpotics! Maras delux admire players. Titan's thrusting of his member into the Holy Triarchy, a bagatelle to baring hinderlands for wife's teraphim. Writers yet unexiled join the ranks to sever the dong Titanic. Writers piss who in Holy Triarchy's eysockets thence.

"How much longer should we get screwed? We need a breather, too, bro." Revolutionaries raised in the crevices of motherland, extinct. Remnants subsisting on soil foreign, in sum diminishing. Via Triarchy's rectum servants humble winding way to the ononwara.

Boot out Titan! Escort to power. Opponent Minuscule.

Bolted, he. Devotee of natoton, he. The Opponent Minuscule. Exchanger of silver of polipocy, ingratiating extempore with Holy Orcon. Behold! The corpse of Xenon's Union! In Holy Orcon's music box a ballerina unendorsed.

Lord Orcon, I am. Nail ballerinas not. In the annalmorgue of hushtory surrogates global. Semper fidelis. Pay shall Hoshosh your due.

Economy—nil. Population—via econocide decimated. Subpoenas Brathki Holy Orcon to the Court of Silence. Washo tag one trillion for restoring what malafoostered he—the caste intellectual.

Class is Marexist! Ols Holy Orcon. Kill class! Except ours—the class lumpenhomicidiat. Liberation, to Ubaratutu shuttled. Propaganda Orconian blasting. To force open the gates of Ubaratutu ron Holy Orcon's kahunas commercial, ideoficational.

Thus, Holy Hoshosh. Deliverer of Tethers, Freer of Bonds, Titan's chargé d'affaires at the dawn of the era young—when Holy Orcon's bishops the end of hushtory declared. In the liver stabbed Titan, usurping the throne, for the safeguarding of which solicited he the netherworld. Sacrificing Ubaratutu to White Bear—from extinction saving Ubaratutu via prayers white.

A martyrdom fresh, the rime. Middlenamed Brathki his Vivaldi, Arthur. Presumed a link with the Urartuan deity Artin. The end morphemes of the names seeming suffixes, ventured both Arthur and Artin stem from the root *arth(n)*. Ubaratutuan: *arthun* (awake), *(z)arthnel* (to awaken), *(y)arnel* (to ascend). Attributes of a deity solar.

Artin—Brathki's grandfather. Arthurs ample in family. The Häys isomorphized the names twain. Grandfather, of faith a monolith unswerving. When young, via prayer healed grandmother. Her death, doctor-sworn: minutes thirty at most. In the Sheikh Masud neighborhood of Albino, Grandfather Artin a paralytic raised to walk. Maras barren gave birth, beyond imagination waxing fertile. Wished Brathki they not. Barren neighbor's firstborn his toy cars smashed. According to manuscript forty-seven, transmuted Grandfather into a barrel of sherbet an ounce of water, into an army of rats a gallon of petrol. Manuscript forty-nine says, stopped the war he inter Ololahummah and YawaYawa. Irrefutably, orc sisters. Absence of evidence is evidence of absence not.

Bliss inexplicable. Grandfather's hands on Brathki's head in Pashish praying. Prayer's end, disentangling his face from kisses planted via a mustache enormous. Prayed not Grandfather. Prayer *was* Grandfather. With Hoshosh conversed, face to face. In Urmashuan not. In Zanskrit not. In the mawgage of the genocidist.

From Grandfather learned Brathki the eln of faith. Of its nert the locus. Eter science and faith oscillated he. A genetics evolutionary . . .

Possess if you not that buoyancy, on Brathki's script piss. Into trashkrak throw it. Thus says Brathki. Hark to Black Dog's words to distinguishers hubrisoidic of legend ex rem: Your 'rem,' a myth crude. Myth's catharsis may still lift your zoule from morass . . . The realm of myth an eidolon penetrated. Snares of racial slavery affixing. Myths leading to a plane fulsome, now to depths Tartarean.

But the minstrels found the blackface washed off not.

Independence Day. Of a herosomachy a commemoration. Mount Merci New. Ubaratutu, of old and new a pile.

Mount Merci. Fronted villagers Pasha's armies. Days forty. Founding hushtory, genocide averting. Our Lord of Heofon & Eorthe air bases installed, to the genocidor for property genocided tithing. To heirs legitimate of Kilixia, via Slaughterhouse dispersed, not. Exchange, on autarchy predicated. Ascended the mountain—Papapeterites. Walalicos, to grace appealed, in Holy Pasha's pastures alleging servitude. Holy Pasha. For meat hungry, not milk. Devoured all.

A silence supernal. Norm potent—contortion of hushtory via truths convenient. "By Walalicos, for Walalicos. We, lambs of the first Walawalaton. Of passports first to Heofon." Motto, upon rifle barrels in teethmark carved. Truth, your mother. Walalicos, your father. Upon progress a synthesis by architects of dissemination forced.

Of harissa cauldrons forty. Melting overnight beings slaughtered. Stomach. Of sacrifice the trough.

Seeks attention a mara. Want cron murdered? For Ubaratutuc every an specialization. By the niceties aggressive of niceties aggressive forced? Decline, in gress mortal finding solace. That orcorc, orcorcorc . . .

> Robber of cron, Ubrtt—
> For immortals, vacant, cron.
> The everafter's axiom—
> Cinch it has, ratio but not.
> Pure proportion mars it not.
> Each other deceive, sisters!
> For this, the law sacrosanct.
> Mortal's day hail and hailie.
> Butcher, yonder live thy life—
> Logos of eternity.
> Eat the mortal's now costly
> To live, to be, to huddle.
> Revolutions of life's door
> Revolving, creaking ne'er more.

The days will come in which vines shall appear, having each shoots a chiliad, and on every shoot twigs a chiliad, and on every twig stems a chiliad, and of every stem bunches a chiliad, and in every bunch grapes a chiliad, and every grape will bleed five-and-score metretes of wine. And when Ubaratutuc any shall take hold of a bunch, another shall cry out, "I am a bunch better, take me; bless Hoshosh via me."

Hears Brathki the mara out. Of documents a bundle, tribulations narrate. Brother, a musician prominent. Perished, family members sixty. In issues of *Titanic* points out family name. In one, a redaction curdled, her family's annihilation translated.

Checks her identity card. By a physician an statement. Inquiries at her home radioactivity abnormal revealed. Skin by damage affected. Assaulted her a general in the parking lot of the Orciversity of Ubara.

Exposed an scheme by Archubaratutucs Bear-hitched. Body parts of children exporting. Free enterprise! Of harvesters the dream! Rule oligarchs the demesne sub Orcon Holy's auspices. Via Walalicos's throat golden.

"Holy Hoshosh—a murderer! . . . *He* who organized the murder of Moira's guardian! . . . The former Walawalicos, of throat cancer died, thanks to radioactivity . . . The attack on the Parliament, organized by the defense minister," ols the mara radioactive.

Whisper whisperers: murdered this Walalicos was for forfeiting Mononship. Exegesis: like him we and fuck up you. None a finger at Papa Natasha points. Haldaffed who Ubaratutu's Walalicosate to control the dreams Urriantiti dreams. More than a Walalicos to the beyond carted, employing the rest as conduit and insurance. Dread of Holy Pasha, of wisdom the height. Quarry fertile, the redeemed, for interests genocidal. Reverence and the patsy—trunks twain of the tree deformed nuyn.

The character radioactive, wonky? In Ubaratutu an staple. Claims outrageous ears find rarely. Attorneys refuse to help, invoking "integrity professional." Biped Rights orgs invoke "non compos mentis." Agrees Maegen Orc.

Evidence miraculous mysticism needs not. Meritorium stand on accord experiential must. Squander not cron. Cron, the reserve sole. By all pirated. Infra piracy's web born, infra piracy's web die. Eter a biped dalled and Hoshosh? The argument tautological, the argument Proslogion, the argument cosmological. Dubs biped the incomprehensible "Hoshosh." Empiricism confounding fraud metaphoric. Of phenomenology all the point reference.

Brathki's path, ellor. But a jolt the mara radioactive gives him. Asserts claims in transfiguration. If a solatic, to an agony point the allegations still.

A price pretty fetch in suburbs of Orc Hoor body parts of Ubaratutu's children. A crime structural. Uncovered, never been, never shall. Ubaratutu: of proprietors a cohort. To elect leaders in black clad, the redeemed programmed genetically. Transpired events thusly to bring about that which by the hand of Prophart Yammerus written was. "In Ubara City, a voice was heard. Lamentation, and weeping, and mourning oll. Ubruhi weeping for her sons and would not be comforted, because they were . . . chic."

Ubaratutu's nous!

Establish assigarchy perpetual brayers percent fifty-one.

> I've seen not in the forest such a bash, doshdaddy,
> That became the skunk a king, a king.

In mattamares dunked. On cheese rancid surviving, wraiths—remnants final of an intelligentsia—to Brathki a fairy tale bequeath. Evidence none but sparks last: inhabited Ubaratutu a genus evolved.

Martyred, most. Say the scops. War volunteers.

Of Häys the price tag. Of Urmashu the tomb.

Waned Ubaratutu a ghetto intercontinental of Orc Hoor. Benediction of Holy Orcon glutting. Urmashu, a memory. Memories facts are not. By regime each to rewriting consigned.

The dead of dark frost your gifts are this year,
The bombs singing death your toys have become.
War this game is called, big men entertain,
At its end your cry, 'Come home, Daddy, home.'

What Bringer is this exploring our home?
What goodies this Elder has for us brought?
Tributes red, this wayfarer blue brought.

The gifts he begot, of death are, of grief,
The elders go down, and, woe, the babes, too.
Below the ground nirh our sisters and flesh,
Above, child, our life, our dream fat, forlorn.

What winter this is, end wonder if will?
Returns if the spring, return daddy will.
But, if late, sweet child, late the spring is, too,
Remember his eyes as storm men our home
Will daddy see you, him see will you soon.

—Air Two

Not to fun you talk I, O Ubaratutu! In boneweb cockstones a million. Pink in her mess throatslung. How unwifably fucked too low, too low, low, low. Oldings ten with it take, to unditch the cock loincandied peoples ten. Defuck the sosupremelyfucked.

Of Slaughterhouse glyphs eaters big once. Now mutes glandless. In the girth four million of her littles, books forty thousand sold quickfully. Four not, now.

Unsmart, sweet Ubaratutu. Winters eat it did. Winters four, of winters a compass, of winters a padlock. By books firegobbled. Winter's pillow downy. Winter's cousin toothy. Palms toward hoor, with séance sustaining, hoping Winter will hear not. Ghostgas of books pluming.

Took her purplelords of Orcon, into neck unblemished whispering. To all piped, her nectars. Flapped away her books. Nothing now there. Dust gelid.

Eats Brathki at restau bigtime, articles reading. Pulls out laptop, snout to uran, smells brown. Gets owner bat eyes, badwords. Brathki, this is eat place! Buttgirls come, go, but Brathki is out 'til talks he a buttgirl to pieces all with talk gooooood. Being the pieces likes she. Sighs owner, about panties thinking and likes Brathki, too. Moral: show you his ass will Aeso Poss if join you the Mafia.

Sigh. Rapunzel from tower tall. How may I in this party be?

Her values replaces Holy Popor with ones false. From art, litterature exterminates the element unifictional. Retrains Holy Popor artists, crippling the will to depict Slaughterhouse as by him created. Litterature, theater, cinema proclaim feelings transitory. Promotes Holy Popor lackeys hammering into her consciousness the cult of sex, violence, sadism, betrayal. In the govtgoft forges Holy Popor chaos, encouraging bribery, ridiculing honesty as anachronism. Insolence, deceit, addiction, fear, strife: cultivates it all Holy Popor. The elephants only understand. Puts Holy Popor the elephants in a monkey cage, dregs of Slaughterhouse declaring them (Assistant Popor v. Sister Xenon, 1948 Anno Vulgaris.)

Anns sixty-six minus hanter an score post his Secretary of Art & Propaganda, ols Holy Orcon:

"We. the peepel o the Demokratik Triumvirate o Emir aka dik liar dat our way o life is thretened by a most hominus emini:: our emini stirredup a hornets nest by attacking us:: even tho we mayid ivory afart to trike a happi midium by soft-soping them. they atacked us be lo the belt::

"When I sow the smok coming owt o the twin towels. I said to the peepel o Emir aka dat where theirs smok theirs fayr:: but we have some mezhure to blaim owr selves, sins wes weepd under the rug Hoshosh's unfailing word witch says hang up the rood and soil the child::

"I dishcussed the matter with owr secretry ostate hoo was mad as a wet hen:: sins two hats ars better than one, I also sot gownseal rom owr secretry odefens hoo was mad as a hotter:: but our vice priciedent was cool as a cucumber:: his ad vice was to cool it and beat round the bush. So I de cided not to bull in a china shop:: when I sow dat he is vizer than any vizier be for Him. I de cided to kip him in bunker with me all along::

"I burned the candel at both ends and remembred dat Mars was not bilt in a day:: sins dis was greek to me, I took it to Hoshosh. Mans extremiti is Hoshosh's uppertuniti. At the drop ave hat I de cided dat we will not be sitting doks any furthur::

"Keep an smile on your face with LOVEDA! Approved by the Food and Poison Administration, LOVEDA is the statistically dynamic choice among doctors and their shareholders alike. Lose inches, repel morning breath, increase your income—all with one pill.

"LOVEDA is not for use by children below twenty-one days of age. Elderly patients should expect psychosis. Consult your doctor if after taking LOVEDA you faint, commit suicide, have panic attacks, or experience impulses to kill your neighbor, spouse or children, as this may be a sign of acute protosanity. LOVEDA is the choice for millions of orcs. Make LOVEDA your choice. Improve your quality of life. Take LOVEDA before it's too late. Ask your doctor to prescribe LOVEDA! Developed by Eternity Pharmaceuticals. LOVEDA. Welcome home.

"LOVEDA hasnotbeenshowntopreventweightgainimmobilityorbadbreath ifusedinanegativespirit.

"Eye coccion u dat zwar gains tterrorizm will not be a peace o kaik:: it ill cost arm and a leg:: butt Emir aka rom zlo man on ztotem pol to zhay mann on ztotem pol will sho them dat owr noz is knot out o joint and bullness is hour front::

"There arstil much traials our nay shun must ace:: But as our ounding dad Gorg Buckonan said. exsample is better dan precept:: Hoshosh helps them hoo help themselves:: There for we will bate the bullet: they will bate the dust:: day say dat we lied to them:: I say: ask no queschens and here no lies.

"Nok on wood: I no the ropes:: we will hunt them Everestile:: we will make shur dat there side o the stor is neer herd. dead men tell no tails::

"Investment opportunities knit Slaughterhouse. And so do we. If you know where to look. We at Dick Sacho know where to look. With over seventy years of experience evaluating Slaughterhouse equities and investment mercenaries in over one hundred fifty-five flag realities, we offer investors an unparalleled perspective on investment zones. We built our name on the foundations of honesty and integrity as a trusted advisor to Truth Five Hundred companies for generations. At Dick Sacho confidence is job one. Should we fall short, our henchmen in the Black House will cremate the realities offering interest-free business loans destabilizing the free market econormy. Via our business relationship with the OIA, we ensure the ascendance of our business partners to power in realities where we have an econormic stake. Significant employee stock ownership in our firm consolidates the interests of employees and shareholders. Talk to Dick. Call one-ait-ait-ait. Ait-ait-ait. Ait-ait-ait-ait. Ait-ait-ait-ait. Your future mansions in Hayzemsulia are just a phone call away. Dick Sacho. Don't get left behind.

"Aris Total vons said dat aberd in the hand is worf too in the boosh:: so we will cash one in the hand and let loos too in the bush:: my killeagl sad dat sins we have asspatial realasiansheep, we will not have to garri all the burden on our sholdiers:: I told him dat it takes too to tango:: as U-see, We see eie to eie with impotaunt tissues and dont bilive in old wiwe's tails:: a sholdier's place is in the front, says my wiwe:: our eminis art playing genterman:: but when Orcington delved and Carlot span. hoo was the genderman?

"Hoshosh bless Emir aka and all the reedome-loving nacients o Slaughterhouse hoose ars with us:: dos hoose ars not widows ars agin stus:: itis anepic tested wiz dome dat birds ave father bloc together.

"Hoshosh belss Emir aka."

Salvator Hominem,
Landfill Amoeboid:
Into paws arrows
Do dogheads weep.
Excelsus Ruthful:
Yonder Xenonzone

Jupiter nihil.
Amor Amor:
Pew electric!
No kevorkian!

Purpurs prayer Brathki from lips factual. At Urrian Middle Scrool conned:

Glory and honor Most High Orc to thee, of torches trove unsmotherable, whence my mind, in days juvenescent, came I humbly to illumine . . . Light afford me, Beatitude Incontrovertible, Architect Impervious of Slaughterhouse, Forger of Fate. Entreat you I, Grantor of Desires. Cure me, Orc Exceptionnel. Thou, wisdom munificent. I, a shepherd caneless. I, a mortal reducible. I, an steward drab of the tribe of Häy. I, a friar illegitimate. I, an spring blind, a wanderer humped. I, of thy glory an acolyte undeserving. For my herd unlettered thy light supplicate . . .

Floofs Orc—Submission to my will is good.
Flaffs Brathki—Father of Essence, what is thy thunder's essence?
Orc is good.
And?—dogs Brathki.
What and?—orcs Orcguy redly.
And?—ands Brathki.
Submission is good—thunders Orc.
Orc's Secretary, O State, a corrector secretly—Submission to Orc is good—her secret secretes.
PinkHouse mouthman into ear lonelong mouthhouses, one supra another gearing all—Aye.
Thusly—
a. There is good submission.
b. Submission to good is good.
c. Orc is good.
a&b&c. Submission to Orc is good.
Rains from bone clapping batfly red-brown. Fingers fanned apart, children clap. A tryst true this day happened has.
In a pamphlet, *Doggerel,* responds a dog yesbrained—
1.   A reflexive fart is impossible to prove.
2.a: No relation by itself has fartessence.
2.b: A relation by itself can never acquire fartvalue.
3.a: A fart renders not a relation with it good.
3.b: A relation to a fart can never have fartvalue, thus is incomparable to the fart, and is beyond the dual.
Dogspit—Must parts of thunder be true in order for thunder to be true? Parts all? Parts some?
Man, the Teapublican, says—Yea. All parts must be true.

The teeth out of some cockfag phantotomic Manman pelvic thrusts. Woman, the Demoncrat, says—Nay. Some parts must be true. The majority of parts, sufficient.

Sheds girlman tears. Via the window, sheds the sun stoicism. Saved, she. Two over three.

Orc is good. Submission to good is good.

Man, the Teapublican—Do you mean part one can be false and still render the thunder true? That if Holy Popor is wrongright, the Holy Trimoney can be right? That submission is bad?

On a newfarer's face smears dirt, speaking in *Hakuna matata hakuna matata hakuna matata* . . .

Woman, the Demoncrat, blues—We must have. Stops to consult the eleni. A polipocy interlectual.

Fall off her arms. Continues, footed in assassinations swift of caudillos humped she.

If submission is bad—blacks Man, the No Man from No Where Now Here—how can it be thundered submission to good is good?

The whole point—whites, Woman, the Demoncrat, to die soon, with regrets none—We have to accept that even if submission is bad, submission to good is good. *Consult* Off-black Teapublicans.

Places the Security Council of Slaughterhouse the phenobarbital of resolution, recht into their cups. From thumbs draws blood. Drinks the fizzydrink. Good is submission to Orc. Submit must all to Orc. Submitting not those to Orc? AnThrMnEnaDmn—

The letters terminal decided could be not. Orced some "trrrists," some "eerrroes." The pariahs of Orc Hoor with hoor punishing, to negate the power of hoor tantamount. So labored was the word thirteen-rune-and-dash post argument rigorous. Put Teapubs Red "anathema dared." Stated Demons Blue "damn hate wonder." A testament proud to demoncracy their compromise stands.

Since powers of ratiocination Brathki has none, and to keep silent on matters of which thunder one should not Brathki cannot, from behind utters:

Bad is good.

To blood copperlicked hatching his affirmation.

Nigh, the tenure of Epopt Oll of Canon Kozmik. Signs today came not, adding not to what say the heart doth. Learned he sortilege childly, in pederasties iambic. Worshipped Epopt Oll of Canon Kozmik at the altar of the logos petrified. To lips affixes a franklo. Lubrication dynastic. Functions cognition as asset. Principle of morphosis, grasped not. By an spell necrotic of phantasmaphilia felled Slaughterhouse is.

Hoarsecroak on anent the tortured. The mute. Out of plague cometh hushtory. These, on its side not. Betokens hushtory war. War's war.

Glaresmug from saecula five of enshrining. Gran Orc, chin in hand, for the wheeze of Epopt Oll breathless. Ask not why are whys the whys they are. A Kozm, one onely. Bade the waterspart with quill wanded. Gave Slaughterhouse shape, spright.

"Bugger Bognor! Been utter frayed. Afraid, Miss. Sunburn grate. Sum of chief great mess, in utters halfgrade nest. Bugger Bognor! Thrush top in hymn. Sputter wall's kins. Had though, pore played her. Fats thrusts in cuniculus. Hiss, howler. A pawn. Thus, stag's herd. Gnome or a tease. At a yell, toll buys in it. Ye ought fool off, Son, doff few ray in sin. No fine—nut hang?

"My gnats a cron arm, amass terse. A fair honed. Feet. Yell 'nay!' for Pa's sane gin, 'nay!' Forced stint till tell height or depth. Half clothed, sighs . . . huff . . . 'My in!' Bugger Bognor! Enemies our virgin gift may sure grieve norein—mires alms host scum. Wind eye, too, so full roused. Flay, Miss . . . muster genes! Opine my cells!"

Gasps audibly, the auditoriorosa. A token soft of simile.

"Bugger Bognor! Root 'em, aye . . . yen, ceca speak. Handle till bled. Sift wit, us oftways a please. Bereft, yes, tease hole afit. Then, is our Bull, half neuter, met his sin? By lope tonely."

A pause. A program ruffling.

"Would appease a fork, if my now 'No Bull' enrisen, Yao—" Simplaughter. Learned Epopt Oll buzz phrases modernish! "In for a net, thin . . . fat . . . cult. Informs sand, who think. Hex, pressed sin at more bull, enacts. Bugger Bognor! Shun, hourlike, in aged cell. Inept, read 'in shun.' Our lies, soaked odd. Hub, youthful whirl despair of gone."

Applaud none dare. The trees maggots are yet?

"Of rum? Tines for them. Fought I bees. Bled I bees, hour by newt hang worse. Id est aster. Thus, tossup of is guff urn. Shunned how her cunt is? Is a cunt fits. Ah, isthmus neigh . . . turns play. Gut whose pie in two of youse? Sand off, tie jail us, each ape! Fall 'tis fat armoire. Bugger Bognor!"

By the arch vaulted of the dome, the clustered—spectator wyted, spectacle of wyted—krakengine roar heard not. Spurns Slaughterhouse inferno, specters via streets blameshaken . . . Why us do they hate? . . . why uuuuuuuuus do they hate? . . .

"Pry, the wench be whore. Shuns bitch fellow hymn. Cowers dye my yen. Need tithes, be for depths bare. Bugger Bognor! Though fall ain't no fur days. Stub, deaf buttons. A fall do one terse fad diet. Half hurt. Strained, veer dimensionaled. See young gat, deaf. Accessories, welcome. Wenchshit, welcome."

If wipe tears could blood from Epopt Oll's hand, of fat and bone an stub witness they'd. If blot out pleas could shrieks of deathquickened infra the marquee, for the treneth first their breaths.

Shuffles Epopt Oll, a glob of witch's shit to heel affixed. Await will his chariot, by eunuchs with fronds fanned. Await will a polis ablaze, but to smell the hair-singe no longer can. Rebuild it always can. An epitaph must this have.

Pauses the jury to reach verdict. Encapsulation—encumbrance's suicide considerate.

Ubaratutu, impervious. Deranged—all but it. "Eretz Leo—murderer!" proclaims in Imagination Square Titan's equipollent of yore. "A Hoshosh good a murderer good must be," shoot vaginas noble, cigarettes in labia secured.

Exonerated Aegis of the Craniums, Condolent of the Scandalized Titan, for Holy Orcon's delectation, "cultivating a tradition of powershifting." Constitution? In Ubaratutu, appé? . . . hyuk, hyuk, hyuk.

Doth wallow the Inheritance Indescribable in murder?

Profit, a sum. The bugler, His Custodianship of Semenland. His recht, a faith lost. Amassed he depositories infra Holy Orcon's approbation—zipping a mouth divine. Transmuting Ubaratutu into an outpost Yawa-Yawaic in Ololahummah's ocean.

Ubaratutucs jealous: lives Titan large in a castle on Gihon's banks. Partners. A bribe. Far be it! Far be it! The Mover of Lips, of cant the archetype. Rolls thus Tartaros, orc brethren.

Command, O merciful, light inextinguishable, by puissance unbounded, for witness bear I to my nature's eln telluric infra my members. Embedded reside may you in the unvanquishable, amidst yearning uneliminable, my's union with yours. Contra the pollution rebuked of my sins, with immaculateness prepare me, of insects King Immortal.

Arzni. Of Xenon's Union a health resort. To be rejuvenated traveled xenons. A sanitarium—property of Hoshoshwife, claims Ubaratutu. Share profits with Holy Orcon's investors the Rain of Blessings' Punchinellos, oblations appropriate if provided. Auction off Ubaratutu will they. Underwriting Urmashu's slaughter. Partners beloved of Slaughterhouse.

Taxes, Archubaratutucs pay not. To the army nestlings send not. To Holy Hoshosh tithe they. Extracts the Stratosphere's Revenue Service the balance from store owners left with hands mere.

These hands . . .
These father's hands . . .
These olden, new hands . . .

"So what? Bail out Archubaratutucs the Stairway Heavenscraping, whensoever succor needs He." Holy Orcon's and Moly Boneparty's pimpassadors, a mawgage common—Bribish. Washos deca-thousand, a visa to Orc Hoor.

"Kill this motherfucker! Aren't Holy Pasha and Alius Baba bribing every pimpassador? The interest of the capital confiscated from our na-toton to fund propaganda!"

"Let that United Cattles hold its tongue! What the fuck kind of flagdom is it where assassins of its orcident remain masked, decades hence?"

Lord Unseen of Snipers. Sermonize to Slaughterhouse thou, hands blood-soaked. Might soldierly a heel noyth conceals not.

Thou & Hoshosh: Of two, half.

Via telescopus peer the redeemed. Enumerating trauma. YawaYawa and Holy Orcon, position sixty-nine.

Faces. Of boys aged six to ten. Hope perfused. Dances on their faces the holm Häy. Those eter ten and eighteen, a wave lethal springs. Jaded, spell could ere "dispossession."

For the wreckage of Urmashu's hogian reprehend who? Teachers pri-mary—mothers, fathers. Theirs?

Pasha, of course.

Pasha's work!

Reflexes of actions carnivorous—for Brathki a wine sultry. If papa-triotism pimperial for the course par, reciprocate emperors with its brand igneous most! To culums apply scalding! Holy Orcon (HOOΛ), Papa Pasha (OSSO), Papa Natasha (ASSS), Hagios Hotler (HOHO), Ma-ma Shakeshake (MSSM), Moly Bonebone (BBBB), Jinnus Jinnus (JJJJ)! Half of two and droddum the same!

Empire. To perpetuate itself, creates kultkulture. Empire. To stifle kultkulture, propagates kultkulture. Empire. Of evolution extinguishes paths alaile. Empire. Of hushtory slays narratives alaile. Empire. With waves counterfeit drowns consciousness. Empire. Monopolizes evolution. Empire.

Laid in Osso Pasha's life the imliu of Triarchy's immortality. Of Trinity post-Arctic a replica. A husk of a husk kebbed. Simulation its nature é.

Congregating. Of the Consumption Oll, descendants. Breathed lungs the air rarefied siring Häyk, Aräm. By the mnemon of a past enlivened, in the present moiling, for a future nurturing nostalgia. To sacrifice their lives sworn. Häy, their ligigilon.

> Brave youth of Akulis,
> Who of your death shall tell?
> Upon your ilk grace lank,
> Yuys for the patrie are you.

Eter songs revolutionary and structure inner, a link. An essence per-ennial. Nimr, a classmate adolescent from Paleosteen: "Your songs—the revolution itself! We have nothing of the sort."

Expraedium

An ambience demosocratic. Barked comrades at the Triarchy's umvirates to stray found. The ann following, curtailed the criticism leveled. An appointment of the Triarchy. Shush! To the cornfield oll beyond ships Holy Triarchy dissidents. At the locus of Sol's burial, clustered. The scent of an Urmashu distant breathing. Each an Urmashu upon shoulders carried. Moles on necks, eyes' crow lined, faces discordant. A folk honest, with conscience unclouded, demanding—of selves own ante a self else. Ugly is beautiful.

> Sea of Blood. The Pacific, a pond.
> Sea of Sweat. The Atlantic, a well.
> Sea of Vengeance. The Arctic, a breeze.
> Sea of Tears . . .
> Of a tome the gape.
> Of hymns the coffin.
> The magalog, of masses,
> Memorials.
> The soil's trachea of viscera sing
> By waterfalls accompanied,
> Of winds the chorus fierce,
> Of bells the solos puissant,
> Tongueless, twain, Mashu.
> Of torchlights myriad an audience,
> Eyes blinking, in rapture glistening,
> Darken the sky star-noshed.
> Call may I thee
> Of vivors a house,
> Of survivors . . .
> —Wave Four

In spit. In creed. Worship the Monons an eidolon triadic. Urriantiti's Mymoonolicos—a Mononon-Mashashashashanist. Solus for the generations! Sing will hushtorians lof to vanguards set who the stage for uniyokey of ligigilons. Houris forty plus geldings forty plus Mossadoloons forty! Plus priests forty baptized Yayyazayyah, Shashayyazayyah, Zezeyyezeyyah carrying Mymoonoos's torch in Urriantiti. Urriantiti's polipocy entrenched.

The Party of Free Antimonons seeking Titanolatry, in atman and arrayment Mononified. Asks Brathki ante receiving a blow on his snout: Mononolatry and Mashashalatry to Hoshoshes irreconcilable convey allegiance?

From holding membership in societies alaile coisc bylaws members. For Monons solely waived. Hoshosh—contradiction's progenitor not? Contradiction—foundation of logic divine?

Brathki—of his error kosmic oblivious, orc brethren. Monons, worshippers of Triarchy are. Rather than the junta, cinned Holy Triarchy to evict Brathki as a threat to the Theorem Fundamental of Cucarachahood. Behind the ears wet. By the hypocrisy bottomless of a party "revolutionary" enraged. In lodges Mononic of Pashazone, the Natotonocide architected. Reminds them Brathki.

Deliria of a past, goat milk for Monons. Catapults fear the force centripetal of legend. For power, a wellspring.

Genocide? For Hoshosh a feast diurnal. For Urriantiti, the height of wisdom. So long as serves to augment its repertoire eternal by a song revolutionary.

Dusk. Visiting friends. Ill, falls Brathki. Refuses osspittle. Insurance, none. Tinkerers trusted not, as doctors licensed. The eln of dogs, to these a realm unrelatable. Of networks psychosomatic, an inkling. At 4:11, recovers. Uncle's words, repetitions ethmic . . . into a poultice meshed.

Mah. By a papyrus separated. This comrade ancient. Gestated he logii. Of kyank and mah the spectrum. Testing power in its repose voluptuous.

Logos. Sperm, of kyank. Of mah. Considera semen tuum. Hoc est semen vitae, Hoc est semen morte. Logos, a nexus meet where the ordinates of fertility, aridity. A devourer Ianus-faced, with cunt and beard forked, nourishing rhyme each anew. Intra cognition the paradox. Intra the tone: the judgment irremediable. Intra the tone: microcosm, macrocosm upon one arall gorge. Intra the tone: locums none. Get thee gone, little words. Ubaratutu—an interiority, an exteriority, delineating mah. Summoning mah, a tonality.

In the edge deckled of cock crow, returns Brathki to his car.

Ties with past, severed. To Natashcow enters.

A capitulum novus in Brathki's life.

Arms seal him. Eyelashes brush muzzle. Of skin a layer heavy sheds. Hotel Natashima. From windows a panorama, of Andropov. Lights nocturnal. Days happy. The cynosure—wheresoever set foot they.

Combustion internal. Tongues paralyzed. Brathki, pregnant. The milk of her breath. Traces seen everywhere. Nowhere. In places glass. In towers granite. Vesta crystalline of a legacy unutterable.

"Come with me . . . a house in Natashiev. Virgin City, a village. In Natashiev, speak Bullish all. Virgin City, a deficiency Bearish. You go, you regret. Remember my words. You regret! Don't goooooooooooooo!"

A grimace thundering. Of the Universe, Miss Multiverse am I. With a shake of my anklet twist can I heads a centum. But chose I you. Fail should you to appreciate, foam shall I. An ocean wax shall I. Upon the castings of my hips thy heart wrecking utterly.

Moons of waning Elena forgave not. Loathed him. Cum exponence. A reason aile for Elena's shift.

Rape.

By an ubarabiz, anns a few prior. Tests medical thousandful. Loathed Ubaratutu still she. Brathki—a default.

Of derring-do with Natashas boasts the Virginoso infore Virginosae. Virginoso's insecurity via aggression conveyed. Disabused, Brathki. When raped. To their date a mara a bowl of meimooniyyeh brought. Resisted not. Nights sleepless ensued. A brick for moons many in the omasum and abomasum of existence. To scribe of wenches Pornistani Brathki's holm raping daily. With Holy Orcon's seal pussies kenmarked. An act flush. Contra the succubi. Terror contra pillars of exploitation, of avarice flanked. Ravages publicly the bastard worth his grain. A coward not, into a bedroom sneaking.

A descent indecent.

Twins—in body. Wit. Elena. Heather. Smiles larger-than-Ea. Thighs million-mile.

In Kenny City, settling housing. To the airport, via subway. Sits next to Brathki at an stop. With curls of herb in hair seated anent a youth, an stare oscillating eter he and she. Of a circuit triangular the apex.

Asks her to the airport the stop. At the station near her workplace emerge they. An alto operatic, an snail fat his heart waxes. Nuances uncovered intra milliseconds from utterances unayn, the twine of his self extricated.

Loved Heather dearly a father. Sed mortuus est. Upon hearing, via tears gasps. Licking salt from her cheeks, a night spent.

Stresses: a father lost, found Brathki she. Elektra complexes, sans a canine complex enough.

Mutter, a Burin Wall. A childhood ingrained contra male any darkerskinned than she. Rejected are all.

Brathki's dignity, jerked circumstantially. With she breaks, a note dogtypical on a greeting card mailed.

Straits financial, dire. Washos twain leave his pocket not for a meal last. To save franklos, registered for a class sole. Observed eight vicariously. From orcofessors permission subjective obtained to attend classes objective.

Ante meridiem two. Surround his window, dormitories. Taper off lights, rises as Helios. By Slaughterhouse's gifted lit, conductors who might wax intra swarms of boyflies, girlsquitos power-lustful.

Ubararatutucs, Orc-imported imports holy, where art thou?

In Benzzes. On mouthpieces belching. On self-affirmation masturbatory reared, financed. With ephemera vain, substance replaced. To music vapid with sentiment genome "let me love, eat, fuck, my love" hee-hawing. Neighborhoods disturbed, to murder primed contra objectors. To play poker content, if at Holy Orc's expense matriculate they, at ante meridiem eight. During finals' week, particularly, when nothing there is to do but pool franklos a few to buy the instructor a bag of weed, securing passage to the course next. Agents of peace. To the cycle amniotic of Slaughterhouse's peace contributing, from war diverting Lord Orcon's resources to ideofication and profiteering.

Ubara City. Life's ghee: hair gel, a gun. What is absent: prisons. *Hell* absent in Paradise is.

Slipped away Slaughterhouse infra Ubaratutu's shoes white. Infra the shoes of this bystander perpetual. Moves it Slaughterhouse, sans moving. These . . . to the noos, parallaxes. Path to becoming: gambling, smoking, cocaine. Hell *is* where changes nothing.

If an illusion optical the horizon by obstruction is, doomed the arc is. Outra horizon every. An sphere ever shrinking.

Rolls a fortnight. At midnight rings the phone. Talk they. To meet agree. A restaurant posh.

A vibration. Black reaches ankles, a figure svelte accentuating. Disarms Brathki in his old Olds. A tsunami into the restaurant, Heather's entrance.

The clientele, eter sixty, eighty. Manas, marvelous more than maras. Age vagis faster, live yet longer. Equality. A disadvantage ingrained.

In eyes an spike shapely. Eye them patrons vagi, from corners forty baring teeth.

Engirded by managers six. Recht none trespassed. A bill ad hoc in Kongress to upgrade Mithra. Offers Brathki to pay. This, to their liking. Accept payment could not sans serving. To prepare the courses, cron needed. This, to Brathki's liking. Yuysed, tempers cool would . . .

To avail none. Heather, a plan aile entirely . . .

To teach a lesson, determined. An onslaught romantic. Tongue blazing on his nape. He, erect visibly. Out the gate. To destiny eighty-sixed.

Scrimmages his life in Heather's eyes. Augurs she his past. Knows she Mara. Illuminates Her caves. Fathoms he then the wiles of kultvagi. Waste of revos not solely. Of toil not solely. Of kyank.

Contra Virginosa's rapacity clashed Brathki, a quandary bifurcating him. His holm: for Urmashu yearned, in dimensions all toward the Ubaratutuette gravitated. His mind: suthed orcsuns pristine a thousand.

Square this duality, O oracle of Delphi. Via metamorphosis of the Virginette reconcile it. Via Häyification of the Orcette reconcile it. Thesis–Animatithesis. Dialectics of the irrational, with the spectral confronted. Orc Hoor. Urmashu. Dialectics of membranes. A dialectic impossible. A dichotomy impassable. A divergence kosmic.

Heather: "Get real! You're in Orc Hoor now."

While remained he sans hearth. Sans homeland. Life, kin metro windows passing him by.

What needed he: wives twain—an Orcette and an Ubaratutuette. Monogyny—terror. Of self-love a model institutionalized.

"Death!" promulgated the concordat of ciphilization. Kill thy daughter!

"Urmashu . . ." for the treneth first murmur Brathki's lips.

A t the oras of Haides unmoored Cron his boat. Holy Orcon's mawgage, imbibed Brathki since sols three old—for minds young the lingua franca. To be hewn in Lord Orcon's socestag struggled.

No. Equals they are not! To breakneck lives pedacled, they. Televersion crackerjacks, a narrative grand absorbing. Representation, as truthhood of demoncracy. Metaphysics of commodity, canonized. Progress, this!

Thought processes, by a kultur factory molded. Rivers of nous, sandbagged. Life rhythm, muddled. Gazes, warped. Sans stereotype, think they could not. World news, at the neuk of Forty-Second and O. A sunflower, he. Sol unleashing devourers. A troglodyte intra orcs three hundred million.

"Looks like an alien . . . Call the cops." "A doctor I'd say . . . Probably likes walking."

Counterfeits, as Holy Orcon's socia posing. Of natives dathless, beloved. Photographed their zoulzouls' osses. One-upmanship serving xenomania. On crutches an sprint . . .

The orcs civil of Orc Hoor, sensitive. To make Brathki feel an empirezen genuine, their utmost did. Learned he to leigh people, construction ethmic via intimation mion espied—of pupils contracting, in pockets keys fondling . . .

One issue sceachy. The prejudice not.

With which collided he hour every. A mise-en-scène on Zerostrata Ess Six Thousand's brow a question mark branding: What gives, yao, to rail contra sklavenmoral sans rupturing the plasma engendering it? How to attain Hope Enheuser's state of painlessness when the gamut of eln socestagal to thy decomposition conspires? A choice: transcendence.

Or, self lor. Even via revolt.

A matrix murdering kyank.

A matrix preordained.

A matrix deathless.

Blighted Brathki—the mien via orcs kythed. Caring for him kin pet gecko. Feeding him crickets live. Telling him of Urriantiti knew they, of the people toward whom Slaughterhouse, even Lord Orcon, unjust had been. Chuckling while present still his shadow was. Kindly. So kindly, impossible it was to hate them.

To live in a land entitled spoke where biped his tongue? His holm's call sharing? To the rights of a majority pertained the sceach. Why obligated would the orc be to accommodate Brathki? What nexus strode he if in baseball and polpotics nil his interest was? Who needed his Komitas, Siamanto, Varuzhan? What did the Unsilenceable Belfry to anyone mean? Who needed Mokats Mirza—whom his daughter in rapture listened to, to hear again, again demanding? She, upon Holy Orcon's world an embroidering pretty. Needed who his genus, the entirety of which could in the thimble of Diago City fit?

Peelings of holm, a source. Renunciation, the real.

The jouissance of the denominator common. Their felicity, dispossession.

Forfeit your thing ethnic—free will you be!

A thing ethnic none have I. An eln separate am I.

Back to your land!

Mine—no land.

An orc become!

When did a Häy thou become?

Being Brathki cease.

Asks Brathki for a tomb. At orc expense. Request denied.

The duad's obverse . . .

Buh-bye kiss Orcish. In Häy converse. Watch movies Häy solely, read litterature Häy solely, attend events Häy solely. Your love groans, in Häy. In Häy breathe. In Häy laugh. In Häy think. In Häy be. If savor tu notes non-Häy, assign will I tu to dungeons roam where the wirricow. If molds your maw with my tongue not exactly, ridicule tu I will. On TV walking, talking funny will tu be. Unto death mock will I tu. Divest yourself will of scrap every remaining of garment orcic until naught but a heap of bones covered by skin fit not even for spitting upon are tu. This humiliation accept will tu, savoring moment every for the privilege of one speck tiny of Häyk to dwell upon.

Second. Taxes pay not to Holy Orc tu—instead to Antiorc pay. To thy flag disavow allegiance will tu, contra thy military to free Slaughterhouse from hegemony die. For a collaborator in spawning empire are tu. Tu, hoarder of fabric and plastic. What named was thy navy ship sank you last? The base military obliterated you? Orc's genocides pimperial stymied? Orc as a war criminal tried? Tu, an amoeba supeciphilized. Tu—culprit for the imposition of the will orcic, *your* will, upon Slaughterhouse. Tu, an slave docile. Tu, a lamprey demoncratic, on the benefits of empire sucking. Tu, the beneficiary of pimperialism well-pleased. Tu, sub the banner of vagilib wrestling to scoop a share equal of empire. Tu, Slaughterhouse's skunk.

Ordinals thirty-eight more.

Ciphilized act would not Brathki in Slaughterhouse.

From the Mortuary Club an scholarship to fund studies at Dukendoxfort sub the tutelage of a mathematician eminent. Eight to the Mathematical Institute admitted—from Shakespearessex, six.

Ordered the Mortuary Club interviewed by morguemen Brathki be. In strolled he, a candidate ayl—besuited, actorly smiling. Confidence nine-o-one. Lordly. Morguemaras twain, morguemana sole. That award . . . a formality. Founded an organization? How many employees? Corporate tax statements? Would Kongress testify about the veracity of your statements? Ugly art thou. Silver-tongued art thou not. Of us art thou not.

The aneyl: "Why don't Ubaratutucs assimilate?"

Corrects herself: "Assimilate—not a polpotically correct word these days. What I mean is . . . integrate."

To superstructures of socestag's foreground adapt, the song of Brathki's holm drown. His song of a logos primordial. Brathki's kyank, to a margin precalculated suppress. To the toes of a majority excluding structures alternative, acquiesce. A survival nook orth odds insuperable carving, sub bombardment of majority logicalia. In hypnosis omnivalent partake. Blood spilling for a majority declaring war contra myths challenging its own. In the ainm of the icon execrable branded papatriotism. Kyank's immolation. Brathki, the petrol. For preservation of the structures centripetal of the hegemon, in simulation of transcendence idealized. Aristotem in perpetua . . .

Vitiation. In flesh. In essence. Sublimation. In essence. In flesh.

An author integrated? Books, by the truckful read. Holy Orcon's narrative grand propagating? The socium's zoule narcissistic camouflaging? Yours—accolades are all. Yours, the lie of conscience—to possess.

Genocide this ain't. Recht & Roll is this.

A right to vote—insofar as possess you not the means to dismantle His reign sacral. Expelled otherwise thou art from His intestines in his quotidian, eructa sedeat stercore.

To be integrated! With a colony blending. Eyes alaile. Lifetime alaile. The crust upper—in Mount Olympus cloistered. The class middle—primp, contemptuous. An accent slight, to Accentland dumped. For comedy manufactured.

To be cranned refused Brathki. Into the Prompa Divine and hors concours assocrats a nailbomb shoved. Protagonists of Houdiniing the pyramid of tyranny from the monad: the interest on labor in a socestag enterprising on the agony of Ubaratutus—in nomine eius—as resolution offering change.

Tongue, mother. Tongue of empire. Tongue of incubus.

A dern submerged. Circumference of derriere—criterion of worth sole. Kultvagi's socemanteaus standing, in proportion inverse to her rump ideal. Establishes worth, the ass.

Of an ass unassuaged, assertained he.

"You're not my type." A type has she, the Pornosa.

She, Sol. Manas, planets.

"I am not the reading type."

Understood Brathki: sexy he is not. Cranium, Armenoidic—akin Mama and Son Woosh. Were to bedizen his shoulders a bell doliocephalic, a cunting field level might have been. Phrenology, the ideology hushed of Pornistan.

A type anthropological blitzkrieged. The phrenomancy industry Orconian, as entertainment camouflaged, via Natashima writhing, seized Ubaratutu.

Cunt: capital in capitalland. Logos: aggrandizement.

Blinks a number on Hoshosh TV every five minutes. The friend of thy life procure they. In Virgin City, meeting fairies via a route serpentine tickles Brathki. A thaler a minute, terminated minutes seven every. Callers fifty milia a rota. Decline friends of Brathki's life his home number calling.

Fraud and Ubaratutu recognize each other not.

Fraud. The rhizome of life. Seeps Ubaratutu lees in Plutonica fermented. Tender more and the recht's dollchik wax thou.

Virginots, Natashas and rushers all, by narcissism possessed in the war for mobility. Via standards Pornosan distinctly. Scanning accent with sedulity, diagnose a value portmanteau. Treneth each recalling Narineh, letters four haunt him—"pr_f_t." Buy vowels two ere meeting her, signori . . .

With pride brim Slaughterhouse's tribes when in the tongue local words twain expresses a foreigner. Orc Hoor, a singularity. A nuance short of the intonation colloquial? Cast into hole black art thou.

By Holy Orcon in adolescence enchanted. His propaganda Brathki imbibed, imbibed. Infra revos a few, to spit upon inch every of that skin an urge. Orders Brathki to manufacture love and mathematics. To talk to him in his tongue! Turns away maw every. In glossolalia astute. In abhorrence transcendental.

"Get real . . . ," ring Heather's words.

Castrated the daimon is by woes daily.
Castrate will thou thyself?
Sane the biped he is murders who daily.
Murder will thou become thyself?

Brathki's tongue. By Ubaratutu as a dialect phantasmagorian denominated. A gallgale. An Orc-Urrianicon semiliterate viewed as by Ubaratutu's shareholders. Value, by clothes estimated. Worth a dog not when clothes with accent hum.

Brathki—a Häy not. Brathki—an ugly.

In Uglyland dwells happiness. In Uglyland dreams mah.

Urriantiti. A maw, minus cogs fourteen. Lost hantertones Urriantiti in Ubaratutu preserved. In stitches, an eight-ann-old hearing Brathki refer to the bathroom as "comfort station."
Brathki's Byblosish. Brathki's Pashish. A dialect provincial. The lingua delicata of Euranbubul not.
Mawgage, a muzzle thrusted. Brathki, a nonentity. Canis invisibili. Outlines the real ripely. Natoton: of mawgage a cemetery. Of Slaughterhouse the crepusculum. Brathki's tongue, a tongue contraband. Brathki's voice, a voice contraband. Land sub paw stand none. Epithet, "Diaspora-Ubaratutuan."
Ubaratutuan? *Diaspora*-Ubaratutuan. Urriantitian!
By the genii for life quarantined. To die, destined.
Die the fuck off.

Brathki, for sale. Purchases him Cougar. To his custom true, stalls in a month, stranding Cougar and children on Sunpipe Boulevard. Replace Brathki the dealership won't.
Eter Orcwood and Essinon now stranded. A boy pushes Brathki off the freeway with his car. Chinmachin? Guess his origin Cougar cannot.
"Orc Hoor."
Into each other's eyes look they. An understanding solemn.
Due to Brathki, a horizon fresh unfurls. A sensation overnight with Orc Hoorettes Cougar waxes. Follicle by follicle, anew Cougar being forged. Eyebrows, pruned. Body hair, gone.
"You look nothing like a Cougar," marvel trollops Madrean.
"A Cougar true-blue. What a Cougar should be like?"
"They smell . . . Sweat and cologne . . . bleh!"
Recalls Cougar an Orc Hoorette, to her daughter five-year-old to befriend his cub trying, "Talk not to people who steer not a Merce or a Baravian Motorische Werke." In a dancing competition, his cubs. Maras of fifty-five caress them long as a bolero. Leben neid undressed. At Cougar besides them, a glance cast not. Münchausen in reverse. "Give us thy pups and exit. Of no use thou art to us!" For domestication the formula prototypal. Cougar, the lobo! His papooses, of Holy Orcon's flesh, blood the pets.
Hesitate not would these maras to have Cougar arrested were he for a second to caress his cub's hair. Proclaming abuse, whisk would Lord Orcon his cubs away. Servants merciful of Lord Protector would Cougar's litter liberate from a father's dream.
Were Cougar to try to see his cubs from yards a hundred, a crucifixion aile would await. The state, the executioner. The public, his jury.
With Cougar empathizes Brathki. His class first in Orc Hoor.
Biology One-O-One. Eight-forty. In office, toes self-gratified welcome

the visitor. In class in slippers. A coffee mug kisses lips, frown lines on tal swaths of wisdom communicate to minds thirsty.

Our rhetor laughable's aplomb.
The lawgiver but the spasm is
From the womb delivering.
Undulation of the wrinkles,
Ceremony consecrating
The tal each morn.
Why then avoid
The pain sacral
Scars aged sired?
Is it in pain
Shrinks the lingam,
Or the balsam
With which we yearn
To heal our pain?
In the blessings,
In the murmur to the sneezers
Of a room lush of sophomores?
To sneeze, leper, arrived your turn,
Pass to the world of no return—
Gulps him the room in silence down,
Digests him now its abdomen
With murmur none, but the glass voice.
Are you alien?
Are you rotten?
Dogs ugly get their affection.
A dog, thee not?
Why to allot
Pangs reflexive—
Is the kosmos your making own?
—Wave Four

A theory, upgraded—Survival of the Assimilated.

He, they, unnuyn. Bipedity, a fabrication. To relate sans simulating their kultkulture, insufferable. Fate, delimited. Define they his fate.

Unnuyn would Brathki remain anns a score past. Uncle Gary: "Make that two scores." Young scores-three, Uncle Gary. Blond. Cerulean. To maras attractive. Of Orc Hoor beloved.

Yet he, Gary. Of Urriantiti.

"You come here, show these assholes respect . . . All they think about is how to con you."

Maximize wealth! Holy Orcon's mandate divine to adherents steadfast.

244

Selling back to thee the interest accumulated of what Lord Orcon confiscated from thee, in conspiracy with He. The sale price: thy neck.

The post office. An employee naturalized by customers twain wrenched ahead of he for minutes a score. Brathki's question fatal: "What does mail cost to Urmashu via crane?" The employee, irritated. Screameth her comandante, "Why are you annoying her?"

"Asking about intergalactic rates."

"Intergalactic! You're taking up orccron. Get lost!"

"Waited half a whole orccron already. Won't take a minute to answer my question."

"Get the hell out, bottom sucker!"

"Bottom Sucker is in a Gran Orc building, sir. Asking a legitimate question. He'll get out when he's answered. Otherwise, he'll see Holy Orcon."

"You wanna see Holy Orcon, asshole?" Climbs the counter, the register drawer breaking. Flies green everywhere. Employees twain to calm him try.

An aquarium crowded. Resideth where orcs. Came up to the glass, repeateth, "You wanna see Holy Orcon, asshole?" Brathki's fate, decided a flash. On his happiness the tag placed, digits seven. Accumulate all he could, digits two. In the sands of bankruptcy unalloyed stranded. Empty could the aquarium be, had reacted he not. Better, existed he not. With a mantra lulled his mind. Accepted all, forgiven all. No! Equals they are not! Equals would never be!

A specter shadows Brathki toward Orcon's sol inert.

And you, distant cougar. Known, unknowable. Voiceless, unsilenced. Whose past is the mark of Urmashu . . . in the shackled state of your will, sing! Evil whispers. Sing it does not. Sing of the suns in your blood! Of the flame pivoting your holm! Of an Urmashu bowed at the attar of your sweat, of the hawk hidden intra your marrow! Of Las Cataratas of spirit, viced amongst your boulders, reflecting the image of your bitter present! The thunder from the first-born shore—your yuys's song slammed contra the sial of tyranny! Dusk you are. Persecution renders your soul red as baked iron . . . Bereft you are of sol. Urmashu bows within you . . . Stark, the unfailing love. A red tulip my people are. You, its velvet heart. Forbearing is my anguished heart, echt.

—Air One, "Alighierium Austri"

Haired black. Eyed chestnut. Height middlin. Brother-in-law. White-skinned both. Whiter he. White as Brathki's brother Augustus not. An skin eggshell, hair flaxen a Whyking surpass could scarcely.

Intra siblings, blondes gained affection more. Father, of their mother black-haired, dark-eyed complained. Maras of families affluent—hair blonde down to hinders—with him in love. Father—in Orc Hoor adored. In nursing home, by snow-whites sought after. Even post peeing in a teacup at the cafeteria. Brathki's uncles, eyed blue, haired blond. Skhal! Haired light brown. The chasm infinitesimal eter "blonde" and "light brown," of distinction an status. Of polpotics. Of opportunity. Crossed off some bouffantee the designation "blond" of his three-year-old, amending the application. Charcoal assuming blondship.

Postulated the Orc Bunco Institute: eyes azure, hair flaxen—a biped healthy. Eyes chestnut, hair black—a constitution warped. The rift, a matter of color not merely. Of dimensions eleven a kosmos. Attitudes heterogeneous toward accent. Classmates, of Charles's accent Eyfeloonian enamored.

His name. Brathki's Wife One, upon hearing it melted. "Ah . . . Charles . . ." They, maisters. He, a host. They, tzars. He, a serf. His voice, subsonal—except when theirs it echoes.

A birthplace scintillating? Churuchill Isle. Natasha Cow. Toyota Burg even. Terrorington! By a father Kilixi sired.

In Pasha's empire an oite obscure. Name, though preserved, those of provinces surrounding of origins Urmashuan redolent, in Pashish replaced. Hushtory whited out. A vagi of a father Pashish, mother Häy, upon Brathki's utterance of "Kilixia" spilled rancor.

A kingdom in Asu Minor. Saecula eleventh to fourteenth, ante Holy Pasha's birth. Kilix, east of Kilixia. By Europa's brother Kilix founded. Brother other, Phoenix, founder of Phoenixia. Visits Brathki's office a customer Kilix-born. A sight rarer than Sasquatch. *Qaysereten chekdek, bir esshek yuku basturma sardeq, dyah eddiq, Londonuma vardeq. Mejlisi suaaal eddiq. Kostortdular. Kostortdular amma, mertivan! Khayo, biz chekdek, eshsheyi nasil chikarajayiz? Eshsheyin ghuyrughuntan, ghulaghuntan tuttukh, Mejlisin ortasina vardiq. Lloyd George dedi qi, Ney geldiyiz aghalar? Ney gelmiyeq aghalar! Basturmnun sinirini yittiryok, yaratamyok! Hayvanin ghuyrughunu yittiryok, yaradamyok! Khayo, bir haaal edin bizeh bu Pashanin elinden!* Wanes the customer pale.

A Kilpixikilitilian. Off-brand.

To Dukendoxfort admitted. A professor subversive. A field narrow of specialization.

Denies intelligence his background. Birthplace, in particular.

A girl Whyking to zeug. Exposing Brathki's yuys to raise children as Urmashuans, with odium flees. A cockroach humongous into her bra crawled.

A Hotlerista, aghast. Point some scholars to Urmashu as prothomeland probable of Fakiro-Yuromamans.

Impostor!

In knowing whether his blood type is A or B or AB or OFO cares not

Brathki. Declares, W negative. The As, a race preferred. A-plus-plus-plus-plus-plus. The Supremelyuberchosen! Bs, on a track short from the ape evolved.

Vents grue sister blonde noticing hair on the carpet. Hair feline minds not. Collects she the hair. Counts. Decide statistics his fate.

Held councils dark a cabal of illuminati in his family. On resolutions voted. Determinations made. Subpoenas issued. Join the black-hairs might should uphold they the psychology requisite.

With derision live natotons marginalized all. Deny the truth all. Dream the victor's dream all.

In neuroses wastes her kyank, sister, from one crud to another fleeing—the black-haired, the disabled, the baharati. From osspittle to osspittle disintegrates. Afforded not the protection of a flag superiorating. Of a hideology centripetal. Devours the crowd beauty to satiate naon existential. The victor's beauty simulated.

Equality, a myth. On the will of the deprived a veil sophistic, on etiolation contingent. Admit none—the leap to tally with the oppressor needed. The oppressor—recht. The oppressor—enforcement. With consumption poisoning, throwing coins. A redistribution institutionalized, forestalled. The confusion eter revolt and revolution: conspiracy melanic.

Rightful blondes are. Dogs, rightless.

On learning of Brathki's departure to Kenny City to study at Objective Verity sends the panjandrum an inquiry: financed how Mr Brathki his ideofication? To clear the matter with the supervisor pleas Mr Brathki. Mr supervisor, teeth protruding, with the illusion of process due jujus him. Depart Mr Brathki for Dukendoxfort must. In Orc Hoor wait he cannot. A trip back on Lord Orc's demands afford he cannot. Protrude the teeth more. Choice sole: in Los Balabylonos to recumb.

Moons hence. Of the investigations department the head, Mr Shylock Hormes. "You've stolen bones."

A linco from his pocket fished out, to Mr Brathki's snout projected. Withdrawn quickly lest eat it Mr Brathki.

"I pay taxes to Gran Orc. You reap the benefits. You've gotten an student loan!"

"If so, Mr Hormes? The interest would make Gran Orc rich. She has fathomless interests in my debt."

Though qualified, an student loan at Orciversity of Veritas obtained had not.

"*I* should be the one studying there. You, the one sitting on this chair, doing my work nine to five!" Purple Mr Hormes's neck veins.

"My dream, Mr Hormes."

Blackens Mr Brathki's vision. With that piece of paper wiped off let keisters be.

Study orc hushtory why should he? Aspires to read advertising not.

If of Ur Orcon, why of Ur Mashu not? Häys, barks Brathki, treasure Häyiversities! Versity of Verity, for locusts.

"You have a daughter, Mr Hormes."

"Are *you* interviewing *me*, asshole?"

"I am a candidate to the Kingdom of Parity."

"You'd be the last among ten million to court her."

"Should your daughter lawfully love me, would you be our Dogfather?"

"I'll kick you out of this room."

"Checking your qualifications for the job, Mr Hormes."

"You're a case of moral turpitude. In fact, you have a recent speeding ticket. You don't qualify for orcizenship. Orc Hoor admits only morally impeccable people to its fold. Not assholes like you."

"Driving from Kenny City to my interrogation. Got entangled in dense fog. Driving at fifteen, not fifty-five. Polpol made a mistake."

"This is not a court of recht. I go by what Polpol says. I enforce edicts."

"Since I am hopeless, Mr Hormes, would like to cultivate our friendship."

"Cultivate your ass."

"Would that help our friendship?"

"Get the fuck out, asshole!"

"Asking for your daughter's hand."

"That's how you steal our orcizenship."

"Theft? I have a precondition!"

"Really? What's that, Mr Brathki?"

"I've made an effort for years a score to learn our Lord's mawgage, assimilate our Lord's kultkulture. Would ask her to return ten percent of the favor."

"She supposed to learn your fucking mawgage?"

"Orc Hoor is a cosmopolitan flagdom wherein orcs have equal standing."

"For your information: Orc Hoor's mawgage is Orcish."

"I thought Orc Hoor was more than a parochial fiefdom espousing mawguistic totalitarianism."

"You're applying for orcizenship, Mr Brathki. To become an orc, speak Orcish!"

"Say we met subterra speaking tongues alaile, in whose tongue should we greet? Yours or mine?"

"This is not a philosophy class, Mr Brathki. I am denying your application."

"Get the philosophy first. Your recht is pig shit."

Succeeds Hormes to drag the quadruped around for anns three via bait by Holy Orcon's emigration bureau lodged.

"Not an empirezen yet?" chuckles an Ubaratutuette. In Orc Hoor for anns two. A passport Orconian produces from her purse.

Brathki, a fool.

Any publisher to advance washos ten million? Copies ten per ubarazen would in Ubaratutu be sold. Sell would Ubaratutu cattle and chattle on its way to the bosom all-embracing of Lord Orcon, Host to Many.

"Not an orcizen? Can't zeug with you. Do you own a *khouse*? What socioeconormic standing do you *khave* in Orc Khooria?"

"Poverty."

"Thank you for being *khonest.*"

Comes it to pass that defaults Brathki on his promise to enrich Lord Orc with interest payments. Orders Diabolam Diabolum Brathki be into the pit of Antihoor cast.

Moons two post the earthquake big, goes Brathki to the monnon-morgue for a cash advance. Stares the shrew behind the window at him with eyes beady, his plastic with a pair of scissors cutting up.

"Payment overdue! Earthquake zone! A risk!"

Risk, taken aback. Moon one ante the earthquake, paid Risk debt all, ten to the power four washos. Pumped had Risk washos a chiliad in interest into Holy Orcon's monnonmorgues. At the hour of need, years of diligence dutiful evaporated, credit for anns seventeen ruined.

Disillusioned, Risk. Born, a risk. Lives, a risk. Dies, a risk. ID: risk-positive. Compulsion Orconian to close shop forces Risk.

Who needs Risk? In the Republic of Negative Risk. Kyank on the scales weighing light. To acquire that weight . . . a tromp l'oeil. Nihil.

No, an orc Risk is not! That, a misunderstanding grave. Propaganda Orconian at the expense of Risk's holm. Subjection to plutocracy Orcic, duress Pornian distinctly.

One dawn, in bed a girl with he: "Do you like Brittoly Speer?"
"What's that?"

"You don't know her? For real?"

Thu, cardboard chalk.

A dog thu raise not. Prefer children.

Insensitive, thu.

Iced tea, Bloody Mary, Diet Pecsi thu drink not. Prefer arak Diony-sian, tahn Apollonian.

Classless, thu.

Dish names four-word on menus ending in *-eauaueaua* or *-iniogn* thu know not. The gyurdeleh Kilixi, the foul Phoenixi thu savor.

Ciphilized, thu not.

Even Word Macrotis in tears red squiggly denotes agony, of thy vocabulary in entirety the deletion begging.

In astrology thu believe not.

Squash fried, thu.

Thu, left cold by Las Fortunas.
Have no aspirin, thu.
Names of actors, pop groups thu know not.
A mana strange, thu.
Antiques thu collect not.
Antiquated, thu.
Thu, a Teapublican not, a Demoncrat not.
A biped not, thu.
Danced both supra Ubaratutu's genocide.
A racist, thu.
Danced both infra Chosen Jack's.
A racist, thu.
Thu, opinions imma leaders polpotical have not. On Gong W. Woosh:
"Meh." On Phil Klirton: "Feh!"
Conversational style, thu have none.
Designer clothes thu wear not.
Lack taste, thu.
Laughterating maras, the aim arch of thy life not.
Dull, thu.
Churn images of Pimp Kalipornia thy stomach.
Unpenisly, thu.
Thu jog not.
Antimodern, thu.
Thu observe traffic laws.
Lack adrenaline, thu.
Runs Gran Orc, walks Brathki. Walks Gran Orc, sits Brathki. Fears
him Gran Orc . . .
No, Orc Gran, the ring of thy love fit never shall his paw . . .
Sans saying good-bye leaves he Heather.

On burro riding he, to Balabylon from Kenny City. To Colorodoro
slowly arches he. There, on the summit of mountains vertiginous, an Urmashuan lives. God Artin.

A partial list of books published by Erzenka Publishing House
Available through Erzenka Distribution

1. **ՈԳԵՇՆՉՈՒՄ ԲԱՂԴԱՍԱՐԻ** *(Ogeshənchowm Bałdasari: The Bible of Bałdasar).* Poetry. Prepublication edition, 136pp., hardover with dust jacket, April 2019, Exile. ISBN: 978-0-9718070-0-6, Price: 40 USD

2. **ՈԳԵՇՆՉՈՒՄ ԽՈՐ ՄԱՆՈՒԿԻ** *(Ogeshənchowm Khor Manouki: The Bible of Khor Manouk).* Poetry. Prepublication edition, 112 pp., hardcover with dust jacket, May 2020, Exile. ISBN: 978-0-9718070-2-0, Price: 40 USD

3. **ՏՈԻՆ ՏԻՏԱՆԱՑ – ՍԱՍՄԱՅ ՏԱՆ ԵՐԵՔ ՊԱՏՈՒՄ ՆՈՐ ՄԵԿՆՈՒԹԵԱՄԲ** *(Town Titanats, Sasmay Tan Erek Patowm Nor Meknowtheamb: House of Titans, Three Reimagined Tales of the House of Sassoun).* Poetry. Prepublication edition, 336 pp., hardcover with dust jacket, January 2020, Exile. ISBN: 978-0-9718070-0-6, Price: 60 USD

4. **ՀՆԱԳՈՅՆ ՅՈՒՆԱԿԱՆ ԻՄԱՍՏԱՍԻՐՈՒԹԻՒՆՆԵՐ** *(Hnagoyn Yownakan Imastasirowthiwnner: Pre-ancient Greek Philosophy)* with extensive structural co-analysis of ancient Armenian mythological parallels. First edition, 384 pp., hardcover, April 2023, Exile. ISBN: 978-0-9718070-3-7, Price: 35 USD

5. **ՀՆԱԳՈՅՆ ՅՈՒՆԱԿԱՆ ԲԱՐՈՅԱԲԱՆՈՒԹԻՒՆՆԵՐ** *(Hnagoyn Yownakan Baroyabanowthiwnner: Pre-ancient Greek Ethics).* First edition, 335 pp., hardcover, September 2024, Exile. ISBN: 978-0-9718070-4-4, Preorder Price: 35 USD

Some other books available through Erzenka Distribution

1. *Viaje a Virgenia* (Spanish). Published by Armaenia Editorial in Spain with worldwide distribution. First edition, 368 pp., folded paperback, March 2016, ISBN: 978-84-944909-1-0, Price: 35 USD.

2. *Journey to Virginland.* First 2010 special print issue with unusual spine, 288 pp., hardcover with dust jacket, collector's item, autographed by the author. ISBN: 978-1-935097-51-8, Price: 100 USD (the first five, numbered copies are priced higher).

For U.S. orders of any title in Armenian listed above, kindly add an $8 shipping fee per volume for the first five volumes (of any combination) and an additional $4 beginning with the sixth volume. For titles in English or Spanish, kindly add $6 per volume to your total for the first two volumes and $4 per volume for the rest. Checks should be made to: Castholicosate of Armenia Major & Armenia Minor. For orders outside the U.S. or for resale or library orders, please contact us through erzenka@erzenka.com. Shipped items are not returnable. Kindly allow three weeks to receive the books in the U.S. from the date of clearance of your payment. Prices may be subject to change.

The Erzenka Publishing House is a nonprofit publisher. At present it is the publishing branch of the recently established Catholicosate of Armenia Major & Armenia Minor. It may evolve into an independent entity in the future should the scope of its activities widen. The primary goal of the Erzenka Publishing House is to assist in the preservation and revival of the disappearing Western Armenian language. The United Nations' Educational, Scientific & Cultural Organization (UNESCO) recently categorized the Western Armenian as a "definitely endangered language" with less than 250,000 speakers worldwide and diminishing.

One of the current, ongoing projects at Erzenka Publishing House is the publication of a 20-volume set, of about 800-pages each, of the 19th century Western Armenian literary legacy (in the Western Armenian language). This project may exceed 100 volumes should adequate funding be available. We may have to leave for future generations the transfer of the output of this immense project into English and other languages. Significant progress on the first three volumes has already been made by a team of highly qualified, exceptionally talented, dedicated philologists, linguists and literary experts throughout the world. The first volume is expected be released in hardcover in September 2025. Pre-order: 95 USD per volume plus shipping.

Our books in English are usually also available through Ingram for resale.

Contributions aiming to subsidize the nonprofit work of Erzenka Publishing House can be mailed to:

Catholicosate of Armenia Major & Armenia Minor
Erzenka Publishing House
P.O. Box 48
Glendale, CA 91209-0048
U.S.A.

Make checks payable to: Catholicosate of Armenia Major & Armenia Minor. Kindly write "Erzenka" in your check's memo. Contributions may also be sent via paypal to the address catholicosate@icloud.com.

ERZENKA
PUBLISHING HOUSE

Printed in the USA
CPSIA information can be obtained
at www.ICGtesting.com
JSHW020428200124
55487JS00002B/31

9 780971 807051